THE PROMISE OF CHRISTMAS

A SMALL TOWN HOLIDAY STORY

STEENA HOLMES

DEAR READER

Ever since traveling to Germany with my middle daughter back in 2015, I've fallen in love with the whole idea of Christmas Markets and towns focused on the holidays.

Who am I kidding - I've always loved Christmas, with the festive lights, the music, the warm feeling I experience deep in my soul...it's my favorite season of the year.

This book was originally a 2 book novella series. I had more story to tell but not enough for another book so I decided to rewrite and turn it into one novel instead. This rewrite took me over 6 months to do - if you can believe it!

I hope you enjoy this story.

Happy reading!

CHAPTER ONE

ASHLEY

Candy cane wishes and mistletoe kisses...fireside dreams as hot cocoa steams...

Christmas can't come soon enough for Ashley Tanna, not just because it's her favorite season but because of what the holiday promises.

Christmas is warm and happy; it's sugar cookies and pepper-mint mochas in front of a wood fire feel. It's Mariah Carey and Bing Crosby, White Christmas, Charlie Brown, and sparkling tree lights, all rolled in one.

Christmas conveys a sense that everything is right with the world, that for a season, there's goodwill and great tidings and all the stuff that places smiles on people's faces.

Like the perma-smile on her own face when she thinks about Christmas.

Christmas is what's going to save her town and rekindle that home feeling she's so desperate to have.

At least, she hopes so.

In two short months, Innsbruck is going to hold its first Christmas Market, and even though Ashley knows it's not going to be a huge event, she has high hopes for it. Those high hopes have everything to do with saving her hometown, a town that's lost is 'homey' feeling for so many of its residents.

Home is supposed to be a town nestled in the mountains with streets full of alpine cabins and flower gardens, walkways lined with cobblestone, and unique mailboxes.

Home is full of town parks, pathways, playgrounds, and winding riverbeds.

Home has to be about family and community, and memories.

The sad thing is that for most families who have stuck it out and sacrificed to keep their homes, Innsbruck no longer feels like a home. One person referred to it as a death sentence more than anything else. Those who have stayed complain about the commute into the city for work and ultimately leave.

Everything here is slowly dying – the businesses, the people.

She needs to change that. As the town mayor, it's her job to change that.

The first thing she needs to do is figure out a way to make this ghost town of a community feel like home again for everyone, and she knows exactly where to start: it all begins with change. Change of attitude. Change of heart. Change that will make a difference.

The idea of change is challenging, complex, and definitely chaotic. Ashley more than understands what she's about to propose, but it'll be worth it; she believes that with all her heart.

All her life, she's struggled with change, even when it's been forced on her. Still, unless she does something about what's happening with her town, soon she'll be included in the mass exodus – especially if her husband has anything to say about it.

Just thinking about that has tendrils of regret using her spine as stepping stones, leaving her shivering in its wake.

Regret because she knows she hasn't done enough to save this town. She can't leave – even if Brett wants to.

The people of Innsbruck rely on her to save their homes and town for one simple reason: she promised she would.

The issue is that it can't be too drastic or different.

No one likes change, not really. It's a hard pill to swallow, erasing comfort zones and rebuilding new boundaries. Ashley knows this first-hand because, for the past two years, all she's done is try to get her fellow council members to embrace change; one by one, they've blocked every idea she's thrown their way.

Every time she complains about it to Brett, he reminds her of another promise she'd made, this time to him. Truth be told, this was a promise she never expected she'd have to keep.

When she's agreed to run for another term, she promised it would be her last one.

The countdown is on now, as Brett pointed out. She has thirty days left to decide if she will run again or step down so they can move into the city. She has thirty days to decide if she's ready to give up her dreams, career, and home for their marriage.

The decision should be easy, but it's not for more reasons than she wants to admit.

She loves her town. One of her favorite pastimes is walking through the streets, saying hello to neighbors, and stopping to chat about life. The town is full of walking paths and small parks, where children play and families walk their four-legged friends like the cute little puppy charging toward her.

Ashley bends down to greet the pup, who jumps on her thighs, slathering her face with kisses.

"Sasha, down!" A man runs up to Ashley, leash flying free in his hand. "Sorry, Mayor, she got away from me." Jeffrey, one of her neighbors, scoops the pup in his arms and is awarded a zillion sloppy kisses.

Ashley's face hurts from the growing smile she can't stop. "When did you get a puppy?"

The next thing she knows, the pup jumps from the owner's arms to hers, dolling out even more kisses than before.

"Just this week. A friend in the city had an oops-litter and has been trying to find good homes for them. I think she likes you." Jeffrey teases. "They have two left they're still trying to find homes for. Maybe it is time for a new addition to the family?" His brows wiggle like a caterpillar.

Hmmm. "Maybe we could start with pet sitting? I'm sure Jordan would love spending some time with this cutie." Ashley rubs her fingers through Sasha's curly hair before handing her back. "What kind is she?" Jordan will probably jump at the chance to dog-sit.

"She's a mix, and I think they have one like Sasha left. The other is black."

Watching Jeffrey walk away with his pup, Ashley feels a longing to jump and adopt one, except she has a feeling Brett wouldn't appreciate the surprise, especially with wanting to move. She can already hear his arguments for why getting a pet isn't a smart idea right now.

Walking through the streets of her hometown, it's hard not to think about how vibrant this community used to be, where generations of families created memories and expanded their family trees.

Once a thriving mining town, it's soon on its way to becoming a historic ghost town.

The main street has more stores boarded up than not. In the new school year, children will attend out-of-town schools because there aren't enough families for it to be financially sustainable to keep their own schools open.

There are only three churches left in town, and there are rumors that two of them are in the midst of deciding whether or not to join together and share a building. The graveyard of the Catholic church had more members than what filled the pews during Sunday mass.

Once, she used to love her walks home after work.

Now, she's close to dreading them.

Ashley notices Frankie, the owner of Sip' n' Sit, the only running coffee shop in town, looking out the window, arms crossed over her ample chest.

"Was wondering when you'd show up," Frankie says as she glances at her watch. "You're a little late tonight. Things okay?" She pulls out a chair for Ashley before bustling to the counter and starting on her order.

Every evening, Ashley stops in on her walk home, sips on whatever beverage Frankie makes her, and nibbles on whatever goodies are left in the display before heading home.

Every evening, Frankie waits for her, eager to chat about local gossip and encourage her to keep up the good fight.

Every evening, Ashley hugs Frankie and tells her to head home before it gets too dark out.

It's a nightly ritual she'll never tire of.

"Did you know my neighbor, Jeffrey, got a new puppy?" Ashley gazes out the darkened window, catching the reflection of passing vehicles and not much else. "She's the sweetest thing and makes me wish I had a dog." A whisper of a smile rests on her face until she remembers what she wants to ask Frankie. "When did the Oars move? I walked down their street tonight and realized there's no one left now." Ashley pulls out her notebook and makes a note to follow up on that street and why it's so empty. Surely not everyone has moved.

"Oh girl, they moved a few weeks ago. Didn't you know? Guess John got a promotion, including an executive apartment until they figure out what to do with their house." Frankie sets a cup of frothy coffee down in front of her. "And yes, you should get a dog. You always had one growing up, and you know Jordan would love a puppy."

Ashley bends down to sniff her drink.

"Peppermint mocha," Frankie says before she catches a faint peppermint scent. "Trying something new."

Ashley stares at the mug. It's like Frankie can read her mind. "I was just daydreaming about sipping a peppermint mocha on my way here. How did you know?"

"Girl, you've been humming Christmas carols all week." Frankie retreats behind the counter as Ashley enjoys her first sip.

The drink is decadent, thick, and with the perfect amount of peppermint.

"This is the best mocha yet," she praises Frankie, carrying a plate of chocolate chip oatmeal cookies.

"Anna picked up some drinking chocolate for me when she and Weiss went home. I guess they had a stopover in Paris, lucky them."

Ashley takes another enjoyable sip and nods. It reminds her of the hot cocoa she'd enjoyed at Angelina's in Paris on her honeymoon.

"They're back? I haven't seen them yet." Ashley adds another note to her notebook. She needed to check on Weiss, make sure he was feeling okay, and find out about their trip home to Germany. Mia, one of her best friends, asked her to check in on her dad before she flies back.

"They just got back today. I'm sure Mia told you about Weiss' cold? Anna's nursing the man back to health. Me, I can't stand when my husband gets the man cold, but Anna, she worries over him like a mother hen. Mia...well, you probably talk to her more than anyone. Is it true she stayed behind to do some more traveling? What about the Christmas Market you two are organizing? Frankie leans forward. "She is returning, right?"

Ashley looks up in surprise. "Of course, she is. Why would you think otherwise? She's just staying a few extra days to..." she has to be careful how she words the next sentence... "for research and to buy more supplies for her booth and her store."

"Research?"

Dang it, of course, Frankie caught her slip.

Mia is one of Ashley's best friends. Mia said something a few months ago that sparked Ashley's recent proposal to the town council.

"You promise she's coming back?" Frankie asks.

Ashley holds up a hand, palm out. "I swear. This market is all her idea, so of course, she will be here. She says she's got a notebook full of ideas and suppliers so we can have that traditional German Market feel." She knows her eyes are sparkling, but she hopes Frankie doesn't notice. She's been keeping a secret from the woman, and it's been one of the hardest things she's ever done.

"Between you and me, I've been so worried that she wouldn't come back at all and that her bookstore would close up like all the others." Resignation settles in Frankie's gaze. "Not like it matters, though. I swear, this place is drying up faster than a houseplant with no water for two weeks."

Ashley pinches her lips together, knowing she has to remain silent.

"You know it's true," Frankie said. "Have you figured out a plan yet?"

Ashley swallows hard. A plan? She has a notebook full of

ideas. Every single one of them shot down by the town council until recently.

Now there are two on the table, but she's been given strict instructions from her fellow council members to remain silent until their town meeting. They don't want her to sway any community members in one direction or the other. In fact, everyone agreed to remain silent.

The one idea is focused on Christmas. The other is turning their town into a retirement village.

She's received a rather substantial offer from a large holding firm that wants to buy up all the property around and in Innsbruck, tear down a majority of the houses and build lodge homes.

She has no problem keeping quiet about that one. It's the easy route to saving their town, but it will mean a mass exodus of anyone who doesn't see a retirement village being their saving grace.

Thankfully, it's not their only option. It's just the easiest one.

"What aren't you telling me?" Frankie leans in and waves a chocolate chip cookie in her face. "Fess up. I know you are keeping something from me."

"We have a town hall meeting tomorrow," Ashley reminds Frankie, unable to say more even though she desperately wants to.

"I'm aware." The frown on Frankie's face speaks volumes. "It's true, isn't it?" She continues. "The whole council is resigning tomorrow?"

This isn't the first she's heard of this ridiculous rumor. Rather than answering, Ashley focuses on her cup, slowly raising it to her lips and sipping the velvet liquid before she looks Frankie in the eye.

"We've known each other too long, girl, for you to go silent on me." Frankie's frown is a fierce one. "Don't bother lying now. It's true, ain't it? Damn it, Ashley!" She tosses her half-eaten cookie back down to the plate. "What's happened to you, girl? You've given up, haven't you? You were supposed to be our guardian angel. Even the pastor said so!"

Ashley recoils from the accusation.

"Sorry." Frankie drops her head to her hands. "I didn't mean that."

"It's okay." The words tumble from Ashley's tongue without thought. It isn't okay, yet she understands the frustration all too well.

She feels it too.

Her next sip of mocha has her burning her tongue.

"I need to ask you for a favor," Ashley says softly. "Will you trust me, please? I promise you I haven't given up. This town means too much to me." She places her cup back on the table, reaches for Frankie's hands, and squeezes. "Do I have a plan? Yes. Will it be one you like? I don't know."

"I want to trust you, hun. I really do."

"Don't give up on me yet, Frankie. You, of all people, I need in my corner." It hurts. It really does, knowing her friends lost faith in her. She pushes herself to her feet. "I should head home. I'm running later than normal. I have dinner in the crockpot, and no doubt Brett and Jordan are waiting for me."

She promised she'd be home for dinner tonight.

Frankie stands to her feet and envelops Ashley in a hug.

"I'm sorry for what I said," Frankie whispers. "Of course, I trust you. Forgive me?"

Ashley nods. "Don't think twice about it." It's the right thing to say, even if she's not sure she believes it. The thing about words spoken out of emotion is that, more often than not, they're the truth. Frankie wouldn't have said it if she wasn't thinking about it.

"Besides, I'm the one who should be apologizing, Frankie. You're right. I've let everyone down. Everything I promised to do hasn't worked, and the result is more empty houses, more boarded-up businesses, and soon we'll be losing the school too. But I promise I'm trying."

The guilt crumbles like an avalanche with fresh snow. She's being buried alive in all the hopes and expectations the town has rightfully placed on her.

Frankie doesn't answer, just heads to the counter and grabs a brown bag full of cookies. "You don't have to share these if you don't want to. They'll do well if you freeze them."

Ashley gives her friend a very thankful smile.

"You're sure you don't want these for the card group tonight?"

Most nights, groups within the town would gather in Frankie's coffee shop. Tonight, a group of men came in to play cards. Other nights, a book club and even cribbage players came in for a warm cup of coffee and something sweet Frankie had baked for them.

"I actually have a group of young bakers coming in to make cookies tonight. In fact, I think Jordan is coming."

Ashley pulls out her phone to check the calendar. She doesn't see anything about a bake night in the family calendar, and Jordan knows to place her plans in there. Their schedule is busy enough, and keeping the family calendar updated is their only chance to take control of the chaos.

Nope. Nothing. The calendar is empty. She sends Jordan a quick text, knowing her daughter always has her phone nearby.

Shoot. Sorry, Mom. I forgot to add it to the calendar. We got home early, and dinner is ready. PS...Dad has a surprise for you!

Ashley's heart slides down to the soles of her feet, and for just a moment, the thought that maybe she wouldn't head home right away flits through her mind.

Brett's surprises aren't always a good thing.

Frankie waits on confirmation.

"Yep, Jordan will be here," Ashley rereads her daughter's text message.

The last time Brett had a surprise for her —a good surprise that was — was...years ago. Back when things were good between them. Lately, his only surprises have been those that break her heart.

She isn't sure she can handle anything more tonight.

She musters a smile that's supposed to register excitement.

"Everything okay?" Frankie asks.

Obviously, she failed.

"All good," Ashley adds a bit of cheer to her voice. She places a to-go lid on her cup and gives Frankie a brief hug before hurrying to the door.

"Why don't you come tonight, too? You can be a taste tester," Frankie calls out before she leaves.

Ashley rolls her eyes. "She's fifteen, Frankie. Hanging out with mom is not her idea of a fun night. Besides, I have a lot to do for tomorrow night's meeting." She gives her friend a wave before leaving.

Thinking about the mountain of work that needs to be done in time for tomorrow's town hall meeting, Ashley stops at the liquor store on her way home. Everything is riding on this town hall: her hopes, dreams, and ability to keep her promises.

CHAPTER TWO

Ten minutes later, she's at home, and the smell of BBQ spareribs from the crockpot she'd prepared earlier has her stomach rumbling.

Jordan is waiting, the table already set, phone turned down on the table.

"Sorry I'm late, baby." Ashley leans down and plants a kiss on the top of her daughter's head. "Dinner smells so good. Where's your father?"

Ashley may be good at many things, but cooking is not one of them. This though is one recipe she knows she can't screw up.

"He's upstairs getting changed. Don't worry, I already tasted it. I added a little brown sugar to the sauce to give it more flavor."

"Of course, you did." Ashley attempts to hide the roll of her eye as she smiles. It would be a miracle if Jordan didn't do something to any meal Ashley prepares.

"I also baked the cauliflower. I figured you forgot about making a side dish."

Ashley can't tell if there's a hint of sarcasm in her daughter's voice.

Is this a battle she wants to fight? Not tonight.

"No, I didn't forget. I was going to air fry some potatoes and make homemade poutine." In fact, she's been drooling over the idea of the gravy and melted cheese curds all day.

"This is a little healthier, don't you think? I tossed them with olive oil, garlic salt, and parmesan." Jordan's eye roll is one for the record book, and she doesn't attempt to hide it.

Ashley takes a nice long breath and recalls something her therapist had said to her: at fifteen, Jordan is trying to find her footing in my busy world. She doesn't just want to be the mayor's cute daughter anymore. She wants to make a name for herself and be known for something that has nothing to do with her mom and everything to do with herself.

If there is one thing Ashley has learned, raising a strong, independent teenage daughter is challenging.

"Absolutely, it's definitely a healthier option. Thank you for making it."

Ashley's phone goes off.

She's about to answer it when she catches the not-so-subtle look from her daughter.

During one of their bi-monthly family counseling sessions, Ashley's therapist suggested creating the dinner meal be an electronic-free zone. There's been a disconnect within their family that Ashley has been trying to fix. Jordan blames it on the fact both her parents are too busy with their own lives to focus on her. Brett claims it's the price to pay for living so far from work. Ashley...well, she can blame it on a lot of things but won't. The truth is, she's juggling so many responsibilities, balls are falling, and she is failing on so many levels.

The first week with their phones in the basket during meals was...difficult. By the third week, she and Brett have enjoyed being unplugged, but unfortunately, Jordan still struggles with the idea.

Brett walks into the kitchen and leans in to place a kiss on Ashley's cheek.

"Getting home early, that's a nice change," Ashley says to him.

"I got out of a meeting early, and Jordan was on time for once. By the way," he glances over to where Jordan's sitting at the table, "she's not allowed to go out tonight until her homework is done." He opens the fridge and motions to a box on the top shelf. "I picked this up for you."

She should say thank you, but he's already turned and is pouring a glass of wine.

Ashley doesn't need to open the box to know what it contains: her favorite dessert from her favorite bakery in the city.

"Thanks for the cheesecake," She finally says. "What's the occasion?" She has no idea why he'd bought it. It's not their anniversary, nor were they celebrating anything, the only times he ever brings home cheesecake from the city.

"Thought we could celebrate tonight since I know tomorrow night will be a mad house." He hands her a glass.

"What are we celebrating, exactly?" Tomorrow night is the town hall meeting; yes, it will be a mad house. Town meetings always are.

"You're kidding me, right?" The disdain in his voice feels like sludge on her skin. "Tomorrow night, you're announcing you won't be running for another term, right?"

Ashley looks at him with surprise. What is he talking about? She never agreed to that. She still has a month to decide, technically. Tomorrow night has nothing to do with her stepping down and everything to do with saving their town.

"Please tell me you're not breaking your word," Brett grumbles, his hand slamming down on the counter. "God, after the day I've had, that's the last thing I need to hear."

Ashley swallows back the words ready to jump out, and forces herself to focus on the emotion behind his words instead. She'll deal with his expectations for tomorrow later. For now, something else is going on.

"What happened today?"

The look in his eyes is cold. Empty. Resigned. She doesn't like it. It's a look she's seen all too often lately, too.

"What didn't happen." He spits the words out like his mouth is full of dirt. "I can't wait until we move. I don't know why we thought this would work; you are being here, while I travel back and forth and have to pick up Jordan from school." His gaze slides from hers. "It's starting to look bad."

"What's looking bad?" She has no idea what he is talking about.

"Me, leaving work early."

What? Since when has it become a problem? He was the one to suggest it. He liked leaving the city as early as possible to avoid the traffic.

"I didn't realize it was causing issues." She keeps her voice calm, her tone soft. She wants to remind him that this was his decision. All of it - from accepting the job to switching their daughter to a school in the city. A decision neither Jordan nor herself agreed with.

"It's causing more issues than I can count." Brett groans in frustration as he runs his fingers through his hair. "I just haven't told you about it."

Secrets. A noose tightens around her heart. What else is he keeping from her this time? The last secret had her threatening divorce.

"Why not?"

The look he gives her is full of exasperation.

"I'm serious, Brett. We talked about this. We need to communicate better, right? How can we do that if there are still secrets between us?"

There have been enough secrets in their past, she can't handle more.

"Um, guys, can we just eat, please?" Jordan's voice is full of frustration, embarrassment, and a hint of sadness. They shouldn't be discussing this in front of her. That's not fair to Jordan.

Her husband closes his eyes for a brief second. For a brief second, she thinks he's going to change the subject and suggest they talk later, but instead, all she sees is anger in his gaze.

"Secrets. Right. Like you should know." He spits the words at her, the accusation unsettling.

What the...? Nope. He's not doing this, not again. She knows exactly what he's trying to do, but it won't work – she will not accept being his emotional punching bag tonight.

"Listen, I get you had a rough day, but coming home and throwing it on me, that's not the answer." She portions out the ribs onto plates with faked calmness.

Jordan's chair scrapes along the floor before she stomps out of the kitchen, up the stairs, slamming her bedroom with enough force the glasses in the kitchen cabinets shake.

Ashley goes to follow, but Brett stops her.

"Leave her be." His tone is cold, uncaring. "She needs to work on her homework."

"I'm not going to leave her be, Brett. She's obviously upset about something." It's pretty apparent what, but she bites her tongue and heads upstairs, knocking gently on Jordan's door.

Jordan's cross-legged on her bed, headphones covering her ears as she bends over her notebook, furiously writing away.

Ashley perches on the edge of the mattress and nudges her daughter's leg.

"I'm not hungry." Jordan takes off the headphones and drops her pen. "I have homework to do, and honestly, I don't feel like hearing you two argue again."

Being a mom is hard, especially to a fifteen-year-old emotional teenager. It's like walking through a farmer's pasture barefoot and blindfolded. You never know when you will step into a pile of manure or a gopher hole.

"How did your math test go?" She'd helped Jordan study last night even though her daughter is a whiz when it comes to numbers.

"Fine." Jordan leans back against her pillow. "Seriously, do I have to come downstairs?"

Ashley nods. Despite this being a rule Brett put into place, it's one Ashley has grown used to. Eating dinner as a family is important to her, even if it is done in silence. Being together, for even a few minutes each night, is better than nothing, right?

"Why do I have to go to school in the city? Why can't I stay here and take the bus to Mountain Head with my friends?"

For the past month, she'd listened to this request daily.

Brett has been adamant that Jordan start the school year off in the city since they'd be moving there. Ashley gave in because sometimes it was just easier that way. Poor Jordan was never given an option, and that's on her. Jordan had every right to be part of the conversation, especially since it directly impacted her, and she wasn't given that opportunity. Why? It was easier for her to go along with Brett rather than argue.

That's not a good enough excuse, though.

"I'm sorry, hun. But the school isn't that bad, right? And you have friends there, so it's not like you're alone."

"Whatever." Her daughter drops her chin, crosses her arms over her chest, and Ashley swears she sees tears forming.

"I hate him, Mom. You have no idea what he's like when you're not around. No idea the things he says when you can't hear him." Jordan mutters, her voice wobbly with suppressed emotion.

"Who?" Taken back, the stupid question comes out before she can stop herself. Jordan doesn't have a mean bone in her body, and the word hate is rarely uttered. Sure, she's emotional and hormonal; what fifteen-year-old isn't? Still, she has the biggest heart and believes everyone deserves a second, third, and even tenth chance.

"Him." Jordan breaks out into full tears. "Dad. I hate him."

Ashley opens her arms as her daughter throws herself across the bed.

She doesn't know what to say, but not having the words to help her daughter makes her feel inadequate. Things have been hard between them all, so she's not surprised at Jordan's outburst.

Sometimes, she feels the same way.

CHAPTER THREE

Forty minutes have passed by the time Ashley heads back down to the kitchen.

Dinner is obviously cold. A bottle of wine sits discarded on the kitchen island with barely enough liquid left for another glass.

And Brett is nowhere to be found.

Go figure.

What's his problem? What secrets does he think she's keeping from him?

She drinks what's left of the wine and makes her way to the back porch, the only other place she can think of him being.

He doesn't look at her as she opens the door.

Doesn't look at her as she sits beside him on one of the wicker chairs, wrapping a cozy blanket around her shoulders.

Doesn't look at her even though she's staring directly at him.

"Did you get anything to eat?" Such a stupid, mundane question, and yet, it's the only way she knows how to start this conversation.

He nods.

"Enjoy it?"

He nods again. Seriously? Can't he even speak to her?

"Calmed down enough that you feel up to talking?" She is really getting tired of walking on eggshells with him.

It takes him a moment or two before he lets out a long sigh. "You put her first all the time. You realize that, right?" He still won't look at her, but she doesn't need to see his face to hear the jealousy in his voice. Is he for real?

"She's my daughter. Our daughter. Of course, I am going to put her first." What is going on with him?

He swigs his wine until the glass is empty, slamming it down on the table beside him so hard she's sure it cracks, and finally lets her see his face.

She wishes he hadn't.

All he reveals is a cold mask of hatred, jealousy, and indifference mixed in with regret and sadness – and it's all directed at her.

"It would be nice to feel important, you know. I am your husband, after all." His lips barely move, but the force of his words pierce hard enough to leave a bruise.

Of course, you are." Where is this coming from? "What is going on with you? You accuse me of keeping secrets, upset Jordan for whatever reason, and now this? What have I done?" Most importantly, how can she fix it for him.

Her therapist often reminds her that she's not responsible for fixing everything in her life, even when it comes to her family, but she needs to. There's this innate need for peace in her home, and when it's not there...she feels responsible.

Responsibility. That's such a tricky word. Responsibility is what runs her world and keeps it from careening into destruction. Responsibility is ingrained so deep into her psyche that not being responsible for things in her path isn't possible. Not for her, no matter how hard she tries.

Her therapist wants Ashley to work on getting out of the

middle between her husband and daughter, between the residents of Innsbruck and the future, between everything she believes is her responsibility.

Ashley hasn't worked out how to do that yet. Sure, she's tried to step away, to not be a helicopter parent, and that seems to be working, but Ashley needs to be involved, to be needed, to help others and make life easier for them.

If she isn't that person who steps up to the plate, who will?

Again, not her responsibility, and yet...

"You have no idea, do you? You're really that clueless?" Brett forces himself to his feet and walks three steps forward, his fists clenched at his side.

Brett's words plow into her with the strength of a rhino, crushing her beneath its stampeding feet. "Clueless? Even for you, that's harsh, Brett. You know you're important to me. So is Jordan. Stop making me feel like I have to choose between you and her because that's not how being a parent works. She's a teenager who needs to know her parents love her. You," she thinks about how the therapist says to avoid using the word *you* during arguments, "and I are adults. We know we love each other, right?" Does she really have to explain this to him?

"And yet," Brett continues, as if he didn't hear her, "she will always come first, won't she? Whatever Jordan wants or needs, that's what matters. What about me? What about what I need?"

Concern for her husband forces Ashley to her feet. "What do you need?" Brr, it's cold out here. She clutches the blanket tighter, wishing they'd gotten the deck heater out sooner. They could move this inside, but there's less for him to break out here.

He scrubs his face and groans. "God, if I know." The words are wrenched from his soul, and Ashley feels a semblance of hope for a moment.

"You're not going back on your promise, are you? To step down from mayor so we can move to the city?" He turns.

"Cause I can't keep doing this, Ash," he says, "the drive, dealing with *her* day in, day out. I need to start staying later for work, going in early...if I don't start stepping up, they will bypass me for the promotion we both know I deserve."

She tries to focus on what he's saying, how it affects him, but she can't get past the *dealing with her* part.

"By *her,* I'm assuming you mean *our* daughter? And you're not *dealing*, Brett. It's called parenting. You decided to pull her away from her friends and drag her into the city for school. Why? Because you thought it would force me to do something I already said I would." Ashley breathes in deep, trying hard to steady herself. "I'm sorry things are tough at work. I'm sorry having to drive our daughter home every day is such an inconvenience—"

"See," he interrupts, "it's all about her. You didn't hear a single thing I said, did you? This has nothing to do with Jordan and everything to do with me and my job." He runs his hands through his hair, pulling the ends until they stick out. "What will happen if I lose that promotion, huh? Do you think we'll be able to afford to live in the city like we do here? We'll have to downsize, trade-in a vehicle, go on a freaking budget..." his body shakes at the words.

Ashley knows this is an issue for him. All of it. Coming from a welfare family, he's worked hard to get to where he is today, but in this case, he's overreacting.

Inside she's seething, but she refuses to show that to her husband.

"If you must work late, then you work late. Jordan will deal. She can work on homework at the library or a friend's house." Again, this isn't a new topic, so why it's an issue now doesn't make sense.

Unless the real issue isn't Jordan or his work, but his fear Ashley isn't going to resign like he hopes she will.

Truth be told, she doesn't want to.

She doesn't think she should have to either.

Yes, she promised she would think about it, if and only if she couldn't figure out a way to save her hometown. He's the one who assumed thinking about it meant yes. He says she's not hearing him, but it goes both ways, doesn't it?

He's not hearing her either.

"I'll walk with Jordan to her bake class tonight at Frankie's. Feel free to join us if you'd like." Ashley tosses out that little bomb she knows will rile him up but laces her voice with sugar in hopes he doesn't.

"I told her homework came first."

Guess she didn't add enough sugar. "She'll be done in time, and what isn't, she can finish on the drive in the morning."

She happens to glance down and catches the flinch of his fists. She steps back, an instinctual response, but doesn't retract her words.

"For once, I'd appreciate being respected. You're not the only parent, as you like to remind me, so stop overruling me when it comes to Jordan." The muscle in his jaw pulses, and Ashley glimpses the ugliness behind the mask of the man she once promised to love and respect.

What does he see when he looks at her? Can he see behind her mask? Does he see the repulsiveness she's feeling toward him right now? The anger that simmers but never boils over? Does he notice her pause? How she works hard to add the right non-confrontational tone to her voice?

Does he even know she wears a mask for him?

Does he know she's barely holding the cracks growing within their marriage together with masking tape?

The words she's about to utter are words he needs to hear, but they're not words she feels. Will he notice?

"I respect you, Brett." *She doesn't.* "I respect your hard

work, and how you want the best for our family." *The best for him, more like it.* "I respect that you've always had to fight for what's yours, and you feel like you shouldn't have to fight with our daughter or with me." *It's called self-preservation and has everything to do with you and nothing to do with us.*

The tightness in his shoulders disappears as she says the things he needs to hear.

His fists relax the more she praises him, too.

The anger on his face withdraws as she says words she doesn't believe and yet falls from her tongue too easily.

"Thank you," he says. "That means more than you know." The way he's now studying her, she wonders if he's finally seeing the lie behind her words.

Once upon a time, he would have. Maybe now he doesn't care. Perhaps now, he assumes he doesn't have to.

"She needs to start caring about her grades." Brett returns to his seat. "She doesn't think they matter."

Ashley closes her eyes and mentally counts to five before feeling calm enough to return to her seat and sip her wine. This roller-coaster she calls "Brett's Emotions" is exhausting on the best of days.

"She does care. Somehow, I think this has little to do with Jordan and everything to do with us, or more specifically, me." She takes that as a sign to continue when he doesn't say anything. "I know you want to leave Innsbruck. You came here to make me happy, and I appreciate that. We said we'd stay for five years, and then I took on being mayor, which has led us to an extra four years."

She can read the words he wisely withholds on his face. "When is it your turn," she continues, "I think that's what you said, right?" He nods, the surprise that she caught that clear on his face. "Why does it have to be you or me? Why can't it be about us?"

It takes exactly three seconds before he barricades himself with a hard exterior. "With this town, there is no us. You've let it consume you, Ash."

Consume her? No, never. Family always comes first. That's one thing she's worked really hard on – to live a balanced life. Family comes first, always. Then work. It guts her that he would accuse her of the one thing he knows she struggles so hard to not let happen.

Does that mean she's failing?

"Yes, what happens with Innsbruck is important to me," she says, measuring her words carefully. "This has been my home for as long as I can remember, and I'm not willing to give up on that. The people here are family, Brett, or don't you see that?"

"What I see," Brett says with rising anger, "is that you're more focused on the needs of this town than your family. What happens here – it's not your problem. Let someone else handle Innsbruck's future."

He might as well have slapped her face with the palm of his hand, leaving a bright red mark on her cheek. His words have the power to cause more damage than anything else, and he knows that.

"Wow." She swallows the bile rising up her throat. "Thanks for telling me how you really feel."

Every couple has a line that, once crossed, tears their marriage apart.

This is Brett's line. He's made that very clear since early on in their marriage and has brought it up again and again during their therapy sessions. It's why she said she'd *consider* stepping down from town council, why she'd agreed to *think* about moving into the city, even though that's the very last thing she's ever wanted to do.

She was willing to, though, for them. To keep their marriage intact.

Was.

That simple word contains so much power.

"What happens to us, to our marriage, is on you!" Brett's voice is cold, like a frozen pond during the harshest of winter.

"What's that supposed to mean?"

His hands fist again. She catches the tightness in his shoulders and the pulsing vein as he clenches his jaw.

She's actually feeling a little afraid.

"You know exactly what that means," he says. "If I mean anything to you, you'll resign tomorrow night."

The way he looks at her, she may as well be dead. He is cold, hostile, and opposite from the man she'd once fallen in love with.

"What's happened?" She has to ask. She has to know what brought this on and why he is so distant with her.

"Tell me," he demands. "Tell me you're going to keep your promise and resign."

"Why are you forcing this, right now of all times?" She won't promise, she won't say the words she doesn't mean.

His lips thin into a single line.

"I thought...I thought I knew you. I guess I don't, do I? I should know you better than him, but..." He whacks his thighs with his fisted hands, causing Ashley to jerk with each hit. "I didn't think it was true. I didn't want to believe him. I thought I could trust you..." Brett grounds the words out as if they wound him.

"What are you talking about?" A knot of anxiety rises inside her as her thoughts dance in her head, weaving through conversations she's had with anyone that might have produced her husband's anger.

"I spoke with Nigel."

She waits. Nigel and Sylvia are good friends of theirs, actually her closest friends, truth be told. Talking with Nigel is no big deal, she was just over to Sylvia's house the other night, sipping wine and talking...oh no.

"Let me guess," she suggests, but his hand rises with his palm facing her, demanding her silence.

"Apparently you told Sylvia just how desperate you were to find a solution for this town. How this is home, and you felt responsible for saving it. She apparently believes you when you say you'll do anything to ensure Innsbruck doesn't die out." His face is like granite now. "You know, Nigel seemed kind of shocked. In fact, he even accused me of lying when I said you were going to resign after sharing news about the retirement complex."

"You what?" Ashley jumps to her feet. "How could you? We'd agreed to keep that between us."

"I figured Nigel deserved to know, seeing how he sits on the council and all." Brett shrugs, trying to appear like it doesn't matter, except he knows it does.

"Brett..." her voice stops, the words stuck, unwilling to come out.

His brows rise, but he doesn't say a word.

She swallows hard, deciding what needs to be said versus what she wants to say.

Like *how dare you*, and *don't you realize what you've done?* Except, she knows he dared, and he knows exactly what he's done.

He just screwed her over. If this were a game of chess, this would be when he'd knock down her queen and call checkmate.

"Mom?"

Jordan stands in the doorway, bag slung over her shoulder. "Most of my homework is done. I can finish the rest tonight before bed or on the drive. Ready to go?"

Ashley smothers, squashes, and subdues every single

emotion simmering inside her. She pastes on a smile meant only for her daughter and breathes deeply.

"Absolutely, let's go." She leaves Brett behind without a single glance.

"You're just going to walk away?" He calls out.

Yes, she's going to do precisely that. She doesn't even hesitate when she hears the sound of glass shattering against the patio stones.

Jordan's eyes grow round. "Everything okay?"

Ashley grabs her purse. "It will be," she says, the promise in her voice as they leave the house. She isn't sure how she'll make it okay, but she will. She has to. One way or another.

What happened tonight is not acceptable. His anger, betrayal, and accusations crossed the line for her. She doesn't know what that means exactly...but she'll figure it out.

She always does.

CHAPTER FOUR

After last night, today is a multiple-pots-of-coffee type of day.

Her first cup was at the kitchen table as she went over her daily planner, struggling to keep her eyes open while figuring out how to find a better balance between family and work.

Her second cup was during breakfast and before making sure Jordan was up in time. The last thing she needed was Brett being late for work.

She finished that first pot of coffee by pouring the rest into her to-go mug before heading out the door.

By the time she made it to work, her mug was empty, her footsteps sluggish, and if someone had told her to have a nap, she would have listened to them.

She'd barely slept three hours last night, thanks to Brett's constant tossing and turning and his mumbling in his sleep about betrayal and spiders. The man hates spiders, and dreaming about them is a sure sign he's stressed.

He barely said ten words to her in the morning over coffee. *Good morning* and *I'll see you when I get home.*

She hates when he acts like that, but the person she really

feels for is Jordan, having to deal with him on the ride to school. She knows Jordan will listen to her music and work on homework, doing her best to ignore her father, but still.

The guilt from Jordan's words lay on her like a heavy blanket. A daughter shouldn't have to ignore her father, nor should it be something she has to get used to.

Whatever is happening within their family dynamic isn't okay and needs to change.

There's an unmistakable feeling of failure wanting to smother Ashley regularly. If there's one thing she hates, it's failing. Right now, she's failing in her marriage, as a parent, and even as Mayor.

What kind of example has she set for Jordan when it comes to relationships? A poor one, that's what.

"Hey, Ashley." Susan Crawford, her assistant, holds the door to the office open for her. "I had a feeling you'd be in early, so I grabbed coffee on my way over," she continues before Ashley can say hi. "Figured you could use it."

Ashley takes the offered coffee and sips the delicious concoction of espresso, cream, and vanilla that only Frankie can make.

"You're a lifesaver," Asley mumbles into her cup.

"Today is going to be crazy," Susan says as they walk down the carpeted hallway. "I stayed late last night and have everything ready on your desk." She flips on the lights as they walk into the main space of their office.

Usually, Susan would already be in the office, lights on, diffuser going, and coffee pot running by the time Ashley makes it in.

Today though isn't a regular day.

Town Hall is tonight, and Ashley has a day full of council meetings and phone calls. Before Susan came to work with her, she dreaded Town Hall days. But Susan has never been more organized and ready to take on a challenge.

"You didn't have to do that," Ashley says, "but you know I appreciate it."

Susan slides her purse into her bottom office drawer, hits the button to start her computer and smiles. "I know. And I appreciate the spa day at the Lodge as a thank you."

Ashley laughs. Of course, she's already made reservations at the most expensive spa in the area. Their last Town Hall had been a little crazy, and Susan basically made herself sick from preparations. Ashley promised her a spa day following every Town Hall she helps prepare for.

"I booked you a massage as well." Susan hands her a post-it note. "It's already in your calendar."

The note read deep tissue massage followed by time in the European style mineral pool, ending with a pedicure. It all sounded like heaven.

A swell of love for this woman fills Ashley's heart. Usually, Ashley is the one thinking of others, so to have someone think of her... means so much.

"Oh, no, you don't. You don't get to cry over this." Susan says, pulling out a tissue from her pocket and dabbing her own eyes.

"Sorry," she stares at the ceiling, willing the tears to disappear. "Today will be a long day, but we've got this, right?" What Ashley's really asking is if they are going to survive today.

"We've got this if you're ready to tell me your plan. Please? I can't help you if you don't let me in." Susan sits in her chair and flips open her notebook as if ready to write down the next words to come out of Ashley's mouth.

Of all people she should be able to talk to, Susan would be it, but council tied her hands, even with her own assistant. Their leash is ridiculous, but if she has any hope of having her plan become a reality, she has to play by their rules.

Well, in reality, it's all because of one man who likes to cause her issues. It's become a contest of wills at this point.

"Tonight. I promise, after tonight, we will have a lot to discuss, plan, prepare... we'll need multiple massages if my plan works."

"Not sure if you noticed, but your council meeting had to be moved to before lunch, by Nigel's request. Maybe you can ask them to take the muzzle off so I can help you prepare properly for tonight?"

Ashley groans at the news. Having the meeting before lunch means they will expect lunch to be provided, except, in trying to save their town, Ashley has placed cuts in every area possible, including council meals.

"Don't worry," Susan says, as if reading her mind. "I've already got it covered. Mom is making her famous German salad, Josie is putting together a sandwich platter, and Frankie is taking care of dessert. Mom is organizing getting everything here in time, so it's one less thing we need to manage. And no," Susan says before she even has the chance to ask, "none of them expect reimbursement. Mom says this is her way of saying thank you for how you organized care when she had her hip surgery, and you know Josie...she loves to be needed."

"Josie is always needed, and as for your mom, I can't believe how quickly she bounced back post-surgery." Ashley knows better than to object.

"You and me both," Susan says. "She has me walking with her every night."

"And you look great." Ashley tries to comment on the weight loss she's noticed in Susan.

Her assistant waves the compliment away.

For the next hour, Ashley works through the messages and

the to-do list Susan created for her and is making a good dent in the pile when her phone rings.

"It's not too early, is it?" Nigel, one of her oldest friends and married to one of her best friends, asks the moment she answers. She is still upset that Brett told Nigel about his plans for them to move into the city.

"That all depends on why you're calling." If he's calling about what Brett said...he should have talked to her directly.

"I hope you didn't mind I requested the time change for our meeting. Sylvia has a doctor's appointment this afternoon I can't miss." His voice softens at the mention of his wife.

"Everything okay?"

"Just another ultrasound. The doctor wants to keep an eye on junior, considering everything." Sylvia's last pregnancy was considered high risk, and although she'd been doing well, she was close to seven months when they'd lost their baby.

"I'm sorry, I didn't know." She should have known. Again, she's dropping all the balls that truly matter to her. Sylvia is her best friend, closer than a sibling. This doctor's appointment is something she should have known about.

"Yeah, I told her that. But she knows how stressed you are, so...just give her a call, okay? Talk her down if you can."

The concern is so clear in his voice that it scares her.

"I will." So many things are running through Ashley's mind about how Sylvia must feel. Terrified. Cautious. Worried.

"Thank you. While I have you on the phone, is what Brett told me legit?"

Ashley gives off a small groan. "Things with Brett are...on shaky ground, and the man only hears what he wants to hear. He shouldn't have said anything to you."

It takes Nigel a few seconds to reply, but when he does, any worry about his reaction disappears. "That's what I figured. I also know you'd be the one to tell us, not him, so I didn't put too much stock in it. Besides, if you were planning on leaving, you wouldn't be fighting so hard for this Christmas idea. This has me asking another question: how concerned are you about the council meeting and tonight's town hall? Do you think you can pull it off?" Nigel's tone is very non-confrontational, which Ashley appreciates.

"I have to. It's the only option."

"No, it's not the only option," Nigel reminds her.

"True, but it's the only good option for our town. You know this, Nigel. You know it, and you agree with me. Taking the offer to become a retirement village is a death sentence for Innsbruck, and we both know it." As much as Brett wants her to run with the offer and place their own lives and marriage first, she knows it's not the right thing to do. Not for her, and certainly not for the people in Innsbruck. Yes, jobs will be created if they accept the offer, but at what cost?

"Are you ready?"

"For tonight?" She barks out a laugh. "Goodness, no." Ready is the last word she'd use about tonight.

Tonight's results will either be sink or swim, take the offer that's presented or grab onto an idea that could be an amazing success or flaming failure.

If it were the council's decision, they would go with the offer and sell everything they could to the conglomerate that wants to build the luxury mountain retirement village.

Ashley would prefer to take a chance on something that could be life-changing for everyone in town.

Thankfully, it won't be up to the council, but instead, it'll be up to the town members. She's fought long and hard for this night to happen but happen it will.

"I have an idea. I don't think you should be the one to..."

Ashley relaxes back in her chair and twirls to face the large windows onto the main street, waiting for him to finish his sentence.

There's no reply.

"Nigel?"

There was mumbling in the background before his voice returns.

"I'll see you in a bit and explain then, okay? Do me a favor and just call Sylvia, please."

Ashley makes some notes while they're fresh in her mind before calling her friend.

"Why didn't you tell me you had an appointment today?" She keeps her voice light and friendly, erasing every ounce of fear and worry.

"It's bad enough I have Nigel coddling me. I don't need to hear the worry in your voice either. Trust me, I'm worrying enough for all three of us at this point." The exasperation in Sylvia's voice barely covers the fear Ashley hears.

"I'm fine. This baby is fine. I didn't tell you because there's nothing to tell. This pregnancy is different than the last one, I know it."

"I know it too. For one, you waddle like a penguin."

Sylvia's unexpected laugh is exactly what Ashley needs to hear.

"A penguin? Really?"

"It's cute," Ashley says. "I think it's all that baking you've been doing."

"Gah. I know. Stress baking is the worst, and I'm running out of space in the freezer."

"Good thing I have a solution for that," Ashley says.

"If your solution is to bring some with me tonight to the town hall, I'm way ahead of you."

"I like how your mind thinks. Listen, be honest with me. Are you really okay?" Ashley isn't about to let the topic slide.

"I'm freaking out inside, but if you mention that to Nigel, you're dead to me forever." Despite the teasing in her voice, it's the underlining fear that Ashley hears loud and clear.

"I wish I could be there with you, or at least see you afterward." Ashley offers.

"Oh, shut up. I'll be fine. You've got enough on your plate. I'll see you tonight, okay? If anything serious happens, you'll be the first one I call. But it'll be fine. I can feel it."

Ashley wants to be the cheerleader Sylvia needs. "I believe you. Hey, I picked up a little something for the baby. I saw it and couldn't wait. How about we do coffee tomorrow morning so I can give it to you?"

The slight inhale, the excited quiver of breath is the exact reaction Ashley wants to hear.

"A gift? I can't wait! Coffee sounds good. Now go. Thank you for calling, but seriously, you've other things on your plate."

Susan knocks on her door and motions behind her, just as Ashley hangs up the phone. Marcus Long, a council member and the one man who ran against her for Mayor, is there, arms crossed, with the largest scowl she's yet to see on his face.

It's her goal to one day bring him over to her side and work together instead of constantly being at odds. When that day happens, they'll share a laugh over how often they've disagreed. One day. They both love Innsbruck and want the best for their town; they just come at it differently.

"We need to talk before the council meeting." His gruff voice stirs a flurry of nerves inside Ashley.

"What's up, Marcus?" She motions to the chair opposite her desk. He walks forward but doesn't sit. Instead, he grips the edges of the seat, his scowl unrelenting.

"Who did you talk to?" The accusation is there, heavy in the air.

She reels back, shocked by his words. "No one. Susan doesn't even know."

The disbelief on his face churns Ashley's stomach. Technically, Brett also knows, but the council is fine with that. Brett wouldn't have said anything, would he? After last night, Ashley wouldn't be surprised, considering he seems intent on sabotaging her job.

"What's going on?" She somehow manages to keep her voice calm.

"I just spoke to Weiss. I ran into him at the hardware store. He's renovating to turn his house into a bed and breakfast. Why would he do that unless he knew something was happening." His eyes narrow as he stares at her.

"I have no idea, Marcus. No one has said anything to me about them opening up a B&B, nor have any permits been pulled."

He cocks his head to the side. "I have a tough time believing that. Mia would have said something."

"Are you calling me a liar?"

His mouth opens like he's about to do precisely that but then closes it.

"Seems odd they would open a business in a town that's all but dying unless they had some insider information, is all I'm saying." His tone is less defensive now, more cautionary.

Ashley, wondering the same thing, keeps that thought to herself. "I haven't said a word, as agreed. If I haven't told Susan, the woman who should be working with me on this, then I for sure wouldn't say anything to anyone else. Other than knowing opening a B&B has always been something Anna has wanted to do, this is the first I've heard of it."

Marcus doesn't reply, something which Ashley is grateful for.

"If you'll excuse me, I still have some reports to put together for our meeting at lunch. I want to make sure I present everything in a fair manner tonight, but to do that, I still have some items to prepare."

Her instinct is to contact Mia or call Anna right away, but she didn't lie to Marcus about not knowing, and she really does need to be better prepared for today's meeting. Everything else will need to wait.

CHAPTER FIVE

The council meeting this afternoon lasted way too long. It could have been half the length if not for Marcus wanting to insert his dominance at every single opportunity.

She'd presented all the requested information, sales numbers, projections, and forecasts, every possible scenario she could think of for both plans, and her head hurt.

She has a stop to make before heading home for a quick bite to eat before the big meeting tonight. Anna called and requested she stop in on her way home, which is perfect considering she has some questions to ask.

If it's true that they are turning their home into a B&B, the timing seems too good to be true.

There are many things Ashley can say about Anna and Weiss Becker, a German couple she's known forever. She was born a day after Mia, one of her best friends, and their mothers were roommates in the hospital.

The Beckers are also one of the founding families of Innsbruck, a solid couple that almost everyone has relied on in one way or another. Visiting with them is always a pleasure, even if the timing isn't the best.

The moment she steps through their door, she's greeted with warm hugs, wet kisses on her cheek, and a plate of fresh bread, cheese, and sliced meat.

"I know you're busy, dear, what with the meeting tonight, so we appreciate you stopping by," Anna says as she busies about her kitchen, making a pot of strong coffee.

Ashley has always loved their home. It's full of antique cuckoo clocks handed down from past generations, hand-woven mats, old plates hanging on the wall, and black and white photographs.

It's the photos Ashley loves the most.

They portrayed days long past, families who lived in one- and two-bedroom homes, farmers, weary mothers, and fathers with too many mouths to feed. They also portrayed hope and devotion to a beautiful country before the ugly war that brought the German families here to create Innsbruck.

"Are you rested from being away? Happy to be home or wishing you were back in your Bavarian Alps?" Ashley notices a shelf on the wall that wasn't there before, full of beer steins just as she's sitting down.

"Are those new, Weiss?"

Weiss grabs one from the shelf and brings it to the table.

"Ya, frome meine Vater." He turns the stein round in his hands.

"Sprich Englisch, Weiss. Wir sind nicht mehr in Deutschland," Anna mutters. "Sorry, Ashley. I told him to speak English as we aren't in Germany anymore."

"It's okay, Anna," Ashley assures her. "My German is rusty, but I understood." She works through the words in her head to ensure she repeats them correctly. "The beer stein was from your father," she says to Weiss with a gentle smile. "I'm sorry for your loss."

While in Germany for their yearly vacation, Weiss's brother

passed away. Mia flew over to attend the funeral and be with her family.

"We live, we die. It's the way of life. His wife said my brother died in his sleep, a smile on his face. So, he was happy, and that's what matters," Weiss wipes a tear that trickles down his weary face. "We found these in the family home, boxed up with my name on them. I always wondered where they went, thinking my brother sold them." His sigh is full of sadness.

"Funerals are always hard," Anna says quietly, "but it's always nice to head home to see our family. We missed home, though."

"And we missed you," Ashley reaches out and clasps Anna's hands between hers. "When will Mia be home?"

The widest smile grows on Anna's face. "Ahh, that girl of ours. She loves to travel. She should be home in a few days. She met up with an old friend in Paris and decided to stay a little longer. She's shipped a lot of treasures home for both the store and the upcoming market. She'll be home in time to help get that all setup, don't you worry."

A twinge of envy stirs within Ashley. "I'm more envious than worried," she admits. "One day, I'd love to take Jordan on a trip one year to Europe. Brett took me there for our honeymoon, and I fell in love with the culture, lifestyle, and whole experience."

"Ahh, Paris," Anna says with a hint of wistfulness to her voice. "We love it, too, don't we, Weiss?"

"Harrumph." Despite the grin on his face, his voice comes off as grumpy. "How many times can you see the Eiffel Tower or walk into old churches?"

The giggle coming from Anna surprises Ashley.

"Don't let the old grump fool you. He's the one who drags me to the tower every time we go so we can get a photo, and said Sacre Couer is the best place for a nap," she teases.

Weiss suddenly begins to cough, a deep hacking sound full of fluid. He pulls out a tissue, covering his mouth. He pushes himself up from the table as he continues hacking and leaves the room.

Anna's gaze follows him.

"Anna, that doesn't sound good," Ashley says.

The smile that has remained on Anna's face dissolves. Worry and fear cross the older woman's face as she focuses on her husband.

"The fool of a man refuses to see a doctor," Anna mumbles. "He picked up a cold from one of his sisters and can't seem to shake it."

There's a silence between the two women as Ashley gives Anna time to gather her thoughts. She doesn't want to hurry her, but...

"Ashley, love," Anna says as if picking up her train of thought. "I want you to know how proud Weiss and I are of you. Since you took on the role of Mayor for Innsbruck, your love for this town has been front and center of everything you do."

A pang of guilt runs over the praise from Anna. Once word gets out about the retirement village, Anna will no doubt change her mind.

"While we were back home, we noticed something as we drove about. There are towns dedicated to Christmas, thriving from the swell of tourists who love the holiday season. Towns that could very easily resemble Innsbruck, my dear."

Ashley desperately tries to hide her smile.

"We already have a Bavarian look on most of our homes here," Anna leans forward. "All it would take is a little remodel, some strategic planning, and we could become one of those Christmas towns that people will flock to...all year long." Her eyes sparkle as she puts Ashley's plan into words.

A little remodel, some strategic planning... that's all Ashley's been doing for the past month, having the very same idea.

Who wouldn't want to travel to a Bavarian town? Especially if it was one close by, you didn't have to pay thousands of dollars for a plane ticket.

And who doesn't love Christmas? Who wouldn't want to be surrounded by Christmas, by its joy and warmth?

"You make it sound so simple," Ashley says, knowing her eyes sparkle with the same intensity as Anna's.

"Oh, I know it's not," Anna swipes her hand in the air. "But it's doable, don't you think so, love?" Anna said as Weiss plods his way through the house and retakes his seat.

"The Christmas town idea? Yes, it's feasible. One step at a time, though. It could take a few years before it's complete, but it might just be the ticket this town needs. What do you think, Mayor?"

Ashley squirms under the intense gazes of both Weiss and Anna.

She wants to scream that she loves the idea, but she promised not to sway anyone, especially before both options have been presented to the town.

What does she think? The answer is obvious. She loves the idea. Ever since Mia made the off-handed comment about focusing on hosting seasonal markets, she always has said that it's too bad they couldn't be a Christmas town like the ones in Germany. That's what sparked the idea and flamed the desire to find an alternative to having Innsbruck become a retirement village.

She loves the idea, but the question is, will the people of Innsbruck? Is becoming a Christmas town the revitalization miracle she's been looking for?

"Now, before you say anything, I want you to know we've already spoken to Nigel, and he says the idea holds some promise. He's even urged us to present the idea tonight at the town hall if that's okay with you?"

So, this must have been what Nigel wanted to talk about but ran out of time.

"I love the idea, Weiss. I really do."

"We know, dear. Nigel told us you already had this idea in the works, but you can't say anything until tonight. I promise, though, that this is between us. We wouldn't want to get you in trouble."

Hmm. Was Nigel the one who spilled the beans then? The one responsible for getting Marcus so riled up? Whomever it was, at least it wasn't her.

Weiss coughs again, his body bending over from the strain. Anna pushes back her chair and stands beside her husband, her hand on his back. "I think it's time for the doctor, love."

He shakes his head. "I'm fine. It's just a stupid cold," he grumbles.

The stupid cold he's complaining about leaves his complexion white as crusted snow on the trails behind their town, and his forehead dots with sweat.

Ashley stands, gathering her bag, and reaches for both arms, giving them a slight squeeze. "Weiss, please see the doctor. I don't like the sound of that cough. I'll see you both tonight, and thank you for bringing the idea forward tonight, I appreciate that. I'd love to hear more about your trip, though, maybe I'll bring Jordan over some night, so she can see your photos?"

Anna's hand covers her chest with happiness. "Oh yes, bring that sweet girl of yours over. I always love when she stops in."

Ashley lets herself out, the sound of Weiss's continued coughing following her out the door.

CHAPTER SIX

MIA

"Mia, what are you doing home so soon? I thought you were in Paris?"

Mia sees Ashley leaving her parents' house with a massive smile. She wishes she could return the look, but she's been sick with worry for the past twenty-four hours that even if she tries to smile, it'll look like a grimace.

"Is Dad inside? How does he sound?"

The worry on Ashley's face tells Mia all she needs to know.

"And that's why I came home early. I didn't like the sound of that cough." Her uncle recently passed away and was initially sick with a cold.

"He's being stubborn," Ashley warns.

"Of course, he is." She looks around the yard and notices her father's truck. The bed is full of lumber. "What does he think he's doing?"

Ashley follows her gaze and sighs. "Rumor is he's about to tackle some renovations."

"Renovations? For what?" Her father is always on the go, needing a project to work on, but he's getting too old for this.

"A B&B."

Mia tears her gaze from the lumber to her friend's face. What is she talking about?

"You know your mom has always wanted to run one."

"That was a goal for when Mom retired, like, years ago."

The moment Ashley shrugs, Mia gets a pit in her stomach. "What is going on?"

Ashley checks her watch. "I have to run. We have a town meeting tonight, but come by after, okay? I'll need a glass of wine or two to relax afterward, and I need to update you on some changes we made to the Christmas Market."

"Changes?" The market is in less than two months, and she can't be making changes at this point.

"Nothing to be worried about, and I've got it handled, trust me. I asked Matt to help with my idea regarding the booths we'll be using. I want this market to have a...certain look and feel."

Mia slowly nods her head, trying to process what Ashley's saying.

Earlier in the year, they'd mapped out the market design. In the past, the markets were always held in the school gym, but this time, Mia convinced Ashley to have an authentic outdoor Christmas market in the town park.

"Right, we'd discussed that look. We were going to wait till next year, though, to use some of the proceeds from this year to pay for expenses." Why is Ashley rushing?

Ashley shrugs slightly, but it's more the glean in her eye that makes Mia suspicious.

"If we're going to do an outdoor market, let's do it well, don't you think? I mean, simple tables won't cut it. Besides, Matt didn't seem to think it would be an issue."

Matt? Matt who? Wait...not her Matt? Well, not *her* Matt

per say, but she can't mean the guy Mia has quietly been interested in for the past six months, right?

"When you say Matt, you mean some guy from the city...right?"

Ashley's brows furrow. "No. Matt Pablo. You know..." Ashley leans forward, "your Matt Pablo."

A fast flush of embarrassment presents itself along Mia's neck and cheeks.

Ashley's eyes twinkle. Oh, her friend is enjoying this way too much.

"He's not mine, and you know it."

"Only because you've barely spoken two words to him."

Mia looks everywhere but at Ashley.

"Now that you're home, I'll set up a meeting between the three of us. How does that sound?"

What? No. No, no, no.

"Don't do this, please," Mia begs softly.

"Don't do what?" The glee in Ashley's smile confirms she knows precisely what Mia is hinting at.

Fine. She'll speak it plainly. "Play matchmaker. Don't do it, okay? You're not very good at it for one, and two, if anything is going to happen, I rather it happens on its own."

Ashley heaves a very long sigh. "No promises. I want to see you happy, you know that. He'll be there tonight, so we can chat briefly then, okay?"

"Tonight?"

"Town hall? You are coming, right? We'll be discussing the market plus...other stuff – that is, if you can stay awake."

Mia yawns as if on cue. "Paris to Calgary is a long flight. Thankfully it was direct, and I could sleep a bit on the plane, but... I'm all for an early night, that's for sure."

"If you can't make it, that's okay. Give me a call tomorrow, okay? I want to hear about your trip and what goodies you found."

Mia hugs her friend goodbye and hurries inside just as her mom walks down the stairs, a finger to her lips.

"What are you doing home?" Mom wraps her in a warm, welcoming hug. "We weren't expecting you for a few more days. Is everything okay?"

Mia pulls away and looks her mom over, noticing the extra weary lines on her forehead, the dark circles beneath her eyes, and the way her shoulders sloop forward.

"How's Dad? I didn't like the sound of his cough on the phone."

"Is that why you're home?" Mom threads their arms together and leads her into the kitchen. "I've got tea on; come join me. Dad's lying down. He's a bit tired, that's all."

Mia follows her into the kitchen and notices the beer steins on the wall and the plastic-covered crocheted cloth on the table, both items they thought had been lost to them after Dad's parents passed away.

"Mom, what's with the lumber out in Dad's truck?"

It takes her mom a moment to reply.

"Mom?"

"Dad just wants to fix the place up, that's all," her mom finally admits.

Mia's brows rise, and she waits for her mother to say more because she knows more needs to be said.

"I know we'd talked about moving back to Germany, but... there's nothing left there but memories, you know? So, we decided to stay in Innsbruck and fix the house a little."

Mia catches the way her mom won't look her in the eyes, how she keeps her hands busy, a transparent avoidance tactic.

"Ashley already told me what you're doing. A B&B? Seriously?"

Mom's face flushes. "Yes, seriously. And why pester me like this if you already know? That's not nice, Mia."

Mia bites back an instant retort, knowing it's not the time to hold her mom accountable. She's worried about Dad, that's clear, and that's the focus right now.

"Dad can't be doing the renovations, Mom. You know that. Especially now."

Anna pours their tea and joins her at the table, smoothing down the plastic as she does.

"You know, owning a B&B has always been a dream of mine. We thought of doing it in Germany, but…why not here instead?"

Is she really asking her opinion or trying to explain herself? All her life, her parents have talked about retiring to the home country where they would run a B&B, following the family tradition.

"I don't know, Mom, maybe because all you and Dad have talked about is going home?"

There's a sadness in her mom's eyes as she stares at Mia. "Home is here, hun. It's where you are. Dad and I realized… we're not young anymore and want to be surrounded by our family. We want to be here, with you, at home."

Mia swallows back a lump that forms in her throat. Why does it feel like Mom is saying more than she's letting on?

"Why would you run a B&B? Especially now? I'm even struggling to keep the store open…."

She's more than struggling if she's being honest. It's why she's so desperate to try something new, to find new and different items to sell. After talking things over with her friend in Paris, a friend who does marketing for small businesses for a living, she has some ideas of where to start, of how to do things. Still, it will take time and money…and if this doesn't work, then doing the unthinkable is her next step.

She dreads having that conversation with Ashley, having to tell her she needs to close shop...hopefully she won't need to.

Anna inhales a long deep breath and looks upstairs. "It's what your Dad wants to do, hun. If it makes him happy, then I'm happy, and really, that's all that matters, isn't it?" Anna wraps her hands around her mug of tea and blinks rapidly.

"What aren't you saying?" Mia's words come out as a hoarse whisper, mainly because she's struggling to fight back the tears she's determined not to shed. That's not what her mom needs right now, her breaking down.

It doesn't take long for Mom's tears to start falling, leaving streak marks along her cheeks. Well, that's it. Mia can't possibly hold her own tears back now.

"Mom?" Mia reads all the words, the emotions, the things her mom isn't able to say. "He's going to be okay," Mia somehow manages to choke out. "He has to be."

Anna nods, but she's still unable to articulate anything. She wipes some non-existent crumbs from the table, unable to look at Mia.

Mia waits, a rubber ball of grief resting in her throat, praying things aren't as bad as she's making them out to be. They can't be.

"I'm just being silly." Anna gets up from the table to putter around the kitchen. "It's probably just a bad cold, but I'm worried. You know how it is. Your father thinks he's invincible when the reality is, he's just an old man that I'm not ready to lose any time soon."

"Neither am I," Mia says. She pulls out her phone and scrolls through her contacts. "If running a B&B is what you want to do, then okay, but Dad can't be doing the renovations alone. He needs help."

"Oh, honey, put that—"

"He needs help, Mom. It's not like you can't afford it, and

I'm sure someone here in town would appreciate the work, don't you think?" Mia's tone is a little cross, but she can't help it.

"Mia Becker. Put your phone away, and don't you dare talk to me in that tone again. Of course, your father isn't going to do it alone." She glances upstairs again, and they both pause, listening for movement.

"I've already taken care of it, okay?"

Mia knows enough to keep her mouth shut. Anna is giving her that don't-mess-with-me look Mia grew up with.

"Sorry, Mom." Apologies go a long way in this house. "I just...I came home early because I'm worried about Dad."

Anna walks around the table and wraps Mia in a hug. "I know, love. I'm worried too. Your father is stubborn, but I am too. So are you, don't you ever forget that. I know you're worried about your store, but I promise you everything will be okay."

Having her mom's arms wrapped around her in a tight squeeze.

"From your lips to God's ears," she whispers.

"Oh honey, He's already answered." Her mom whispers a saying she's said all her life. Usually, Mia would smile and nod, but lately, she can't help but feel that sometimes, her mom's belief is misguided.

She'll never admit that to her parents, though.

"Tell me you believe that, Mia. Don't you give up on God because He hasn't given up on you." There's a sternness in her mother's voice Mia hasn't heard in a long time.

"I believe Mom. Maybe not as strongly as I once did, but I believe." Even though she says the words, the truth is that she's not sure what she believes anymore or if it even matters.

For her parents' sake, though, especially when it comes to her father's health, if believing is what she needs to do, then she's all in.

CHAPTER SEVEN

ASHLEY

Ashley winces when the front door slams behind her as she walks into the house. She's always after Jordan about slamming the doors, and now she's doing it too.

She was lost in thought her whole walk home from visiting Anna and Weiss. This Christmas idea of hers must work – if others are coming up with the same idea, it's destiny, isn't it? It's meant to be. It has to be.

There are a lot of cons to go with the pros regarding her reinvention idea – but the good outweighs the bad, right? Sure, the cost is a factor. Renovating a whole town will cost more than most will expect. It's the main reason Marcus is all for the retirement village; there's no cost involved other than losing the essence of their town.

"Hey Mom, you okay?"

Ashley jumps. Jordan's sitting on the stairs, arms wrapped around her knees.

The look on her daughter's face brushes everything else

from her mind. Ashley heads toward her daughter with her arms open and is so thankful when Jordan jumps up and throws herself into them.

She's still her little girl.

"Are you okay?" Ashley is getting squeezed tighter than the elastic band in her hair, which tells her no, Jordan is not okay.

"It's just been a long day," Jordan finally admits. She glances toward the kitchen, rolling her eyes. "Dad's making dinner."

So many emotions roll over her daughter's face, but before she can prod any further, Brett appears, dish towel slung over his shoulder, a broad smile on his face.

"Hey, welcome home. I started dinner. I figured you'd be slammed at work, and knowing you, you'll need to rush out the door soon anyway for that meeting tonight." He approaches her, edging out their daughter, and wraps her in a hug.

She wishes she could relax in his embrace, but her nerves are so on edge that his touch only intensifies her anxiety.

"How was your day?" He asks. "Looking forward to tonight? Wine for later is chilling, but I poured you a glass of red when I heard the door close." He babbles away, not even looking at her directly. He knows there's a disconnect between them but doesn't want to admit it.

Ashley tosses her purse on the bench and heads into the kitchen for that glass of wine. She drinks half before feeling a semblance of readiness to take on Brett.

"I'm about as ready as I can be."

Brett stands at the stove, wooden spoon in hand, sauce dripping onto the floor as he waits for her to continue.

She doesn't. She sips wine instead while the conversations from today swirl in her head.

"Well, I'm sure tonight will be fine," Brett says, his voice full of confidence. "That retirement village offer is virtually the answer everyone's been looking for. They must see it's the only way to revitalize this dying town."

Jordan slips into the kitchen as quietly as a toddler hiding behind the couch with a set of Sharpie markers. Ashley gives her a smile.

"It's one answer, Brett. We've talked about this."

"It's the only smart move, Ash." Brett's smile is forced. "Sure, you'll present both options but make sure as Mayor, your preference is—"

"That's not how this works, Brett," Ashley interrupts. "You know that."

His brows draw together until they make a straight line across his face.

"You have the deciding vote," he argues.

Ashley struggles to remain calm. Why are they having this discussion again?

"What's not to like about the idea?" He won't let up, like a friggin dog with a bone...

In her head, Ashley runs through all the arguments brought up today during the council meeting. There are definitely council members who agree with Brett that this is the best and only option for their town. This council meeting was probably the most volatile session she's experienced since her tenure as Mayor, and that's putting it lightly.

What's not to like? So many things. It's bad enough she has to fight with some council members about the idea, but with her own husband too? It's exhausting, and this conversation shouldn't be happening – especially right before she has to leave for the town hall.

"For one," she says, "the idea that Innsbruck has always been a town focused on family seems to get lost in the big picture, don't you think?"

He dismisses her words with the wave of his hand. "That

won't change. Families will still come to visit their elderly parents. It'll be better than what we have now, and businesses will prosper, too. Surely they see that." He parrots word for word what Marcus said today.

"You talked to Marcus, didn't you?" A cyclone of frustration boils inside her. Why is Brett going behind her back like he is?

Brett dares to shrug like it doesn't matter, increasing the turmoil inside her. She should keep her mouth shut, she should leave things be until later, but she can't.

"What happened to supporting one another? To trusting the decisions we make when it comes to our careers? To being partners?" The questions fly out of her mouth with zero regrets.

"I am supporting you."

She would love to smack the look on his face off. "I figured it wouldn't hurt," he continues, "to have a few allies on your side." He sounds offended.

Offended. Him.

Her mind is blown. Her blood boils. It's been simmering all day in the background, but she's dialed up now, and his words, actions, and reactions are too much. Her cheeks burn as her blood pressure rises, and the headache she's been nursing all day is now pounding with the strength of a jackhammer.

The intensity increases, intensifies as she stares at a man she no longer recognizes.

Where does this leave them? What is she to do with what's happening between them?

She can't think about that right now. That's an issue for tomorrow.

"That's undermining me, Brett. Not supporting me." She can't believe she has to explain this.

"More and more, I'm feeling like we're not on the same page here, are we?" There's a coldness to his voice, a tinge of hostility with a touch of anger.

"Same page?" She asks. "Are you kidding me?" They are residing in separate chapters or even in two completely different books.

Who's to blame, though? Her? Him? Both? No one seems to be listening to each other lately, not truly listening.

"I know you want to move. You are more than ready for the next chapter of our lives to start. But I'm not there yet. I'm trying, Brett, I'm really trying...." She stops when he turns away, giving her an apparent cold shoulder.

"I'm sorry, but I'm not ready." Saying the words, admitting them out loud, frees something inside of her, something she hasn't been ready to accept.

Brett's shoulders tense, a tight line from one shoulder blade to the other, his back taut, his movements tense as he stirs the sauce.

He's angry.

So is she.

Jordan has slipped away at some point. Hopefully, she didn't hear too much. She doesn't need to see this ugliness between them. Ashley needs to be doing a better job at protecting her daughter.

Just another thing she's failing at.

"I knew it," he mutters. "You've strung me along, all this time, made me believe you were willing to put me and our marriage first, for once. You've lied to me over and over and over again, even though I've given you so many opportunities to be honest."

Her grip on her glass tightens at his words.

"Lied? Oh, that's a good one. When has our marriage ever been first for you? In between girlfriends, maybe?" She regrets the words the moment she says them. She's never wanted to fling their past like that, not after all the counseling they've done. Forgive and forget, right? She promised to move past the pain of his affairs, believing he'd never hurt her like that again.

Deep down, though, she's always known there's no forgetting. There's forgiving and putting to the side, forgiving and moving on, forgiving and praying it never happens again...

"I've never lied to you, Brett." He'll be waiting a long time if he's expecting an apology. There's nothing for her to apologize for. "I've always been as upfront as I could be. You just haven't wanted to hear what I've had to say."

He flings the wooden spoon in the sink, pulling plates out of the cabinet, and slaps them down on the counter. Surprisingly, none chip from the force.

"Dinner is ready. I hope you enjoy it. I'll be in my office." He pulls a beer out of the fridge and storms out of the room.

Of course, he runs from the conflict between them. He's like a little boy not allowed a second bowl of ice cream.

"This is the last thing I need right now, Brett. Tonight, of all nights...come on." She says to his retreating back.

Ashley usually loves town hall meetings, but not tonight. Tonight has her anxious, worried, and a ball of nerves. Tonight has the power to be explosive, full of angst, and she's afraid of what the outcome might be.

Marcus is determined to do what he can to see the retirement village become a reality, and apparently, he's managed to convince her husband to help him.

His threat hovers over her, hangs on her like a weighted blanket. If the town doesn't vote for the retirement village proposal, he will fight her every step of the way. He's made it very clear that he disagrees with her vision, claiming she's stuck in the past, and if she doesn't move their failing town into the future, then he will.

It doesn't hurt that his property is one of those that will be bought out. All he can see is the money, while she focuses on the people in their town.

She has this niggling fear that Marcus will go over her head and contact the corporation behind her back. He all but said he would today.

"Mom?" Jordan returns to the kitchen.

"Hey." Ashley forces a cheeriness she doesn't feel. "Come have dinner with me. Dad is...working or something."

She spends the next few minutes dishing up their plates, happy to have something else to occupy her thoughts. Jordan seems to understand. She chatters away about school, homework, and friends; nothing about the tension in the home, the meeting tonight, or what their future will look like.

Ashley appreciates the normality Jordan attempts to create for her.

"I'm in the mood to walk to the meeting tonight. Want to join me?" She asks Jordan. At this point, she doesn't care if Brett joins them or not.

Jordan hesitates. "I'd rather stay home if that's okay? Arielle and I were going to get together and work on homework together."

Ashley pulls her hair into a ponytail. "Of course, sorry. I wasn't thinking. Why would you want to be there tonight?" She laughs, but it's more half-hearted than anything.

"Thanks, Mom." Jordan gives her a brief hug. "Mind if I have Arielle come here? I'll clean up the kitchen before she gets here."

"Just give your dad a heads up, okay?" Ashley says before heading upstairs, by-passing the closed door to Brett's office without missing a beat.

CHAPTER EIGHT

MARLEE

Every time they drive up the mountain road to Innsbruck, Marlee gets hit with an overwhelming nostalgia for returning home.

Every. Single. Time.

Maybe it's the familiar sense of remembrance as she catches sight the trails she hiked with Jared, the field with trees she helped plant as part of a school project when she'd been a teenager, or just that this is where her heart remains, despite having moved away six years ago.

Every day since they left, she's prayed they could return home, but more and more, that appears to be impossible. She never wanted to raise their children in the city, to be enveloped by that bubble of busyness that comes with being in the city. Yet, that's precisely what they've done.

"I heard that sigh," Jared reaches across and squeezes her hand. "I heard it, and I feel it too," he continues, his voice a little wistful. "You know if we could, we'd move back."

She tosses him a smile but keeps her thoughts to herself. He says it, but would they really? There's so much history here, and not all of it is good. Secretly, she doubts Jared will ever want to move back, mainly because it means being close to his family again.

They are on their way to Jared's parents to celebrate their son Julian's birthday. He's such a good boy, he hasn't once complained about canceling his birthday party with friends, even though she knows he's disappointed.

They'll make it up to him by having the best weekend ever. Tonight is all about sleepovers with the cousins. Tomorrow is his birthday celebration and maybe even a hike on some trails. She'll make sure it's fun for all the kids.

"It'll be nice to see everyone again, don't you think?" She half turns to her husband and watches for his reaction.

He gives a brief smile. He was the oldest of three, and whether he admits it or not, he bears a sense of responsibility for his siblings and family.

Jared drives through the back streets, the fastest route to his parents' home,

Josie is there, waiting on the porch when they pull up. Her arms are wide enough for her grandchildren to launch into and her laughter at seeing the kids is infectious - for Marlee at least.

Jared stands there, hands in his pockets, as he looks around.

"Come and give your mother a hug," Josie says the moment she lets go of her grandchildren. She's already given Marlee a hug and a kiss on the cheek.

"Hey, Mom." Jared wraps his mom into his arms, holding onto her for a few moments longer than usual.

Even if he never says it, Marlee knows he misses his family.

"Yard needs cut," Jared mumbles.

"You know where to find the mower." Josie pushed her chest forward, clearly affronted.

"Why hasn't my brother taken care of it?"

Josie shoos him into the house with her hand. "Your brother has his own family to take care of. The yard will get done when it gets done. It's only grass, and God knows it always grows."

The minute they enter the house, chaos reigns. All the cousins are here, and this is the official grandchild-sleeper weekend.

"We should have gotten a hotel, just for the two of us," Jared says to her.

"What do you think your siblings did?" Josie nudges her son with a twinkle in her eye.

The kids run through to greet everyone, digging into the bowls and plates of snacks Josie set out, and of course, a few cups of juice manage to get spilled.

"That's it. Outside," Jared's raised voice has all the kids, including their nieces and nephews, stop in their tracks. "This isn't the zoo, and you're not a herd of zebras. Apologize to your grandmother and then skedaddle."

All seven, from ages three to thirteen, apologize to Josie. The oldest grandchild grabs paper towels to clean up the mess before joining the others outside.

"Don't be too hard on them, Jared. They haven't seen each other in a few months." Josie taps her son on the shoulder as he helps to clean up the mess on the counter. "You were no better when your cousins came to visit if I remember correctly."

"Is there anything I can do," Marlee asks, diverting the conversation as best she can.

Josie looks like she's about to say something, then notices the time. "Jared, I need you to take care of grilling the burgers and hot dogs for the kids. Marlee, you can help me set the table and wrangle the kids back inside to eat. I then want you both to join your father and me as we head to the town meeting tonight. The kids will be fine while we're gone."

Jared looks like he's about to argue, but the glare from Josie has him closing his mouth with a snap. He takes the tray of meat and heads outside.

"Durwood should be back any minute. I expected him here before you arrived, actually. That man..." Josie shakes her head as she tsks at the time. "I think he expected you all to be late."

Marlee is taking things out of the fridge and chuckles. "Late? You do know your son, right? He wanted to take the kids out of school early so we would miss the traffic, but I put my foot down."

"Oh, you should have," Josie says.

Marlee shakes her head. "Julian has been looking forward to celebrating his birthday in his class. They do a whole thing to make the kids feel special. I didn't want him to miss that, especially since he's not having a birthday party with friends this year."

Josie presses her hand to her chest. "I hope he's not too disappointed to spend it with family?"

Marlee hears the hurt in Josie's voice and rushes over to place a hand on her mother-in-law's arm. "I think the fact he gets one of your cakes for his birthday rather than a store-bought one more than makes up for it," she smiles, her eyes twinkling. "He's not disappointed at all, considering he's been begging to come here for a visit."

That brings a smile to Josie's face. "Did you know he called me the other day and asked if he could help make it?"

This is news to Marlee. "Why am I not surprised? Did you know one of his dreams is to open a bakery when he's older?"

"Oh, a boy after my own heart. Bless him. He can come to Grandma's anytime he wants to do some baking."

Jared and Durwood walk into the kitchen carrying platters by the time they get the food out on the table, and the kids are corralled onto their seats.

"You're late," Josie says as she gives her husband a kiss on his cheek.

"Sorry about that. We need to hurry, though, or we'll be late for the meeting." He apologizes to everyone, but his gaze lands an extra second longer on his son.

"You're here now, that's what matters," Josie says, taking his hand and leading him to the table.

Marlee watches the two, searching for...something, she's not sure. Are they doing okay? Is Durwood doing too much? Taking on too much? There are no signs of tension between the two, which is good.

The same can't be said about Durwood and Jared, though. You can cut the tension between them with a steak knife. She wishes she knew what was happening, but she's been left in the dark. Jared says it's not worth getting into, except she knows it is. It has to be.

Family is everything; she hates that their kids are growing up so far away from family because of a rift. Despite all the excuses Jared gives her about why they moved to the city and can't move back home, she knows they're exactly that, excuses meant to hide something.

She just wished she knew what those excuses were covering.

CHAPTER NINE

ASHLEY

Innsbruck Town Hall is plain in decor. For years, it's been used for meetings: Boy Scouts, Girl Guides, weekly bingo games, church youth groups, wedding receptions, weekend game tournaments, Santa photos, and just about everything else.

Susan tinkers with the food tables at the back of the room, moving trays of goodies around.

"It looks fine," Ashley says, setting down the plate of cookies Jordan made the night before at Frankie's.

"I need to keep room for Sylvia's baking, I just don't know how much she's bringing," Susan mutters.

"Expect a lot. She's out of room in her freezer, I'm told."

Susan groans. "Great. What does that mean? Three plates? Five? More?"

Ashley glances around the room surprised Nigel and Sylvia haven't arrived yet. The game plan was for council members to arrive early and greet everyone as they arrived to get a feel for the temperature in the room.

The goal is to see how everyone feels about an Innsbruck reinvention and if they have any ideas.

They've plastered posters all around town, inside shops, and even sent out a blast via email about the concept of Reinventing Innsbruck, hoping if they could get people thinking of it, some ideas would come to light.

"Where's Brett?" Susan asks.

Ashley keeps her gaze focused on everything but Susan. "He'll be around later. He had some work to finish up first." She has no idea if that's true or not. She'd left without saying a word to him.

Truth be told, she really didn't want him here at all.

Ashley surveys the room, surprised at how quickly it's filling up, and they still have twenty minutes to go.

Ashley quickly checks her phone, forgetting to turn it on after she'd arrived home. Twelve missed text messages and three phone calls from Sylvia. Her heart sinks. She never followed up after Sylvia's appointment, and she should have.

Friend rule #101: You are there when your friend is in need. Always.

About to call Sylvia back, she pauses when she realizes her friend has arrived.

In a wheelchair.

Ashley's heart bottoms out.

Nigel's fingers clutch the handles of the chair like a lifeline while Sylvia holds a box on her lap, her face as serene as an angel.

"Oh my gosh, I just noticed your messages. I am so sorry," Ashley gushes with guilt as she runs to her friend's side. "What happened?" Her gaze flies between Nigel and Sylvia, needing one of them to answer.

"Don't worry, I figured you were busy." Sylvia hands the box full of baked goods to Susan. "I meant to have these here sooner," she apologizes, "but someone," she glances over her shoulder to Nigel, "thinks I'm as fragile as a blooming sunflower." She frowns with a fierceness that matches the same look on Nigel's face.

"Bed rest doesn't mean going to town meetings you really don't need to be at." Nigel grinds out between a clenched jaw.

"I'm not on bed rest. I have to take it easy." Sylvia looks up at Ashley as if looking for support.

Ashley holds up her hands in surrender. The last thing she wants is to get in the middle of this argument. She'd been there before when Sylvia had to be on bed rest, and her friend did not do well with inactivity.

"What does 'taking' it easy mean, exactly?" Ashley asks.

"Not being on my feet," Sylvia says.

"Bed rest," Nigel counters.

"So, the wheelchair is...a compromise?"

Nigel's eyes close while Sylvia purses her lips.

"I will not be stuck in bed again if I don't have to. And," she says, twisting around to speak to her husband, "I don't have to. The baby is fine. I am fine. But a certain someone is being a tad bit overprotective." She crosses her arms and looks like she's about to pout.

To break the tension between the two, Ashley gives her friend a hug. "If the baby is okay, and you are okay, then I say thank God it's not bed rest again because, as much as I love you... you're not the nicest person when you're confined." She blows Sylvia a kiss.

Ashley notices the growing crowd forming around Sylvia, no doubt curious about the wheelchair.

Nigel notices, too.

"All right, beautiful wife of mine, let's get you out of the doorway, so we're not blocking traffic any more than necessary."

Nigel pushes her forward, the crowd following behind until he parks her at the front.

"Everything okay?" Susan whispers.

"Other than her being a tad bit grumpy, there are no tears, so I'm going to go with yes." She really hopes everything is okay, she really does.

Susan hands her a bottle of water. "There may be no tears now, but we'll keep an eye on her. Now, it's time you head to the front and get this show started."

Ashley breathes in deep, closing her eyes, and mentally counts to ten. Her stomach is all in knots, but she's determined to ignore the anxiety that keeps wanting to crank up a notch or two. She has no idea what will happen tonight, but whatever it is, it'll be out of her hands.

By the time her eyes open, she's got a smile on her face – it's time to get this show on the road.

She waits as more council members join her, seated in their chairs behind her, while she stands at the podium. Susan placed a sealed envelope there for her. Sealed, so people wouldn't be tempted to sneak a look like they used to when a regular file folder was used.

Once everyone takes their seats, Ashley goes through the official motions and notes and then pauses.

"When you elected me to be Mayor of Innsbruck, I made you a promise that the revitalization of our town would be my number one priority. We have so much to offer as a town, and there's no reason why we should continue to dwindle in numbers as families move away. I want to tell you that I have worked hard to keep my promise, and we have received some outside interest in helping us to save our town." She looks out at the crowd and realizes the heavy weight she's been feeling the past few months isn't just about her and keeping her promise.

It's about the very people in these chairs, their families, their children, and the business represented here.

The responsibility of that weight feels almost too much to bear.

"Before I present the offer, I want to share with you something I've realized." She chokes up a little. Each seat is filled with someone she's known for years, some since a small child, generations represented within one room...and tears spring to her eyes.

"The heart of Innsbruck is you." She points into the crowd, hoping to make the point personal. "We are a town that consists of families, and that is what we are about. One person alone can't save this town, but with all of us combined...anything is possible."

She catches the way Sylvia nods, sees the thumbs up from Frankie and the smiles from others. She also finds herself looking to see if maybe, just maybe, Brett has placed aside his anger and is there to support her.

He's not. His chair at the front is empty, and he's not one of the few loitering at the back.

She's alone, and that's a hard pill to swallow.

She does the only thing she can now - she pushes that tiny seed of betrayal to the side.

"We've received an offer to turn Innsbruck into a retirement village. Three condo buildings would be built along the east side, along with a medical facility and an assisted residence." She glances down at the points the council wanted her to make. "It would mean the town would sell some of our land and various properties throughout town, and yes, several of you would probably receive offers to sell. Before you ask," she holds up a hand, "yes, it would be financially profitable for our town and overall business throughout town." Ashley pauses, reading the emotions that cross the faces in the crowd, hearing the audible reactions from those around her.

Are they excited, or are they upset? She can't tell.

A few shake their heads. Others nod, but the majority just sit there, arms crossed, and Ashley feels a small measure of hope.

Marcus takes to his feet and her heart rate increases, worried about what he has to say.

She wants to give the other option, to explain to them her vision, and quickly looks to Nigel. As if reading her intentions, he shakes his head slightly.

"There's a microphone in the aisle for questions," Marcus says, "and suggestions. Remember, we are here to discuss the opportunity, pros, and cons. It's a great offer and one we don't want to dismiss out of hand."

Ashley's surprised he isn't being more vocal about his support for the proposed village.

One by one, people stand behind the microphone to ask questions or voice their concerns. Many see the benefits to their businesses, while others worry that the younger ones will be lost by catering to the older generation.

All very valid concerns, and none of it surprises Ashley in the slightest.

The evening drones on like that as, one by one, people have their say.

Marcus is ready to have Ashley concede that the village idea may become a reality, but she's not. She's still waiting for one person to speak up, and until he does, she'll remain.

Of course, Weiss Becker waits until the last minute, but she understands why as he makes his way toward the microphone.

He doesn't look too good. He's pale, worn, and looks worse than he had earlier today. He coughs, mouth covered with a cloth he pulls from his pocket. Anna stands by his side, worry lining her features.

"Weiss, let me grab you a chair." Nigel carries a chair over to him and then starts to pull the microphone from the rod when Weiss stops him.

"I'm not that old that I have to sit. You go on now." He shoos Nigel away. "We've been away for four months, as most of you know. We went home, to Germany, for what will probably be my last trip home." He coughs again, body bowing from the effort.

"Weiss, sit down, you old fool," Anna whispers, but loud enough that everyone hears.

"Love, save the babying for at home," Weiss pats her on the arm.

Many people in the room, including Ashley, chuckle at the tenderness between the two love birds.

"How many here have heard of the German Christmas Markets?" He glances around, and many raise their hands. "There are towns in Germany that focus on Christmas year-round, did you know? Not just Christmas towns, but towns that also focus on specific fairy tales. These towns... reminded Anna and me a lot of Innsbruck. Old, nostalgic, full of promise...they did what we've not yet been able to do: they found a way to stay relevant, to remain alive and provide security to those who live there." He pauses, catching his breath, turning his attention from the crowd to Ashley.

She gives him a slight nod, thankful for his words. They give her hope, and she can't stop the smile from growing on her face.

"Mayor, you've talked about Innsbruck having the strength to reinvent, that the families, the people here...the heart of this town...if we could all come together, anything was possible. So, why not this? Why not become a year-round Bavarian Christmas Town?" He turns to face those around him. "You realize this town has a sister town, right? In Germany, too, where many of our families came from. Why not go back to our roots?"

Weiss, a retired teacher, holds a place of authority within this town. Many know him as someone they can trust for a good reason.

"It means changing our focus, but would that be so hard to do? I mean, who doesn't like Christmas?"

Someone in the crowd raises their hand.

"Is there really a demand for a year-round Christmas town?"

Weiss rubs the back of his neck. "Well, that's a good question, isn't it? It's not like people don't come to the mountains year-round, right? Winter is about skiing. Summer is about the beauty of the outdoors...why not find ways to cater to both types of tourists? Become known for something, you know? It'd take a lot of work, and we'd all have to pitch in and help, but why not? The logistics we'd leave to the council, but I'd imagine we'd want to alter the look of our town to have more of a Bavarian feel than it does now. Perhaps we could reopen some of those businesses that closed, theming wouldn't be that hard, I'd imagine. It could work if we put our mind to it. Would make the place livelier too, with a little bit of marketing? Those who can't afford a trip to Germany to experience the Christmas Markets could come here instead. We'd make it as authentic as we could."

Out of breath and wracked with another round of coughing, Anna all but drags him back to their seats.

A low murmur fills the room as people talk amongst themselves and those around them.

Ashley notices a slight motion from Sylvia to Nigel.

"As many as you know," Sylvia says as he hands her the microphone, "my background is in marketing. I've worked with some coastal towns to grow their tourism portfolio. This idea of reinventing Innsbruck into a quaint German town..." she pauses as unspoken communication happens between her and Nigel.

Everyone seems to hold their breaths, including Ashley.

Please let this miracle happen. Please, please, please...

"It's doable," Sylvia says. "If we all pitch in, we can make it happen."

The longest sixty seconds of Ashley's life occur as there's utter silence in the large room.

Until Marcus walks forward.

"While reinvention toward a holiday town sounds exciting, it will also be expensive, probably more than what we can afford. Do we really want to go into debt over this? The retirement village will be paying us, which means, as a town, we will survive. As Mayor Ashley mentioned, families will also prosper from this if they agree to sell their homes and land. It's a win-win scenario."

Ashley feels the excitement in the air deflate when he brings up the financial aspect. Knowing Marcus, he probably intended for that to happen.

Not on her watch, though. It's time to take back control.

"The goal tonight," she says, "was to discuss possibilities. So far, we have two ideas. Both come with positive and negative aspects. Would anyone else like to present another option?"

No one responds. She waits another thirty seconds. A few people whisper amongst themselves, which she takes as a good sign.

"What I'd like to propose is this - let the council do a little homework. We will focus on both options and hold another town meeting to present our findings."

A voice from the back interrupts her from saying more. Marcus' wife stands.

"We elected you all to make these decisions," she says,

projecting her voice. "Why waste our time when you're going to decide anyway?"

Marcus beams a bright smile toward his wife, which doesn't surprise Ashley. He then brings the microphone toward his mouth.

Oh no, he doesn't...

"That's true," the words rush out of Ashley's mouth like a horse from the gate, "but since this decision will affect everyone in our town, I think it's only fair that you are allowed to be part of the decision process.

"We have a month before the deadline on the retirement village offer expires," Nigel says. "That would give us time to pursue each option and present our findings to you. I think," he glances toward Ashley, "what our mayor suggested is a good idea."

Thankful for his help, Ashley gives him a slight nod.

"In the meantime," Ashley says, "if anyone has other ideas or would like to help with the research, please feel free to talk to me or any other council members." She goes through the motions to close their meeting, knowing things can continue for another hour if she doesn't.

The first person to approach her is Marcus.

"I'd like to head up the retirement village proposal if you don't mind." He isn't asking.

Butting heads with the man is something she's used to but not something she enjoyed.

"Let's discuss tomorrow afternoon during our follow-up meeting, okay? We will divide responsibilities and scopes then."

He sticks his hands in his pant pockets and frowns.

"This is our only option," he says below his breath. "Even your husband agrees with me." Marcus' face holds no smile, no softness, no semblance of friendship or familiarity.

Ashley grinds her teeth. Damn Brett for opening his mouth.

"Unfortunately, Brett wasn't elected mayor, nor does he sit on the council." She isn't going further with this discussion, not with Marcus.

She will, however, continue this discussion with Brett himself tonight. Regardless of the consequences.

CHAPTER TEN

Brett is waiting for her when she walks in the front door. He's got his phone tied to his ear, but the frown on his face tells her more than she wants to know. She can only imagine who he's talking to. Best guess - it's Marcus.

Suddenly, she's more worn and wearier than expected and wants only to head to bed, rather than step into the fighting ring.

"Thanks for the warning, buddy. Talk to you later," Brett says before getting off the phone and facing her, like a man ready to take down the world.

"Thanks for the heads up," he says to her, the tone of his voice saying more than his words.

For the heads up? She's obviously too tired to comprehend what he's saying. Her brain is exhausted, and the last thing she wants to get involved in is a heated argument with her husband. Again.

"A Christmas town? Really, Ash? You mentioned something about markets, but I didn't expect you to go all hog crazy on some hair-brained idea like this. You should have told me, don't you think? Considering everything... I think I'd be the first person you would have told."

She wants to answer, but there's nothing there, like he's siphoned all her energy. She heads to the kitchen for water, and he trails after her.

"What happened to resigning? What happened to keeping your promise? Marcus says the idea isn't going to happen, that the town can't afford it even if they wanted to. Which is something you should have said rather than give false hope." He's scolding her like a child, which is entirely inappropriate.

"False hope? I don't know what Marcus told you, but it sure wasn't that." She drains the glass of water, guzzling it like she's dying of thirst.

What she'd really love is a big glass of wine, but then she'd say more than she should tonight, and it's better to keep a level head than say words she'll later regret.

Words like: *why didn't you come? Why didn't you come to support me? What is happening to us?*

"It has its merits," she says instead. The idea has more than just merits, but she really isn't in the mood to discuss or try to sell it to Brett tonight.

"Really? I see more negatives than positives." Brett stands there, arms crossed, eyes shooting daggers full of condemnation at her. "Seriously, Ash, you need to step down like you promised and let someone else take the reins on all this."

He sure is ballsy, she'll give him that. Like a dog with a bone...

"If you wanted me to step down, you would have been there tonight to ensure I did. I would have needed your support, Brett, don't you realize that? That would have been one of the hardest things for me to do, and I would have needed you there, by my side, supporting me. So where were you? Here? Doing what? What was more important than being there with me tonight?"

At her accusation, he scrubs the back of his neck, looking at anything and everything but her as his lips twist into something, something that resembles a secret smile.

Her heart sinks, and she doesn't want to let her thoughts go where they shouldn't. Maybe it's not a question of what's more important, but maybe who?

Please God, no. She can't go through that again. They wouldn't survive another affair.

It can't be that, though. He wouldn't be pushing her like he is if he's involved with someone else. She needs to believe that.

"You're right," he says, completely surprising her. "I should have been there. I meant to be, but I got distracted."

Ashley's brows shoot up like a ten-story express elevator.

"I think I found us the perfect house in the city and it's not too far from Jordan's school. It has everything we could want, and if we get the right price from the retirement package, we can afford it no problem while you look for another job."

He's got this wide, crazy look in his eyes. She didn't recognize the man standing before her. "And there's a few other homes on that street listed as well, so we could get Nigel and Sylvia to move, too. Wouldn't that be great?"

Is that what he'd done all night? Look online for a house in the city? When he should have been at the meeting with her?

Incredible.

"We're not selling." Her flat voice says everything she needs to say. In fact, if he'd led with the point, he'd found them a home in the city, she could have headed directly to bed and avoided this whole discussion.

"Like shit, we aren't."

Ashley stares at him in surprise. Brett rarely swears and never at her.

"You made me a promise," he growls.

She blinks several times while trying to decide if it's even worth continuing their argument at this point.

He hasn't heard a word. Not. One. Single. Word.

Every time she tells him she isn't ready to leave, she isn't ready to give up her career, that this is her home, he ignores her.

It's partially her fault, for not making it clearer, for going along with him in letting Jordan go to school in the city, for not putting her foot down stronger, for hoping that things would magically change and she wouldn't have to deal with his anger and disappointment in her.

That or... she's been hoping he would leave her, and none of this would be an issue. Could that be true? A mountain of sadness falls on her, crumpling her inside at the realization. How long has she wanted her marriage to be over? Why is she just realizing it now?

She's done. Done with this conversation, with today and tonight, and everything else that's going on right now. All she wants to do is go to bed and start fresh tomorrow.

Is that even possible?

"How did things go with Jordan and Arielle?" She steps back from him, creating space between them and changes the conversation.

When he frowns, she realizes she's caught him off guard.

"Fine. They just worked on homework and made popcorn," he grumbles.

"I'm going to say goodnight to her and get ready for bed." The day had been long, the evening longer, and she has no energy for anything else, including continuing to fight with Brett.

"So that's it?" He stops her from leaving.

"That's what?"

"You're just going to ignore what I said? Walk away from me and not discuss this?"

So many things should be said, but none of them are what he'll accept.

"I'm not saying the words you want to hear," Ashley tells him, "I doubt I will go despite whatever house you've found."

Brett's shoulders bow. "Don't do this, Ash," he says, eyes downcast. "Please." The pleading in his voice is raw.

"What am I doing, Brett? I thought I was pretty clear earlier about how I felt."

"But you—"

"Promised," she finishes for him. "Yes, I know. How could I forget with you shoving it in my face all the time? I shouldn't have. Trust me, I regret it more than you can imagine."

"You regret it?" The incredibility in Brett's voice surprises her. "You regret our marriage, our family," he swallows hard, his hand coiling into a fist at his side, "me?"

"Regret you?" How had he put that together from what she just said? And where is this anger coming from?

"Putting me first. God, Ash," his fist pounds his thigh, one-two-three times. "Don't act like you didn't know what I mean."

Weary, Ashley doesn't have any fight left within to repeat everything she'd already said. How can she help him understand?

She loves this town. She's never kept that a secret from him. From the very early years of their marriage, moving back here was always her goal, something he'd always been aware of. He'd known and agreed that starting a family here, in a small town rather than a city, was the right thing for them to do, regardless of the sacrifices they'd both need to make.

"Honestly, Brett, I just want to say goodnight to our daughter, crawl into bed and go to sleep. We keep going around this issue, and I'm too tired to argue anymore."

She leaves him then but not before she hears him mumble something.

"I'm sorry, what did you say?" She half turns.

"You wonder why I strayed before, is what I said. You never seem to realize I have needs, too." His lips snarl with an obvious dare for her to deny his words.

She bites her lip to stop the rush of words that wants to pour out.

She will not accept the blame he continually casts her way as an excuse for his past infidelity. He is the one who cheated. Not her.

She doesn't need to say any of those things because he obviously reads them on her face.

"Whatever," Brett grumbles before retreating into his office, the door slamming behind him.

Rooted in spot by his reaction, Ashley contemplates apologizing. If she wants to save their marriage, she will walk into his office and say the words he wants to hear.

Can she say them?

Everything inside her screams no.

Saying something she doesn't mean, only to appease him, means accepting a life she doesn't want to live.

Leaving Innsbruck. Stepping down as Mayor. Moving to the city. Being his wife.

That last sentence is a knife with a dull blade straight through her heart.

Does she really feel that way?

Is she ready to end their marriage? Does this town, her position mean more to her than her family? What kind of person does that make her? What does that say about her marriage?

Then she thinks about Jordan. Her daughter doesn't deserve to have her family torn apart. That isn't fair to her.

Marriage is about giving and taking, making sacrifices for the one you love, and being life partners.

With footsteps as heavy as her heart, Ashley makes her way

up the stairs, one step at a time, and swallows the swell of tears blurring her vision.

Say goodnight to Jordan and then cry.

Sob into the pillow if she needs to.

But first, the only thing necessary is to remain strong and tell her beautiful daughter just how much she loves her.

CHAPTER ELEVEN

MARLEE

For the longest time, no one said anything as they sat at the kitchen table following the town hall meeting. Their walk home had been quiet; everyone lost in their thoughts, processing the options and what it means for them.

The one thing that keeps running through Marlee's head is – regardless of the town's decision, there will be plenty of job opportunities for Jared – if she could convince him to move back.

Rather than continue to stare into her cup of decaf coffee, Marlee broaches the subject they're all thinking about.

"I don't know about you, but I kind of love the idea of Innsbruck becoming a Christmas village." She infuses her voice with excitement and is thankful when Josie gives her a matching smile.

"What is Weiss thinking of," Durwood's voice is both gruff and grumpy. "Who can afford to do all that work? The coppers are dry, or don't people realize that? This town is dying slowly, and it'll take a miracle for what they want to happen to happen."

"Oh, stop being a Scrooge," Josie slaps her husband's hand. "Instead of listing all the problems, how about you figure out a way to solve them?"

Marlee notices Jared isn't saying anything, just staring at the table. She nudges him with her leg.

"It could work," Jared finally says.

His dad scoffs. "In what world would something like that work? Wouldn't it be better to let those retirement people set up shop? We've got a good selection of people our age in this town, we could probably use some of the services they'd provide." Durwood leans back in his chair and cracks his neck.

"What about everyone else?" Jared's tone is a bit snippy. Hopefully, Marlee is the only one who notices. She's tempted to nudge her husband's leg again but doesn't. He's an adult and knows how to navigate conversations with his parents.

Durwood's brows knit together as he thinks about Jared's comment.

There's so much Marlee wants to bring up, but it's not her place anymore.

"Say this Christmas thing happens," Durwood says. "Who's going to do the work? They can't afford to hire some big city contractor. At least with the village idea, they have the big bucks to build what they need. The cash will flow downward, they'll need to hire people from here to do the work, and some stores will reopen to service the needs of those who move here." He leans forward and looks straight at Jared. "Everyone who could do the work has left. Our town Mayor needs to realize that."

Marlee flinches at his words because she knows they're explicitly directed toward them.

For years, Jared worked alongside his father at Holms Construction, a family-owned business that has been in the family for generations. Out of all the kids, Jared is the only one handy with his hands, the only one with any interest in running the business alongside their father.

To say them leaving town was a massive sign of betrayal would be kind. The divide between father and son happened long before their move, but that only cemented the wedge, and Marlee isn't sure this hurt can ever heal.

"I have a family to provide for, Dad." Jared gets up from his seat and heads to the counter, where he refills his water. His words are full of hurt, and everyone in this kitchen can hear it.

"We understand, Jared," Josie says, doing her best to smooth ruffled feathers. "Everyone understands that."

It may be understood, but the hurt is still there and still as raw if the sour frown on Durwood's face is any indication.

"Maybe reinventing Innsbruck would help to bring some new work to the town? A local contractor would be cheaper than a city one, don't you think? There have to be skilled workers still in town." Marlee offers up a different thought, but at the way Durwood's shaking his head, it's obviously not a welcomed one.

Durwood pushes back his chair, palms tight against the table's flat surface, and hoists himself to his feet, grunting at the same time. "I'm headed to bed. Your mother has a full day of activities planned for the kids, and she's already given me her list of tasks to take on."

"Anything you need help with, Dad? Thought I could tackle some yard work, too."

Marlee watches as something unspoken occurs between father and son. Finally, Durwood gives a dip of his head.

"Appreciate that, son."

With no other words, Durwood heads up the stairs, each creaking step sounding like a clap of thunder in the otherwise quiet kitchen.

"Well, I, for one, love the Christmas idea. Your father does too." Josie says once she hears their bedroom door close.

Jared snorts. "That's not what I took from that conversation."

"Oh, you know your father. He needs to think of something for a bit first. He's never done well when something is thrown at him. Give him time to process. If I don't know better, I think he'll be contacting the mayor and offering up his help." The smile on Josie's face grows with her words.

There's no smile on Jared's face, though. Marlee notices that right away.

"With what? Dad closed the company, remember? He's got no workers, and he sure as hell can't do the job himself, not something of this size."

"Watch your language," Josie says, giving Jared a glare. "He may have closed shop, but that means nothing. He did that because you left. You realize that, right? This self-imposed retirement is solely for your benefit." Josie gives one of her famous *you-know-better* sighs before shaking her head at her son. She, too, gets to her feet.

"Mom." There's so much being said in that single word. Regret. Guilt. Hurt. There's even a hint of apology.

"Just because kids get older, move out of the house, and start their own family doesn't mean you stop putting them first in your life. That's something you still have to learn." She first looks at Marlee with a soft smile that quickly disappears as she focuses on Jared. "Your father would have died on the job if it meant working beside you. That was always his dream, Jared. You may have moved to the city to follow your dreams, but doing so meant you destroyed the one dream your father always had. He'll never tell you, though, because of that stupid Holms pride. All you kids have it, and it'll be the death of me trying to be the peacekeeper in this family."

She rinses her cup in the sink and then sets it in the dishwasher. "You two should head up to bed too. I made up the room, so it's all ready. We have a busy day tomorrow celebrating that boy of yours, and I will not have you and your father squabbling, do you understand?" She heads over to Jared and wraps him in a hug before kissing him on the cheek.

"I love you," Jared says to her.

Josie pats him on the back. "I know you do, hun. I love you too."

When it's Marlee's turn, she wraps her mother-in-law in a tight hug. "I appreciate you," Marlee whispers.

"You and me, we have to stick together when it comes to these men of ours," Josie whispers. "Now, go to bed. I'll have coffee on by the time you come down in the morning."

Once Josie is up the stairs, Marlee takes the time to clean up the kitchen, wiping the counters, the sink and finally turning on the dishwasher.

"Do you think she's right?" Jared asks as he waits for her.

Marlee doesn't need to ask for clarification because she knows exactly what he's talking about.

"Your dad isn't a man who can settle into retirement," she says, knowing that's not really the answer her husband wants.

Coming to the decision to leave Innsbruck hadn't been an easy for one for them as a family, but believing Durwood had been ready to retire had eased some of the discomfort.

"I think that's something you would do for your children, don't you?" Marlee places a hand on Jared's arm and slightly squeezes it.

"I'll do anything and everything for my family, you know that." He wraps her in a hug, holding her tight to his chest. She snuggles in tight, dipping her head, so it rests just beneath his chin.

"Even if it means putting their needs above your own?" She asks.

He's quiet for the longest time, and Marlee wonders if he even heard her.

"Guess I learned from the best, eh?" The weight of his head as it rests on hers is a welcoming feel.

In his arms, she's home. It doesn't matter if they live in the city or in Innsbruck. As long as they are together, they can get through anything, even if it means having to readjust goals and dreams.

CHAPTER TWELVE

ASHLEY

It's a new morning, which means new challenges. There's one change, though, no more sidestepping issues, regardless of how painful facing things might be.

That includes asking Sylvia the tough questions, questions Ashley isn't sure anyone wants the answers to.

Nigel answers the door to her and points toward their living room, where Sylvia sits curled in an oversized corner chair, blanket wrapped around her legs and growling like a caged tiger.

"Hopefully, this will put a smile on your face." Ashley hugs her friend before handing her the coffee she picked up from Frankie's place, making sure to grab decaf for Sylvia.

"Your lips to God's ears," Nigel whispers as he stands by his wife's side.

Sylvia glares at Nigel as she takes the offered cup. "Isn't it time for you to go to the office?"

Nigel plants a kiss on the top of Sylvia's head. "I'll be home for lunch. Please behave." He waves at Ashley, then closes the door firmly behind him.

"Sorry," Sylvia says. "I'm a bit..." she doesn't finish her sentence, instead lifting her shoulder in a shrug.

"Grumpy?" Ashley suggests. "Pregnant, hormonal, and tired of being treated like you're fragile?"

Sylvia rolls her eyes. "That obvious?"

"Nope." Ashley doesn't even bother to smother her smile. She can handle Sylvia's grumpiness.

"He's hovering."

"He's being protective," Ashley counters.

"He's overprotective, then."

"He loves you," Ashley points out.

"I know." A soft smile surfaces on Sylvia's face.

Ashley mirrors her friend's look. "Don't be too hard on him, okay? The poor guy probably feels helpless."

"God, I am being horrible, aren't I?" Sylvia covers her eyes with her hands.

"Just pregnant. Right now, you can blame everything on hormones. A smart woman would use it to her advantage," Ashley says, repeating words Sylvia had once told her when she was pregnant with Jordan.

"And this," Sylvia raised her cup in a salute, "is why I love you so much. I don't want to know if there's no caffeine in it. Ignorance is bliss, as far as I'm concerned."

Ashley notices but ignores the dark circles beneath her friend's eyes and how her gaze drops to her extended belly.

Sylvia isn't okay, and while that worries Ashley more than she wants to admit, Sylvia doesn't need or want to be coddled right now. She needs to be treated like a regular person, not one whose body isn't handling being pregnant very well.

Ashley will have to do all her worrying in the quiet and trust Nigel to be honest with her about Sylvia's health.

"What did you think of last night?" Ashley asks. This morning, she'd reviewed her extensive list of things needed to make the Innsbruck transformation possible. Still, she wants Sylvia's honest input before she goes any further.

She wants another opinion other than her husband's. The same man who hadn't come to bed last night or even acknowledged her when she said goodbye before leaving this morning.

Sylvia leans forward, her face transforming into something that looks similar to cautious excitement.

"For one, I wish you had told me, but I get why you didn't. Nigel didn't even spill the beans, can you believe that? The man is a vault, and that's not always to my advantage. Two, the idea of turning Innsbruck into a Bavarian-themed town is interesting. Nigel and I were up quite late discussing it. It could work, Ash, but it will take a lot of work." She leans back and cocks her head. "It also won't be cheap, but...it could work."

Ashley lets out the air she'd held at the word *but*.

"It really can, Syl. And I know we could hire an outside company to come in, charge us through the roof to rebuild, but I think we should keep everything as local as possible."

Local would help the town more.

Sylvia nods. "We have more than enough talent in this town," she says. "And who knows, maybe some of the businesses that left would return."

Mentally, Ashley goes through the list of families who'd moved away in the past couple of years. Especially those with homes that currently sit empty, unable to find new buyers.

"Jared Holms is one," Sylvia continues. "They were there last night. You should talk to Marlee, see if they'll come back."

Losing the Holms' business had been a hard hit for the community. Holms Carpentry had been a generational-run business since the town's founding. To have the shop close and

Jared relocate to the city...many felt betrayed even though it made sense.

Jared has a young family and can't make a living here in Innsbruck. Ashley understands. It's the same reason so many other families have also left.

"They're original family. Their ancestors were the ones who helped build the town, remember? What a story that will be if they were to help with the rebuild, too,"

Ashley adds that to her mental file.

"I think it would be a hard sell, though, don't you? Jared has been gone for a few years now, more than enough time to get his business settled in the city. We might need to think of another option."

Sylvia shakes her head. "I think it's the only option, and we can make it happen. I know we can. We will need to track everything," Sylvia says, her eyes alit with excitement. "Record it for posterity. It would make a great video, book, or use for promotional purposes."

Seeing Sylvia's eyes light up like that, Ashley can't help but smile.

"I know, I know, my marketing hat is on. Nigel doesn't want me to be too involved, he's worried about the stress, but this... this is a long-term thing, you realize, right?"

Ashley nods. She's known that since the beginning, realizing that issue was both a positive and a negative. This would be no Christmas miracle, not for this year. It will need to be done in stages and will take years before the complete transformation occurs.

It's a commitment of time, that's for sure. Time for everyone, herself included. That's something Brett doesn't like. If it happens, if this is what the town decides, there's no way she'll walk away from it. How can she? Her own family had been one of the founding members, and with her parents now gone, she's the only Weber left of her family.

Ashley pulls out her notebook. "I've been working on a list, an exhausting one, to be honest, of everything that needs to happen, projects to tackle, timelines, and such. It's overwhelming

"Of course, it is. You can't do it on your own, you know that, right? You need to create a committee to handle that."

"I know. If this is the direction the town heads, I've started to list those I want on the committee."

"Count me in for marketing, and don't listen to my husband if he says otherwise. Can we afford this financially, though? What if we were to sell off some property that the town owns? Is that possible?"

Ashley taps her pen against her forehead as she goes through her mental list of land that sits empty. It's an idea, not one she really wants to contemplate, and it wouldn't be enough, but...it might be a start.

"We need to start with something that can be completed early, to draw in some visitors. We can start with the Christmas market in the town park. That would be easy to do, and if we market it on social media, we'll have tons of traffic from the city. We could do an old-fashioned Christmas party or a tree lighting ceremony and definitely start fundraising—"

"Whoa, slow down," Ashley stays, stopping her friend. Her head is swimming, her brain a white water rapid-ride full of ideas and concerns. This will take up so much of her life, but now is not the time to focus on this. It's time to get off the ride, slow down and refocus on something else. Something that has nothing to do with town council business.

"Let's put on the brakes," Ashley says, closing her notebook with a snap. "Council is meeting today, and I'm sure this is all I'll be talking about the next few months. I'm feeling a little overwhelmed if I'm being honest, although I love your ideas, and I'll for sure bring them up at the meeting."

"Okay." Sylvia draws out the word as she gives Ashley the eye, the one that warns her she's about to play with fire. "You want to talk about me instead, right?"

Ashley sweeps all emotion off her face, so it's a clean slate. Yes, she desperately wants to talk about Sylvia's doctor's appointment and what's going on with her and the baby.

"First off, I'm fine," Sylvia says, reading her thoughts. "The baby is fine. We're fine. Everyone is just being overly cautious, and if I have to spend the next few minutes with you talking about me, I will scream."

Ashley bites her lip hard and manages to keep her mouth shut. She knows her friend too well to believe she is anything but fine.

"Don't look at me like that, please?" Sylvia pleads.

Ashley raises her coffee to her lips and sips.

"Honestly, I'm fine," Sylvia repeats.

Ashley nods, but her brows do all the talking.

"Whatever," Sylvia huffs, realizing Ashley doesn't believe a word she's saying. "My cervix is a little weak, the membrane thin, and the doctor is concerned the baby may be breech. Not a big deal. I need to stay off my feet and remain calm." She spits that last word out.

"This is your version of calm?" Ashley has to ask, even if it earns her a glare.

That glare turns into alarm as Sylvia's back straightens, her hands grip her belly, and a long keening sound escapes through her pursed lips.

Ashley rushes to Sylvia's side, her heart almost stopping from fear.

"I'm okay, I'm okay," Sylvia breaths.

Sylvia is not okay...all the color has drained from her face with that low keening wail, and her hands shake as she rubs her belly. Her chest rises and falls too quickly for Ashley's taste, and if that panicked look doesn't leave her friend's gaze in the next two seconds, she will call emergency services.

"Don't you dare," Sylvia reaches out and stops Ashley's hand from reaching for her phone. "I'm. Okay." She stresses the words even though her voice sounds anything but okay.

Thankfully, a flush of red seeps back into Sylvia's face, so she no longer looks like Casper the Ghost.

"The doctor said this was normal. It's a sign I'm overdoing it. I'm fine."

Lies, lies, and more lies.

Ashley knows it. Sylvia knows Ashley knows it, too.

"Okay, I'm not fine, but I'm not dying either. Please...sit back down, okay?

Nothing will happen to my baby. I'm just...too stressed, or something." Sylvia rolls her eyes, but Ashley's gaze never strays from her friend's face. She needs to know she's all right, and only then will Ashley calm down.

Her heart is racing a million miles per second, and she feels guilty for not making the call.

"Ash, please..." Sylvia's eyes are bright and clear with confidence that eases the beat of her heart.

"Okay," Ashley says, "I believe you. I won't call the doctor, but I want you to tell Nigel." She doesn't take her gaze off Sylvia and makes sure she understands just how serious she is. "Send him a text, now, please."

With pursed lips, Sylvia reaches for her own phone, her fingers flying over the keyboard. Within seconds, the theme song from Mission Impossible sounds, the ring tone associated with Nigel. Sylvia's brows knit together as she reads his message.

"He wants you to confirm I'm okay," Sylvia says, reluctance in her tone. "And he wants you to tell him the truth."

Ashley's tempted to chuckle but squashes the desire at the look on Sylvia's face.

"He's allowed to be worried," she reminds her friend as she pulls up Nigel's contact and tells him what he needs to hear.

She's resting. She was in pain, but it passed. She says she's okay, and I believe her.

"I really am fine," Sylvia repeats, rubbing her belly with a sweet smile.

"I believe you," Ashley says quietly, but it's not until the tension around her friend's eyes disappears that she knows she'd been heard.

"Thank you," Sylvia says.

Ashley leans forward, elbows resting on her knees. "I believe you," she reiterates, "but that doesn't mean your husband does."

"I know. I don't think he'll relax until our baby is safely in our arms, not that I blame him. But this time, it's going to be different."

"What can I do to help?" Ashley asks.

Sylvia chuckles. "Funny, you should ask. Nigel said to ask you for help. In fact," she hands Ashley a folded note. "He's instructed me to give this to you."

Ashley opens the note and laughs.

How to help Sylvia...please remind her of the following:
- *I only want her to be okay.*
- I'm *not an ogre.*
- *No stress. If she needs to keep busy, computer work, reading, or knitting are the only options.*
- *Remind her to smile - she's so beautiful when she does.*

"Smile," Ashley says out of the blue.

"What?"

"Smile."

"Why?" The look on Sylvia's face is priceless.

Ashley turns the note so she can read for herself what Nigel wrote.

The sweetest of smiles spread across Sylvia's face. "He loves me."

"He loves you," Ashley repeats. The love between the two strikes a clashing chord in

Ashley's heart at the same time.

It must have been written on her face because Sylvia reaches her hand out. "What's wrong?" A set of wrinkles line Sylvia's forehead. "Why wasn't Brett there last night?"

Ashley turns her attention toward the large bay window.

"Ash, what's going on? Please don't tell me he's cheating again." The disgust in Sylvia's voice is unmistakable.

"I don't think so. I hope not. Brett's just...a little more than upset with me."

"Why?" Sylvia asks. "Because you're not capitulating and giving up your life for him? Did he throw another temper tantrum?" She rolls her eyes. "Wait, let me guess - you have to choose between your dreams and his, right?"

It's uncanny how often Sylvia does that.

"Him or the town, basically," Ashley admits. "He feels that since I didn't resign last night, I chose Innsbruck over our marriage."

Sylvia purses her lips into a frown. Her nostrils flare, and her baby blue eyes narrow. "Do you need me to be sympathetic, or can I be honest?"

Ashley appreciates the question. Their friendship has always been based on being honest and open to the needs of each other.

"Honest." Hopefully, she wouldn't regret it, especially considering the mood Sylvia appears to be in. Even as Sylvia collected her thoughts, her mouth opening and closing without words, tells Ashley she might not like what she's about to hear.

"He's made it very clear he doesn't like living here. Everyone in town knows it. Him not being there last night, unless he was stuck in the city for work, showed that." Her frown traces up to the creases on her forehead. "Don't get me wrong, I like Brett. But...how are you okay with any of that?"

"I'm not." Ashley shakes her head. "I thought I was, or that I could be...or maybe I've been living in denial and never thought this day would come."

"But now that it has?"

Ashley finds it interesting that Sylvia doesn't ask for specifics on what *the day* means.

"I don't see myself leaving Innsbruck. This is my home." It feels so much more complicated than that, but is it? Truly?

"What does that mean for your marriage?"

Ashley twerks her lips into something that resembles a half frown. She doesn't answer.

"What if he asks you to choose between him or the town? Like seriously force you to make that decision?"

"He already has. He seemed pretty serious last night, and honestly, I've been wrestling with having to choose for the longest time."

"Really?" The shock on Sylvia's face is dramatic.

"I finally stopped wrestling last night and decided to make a choice. I chose myself. My dreams. My goals. My desires. But I wonder if that's the right choice? It seems selfish. Am I willing to give up my marriage, the years with Brett, and break up our family because of my selfish desires?" Ashley inhales deep, waiting till her lungs ache before releasing the air.

"Marriage is about give and take." Sylvia echoes Ashley's

own internal struggle.

"But he's given a lot already. He's stayed here, in this town, made the drive to the city for years. More years than we'd originally agreed upon. We moved back because of my parents, but he's wanted to return to the city for a long time. I made him a promise...." A promise Ashley has regretted for the longest time.

"To consider leaving when your term was over. I remember," Sylvia said. "Except, no one else ran against you, so you were re-elected a second term, and now...."

"Now, I don't want to leave. Does that make me a horrible person?" She doesn't need an answer to that. "I feel horrible."

Sylvia winces in response.

"He has every right to be angry," Ashley says.

Sylvia's nose scrunches in pity as she nods.

"Honestly," Sylvia said, "if it were Nigel and me, I'd feel betrayed, hurt, angry...wonder when it was my time. So, I get it. But—" she holds up her hand, stopping Ashley from interrupting, "your marriage has been on rocky ground for a long time. I've seen your sacrifices and watched you become less of who you are inside to be enough for Brett."

Tears gather, pool, then run down Ashley's cheeks.

"I'm all for sticking together through the hard times, marriage takes a lot of work, and you shouldn't throw in the towel when it feels like that's the easiest course of action...but I also believe we fall in love with people for reasons and seasons, and sometimes love isn't always meant to be forever."

Ashley lets that sit in her soul, in her spirit, until the smile that blooms on her face holds a little bit of truth in it.

"I guess I need to decide what I want. Should I move, keep Brett happy and find a way to be myself in a city I've no interest in, or... is staying here, revitalizing the town, what I want to do?"

"It might not only be Innsbruck that needs revitalizing,"

Sylvia says softly.

Ashley's alarm goes off, reminding her she's running late.

"What is your heart telling you, Ash?" Sylvia leans forward, concern creasing the corners of her eyes.

Ashley hugs her friend with a heavy weight settling on her shoulders.

"If I'm being honest, in this moment, my heart is being pulled in so many directions, there's no clear answer. Last night, I chose me. I chose Jordan. Today... I need to put my marriage and its future in a box and focus on Innsbruck. That should work, right?"

Sylvia chuckles. "I wish. I think you'll just have to take it one day at a time. Do what you need to do right now, then deal with Brett tonight."

Ashley squares her shoulders and flings off the weight and uncertainty that wants to settle on her. "One thing at a time."

As she heads to the office, the wind picks up, swirling around her, and she zips up her jacket, wishing she'd worn something heavier. The fact there's no snow on the ground at this time of the year is surprising, but that can change any day.

About to check the weather app on her phone, it pings with a message from Brett. She swallows hard before opening his message.

Jordan opted to remain home today. I'll stay in the city tonight. Not sure when I'll come home if I do. You've made it clear I'm not important anymore. It's time I focus on myself.

Her feet continue down the sidewalk, one step at a time, but she might as well have been frozen in a solid block of ice. Brett isn't coming home. He left her and Jordan behind and isn't coming home.

Her husband left her.

CHAPTER THIRTEEN

A cloud hangs over Ashley as she walks into her office, past Susan, without acknowledging anyone on the way.

Brett left her.

She hadn't expected that. Not...that. Sure, they're having problems, and things are tense right now, but leaving like this... she's struggling to process it.

Her heart hurts. Hurts like walking-through-the-Nevada-desert-in-the-afternoon-without-shoes hurt.

She sends Jordan a text, asking what her plans for the day are as if it isn't odd for her to remain home. She has no idea what happened this morning at home or how Brett was with Jordan, but trying to get that information via text isn't the smart move here.

Dad ditched me. I'm scrolling through Netflix and eating cookies. Want me to come by for lunch?

One glance at the papers covering her desk and knowing her schedule for the day, Ashley doubts she'll have enough time to head home for lunch, but...

Let me see what I can free up.

"Everything okay?"

Startled, Ashley drops her phone on the desk and forces a smile on her face before she faces Susan.

Is everything okay? No. She's in a haze, everything clouded by Brett. Blindsided by his text, sliced and diced, his sucker punch has knocked her world apart.

Buck up, woman. This isn't a worry for the moment.

She will not allow Brett to interfere with her day. One thing she's learned since taking on the role as Mayor has been to prioritize responsibilities and push unnecessary tasks out of her mind until she's ready for them.

Which is precisely what she's going to do right now. Sidestep the...landmine...and return to its devastation later.

"Good morning," Ashley says. "Sorry, I didn't say anything when I walked in."

Susan hands her a mug full of coffee.

"Thank you," Ashley barely gets the whisper out before taking her first sip.

"I have a stack of messages for you. Drink that up. I'll bring another when I've finished prioritizing everything." Susan's eyes are sharp and pointed, and her look worries Ashley. Something has happened, but what? What has she missed?

She's grateful for the caffeine jolt as she waits for Susan to drop another bombshell on her. As much as she doesn't need more bad news, it might be exactly what will help her get through the day.

Something else to focus on.

"All right, what's wrong?" Ashley finally asks when it's obvious Susan won't say anything.

"Some people," Susan pauses, sighing, "think they have all the answers. Don't worry, I've got it handled." Susan stares at the notebook in her hand. "I've scheduled the follow-up meeting with the council for this afternoon, it's already blocked off. Your morning will be busy with emails and phone calls, not to mention you have a lineup of those who *need* to speak with you." She shoots a glance over her shoulder with a frown on her face.

Ashley tries to remember who she walked past in the waiting area but can't recall a single face. Someone out there is obviously on Susan's bad list this morning.

"I imagine today is going to be crazy, but I need you to block off my lunch, please."

Susan starts to write this down in her notebook, then pauses. "Everything okay?"

"Jordan's home, and well, I just need to have lunch with her." She knows being cryptic isn't something Susan will accept, but she's not sure she's ready to say more.

"Is everything okay?" Susan repeats her question, and despite trying to remain stoic and locking this away in a box, a tear escapes down Ashley's cheek

"Brett," his name slips off her tongue way too quickly.

She wants to push him into a box, but it's not working. He's there, always present. Her stomach flip-flops, and nausea twists up toward her throat. She swallows past it or tries to, at least.

"Brett headed into the city early and left Jordan at home."

Susan's brows crunch together. "Left her home? The girl has school. What's he thinking?"

Usually, this would be where Ashley agrees with Susan, and they'd mutter about men and being clueless, but not today.

"Regardless, make sure I'm free for lunch, will you?" Ashley doesn't want to talk about Brett anymore. She doesn't want to think about him and what he did. Not now.

"Will do. It won't be easy, but I'll figure it out. On that note...are you ready for the craziness to start?" The way Susan's brow lifts...Ashley isn't sure she wants to answer.

Taking a deep breath, she reminds herself all of this is good.

Being busy means people are excited, or at least have an opinion.

Hopefully, they are more excited than upset. It will make her job that much easier. Enthusiastic members of Innsbruck are exactly what she needs for this idea to be successful.

"Who's coming in first?"

"Old man Holms." Susan almost growls but with a smile attached. There's history between the two, a history full of administrative issues and drama.

Speaking of the devil, she'd just discussed him with Sylvia earlier.

"Take a few minutes with that, first." Susan gestures to the pages of typed phone messages on her desk along with her coffee. "All the important ones, with ideas and suggestions to Innsbruck re-invention, are on the first two pages. The last page is basically questioning and comments I'm able to handle - just wanted you to see my responses in case I'm off base."

Ashley rifles through the pages.

"Things like timeline, cost, questions about the retirement village offer. A few just wanted to offer you some encouragement." Susan rambles off the list on her fingers as Ashley attempts to follow along.

A bell sounds out in the central area. Ashley and Susan twist to peer out through the partially opened doorway to see Old Man Holms, otherwise known as Durwood Holms, standing at Susan's desk, arms crossed, face creased with a frown, staring back at them.

Ashley gives him a little wave.

Susan grumbles something about learning patience. "I told the man to grab a coffee, that you needed some time. He doesn't listen very well, does he?" Susan whispers.

"He never has." Ashley walks out into the main area to greet the frowning man, ensuring a smile is solidly fixed on her face.

"So nice to see you, Mr. Holms."

"Durwood." He gives off a huff. "If we're going to be working together, you might as well call me by my first name. You know that." His grumpy, gravelly voice reminds Ashley of her grandfather's sandpaper whiskers and hot honey tea memories.

"Working together?" She glances at Susan, who shrugs. "I thought you'd retired?"

"Retirement" means sitting on my ass completing tasks my wife has for me. Of course, we're going to be working together. Who else do you think can transform this town into a ginger-bread village? My family helped build this town, and my family will help rebuild it, too." Durwood walks past Ashley and heads straight into her office. He takes a seat, not even waiting for her to join him.

Ashley trails after him, trying to process the fact he just announced they'd be working together, even though she has yet to ask him for help.

If this is the universe's way of directing her path, she'll take all the offers she can get.

"Durwood, are Marlee and Jared moving back then?" Ashley crosses her fingers in her lap, hoping for the news she needs to hear. To have Jared come back and spearhead their building needs will be a miracle, the same miracle she's been needing.

"Who said he'd be involved? My son chose the city. I'll take the lead. I've a few people in mind to run some teams. I may be old and retired, but that doesn't mean I can't get my hands dirty again. Besides, Josie will kick my ass if I don't volunteer." He mutters.

Volunteer? She heard him, right? Will he really take on the most essential role without pay?

"Yes, you heard me right," he says, reading her mind. "What

does it take for an old man to get a glass of water around here?" He twists and looks around for the water.

Ashley jumped up to pour him a glass of water from her sideboard tray.

"The men who work under me, they'd need to be paid, of course."

"That is so..." Ashley searches for the right word, "generous." Generous feels insignificant when what he's offering to do will make a world of difference for their bottom line.

"Holms Carpentry has always been there for our town, and while I'm still alive, that won't change." Durwood's voice is edged in bitterness.

The question about Jared rests on the edge of her lips, but she refrains.

"Thank you," she says instead. "I can't tell you how much this means to me, to the town."

Durwood shrugs. "Don't be thanking me just yet." He pulls out a folded piece of paper, smoothing it as best he can on his leg.

"What's this?" Ashley asks.

"Pretty self-explanatory," Durwood grunts. "Things will need to be done in stages. What you see there is a rough estimate. I think we need to start on Main Street. Update the facades, add trim work, and redo signs. I figured we should prioritize...what will make the town money first, and that's the stores."

Ashley gives what he gave her a more thorough look, liking what she sees. It's very close to what she's also put to paper, with a few minor exceptions.

Durwood coughs. "It's rough, but it's what I came up with this morning."

"I'll talk to the council this afternoon, figure out how much we have to spend at this stage...." She can't get over the level of detail Durwood has down for a man who claims he just created it this morning. She's been stressing over a timeline, where to start, and how much it will cost. He not only drew up samples of signage and different trims for the storefronts, but he even sketched out a few Bavarian-style buildings and has some rough pricing suggestions listed.

"I won't be cheating the town, unlike other firms you can hire." Durwood's gruff voice has her giving him her full attention.

"Of course not, Durwood. This...are you sure you'll have enough help for this?"

Durwood snorts. "You pay the men, and we'll be fine. Lots of them are out there looking for honest work. Not everyone believes the city is the answer. Most of us trust you. It's why we re-elected you. Don't you forget that."

A smile creeps along her face. "I won't."

"No doubt you need council approval or something," Durwood says. "And I'm sure you'll want to hire a big firm to do drawings and all that, but you'll just be throwing money away. We have plenty of talent right here, you know that, right?"

He's right. They do. If this is to work, then everyone needs to feel invested and involved, and the best way to do that is to source local for help.

"Any suggestions then?" Her pen is poised to take names.

"Turn the page. Josie wrote down some for you."

Ashley tries to lock her jaw to stop it from dropping. How could she say no to a family who helped build the town from the ground up?

"Durwood, it would be an honor to work with you and have you help guide this. Thank you for this," she indicates to the notes, "and for the names. I can't thank you or Josie enough."

Durwood coughs but from the sudden redness of his cheeks, she wonders if he's actually blushing.

Old man Holms blushing. Imagine that. He's known for his sharp tongue, heavy hand, and honest reflections. But softness?

"You thank Josie for that," he points to the list of names along with notes on how they can help. "She was on the phone chatting with her women friends, drafting up plans, and all that."

Ashley makes a mental note to give Josie a call and set up a coffee date.

This is the miracle she needs, the answer to the many prayers she's whispered in the quiet nights. It's this: the community involvement, the excitement, and the passion for their town that confirms everything for Ashley.

A part of her wishes she could call Brett, share the news with him, and talk things through, but he's no longer that person for her. They passed that stage of their marriage a long time ago. Even before now, they led separate lives and have for a long time. Is it any surprise that he left? They've been fooling themselves into thinking they could make it work.

It hurts, him leaving, but it's the right thing. She doesn't feel devastated at the ending of their marriage, not like she had years ago when he first cheated. That tells her something.

It tells her that Sylvia is right. Their season for being together is over.

"I'd like to get started as soon as possible. It will be difficult to do much when the snow starts to fly." Durwood's question forces Ashley out of her own head.

"The council meets this afternoon," she reminds him. "I'll be able to update you afterward."

His lips crease together, and the wrinkles on his face become more pronounced.

"I'm not going home and telling Josie to hold her horses, you hear? I don't see anyone else stepping up to the plate."

Ashley contains her chuckle but not her smile. It grows wider than before.

"Now, Durwood, it hasn't even been twenty-four hours yet."

He gives off a wolf warning growl, a sound very similar to one she's heard many times while hiking.

"I have no doubt," she continues, "that the council will appreciate having you on board. We did say last night that we would need a month of research, so how about together we spend that time and come up with a concrete plan?"

She can see he wants to argue, and she's really hoping he doesn't.

With a grunt and a nod, he pushes himself to his feet, sticking his hand out and waiting for her to shake.

She hesitates. Not out of rudeness, but because she understands shaking would be considered an agreement in his books.

Yet, by not shaking, that could be an issue too, an issue she doesn't have time to deal with.

His grip is firm, solid, and steady.

"Missed that husband of yours at the town hall," Durwood says. "A man should stand by his woman at all times. Better be at the next one." The displeasure on his face reminds her of her father and his belief in how a marriage unit should work. It warms her heart, and she touches Durwood's arm lightly.

"Brett," she clears her throat, "couldn't make it. Unfortunately." She adds that last bit at the look on Durwood's face.

He knows the truth. She can see it. How, she didn't know, but it was as if he's managed to look beyond her words and peer into her bleeding heart.

"That there, it's too bad." Durwood looks her clear in the eyes. "He's a good man, but he's got that yearning for the city. It's in his eyes."

"Not mine, I hope," Ashley whispers the words, trying very hard to push back the tears.

"Just the look of a woman who tries too hard."

Ashley has no words, but it wouldn't have mattered because Durwood takes that moment to leave. He stops at Susan's desk, slaps down another sheet, then leaves, the door closing behind him with a thud.

CHAPTER FOURTEEN

MIA

Standing in the doorway, Mia watches her father sleep in his recliner. His chest rises and falls, but the wheezing and sputtering sounds he makes isn't normal.

This cold is more than just a cold. It's settled deep in his chest. She can hear it.

"Come into the kitchen and leave your father in peace. The man is finally sleeping."

Mia follows her mom, keeping her steps light. "I take it he didn't sleep last night?" It's not really a question she needs to ask, considering her mom's bags beneath her eyes. "Looks like you barely got any sleep either."

Mom turns on the stove and fills the kettle. "Hard to sleep with him hacking like you used to when you had croup. I finally convinced him to sleep in his recliner, and I got a few hours of shut-eye."

Mia pulls out a chair and curls her leg beneath her. "You should call the doctor."

"I will."

Neither says anything as they wait for the water to boil.

"You're here early," Mom finally says after she fills the teapot and brings it to the table. "I figured you'd be sleeping in, fighting jetlag."

At the mention of sleeping, Mia yawns, one of those deep, full-body yawns that could have her asleep within minutes if she could.

She doesn't have time for jetlag, though. She's got a business to open, supplies to stack, money to make...hopefully.

"I thought I'd check in before I head to the store."

Her mom gets up and opens a container. "Here, I took this out last night. You'll need your energy if you want to stay awake." She hands Mia an oatmeal chocolate chip muffin, also taking one for herself. "If you need help, let me know. I can come in and put your orders together or help stock shelves or...."

"Thanks, Mom," Mia says, stopping her from saying anything else. "Dad probably needs you here more than I do at The Wandering Aisle, though. If you're not around to supervise, he'll do more than he should, and you know it."

Her mom nods. "All that man should be doing right now is resting. I plan on calling his doctor to see about getting some medication."

Knowing this eases the tension knot that's settled in the middle of Mia's back.

"How much do you think Dad will get involved with the whole Innsbruck transformation idea?" Mia nibbles on her muffin.

Her mother's face transforms at the question, her eyes alight with passion and excitement.

"Isn't it a wonderful idea? Who doesn't love a Christmas town? It's all I could think about last night, Mia. I wish we were younger and could really be involved, you know? I'd love to be on a committee and in the thick of things. I hope you will be?"

Mia plans on it. She was raised that doing something was better than doing nothing, and if you want to be part of change, you must be willing to do the work.

"I'm hoping to convince Ashley to join me for drinks one night and get more details. I'm sure she's swamped now with everyone suggesting things to her."

Mia's mom leans back in her chair. "This is exactly the energy level this town needs. It's a shot of adrenaline, something to wake us up." She rubs her hands together as her smile widens. "It's also the perfect time to get our B&B idea running, don't you think?"

Her mom's excitement overflows with energy as her fingers tap-tap-tap on the table.

Something's up. Mia eyes her mom, taking in the satisfied smile, the ease around her eyes, and the notebook left open on the table full of to-do lists.

"You've been planning this for a while, haven't you?"

The way her mother's eyes round with faked innocence confirms there's more going on here. "You know we've always talked about doing this, Mia. The only thing that's changed is the location."

Mia doesn't buy it. There's something else going on here. Something her dear, sweet, in-the-middle-of-everything mother isn't saying.

"So, who came up with the whole Christmas village idea?" She was surprised, just like everyone else last night when her dad went up to the microphone and suggested the idea.

She'd been a little more than just surprised, truth be told. She still is. But the more she thinks about it, the more she dwells on the idea, and the more she realizes she shouldn't be surprised.

All her life, her parents have talked about the Christmas markets in Germany, sharing stories from growing up and visiting family during the holidays. Every time they would go home to visit, they would come back with new mugs from the markets they saw, and then they would make gluhwein, spiced mulled wine, and drink from these small mugs.

In fact, Mia twists to look at a shelf on the wall behind her; all her favorite mugs are still on that very shelf.

"When we host our Christmas Market this year, we should create a mug for Innsbruck. What do you think? Should we do gnomes or a Christmas tree or...oh, I know," her mom leans in, grabbing hold of Mia's arm, "we could get the art class in the school to do a contest to design something. Wouldn't that be fun?"

Mia pats her mom's hand. "I love the idea. We might need to do it for next year instead, though. We're kind of pushing it for this year."

"I think having a year-round holiday spirit in our town is just the answer," her mom says, clearly not hearing her. "Like my hometown." The sigh her mom gives is whimsical and full of memories.

Her mom grew up in Rothenburg ob der Tauber, a town known for its year-round holiday spirit.

"I love the idea. I really do. It's going to take years before anything will happen, don't you think? Where will Ashley find the funding for something of this nature?" She's sure her friend has already thought of that and is stressing over it.

"Oh, don't worry your head about that. Your father will help."

Wait, what?

How can Dad help unless he knows people or...

Just then, he starts to cough, a deep, hurtful cough that has both Mia and her mom wincing in pain.

"Your father is going to donate the money anonymously, Mia. We have more than enough, you know that." Her mother's voice is now low, quiet, both of them waiting to see if her father needs help or not.

"You're not personally going to be able to fund the entire project, Mom." She knows her parents are well off. Her father has always been wise regarding saving, but they aren't millionaires, and that's what this town will need. Millions, if not more.

"Oh, of course not. We'll help get it started, though. Sometimes, that's all people need, is a little help, you know?"

The recliner foot snapping shut, followed by a large hacking sound, has both women to their feet. As her father coughs, there's a point where it's evident he can't catch his breath. As mom rushes out of the room, Mia is on her phone, calling up the personal phone number of their family doctor, who also happens to be a neighbor.

"Hey Chuck, it's Mia. Are you still at home?" She didn't remember seeing his truck in the driveway, but she wasn't really paying attention either.

"No, I'm at the clinic. What's up?"

"It's Dad..." she heads into the living room, where Dad is bent over, body shaking as he continues to hack.

"That's him I'm hearing? Doesn't sound good. A few people told me they didn't like his looks last night. Sorry I wasn't there. How long has he been coughing like this?"

"Mom says all night. He's only slept a few hours, and those were on the recliner. He's really pale, Chuck, and struggling to breathe."

There's a pause, and Mia's unsure if Chuck even heard her. "Chuck?"

"I'm sending the ambulance, Mia."

Those four words fill her with both worry and relief, but as she watches her dad struggle for air, those two emotions turn straight into gut-wrenching, heart-pounding fear.

Fear that she's going to lose her father and that's not something she's prepared to do.

CHAPTER FIFTEEN

ASHLEY

Ashley gives her daughter a long hug when they meet at Frankie's for lunch.

Tears pool in Ashley's eyes as the hug lingers, but she pushes them away - now is not the time for crying.

What is this going to do to their daughter? Divorce is never easy, especially for kids, but it must be healthier than the atmosphere they are living now, right?

Divorce. That word hasn't been spoken between them, but it might as well have. That's where they're headed, and deep down, she knows they're both on the same page – finally.

Does Jordan know? Does she understand why Brett left without taking her to school? Her daughter is clever, smarter than she's given credit for, but that doesn't make this easy. On the one hand, she's hoping and praying that she has no idea; on the other, she realizes her daughter must know.

Leaning back from the hug, all it takes is one good look in

her daughter's misty eyes, and she's got her answer. *Damn you, Brett.*

She knows.

Jordan knows her father left her. Left them.

Ashley's heart constricts, realizing there is nothing she can do to protect her daughter's heart from the wreckage about to come.

"You okay, hun?" She asks Jordan, her voice soft, her grip strong as she takes hold of her daughter's hands.

"Okay? I should be asking you that." There's something in Jordan's voice that has Ashley pause. She doesn't like what she hears: anger, bitterness, disgust.

She wants to fix this. She should fix this, but she can't.

At least the cafe is empty. Today, of all days, she needs some quiet and peace. As expected, things are crazy hectic in the office, and it's a welcome diversion. Still, right now, she needs to be present, in the moment with Jordan, and focus only on her.

They both deserve that.

"Why don't you two sit?" Frankie calls out from the back, her head briefly popping over the swinging door. "Susan called and gave me the heads up you were coming, so lunch is almost ready."

Ashley throws her friend a smile of appreciation, thankful for Susan's intuitiveness to call ahead.

Ashley struggles with how to begin the conversation and almost doesn't notice her daughter's readiness to explode with words she needs to express.

Jordan worries her hands, tearing apart a napkin, one little piece at a time, while she biting her lip, tearing off dry skin with her teeth, something she only does whenever she's upset.

"Honey, I... I'm sorry," Ashley starts, the two words meaning more than she can possibly ever say. "I—"

"You're sorry?" Jordan interrupts. "Why? Why would you

apologize for something Dad did? He was the one who left. He was the one who threw us away. He's the one who is being the jerk. He..." she pauses, and Ashley can tell she's measuring her words, thinking about either what to say or how to say it.

Ashley hates that her daughter feels the need to protect her.

"Out with it," she tells her. "Say whatever it is you're holding inside. I promise I can handle it." The reassurance is exactly what her daughter needs if the slight leaning back in the chair is any indication.

"Do...do you know he has a girlfriend in the city?" Jordan's voice wobbles as she drops the bomb destroying everything in its wake. Ashley blinks, completely taken aback, struggling with how to react. She drops her hands into her lap and clenches her fist until she feels her nails dig into her palms.

"He threatened me not to tell you," Jordan continues, "told me I'd be tearing our family apart if I did, but..." her words run together in a harried rush, along with tears that fill in her eyes, trailing down her cheeks.

Girlfriend? Threatened? What the...

She's still trying to process everything, to find a single nugget of strength inside of her. Still, she's a field of emptiness inside, utterly barren of everything - words, feelings...any type of reaction Jordan needs.

She finally swallows and drops her gaze.

"I'm sorry. Mom. I should have told you before now, but I just...I hate him. I'm glad he's gone. I hope he never comes back."

This grabs Ashley's attention. Tears stream down Jordan's face as she reveals everything she's been hiding for so long. Her poor girl, having to carry this for so long.

She needs to say something. Do something. Act in some way, and yet she can't do anything. She's frozen.

"Mom?" Jordan grabs her hands, her grip shaky, unsteady, and that's all it takes for Ashley to break out of her stupor.

"Oh honey," she gets up and hugs her daughter. "This isn't on you, not one bit." She rubs Jordan's back in small comforting circles, hoping to quell the shaking. Her daughter, her usually strong and independent daughter, is broken, and that, in turn, breaks Ashley's heart.

All morning, since finding out Brett left, she's felt...empty, stunned, almost blasé about what's happening, but all of that disappears with her daughter's tears.

Now she's angry. Seething tendrils of rage, fury, and something she can't pronounce wrestles inside her. How dare Brett threaten their daughter with something like this.

She should have known. The fear, the insecurity that he'd cheat on her again, haunts her like an unwanted ghost, but she's tried to ignore it.

That's on her.

Him cheating and then threatening Jordan... that's on him.

"I hate him," Jordan says.

Hate isn't a strong enough word for either of them, not right now.

"Yeah," Ashley says. "Right now, I'm there with you. He was wrong, Jordan, he was...." Ashley pushes down some anger to soften her words, "he should never have placed you in that situation."

"Did you know?" There's a level of accusation in her daughter's voice that challenges her to lie.

Which she won't. That's not fair.

Ashley's eyes close for one second before she admits the truth. "I'd wondered, but I wasn't sure."

Jordan's lips tighten until they're almost white. "How could you stay with him then?"

"It's not black and white, honey," Ashley struggles with how to explain the complexities of marriage to a teenager. "Your father and I...have had issues, but we are...we were trying to work through them. That doesn't excuse him, though. Him threatening you...that isn't okay. Placing you in that position because of something he's guilty of... that's on him, not you. Never you."

Ashley wants to wring his neck. Not just wing it but twist it into a tight spiral until he feels a small semblance of the pain he's putting his daughter through.

Frankie clears her throat as she exits the kitchen, oblivious to the tension in the room. "Hope you're hungry. I made my very special BLT and cranberry salad with goat cheese. I also brought some flat whites."

Ashley and Jordan place the fakest smiles they can produce and wait while Frankie sets everything down on the table.

"You look like you're having a serious conversation, so I won't disturb you. But I want you to know I'm here if you need me." She pats Ashley's shoulder, and from how she smiles, Ashley feels she overheard their conversation.

"What are we going to do now?" Jordan brings up the one question Ashley has been asking herself all day.

Now what?

As a woman of lists and plans, she knows she needs one for this situation if only to get her head in the game and not feel like she's floundering.

"First things first, tonight, once I'm home, we will spend the evening eating pizza, drowning our emotions in root beer floats, and eating a whole carton of ice cream while binge-watching whatever shows you want to watch. Then, tomorrow, we will run into the city to grab your things from school and then re-register you into school here."

A spark flares in Jordan's eyes before it just as quickly disappears. "What about Dad?"

Ashley's chest caves as she hears the tears in her daughter's voice.

"Your father," Ashley pushes away everything she feels toward Brett and focuses instead on loving her daughter, loving her enough for them both. "Your father," she repeats, "has made a decision that doesn't include us. Which is...fine." She winces at the word, realizing just how inadequate it is. "No, it's not fine, hun, and we can't pretend it is. What's happened, what he's done...it hurts, doesn't it?" She waits till Jordan nods. "I think the only thing we can do right now is to give ourselves permission to feel. Whether it's anger or sadness or..." she pauses, searching for the right word. "Betrayal – that's how I feel right now. Betrayed and very angry. We don't need to do anything else but be in the moment, even though this is a moment that really sucks." She attempts to make a smile, something genuine, but it probably looks more like a grimace.

Jordan wipes her eyes with a napkin. "Yeah, it sucks. You won't forgive him, though, not for a while, right?"

The realization that Jordan isn't just expressing her feelings, but she's searching for answers on how to navigate the minefield called a broken family hits her.

Ashley has two options. She can let her daughter feed on the hurt and pain, stay on the same playing field Brett is on and let the destruction of their marriage fester into every aspect of their lives. Or, she can take the high road, help her daughter to learn what forgiveness and healing really means, and together they can find happiness.

The choice is pretty straightforward.

"You know what Grandpa used to say to me? The choice to forgive is a personal one that can hurt you or help you heal. By not forgiving someone, you choose to hold on to the anger and hurt, and that's never healthy, not long term."

Jordan frowns. "So, we can't be hurt by what he's done?"

Ashley snorts, unable to help herself. "Oh hell, no. I'm hurt and angry and furious and...I want to lash out at him in the worst ways right now. But eventually, these feelings will pass."

"Not too soon, I hope," Jordan mumbles.

"No," Ashley agrees, "not too soon."

"Anyone ready for dessert?" With perfect timing, Frankie steps out of the back of her cafe and holds a cake plate.

Ashley leans back in her chair, checking the time. She doesn't want to rush lunch, but she will eventually need to get back to the craziness in the office.

"Is that chocolate?" Jordan asks as she gets up and clears their dishes, carrying them to the counter. That small act, being so helpful, touches Ashley's heart.

"Girl, would it be anything else with you here?" Frankie sets the cake plate on the table and lifts the lid. "Jordan, honey, would you mind grabbing plates in the back?"

Jordan takes off as Frankie sits down.

"Mind if I join you? Things felt tense, so I didn't want to intrude earlier." Frankie looks at her with an intensity that has Ashley squirming in her chair.

"You know you're always welcome," Ashley says, dropping her gaze to the cake.

Yes, okay, she's a chicken. She's not ready for Frankie to read her like a book, even though she knows Frankie already has.

"A few months before your mom passed, she invited me over for coffee. Did I ever tell you that?" Frankie says in a very ho-hum tone.

Ashley lifts her gaze, and just like that, all the feels she's tried to squash come flooding up. Frankie and her mom were best friends, and while she might never have said it, she views Frankie as a second mother.

"I won't ever forget that conversation. She had some harsh

words for me, and you know your mom, she never minced words when she had a point to get across."

That sounds exactly like her mother, known for her brutal and blunt honesty.

"She made it very clear that I am responsible for you with her gone. And not just, make-sure-she's-okay, kind of responsible, but in a you-mother-her kind of responsible. She said you tended to take on too much, carried others more than you should, and would sacrifice yourself for everyone else. It became my responsibility to make sure you don't take on too much and that when you do, you have someone supporting you." Frankie swallows before scrunching her nose and looking upward, "God knows I haven't kept my end of the bargain the way I should have, but I am now." She purses her lips.

Ashley remains quiet, keeping an eye on the door to the kitchen.

"Don't worry about Jordan. I left her a message in the back to give us a few minutes." Frankie catches her glance. "Listen, you are one of the strongest women I know. You deserve the world and a man who will offer it to you. You want someone who will remain by your side no matter what you face together, and if Brett can't stand with you, then he doesn't deserve you."

Ashley's lashes coat with tears, and her throat clogs with a sob she won't allow to escape, which means she almost can't open her mouth to reply.

"If your parents knew he'd cheated on you...." Frankie's lips are now a straight line, "well, you know your father would give him a good ass-whoopin'."

The foreign sound of laughter mixed with a sob burst through Ashley's mouth, and the tears running down her cheeks make a small pool on the table. Ashley wipes them away with the palm of her hands.

"He certainly would, wouldn't he?" Her father had been a big man with muscles that used to make her feel warm and safe.

"If he's not already there, you kick that man to the curb, you hear? We've got your back. You won't be alone." Frankie reaches forward to grab her hand, holding on tight.

With a long breath, Ashley focuses on unwinding the tension through her shoulders and smiles at the woman across from her.

"He kicked himself to the curb and left this morning. I'm furious and calm all at the same time if that even makes sense. I don't need his cheating ass in my life."

"Makes perfect sense to me. You're a smart woman—"

"Can I come back now? I really want some cake." Jordan pushes through the door, a puppy dog look on their face.

Frankie jumps up in a whirl of movement, almost knocking her chair over. "Come eat cake. I'm going to box it up for you so you can take it home," she glances over her shoulder to Ashley and winks, "just make sure you leave some cake for your mom to enjoy tonight, you hear me?" She teases.

Jordan's eyes light up like the solar balls they'd hung on their outdoor trees last Christmas. "Take it home? For realsies? You know you're the best, right?"

The smile on Frankie's face, the joy in her daughter's eyes, even if it only lasts for a few moments, is all Ashley needs. It's enough. Right here, right now, amid the whirlwind of her day, it is enough.

She didn't lie when she told Frankie she's both furious and calm. She knows it will all hit her tonight when she's alone with a glass of wine, but for now, she will be okay.

Brett cheating on her again is the nail in the crate of the ending of their marriage. Their therapist told them to have a line that can't be crossed and be open and honest about where that line is.

His cheating has always been her line. He crossed it, and there's no coming back from that.

She can forgive him for tearing their family apart like this. One day.

But for threatening their daughter with his secret... she's not sure that's a forgivable action. Not from her.

Frankie and Jordan are whispering about something over at the counter.

"Can we hurry up with the plates, please?" She raises her voice, so her teasing tone catches their attention.

"Sorry," Frankie calls out. "Just making plans with this girl of yours."

"Oh...what kind of plans?" She raises the glass dome off the cake plate, setting it to the side, and her mouth starts watering as the delicious scent of chocolate wafts her way.

"Rather than sit at home all day watching television, I'm trying to convince your daughter to spend time with me. I have an order for a few sweet trays, and she can help me with the baking and packaging." Frankie comes over to the table and cuts pieces of the cake.

Ashley doesn't waste time sinking her fork into the cake and bringing it to her mouth.

"If that means you keep her busy enough, so she doesn't inhale most of this cake until I'm home, I'm all in," Ashley mumbles around a mouth full of the moist cake.

A quick glance at her phone has her groaning and trying to stuff another forkful into her mouth. She needs to return to the office if she wants to make it home for dinner.

No, there's no if. She will be home for dinner tonight.

"Let me grab a refill you can take with you and package up Susan's order. I'll be right back." Frankie heads into the back.

Ashley looks at her daughter.

Jordan stares back.

They both smiled in unison.

"We'll be okay, right, Mom?" Jordan asks.

Ashley reaches across the table for her daughter's hand.

"This is just a bump in the road, love. A big one, one I'm not sure how to handle right now, but it's still just a bump. Not a dead end. If we remain strong, we'll be okay."

These seem to be the words her daughter needs to hear. With a long sigh, she pulls out her phone. "So, I can tell my friends I'll be moving schools?" There's an uplift to her voice, a bit hesitant, a bit sad, but it's there.

Ashley smiles. She knows she'll need to do a lot of smiling in the next little bit, a lot of encouraging, and even more crying when things finally hit her.

But she's a strong woman. She can and will get through this. She can be honest, be strong and be the support her daughter needs as her jackass of a father walks away from the one gift he doesn't deserve. Not right now, at least.

"You tell your friends whatever you'd like, love."

CHAPTER SIXTEEN

The scene in front of her is not what Ashley wants to see following her lunch with Jordan.

"Damn it," Ashley grumbles, stepping into the reception area, coffee tray in one hand, bagged lunch for Susan in the other. "Why? Come on, people, respect the schedule, would you?"

The boardroom is full. The whole council all arrived before her.

Susan is at her side in an instant. "Sorry," she says. "I called the cafe hoping to warn you. Frankie said I'd just missed you, and you had your hands full."

"I would have been here sooner," Ashley admits, "but Frankie made her chocolate cake, and I couldn't resist." She didn't admit the real reason she took so long.

After saying goodbye to Frankie and walking her daughter halfway home, Ashley stopped in the park by her office, found a secluded bench, and allowed herself a good cry.

Not for herself but for her daughter. For the hurt she'll live with for the rest of her life—-the feeling of betrayal—-wondering if she'll ever be enough for her father.

Her tears were not for herself. Not yet.

A look of envy flitters across Susan's face. "I could really use some cake right about now," she says.

"Then you're in luck because there's a big slice of it in the bag. Why are they all here early?" A glance over her shoulder forces her to give Nigel a little wave as he watches her. He beckoned his head with a tug, telling her to get her butt in the room.

"Blame it on Marcus. I warned them all you were having lunch with Jordan and that if anyone attempted to call you, they'd have to deal with me." Susan's eyes narrow as she glances into the boardroom full of town council members.

"I'd better get in there, then." Ashley isn't sure she's ready to deal with any nonsense from Marcus. She'd rather run home, curl up on the couch with Jordan, and binge-watch shows on Netflix.

When Ashley opened the door, everyone turns their attention her way. Some wore expressions of excitement, others a bit more jaded as if preparing for battle.

She doesn't want to fight, not about this, not with those who promised to serve the town of Innsbruck alongside her.

She barely takes one step into the room before Marcus verbally pummels her.

"You can't tell me you're seriously considering letting a man who should remain in retirement oversee the vast project this ridiculous Christmas idea would entail?" Marcus slams a stack of papers down on the table and sneers. "You're not that desperate, are you?"

Keep your cool. It's a hard mantra to keep, despite understanding that Marcus is worked up and needs an outlet. She doesn't need to be his punching bag, though. The fact he thinks it's okay to talk to her in this manner says something. Something she obviously needs to address.

Deep breaths. Deep, deep breaths.

"Desperation has nothing to do with any of my actions. I'd appreciate a little respect, Marcus – you expect it from me, don't you?" The impressive feat of keeping her tone level, questioning but not demanding, calm and not furious, is surprising.

Nigel tries to grab her attention with small movements of his fingers, but she ignores him. She didn't need him or anyone else to tell her to calm down.

"You're out of your league here," Marcus says. His disdain for her is loud, his un-acceptance evident. He's been after her position for years, running against her during both elections, and he's never let her forget it. She would love to remind him that the people were very clear with their votes, but that would be stooping to his level.

"I disagree." She's not out of her league. She will continue to put the interests of Innsbruck ahead of her own, something she's not sure Marcus can say with complete accuracy.

Marcus shrugs. "There is no possible way this overhaul of Innsbruck is financially feasible. We simply cannot afford it."

Here we go.

Ashley sips coffee, shuffles some papers on the table, and lets the silence in the room grow.

"I think we can." She lets those four words sit there, percolating as hope settles in her voice. "If done in stages." It'll be a stretch, but...

"Why are you so against the retirement proposal?" Marcus asked, elbows on the table, shoulders forward, hands clasped. He gives off the appearance of being attentive, of wanting to know, pretending he's willing to listen...but Ashley knows him better.

She tents her fingers and gives every other council member a good look. How many others agreed with Marcus? A few, if the downward gazes are any indication.

"It's not the only proposal, or have you forgotten?" Marcus

sneers. He shoves the papers in front of him forward, reaches into his briefcase on the floor, and pulls out a file folder.

A triple knot the size of a soccer ball lodges in Ashley's stomach.

"I contacted the lawyer for the retirement village with questions regarding their offer." A smugness settles on his face. "They've increased what they'll pay for each piece of land within the town limit and will even lease a number of our abandoned storefronts. From what I see, they aren't here to destroy what we've built; instead, they'll help regrow and rebuild." Pride fills his voice, like a little boy who went behind his parents' back and thought he'd get away with it.

He turns to look around the room, giving everyone a look Ashley is very familiar with. It's the one that got him elected to council, pulling people in and making them believe in what he has to say.

"Our population will grow. It will thrive," Marcus continues, hope and excitement pouring out of him.

He's avoiding her gaze, which is almost comical. Almost.

"After losing how many of our families? Is the price we'll pay as a community worth it?" Ashley counters. He couldn't be serious. No amount of money will be worth that loss. Not for her.

"We'll rebuild and regrow." Marcus shrugs, everything in him making it clear the price doesn't matter to him.

Ashley pushes herself to her feet, walks around the desk to where Marcus sits and picks up his file without asking permission. She doesn't care about the disgruntled sigh he directs her way as she rifles through the papers.

It only takes for Ashley to wave her hand, and Susan opens the door. "Can you make copies for everyone, please?"

That wall of windows made it easy to communicate with her assistant as needed.

"While we wait for Susan to return, let me ask you all a question." Ashley faces the wall of windows that looks out over their small town.

It's a quiet afternoon with a cool wind brushing against tree branches, teasing the ends of the flags and potted fall foliage lining Main Street. Mia must be back because the bookstore had set out its sign and the tea shop has a few tables set up outside.

This is the street she walked down holding hands with her boyfriend at fourteen. She got her first job at the stationery store, now closed. Her mother used to take her to the craft store every Saturday morning for a new paint-by-the-numbers set after the morning chores were done. It, too, had closed several years ago.

Innsbruck is home. She isn't ready to give up on it.

"How much of our community can we afford to lose?" She keeps her gaze on the shops below, her back to the group at the table. "This offer, yes, for those who sell their homes, they will make more money, but we would be agreeing to sell three-quarters of our town property to them. A huge corporation—"

"Lease," Marcus interjects.

"Sorry?"

"We're not selling. We'd be leasing for fifty years," he says, clarifying.

Ashley doesn't respond. She can't. They will lose their identity, who they were as a community, to a large corporation. How could he believe that is even remotely okay?

"Then what?" Nigel speaks up. "Ashley's right. We will be losing three-quarters of our town. That's not what we promised we would do when elected."

"We promised to find a way to save Innsbruck," Marcus counters, his voice an octave higher than before. "That's what this offer is."

"You," Ashley says, finally turning from the window, "see

the town and families here as two separate things. I see them as one. Without our community, the families who live here, there is no town. No town, Marcus." She wants that to sink in. Not just for Marcus but for the other silent council members. "I won't sell out. No matter how much the offer increases."

The tension in the room stretches, no one saying a word.

"Brett would accept the offer." Marcus' voice may be low, but the challenge in his eyes is loud and clear.

Oh, for fudge's sake.

"I'm not Brett. Nor was he elected as mayor. How many times do I need to remind you of this?" Ashley's irritation for the man grows until it becomes a cancerous tumor on her tongue.

"And yet," Marcus says with a slight shrug to his shoulder, "aren't you supposed to step down as Mayor and move into the city?" He lets that bombshell drop with a hint of satisfaction. "So, technically, this isn't your town to be concerned about."

He didn't.

He wouldn't.

She can't believe he'd say such a thing out loud.

The knot in her stomach tightens. Her hands shake as she attempts to squash the rising anger. It won't be fair to lash out at someone who isn't the actual cause of her anger.

"I haven't resigned, nor do I plan to, regardless of what you might have heard whispered about. This is my home, and I will continue to fight for the wellbeing of our families as long as they allow me to." Ashley swallows the ball of unspoken emotion nestled tight in her throat.

"Is it true?" Another member speaks up. "You're stepping down?"

"No. It's the furthest thing from the truth." The honesty she's trying to convey rings loud like the Notre Dame bell in Paris on a clear spring day. "I am not leaving. This is my home, and I promise, it is still my top priority."

Several heads nod just as Susan enters and hands out the photocopies from Marcus' file.

"That's not what I heard," Marcus mumbles.

Ashley ignores him. He's prodding her, trying to get her to lose her cool, and she isn't about to let him win.

"Marcus," Ashley points toward the distributed papers, "why don't you walk us through these," she tells him.

He's gauging her reaction, unsure whether he's winning or losing.

According to her, he's definitely losing, but she'll let him figure that out himself.

"If everyone would look over the first three pages," Marcus says, clearing his throat, "I think most of you will agree that this is the best financial decision we could make for our town. We won't lose our sense of identity, regardless of Ashley's initial thoughts; instead, we'll expand it." He wears a cat-caught-the-mouse-grin of satisfaction on his face.

"What about a compromise?" Nigel suggests, his gaze on the papers, his fingers tapping on a calculator.

"Why?" Marcus' forehead crinkles as he frowns.

"How?" Ashley asks, interested in the idea.

A compromise is a healthy alternative; looking over the new proposal, she can see where Nigel is going with the idea.

The town owns a section of land north-east of downtown. The land is on a hill, where kids toboggan in the winter and families picnic in the summer. Despite the use, leasing the land can help the town financially.

Ashley catches Nigel's gaze and nods.

He proceeds to lay out the idea to the rest of the council.

Ashley measures the reactions, curious to see the nods, smiles, and notes taken as he speaks.

Marcus is the only one in the room who isn't reacting.

Her phone buzzes with a text. One look at it has her

jumping from her seat and heading toward the hall, not bothering to excuse herself as Susan stands there, phone in hand, concern crossing her face.

CHAPTER SEVENTEEN

Susan's ashen face tightens the noose around Ashley's chest.

So many thoughts flash through her head, but she knows whatever is happening, it's bad.

"What is it?"

"Weiss," Susan mouths. "It's Mia."

Mia? Weiss? What happened? Ashley starts to tick off possible scenarios, not liking any of them.

Mia's store, The Wandering Aisle is open, she'd just seen people walk out the door earlier, so she'd assumed Mia was in her shop.

"Thank you for calling. I'll check in later, okay? We're here for you, love." Susan hangs up, her hand a little shaky.

"It's Weiss," Susan says, clarifying. "He's at the hospital."

"Weiss?" Ashley rubs the area between her eyes. She can feel the beginnings of a headache forming. The sound of his cough and the paleness of his skin at the town meeting worried her. She should have checked in with him this morning.

That's what a good friend does, checks in on friends, especially when she knows they aren't feeling well. Even though her life is upended and she's living in a twister of craziness, that doesn't excuse the fact she keeps dropping balls. She needs to do better.

She has to do better.

"Mia is shaken up. She's headed to the hospital with Anna." Susan pauses and stares up at the ceiling, blinking rapidly. "Dr. Chuck had him rushed to the clinic this morning and then sent him off to Mineral Springs Emergency."

The band around her chest, the pit in her heart, all that pain cramming into a single space, breaks loose.

Sinking into the nearest chair, the casket she's been stuffing all her emotions into opens, and large body-bending hiccups surface along with a wallop of tears.

"Oh, you poor thing." Susan wraps her arms around Ashley, rubbing her hand along her back. Ashley tries to still the flood of tears, but they won't relent. "I've no idea what's going on, but this seems to be the final straw, isn't it?"

It takes a few moments for the tears to abate, for her breathing to slow down enough that she can speak. Wiping the tears away, Ashley wraps her arms around Susan in a hug, thankful for her friend. "Will he be okay?" Ashley whispers. Her throat feels raw like it's been sanded down.

"Mia sounded worried. Come on, let's get into your office and away from prying eyes, okay?" Susan leads her into her office, closing the door behind her. "She'll call when she knows more. We can't let ourselves assume the worst, okay?"

This is the Susan Ashley needs right now. The no-nonsense, fact-finding friend has always been her strength whenever she's been weak.

Ashley considers herself fortunate to be surrounded by so many strong women to have these relationships in her life. If she doesn't want to keep crumbling, she needs to let these women in, hold her up when she needs the support, and remind her that she's got this, she can get through it all, and that this won't destroy her.

"So, want to tell me what's going on? You've been very secretive lately, and that's not like you. Not with me." Susan hands her a box of tissues, which Ashley accepts.

"Brett..." her mouth is suddenly dry, her tongue sticking to the roof of her mouth. She reaches for a glass of water she'd set down earlier and takes a long drink.

"Brett left me. This morning. By text message." A bubble of hysterical laughter bursts from Ashley's lips, even though there's nothing remotely funny about it.

Susan says and does nothing. No words. No hug. No reaching out for a touch of understanding. Her only reaction is an exhibition of anger that crisscrosses Susan's face.

"He. Is. An. Ass." Susan finally manages to say. "What kind of man, a man in a decade-old marriage, just runs like that? And in a text message? If he were here right now, I'd ram that phone so far up his ass he'd never want to use it again."

Ashley loves this woman. She loves her for being on her side, supporting her, and being so angry with her.

"He's gone, Susan. He's not coming back. He left Jordan at home, too."

Susan nods. "I'd wondered."

"I just..." Ashley sighs. "I don't know what to do. About him. Me. This..." she spreads her hands before they fall with a thud against her thighs.

"One thing at a time, love," Susan says. "The good news is that not everything can be fixed right away, which means you have time to breathe and format a plan. You know I'm here to help with anything, right?"

Wiping the last of her tears, Ashley reaches for Susan's hands and squeezes tight. "I cherish you, you know that, I hope. I can't imagine doing this job, getting through every single day, without having you by my side. I knew talking you into taking this position was the right move." She attempts a smile, weak as it is.

"We are a power team, which is exactly what you said would happen." She closes her eyes for a solid second. "If you hear from Mia before I do, please keep me updated. I'll work on a plan to take care of Weiss and Anna while he's in the hospital."

A plan. A plan is what will get them through all of this.

"I'll also chat with the Hands of Love group, get a meal schedule started so Anna won't have to make any meals, and I'll organize a team to look in on the house, water the plants, and such. Hopefully, none of this will be needed, and Weiss will be home within days, but...." Susan starts scribbling notes on her pad of paper as she speaks.

This is why she loves this town so much and will fight with every breath of her being to keep this town intact. Innsbruck is a family, a family that looks after their own.

Susan runs a neighborhood network called Hands of Love. Its design is to care for families in need, whether with meals, support, or anything else.

"I have to run into the city with Jordan tomorrow, we're going to transfer her back to school here. I'll stop at the hospital and check in on Mia and everyone. If you need me to do a grocery run for any meal supplies, I can stop in and get some of the ready-to-go ones. Just give me a list."

Susan waves away the offer. "As if. My husband will be heading into the city for his weekly meeting, and he'll already be stopping for me. He can pick up what is needed. You just focus on you and Jordan, and we will take care of the rest."

There's a slight knock on the office door before Nigel opens it. "Everything okay in here?"

Ashley motions him in and hopes her face isn't a bright mess. She's an ugly crier.

"Weiss is on his way to the hospital." Ashley wipes the tears off her stained cheeks, thankful her voice doesn't betray just how emotionally fragile she is. "I'll keep in touch with Mia to find out how he's doing. Susan will coordinate a meal schedule and whatever else we can do to help them, depending on what happens."

"They're family," Nigel agrees. "Just tell me what you need from me."

"Perfect, thanks." Susan gives Ashley another hug before leaving the room.

"Sorry," Nigel says. "I didn't mean to interrupt; I hope everything's okay?" His voice is warm and concerned, and she's reminded that it's not just strong women surrounding her.

"Did everyone leave?" She notices the time but feels zero guilt for leaving the council meeting like she did.

"Hope you don't mind, but I ended things for you," Nigel says. "I suggested to Marcus that I handle the proposal and offer our new idea. He didn't like it, but...."

"Being Deputy Mayor kind of gives you that right." Ashley finishes for him.

"Seriously, Ash, are you okay?" He pulls a chair closer to her desk.

Ashley thinks about his questions. Does she continue to step out of her comfort zone and share what's happening in her life? It's that, share the news with an old friend or remain stoic and push those closest to her away.

"Brett left me." She decides honesty is the only way to go. He's going to learn the truth, anyway, once she confides in Sylvia. "He wasn't thrilled with this whole idea of reinventing the town, and well...apparently, he also has a girlfriend in the city."

Nigel's shoulders hunch forward in obvious dismay.

"Does Sylvia know?"

Ashley shakes her head. "I haven't had time to process it yet, you know? It's been a busy day."

"Why don't you and Jordan join us for dinner tonight?" He suggests. "Sylvia texted she's in the mood for pizza. Come, okay? You guys don't need to be alone right now." The take-charge-and-take-care-of-everyone Nigel is in front of her now, and as much as she appreciates him wanting to fix this for her, that's not what she needs.

Ashley appreciates the offer. She really does. But having alone time with Jordan is exactly what she needs right now.

"Jordan and I need some time to process things. We were able to talk a little over lunch, but...right now, I'm more worried about her than me. I'll be fine, but her dad, the man who was supposed to stay on his pedestal for life, just jumped off it, and well... she's hurting."

She can tell he doesn't buy what she's trying to sell.

"Okay, no pizza. So, I'll bring Sylvia over later. You know she will want to be by your side."

She smiles in relief. Yes, she will need her friend, and the fact he gets that without her having to admit it says everything about their friendship.

CHAPTER EIGHTEEN

A knife is wedged tight inside Ashley's heart, and the longer her daughter sits on the couch and cries over how betrayed she feels by her father, the more that knife digs in.

Her simmering anger for Brett increases in strength for what he's done to Jordan.

She's still not ready to process what he's done to her, to that level of betrayal, his affair...

"Jordan, honey, don't ever apologize for how you feel, okay?" Ashley whispers as she lightly rubs her daughter's back.

"I should be stronger," Jordan says, forcing the dull blade deeper into Ashley's heart.

"Why?"

"So, you don't have to be the only one."

The knife twists, turns, and tears through Ashley like melted butter.

"I don't want you to feel like you are alone," Jordan continues, "like you have to be careful with what you say around me, you know? Dad is a jerk, and there's no sense in hiding that." Jordan uses the pad of her hands to wipe away the tears trailing down her cheeks.

"Jerk is kind of putting it mildly," Ashley says without thinking. Her daughter's maturity level right now is astounding.

"How about we make a deal? We feel what we need to feel. We create a safe place between us, and whatever we say and feel stays in this safe zone, okay?" Ashley holds out her pinkie.

She really wants to wrap her daughter in a tight hug and never let go, but something tells her that's not what Jordan needs right now. "No matter what happens, you've got me—"

"And you've got me," Jordan says, interrupting her. "You don't need to hide your emotions or watch your words with me, Mom. I can handle it. I promise."

Ashley's eyes swell with tears that threaten to crest over her lashes. Of course, she's going to watch her words – she won't be the one to ruin the relationship Jordan could have with her father if he manages to salvage what he's done. Berating Brett isn't fair to him, her, or their daughter. He will always be Jordan's father, regardless of their marital status.

"What your dad did to us, as a family, was..." struggling to find the right word, she sighs. "Disgusting doesn't cut it."

"More like despicable," Jordan says.

"Yep, that's it." Ashley nods. "We will get through it, though, eventually."

Jordan nods, looking off into the distance. "Ice cream will help." Jordan jumps up from her spot on the couch. "Want some? I promise to give you a large bowl."

A bowl? Who needs a bowl? Just give her the whole container, that's why she bought so many small ones. The intent is to drown her sorrows with each spoonful and not feel guilty for eating a whole container.

Ashley leans her head back on the couch. She's exhausted. Empty. Expended. She's not sure she can handle any more heart-to-heart talks without ending up on the floor a sobbing mess.

She picks up her phone and finally looks at the text messages she's been trying to avoid most of the day.

Most of them are from Brett.

The firm has an apartment I can rent until we settle things.

If the weather cooperates, I'd like to come this weekend for my things.

I know it will be awkward. Try not to make it, okay?

Jordan is upset with me. I get it. But she needs to be respectful even in her text messages.

Ignore me if you will, but it doesn't change things.

By the time she finishes reading the last message, Ashley's hands shake so hard she almost can't read the one that pops up: *Try not to make it awkward, okay.*

Is he for real? He's the one who simply walked out the door and didn't come back. He's the one who told her he'd left her via text. He's the one cheating on her.

Try not to make it awkward? Why would he think saying something like that is even remotely okay?

A cyclone of emotions whirls inside her: rage, hurt, frustration, and even shame. She's trying hard to contain them, to only let a trickle of what she's feeling show, not wanting to burden Jordan with watching her mother crumble, but damn, Brett is making it hard.

She wants to yell. Scream. She wants him to know exactly how she feels about his messages and stupid expectations, but if she does, Jordan will hear.

Even though she promised to always be honest with her daughter, Jordan doesn't need to know every single dirty detail.

Praying for strength, she finally replies. She's tempted to explode and tear a strip off him, but why bother? She simply types back *this weekend won't work. I need time and will let you know when I'm ready for you to come by.*

Simple, to the point, and doesn't leave much room for discussion.

There are files in my office I need.

She lets out an exasperated sound of laughter. Guess he should have thought of that before he'd left this morning.

If he'd done this last week, if she didn't know about him having an affair or the fact he'd threatened their daughter into silence, she might be reacting differently.

She might be begging for a second chance, for time to talk, to work things out; she might even have given in and agreed to look at houses in the city...

Thank God this didn't happen a week ago.

It's on the tip of her tongue to reason with him, wanting, needing to know why he's done what he's done, why he betrayed her and their marriage again, why he would place the responsibility of their failed marriage on her shoulders...but she stops herself.

The only outcome will be one full of regret.

She will regret giving in to him.

She will regret giving him the upper hand.

She will regret giving their marriage another chance.

It's crazy, that she's okay with them being over. She never thought she'd feel this way. The first time she'd caught him cheating, she'd been willing to look the other way, to do everything she could to fix whatever issues led him to stray.

Now, she realizes the issues are on him. She won't look the other way because she shouldn't have to. If he tries to use the issues in their marriage as an excuse for him cheating on her...it will only show his true character, and she's not responsible for that.

That realization hits her with such force, it knocks any remote feelings of guilt out from her soul.

She is not responsible for him. She inhales a long breath of air and lets that freedom fill her. The anger, the betrayal, the hurt, and the resentment are not as intense now. Sure, they're still there, hovering, watching, waiting for a moment when it's safe to come out, but for now, there's a satisfying release of sorrow.

With her eyes on the kitchen, her fingers fly over the phone keyboard with barely a glance.

Tell me which files. I can drop them off tomorrow when I'm in the city.

She hesitates to say more. Does she need to? Should she explain why she's coming to the city, or will he assume it's to take Jordan to school? Does she need to tell him? The answer is obvious...yes. When it comes to Jordan, he has the right to know and be involved.

I'll be transferring Jordan to the school here in town.

"Why are you frowning at your phone?"

Jordan stands directly in front of her, holding two bowls of ice cream in her hands.

"How long have you been standing there?" Ashley asks.

"Why the frown?" Jordan repeats.

Ashley takes the offered bowl Jordan shoves in her face and sets it on the ledge of the couch. "Your father texted that he needs some files from his office. I offered to drop them off while we're in the city tomorrow."

Jordan shoves a spoonful of ice cream into her mouth. "Did he say anything about me?" The question comes out a bit muffled.

Ashley pauses, thinking of how to word things. How much did she say? The whole truth? Part of the truth? If she expected honestly from Jordan, she should give it in return, right?

"He mentioned you've been in touch and haven't tried to hide your feelings."

Jordan shrugs, her face buried in the bowl. "I wasn't very

nice," Jordan admits. "But then, he wasn't very nice to me either." She stirs her spoon in the bowl a few times. "I told him he needed to apologize for what he'd said to me, for how he treated me in the car, and for leaving us like he did."

When Jordan meets Ashley's gaze, she can see the hurt, anger, and resentment simmering beneath the surface.

She's proud of Jordan for sticking up for herself, even though it must have been hard to do.

"You're right," Ashley says, "he does need to apologize to you. But," her stomach twists into a sailor knot, and it's all she can do to breathe through the pain, "he's not going to. Not for a long time. Not until he realizes what he's done is wrong and that he's hurt you."

Jordan sucks on her spoon, enjoying the ice cream, an obvious ploy to give herself time to let Ashley's words register. Finally, she nods.

"Still doesn't make it right," Jordan says, a pout in her tone.

"No, it sure as hell doesn't."

"I'm not going to act all nicey-nicey either," Jordan says, her gaze locked onto the bowl she holds. "He's hurt me, and he needs to own that. He's the parent, or he's supposed to be," she mumbles.

A single tear dangles on the edge of Jordan's lash. When it drops, Ashley leans over and gently wipes her daughter's cheek.

"You don't have to be anything you're not, but try to remember he is your father. You can be angry and respectful at the same time," Ashley says, trying not to wince as she finds herself backing Brett up with his earlier comment.

Gah, parenting is way too hard some days.

"So...I can say I hate you but not that I f'n hate you?"

It's hard not to smile at her daughter's suggestion. "Exactly."

Ashley fills her mouth with another spoonful of ice cream

while considering what else to tell her daughter. "He also said he wants to come and grab some things this weekend."

Jordan's hand freezes mid-air, with ice cream dripping from the spoon back into the bowl.

"I told him this wasn't a good time to come."

Jordan's chest deflates as she lets out a long breath, confirming Ashley did the right thing for both of them.

"I don't know if I want to be here when he does come," her daughter whispers. "Is that bad?"

Ashley sets her bowl on the coffee table before wrapping her arms around Jordan's shoulders. "Oh goodness, no, that's not bad at all. I really don't want to be here either." She could ask Nigel to be here instead. Is that being chicken? Cowardly? Cold?

It doesn't matter. It's how she feels.

"Where is he staying?"

Ashley runs her hand along Jordan's long hair. "He's renting an apartment his firm retains, which means he's fine. I'll pack a suitcase of his clothes and toiletries, and then he probably won't need to come by for a while. Not until we are ready to see him."

Jordan swallows hard before pushing herself up from the couch.

"I'm going to my room, is that okay? Shelby and I will video chat and do homework together."

Realizing her daughter needs time away from the discussion and possibly away from her, she nods just as her phone buzzes with another message.

I'll email a list of things you can bring me tomorrow. I figured you'd move her.

An inexplicable need to throw her phone across the room grabs hold of her. She refrains but only barely.

Can he say thank you, at least? Sure, he can send a list, but she's not his personal mover, so he gets what he gets.

And, he *figured* she'd move her? Of course, she will. It's the only option. Can he not be polite about it, though, say it's a good idea or, oh, how about I'm sorry this is happening...no, of course, he can't.

He left her. He's having an affair. Yet, he'll blame her. It's what he does.

He's the only one who should be apologizing.

Will that make things better, though?

Will it make this hurt any less?

No and no.

What she said to Jordan earlier had been the truth...he won't apologize until he realizes the wrongs he's committed.

Her heart hurts. Her eyes hurt. Her body hurts. Her soul hurts.

He hurt her, and it doesn't seem like he even cares.

CHAPTER NINETEEN

The container of mint chocolate chip ice cream is empty. So is the double fudge Oreo, and Ashley's fork full of left-over cake from Frankie is halfway to her mouth when her doorbell rings.

Yes, she's eating her emotions.

No, she doesn't care.

With the fork in her mouth, Ashley opens the door and steps out of the way as Nigel pushes the wheelchair-riding Sylvia into the hallway.

"First off," Sylvia says without so much as a *hi-how-are-you,* "It's freezing out there. If it doesn't snow overnight, I'll be shocked. Second, Brett is an ass. Third, I'm here, and I love you." She stands up from the chair, with Nigel supporting her, and she wraps her arms around Ashley.

It was the exact hug she's needed all day. It's the type of hug giving permission to relax, let down her guards and feel if she needs to.

"First, I agree," Ashley smiles after they've separated. "Second, I love you, too." She leads the way into the living room, shutting off the television as Nigel carefully helps his pregnant wife down on the couch.

"Ash, would you mind if I holed up in Brett's office? I have some work to catch up on, and I'd prefer to be close to Sylvia if you don't mind." He kisses the top of his wife's head. "She won't admit it, but she's exhausted and in pain, and since she won't let me hover, being close by is better than being at home."

Pain and exhaustion flit across Sylvia's face. The dark circles beneath her eyes are more pronounced than before, and her skin is pale, translucent. The woman needs to be in bed or back in the hospital, not here consoling her.

"You shouldn't have come." The sternness of her voice has Sylvia jerking in surprise.

"What? Of course, I'm going to come. That's what we do. That's who we are."

"We don't live in the dark ages, Syl. There's such a thing as technology." Ashley pulls a blanket off the back of the couch and tucks it around Sylvia's legs. Nigel continues to hover, concern etched on his face like a burnt wooden house sign. "Feel free to use the office, Nigel," Ashley tells him. "It's not like Brett needs it anymore," she mumbles.

"I can't give you a hug or hold your hand or eat brownies with you if I was home on my couch looking at you through a screen." Sylvia rolls her eyes before she points toward the bag Nigel holds.

He hands it to Ashley. She pulls out a container and lifts the lid, inhaling the waft of freshly baked brownie slathered in buttercream icing.

"First course was ice cream, main course chocolate cake, and now brownies for dessert," Ashley beams a smile at her friend, "I know I'll be paying for it tomorrow, but I don't really care right now."

Nigel hands over two forks he must have retrieved from her kitchen.

"Thank you," both women mutter before digging into the brownie.

"Seriously though," Ashley says after swallowing the decadent delight, "you didn't need to come."

Sylvia snorts in reply. "As if I wouldn't. You need me and these. What's the difference if I'm sitting on your own couch or mine?"

Nigel groans as he leaves the room. "I'd be happier if it were our couch, just saying." He calls out over his shoulder.

"Honey, I love you, but I'm quite happy where I am, okay?" An unspoken message is said, something only he can understand. It takes him a moment to smile, but it's one full of love when he does.

Ashley averts her gaze. She's happy for her friend, always has been, but she's also been a little jealous about the connection Syliva and Nigel have.

A once-in-a-lifetime love, words Nigel spoke at their wedding, and Ashley didn't doubt it. Not everyone is that lucky, but if anyone deserves to be loved like that, it's Sylvia.

"Did he really tell you he was leaving over a text?" Sylvia asks. "I mean, I know we talked this morning about how rough things were between you and Brett, but for him to just ...I just can't...God, how are you staying calm? I'd be a mess if Nigel did that to me." She reaches for Ashley's hand and squeezes hard.

Ashley blows air through pursed lips. "We both know Brett is no Nigel."

"No, that's true. They are both so different. I know you're not okay, no matter how calm you appear on the surface. You don't have to be strong now though, not with me."

Having Sylvia here is exactly what Ashley needs. She doesn't need to explain all the emotions rolling through, which is good because she can hardly explain them to herself.

"Are you talked out? Emotionally numb? Need to focus on

something else, or do you need to vent and plan? How is Jordan? How is she taking it all?" The words tumble out past Sylvia's lips before she stops to inhale.

These are good questions. What does she need? She's a little numb, so talking about emotions she's not feeling is pointless.

"Vent and plan." That's a no-brainer. Venting and planning will help her focus on something other than this disassociation. She needs to cry, really cry, the hard cry that wracks her body, leaving her feeling bruised, but that type of cry isn't available.

Yet.

A plan. Yes. That's what she needs. She always feels better with a plan in place, and she will need one for the upcoming days, weeks, and even months if she wants to keep any semblance of sanity.

"I'm taking Jordan into the city tomorrow to pull her from school and then dropping off some things Brett needs."

"You're what?" The look of shock on Sylvia's face has Ashley second-guessing herself.

"She wants to go to school here," Ashley says, instinctively knowing that's not what her friend is meaning.

Sylvia shakes her head. "No, not that. That makes sense. It's not like you're going to drive her to and from school every day. It's the part about dropping things off for Brett that I don't understand. Why didn't he take them with him yesterday? It's not like he didn't know this was happening, right? He had enough time to gather his things, and I can't see Brett making this a last-minute decision."

Honestly, Ashley never thought of that.

Sylvia's right. Brett has been planning this. He might not have known the exact date, but walking out was always his goal.

The next words out of her mouth will hurt like a barbed-wire-rolled-into-a-ball-the-size-of-a-jawbreaker, type of hurt.

"He has a girlfriend in the city."

Sylvia says nothing. The woman closes her eyes, and her lips move as if she's speaking, but there's no words.

"Syl?"

Sylvia holds up her finger, needing a moment. It isn't hard to read the anger simmering below the surface.

"No. Absolutely not. There is no way I'm letting you do that. No." She leans forward, jabbing her finger into the air. "Don't you dare take anything to him, drop anything off, or give him any concessions. He. Cheated. On. You."

Ashley nods. "But—"

"Nope. No buts. God, he's guilting you, isn't he? Saying it's your fault for not quitting your job? He obviously didn't want you to, not truly."

Does she feel guilty? Absolutely. It's eating at her, nibbling away, little chunks at a time, and if she's being honest, she feels the weight of this failure. Was there something else she could have done? Did she drive him away because she put her job ahead of her marriage?

"Ten bucks, he's going to say you were the one who made him turn to someone else for love." Sylvia voices the very concerns Ashley didn't want to think about. "Don't you dare let him do that. Promise me," she grabs Ashley's arm and holds tight, "promise me you won't take that on."

Ashley bites her lip, not wanting to lie to her friend. There are always two people in a marriage who makes mistakes.

"It's not your fault," Sylvia continues as if reading her thoughts. "He made that choice. He decided to end your marriage, to not be faithful, again...all that song and dance about you quitting and not placing him first was smoke. You would have quit, moved to the city, and he still would have left you. You realize that, right?"

Eventually, Ashley knows she would have come to that conclusion, but hearing her friend say it helps.

It helps more than she can admit.

"You are the best, you know that? I'm so glad you're here."

Sylvia releases her hold on Ashley's arm and fluffs her hair. "I know," her voice carries a smile Ashley so desperately needs.

"So, where is he staying? I'm assuming with his girlfriend?"

Ashley shakes her head. "He's renting an apartment from his firm, apparently. No idea if the girlfriend is staying with him or not."

"Then why does he need things? Those are fully furnished, right? No. No way," Sylvia pinches the bridge of her nose. "Clothes maybe...empty out that closet of his with all his ties and shoes, but drop it off at his office, making him come out to get it all. He doesn't get to call the shots here, not now."

Ashley lays her head on her friend's shoulder. She's so thankful for her, for the brutally honest words, for being exactly what Ashley needs right now.

"What would I do without you in my life?"

"Good thing we'll both never find out," Sylvia whispers, her voice mirroring all the feels that contain the foundation of their friendship.

CHAPTER TWENTY

MIA

The tepid, vile taste of hospital coffee isn't sitting well with Mia, but she can't seem to throw the cup away. It's keeping her hands busy, which is at least something because otherwise, she'd be doing nothing.

If there's one thing Mia hates more than anything, it's doing nothing.

Nothing feels like failure. Nothing means she's helpless. Nothing confirms she has no control.

"Your father will be fine." Mom pats her knee with a gentle sigh. "Stop worrying."

Stop worrying? Her father is hooked up to a breathing tube, unconscious, and it feels like she's slowly watching him die.

Stop worrying? Not likely.

Mia can't say that though, especially not to her mom.

"I wish he'd gone to the doctor sooner." Mia finally places the cup of undrinkable coffee on the table beside her. "I hate seeing him like this."

This is him hooked up to a machine, lying almost lifeless, covered in a thin sheet and a blanket brought from home. *This* is something she'll never be able to forget.

The two of them had sat like this most of the night, shoulder to shoulder, watching over the man they both love more than anything else. A nurse had come in at one point and led her mom to an empty hospital bed so she could get a few hours of sleep in a comfortable position.

Mia refused to leave Dad's side. She'd rather sleep upright in the most uncomfortable chair than leave him alone.

"He can't die like this," Mia whispers, the thought constantly hovering, demanding more space in her heart and mind than she should give it.

"Hush. I won't have you talking like that, not here. Your father is not dying." Mom sets her book down on her lap and twists toward Mia, a firm frown fixated on her face. "He's sick but where he needs to be, getting the best medical attention he can. Your father is too stubborn to leave the world like this, and you know it."

Properly chastised, Mia wipes at a tear that slides down her cheek and forces herself to sit straighter in her seat.

"Honey, why don't you go home? I'm sure you're itching to get into your shop and return to work. I'll be fine here."

It's frightful how well her mother can read her. Getting lost in delivery boxes, registry receipts, or stocking shelves would be a welcome respite to the hours she's spent in this room, watching her father breathe through a tube.

"I'm not leaving you here by yourself. What if Dad wakes up? Or gets worse?" She shouldn't have said that. 'Don't speak into being things you don't want to come true', something her father always said when she was a child.

"Your father is out cold, Mia. He won't wake up for ages, which is good because we need the antibiotics to work. I'll sit here and read, and if I get lonely, you know, all I have to do is go for a walk. Go for a few hours at least, you're too antsy, and it's making me uncomfortable."

The lines on Mia's forehead deepen into a scowl before she gives up. Mom is right. She is antsy and feels helpless.

"Call me if you need anything or if he wakes up, okay? Promise?" Mia reaches for her purse and slings the handles over her shoulder. "I'll only be a few hours, and I'll bring you some fresh clothes to change into and something to eat."

Mia leaves the room with a hug, a kiss, and a promise not to come too soon and finally lets the tears fall as she walks out to her car.

She's not ready to lose her father, not yet, not like this. Not over something that started out as a stupid cold he was 'too manly' to take medicine for. Why do men have to be so stubborn? When will her father realize he's not immortal even though she needs him to be?

It's not until she's in her car that she finally looks at all the text messages she's ignored since coming to the hospital. So many well wishes, prayers, and people wanting updates... it's too much. The idea of responding to everyone...she can't do it.

Her parents are loved, and she's so thankful for that. Still, she can't possibly update everyone, saying the same thing, having to reassure everyone.

She pushes her phone back into her purse without replying to anyone. She cannot muster even that much energy and takes the backroads toward home.

Driving through the mountains calms her typically. There's something about the rustic beauty of the woods, the rugged backdrop of the towering mountains, and the windy roads edged in a light dusting of snow. It's mesmerizing...but not today.

Today, all she sees is her father in that hospital bed, his pale features blending in with the sheets on his bed and the whiteness of the walls.

Today, all she feels is fear.

Fear of what the future will hold without having her father stand beside her, supporting her at every step. Fear of what would happen to her mother if she lost the love of her life.

She's not ready. She'll never be ready to lose a parent. How does one even prepare for that? She doesn't want to find out.

Somehow, she makes it to The Wandering Aisle, a name her father helped her select, on autopilot. The door is open, with their sign out front. Belle, a teenager she hired to assist in the evenings, squats down in front of the sign, writing something in chalk.

"Belle, shouldn't you be in school?"

"Hey Mia, I've got a free period. I thought I'd come down and redo the sign. I heard about your dad. I hope he's okay," Belle says as she gets to her feet and brushes her chalk-covered hands all over her jeans, not noticing the marks she leaves on herself.

"Thanks, Belle. The temperature is dropping, why don't you bring that sign inside."

Belle shakes her head. "It's not that bad."

Teenagers.

"What are you adding to the sign today?" There's an outline of a stack of books with only a few letters.

"Treat yo' shelves." Belle pulls a folded piece of paper from her back pocket and shows her a copy of the design. "I thought it was cute, and we all need something to smile about, right?"

"It's going to look great. Thanks for giving the sign a refresh, but don't be late for class, okay?" She lightly pats Belle on the arm before she walks into her shop.

Stepping into the store is like coming home. A deep sense of peace rests on her shoulders, settling in and sweeping down her spine until she can let go of her fear and breathe with freedom in her lungs for the first time since she stepped off the plane only a few days ago.

All her life, she'd wanted to own her own bookstore. Opening The Wandering Aisle was and continues to be a dream come true. This dream would never have become a reality if it weren't for her parents. Dad helped to build the shelves, Mom helped with the decorating, and even went vintage shopping to find accessories to outfit the store. Together, the three created a place for people to wander, browse and even sit and read.

You see books, comics, stationery, and home gifts everywhere you look. There are nooks with chairs and tables, a children's area where they can read and play, and a corner area dedicated to all things social media promotion – not that many in their small town take advantage of it, other than the teenagers.

"What do you think you're doing?" Tommi, her full-time assistant, walks toward her from the back of the store. "Didn't you get my text? I told you I had it all covered."

Tommi holds up a hand, and Mia copies her. They don't touch, but it's close. Tommi has a thing about physical touch, it's not something she likes doing, so this is her hug.

"Mom kicked me out of the hospital room, said I was making her antsy."

The look on Tommi's face is a mixture of sympathy and understanding. "How is Dad?"

The sound Mia makes is almost unrecognizable, especially to her own ears. It's a mixture of a sharp inhale and piercing cry that inhabits three seconds of time.

"Oh, no." In a rare gesture, Tommi's arms wrap around Mia, which brings on the tears.

All Mia wants is to sink into her friend's embrace,

welcoming the hug, but she knows this is stretching Tommi out of her comfort zone.

"What do you need from me? Other than the obvious?" Tommi releases her and steps back. She's got tears in her eyes, matching the ones in Mia's, along with a hint of fear.

Mia totally understands. Tommi is family. When she moved back to Innsbruck as a single mother, her parents took her under their wing.

"I want to stay busy." She needs that image of Dad out of her brain to stop hearing the beeping of the machines.

"Well then, I have the perfect job for you." Tommi attempts to lighten the vibe with a wobbly smile. "We just got a shipment in. The boxes are all in the back. I wasn't sure if you wanted me to save them for you or not, considering they came from Germany."

This is exactly what Mia needed to hear.

"Do me a favor? If anyone comes in wanting to talk to me, cover for me? I just don't think...."

Tommi waves her off. "Don't you worry about a thing. I've got your back."

Without a backward glance, Mia beelines it to the back and lets out a little squeal at all the boxes piled up.

Yes, this is perfect. One of her contacts promised to send over samples of items, and not only are they perfect for the Christmas market, they're also exactly what she'll need for this new venture the town is about to take on.

The more she thinks about Innsbruck becoming a Christmas town, the more excited she finds herself, with idea after idea running through her head of how she can transition her bookstore into something holiday themed.

The doorbell from the front of the store rings over and over, alerting Mia to customers as they come in, but she hides in the back, not ready to face anyone, trusting Tommi to play defense as needed.

It's in the middle of unpacking a hand-carved Nativity scene from a shop in Oberammergau, a village known for hosting the Passion Play every ten years in Germany, when Tommi opens the door, squeezing her tiny shell of a body through the door.

"Hey, sorry to bother you, but...oh my, that is amazing," she says, gushing over the wood nativity Mia has been setting up. "That's the hand-carved one you sent me photos of, isn't it? I can't even..." she gently picks up a shepherd, her fingers tracing all the lines. "These are gorgeous, Mia. Please tell me you ordered more than one set?" She sets down one shepherd only to reach for Mary, Joseph, and then baby Jesus. "I can't believe someone made these by hand. The one I have at home doesn't even compare to these."

Mia holds one of the angels in her hands, her fingers caressing the wood wings, and thinks back to when she and her dad stood in a small, tucked out of the way store, looking at all the selections. Her dad had a wistfulness in his gaze, telling her he had a story to tell.

Once they were back at the family home, Dad brought down a container from the attic. It was a rough, hand-carved nativity scene that he'd created with his father as a teenager.

That was one of the first things they shipped back home, and Mia can't wait to see it out this Christmas on display.

"So... there's someone out front that I think you should come say hi to. A lot of folks have come in wanting news on your dad, making sure I give you hugs and let you know they're all praying."

Mia smiles. "Thanks for being my referee. Who's outside?" A thread of tension knots tighter inside. She knows people are worried. She gets they want updates and to be there for her and her family, but even just having her phone blow up with messages feels suffocating.

"Susan."

Yes, she definitely wants to say hi to Susan. She had a few email messages from the woman letting her know how she'll be helping to take care of her parents. Of all people who deserve an update, it's Susan.

She heads out of the backroom and expects to be greeted with a hug and words of comfort, but expectations and reality are two very different things.

There's no hug. No smile. No words of comfort.

"I hear you're hiding. Why?" Susan stands there, purse slung over her shoulder, arms clasped at her waist.

"What do you mean, why?" Mia copies Susan's stance, suddenly feeling like she's being attacked and must justify her actions. "My father is lying unconscious in the hospital, and I can't handle all the text messages and phone calls."

"So, if not you, then who?"

"Excuse me?"

Susan drops her purse to her elbow and then sets it down on one of the display tables. "Mia, if you're not answering those text messages and phone calls, who do you think is?" There's a hint of impatience in Susan's tone, and Mia backs up a step.

"Your mother, Mia," Susan says with a very long and tedious sigh. "Your mother is the one answering."

Mia's face scrunches up into a full-fledged frown. "What? I told her not to. She doesn't need to deal with this."

Susan nods. "Exactly. She doesn't need to. She shouldn't be, actually, and yet she is. Why?"

Tommi slinks away, back toward the front of the store.

Mia's mouth opens, but before she can say a word, she wisely closes it again. If there's one thing she knows about Susan, it's that she doesn't put up with nonsense. She has the biggest, most caring heart, but she doesn't suffer fools, and, at this moment, that's exactly how Mia is feeling.

"I have no doubt you're scared and worried about your father, we all are, but you need to pull up those big girl panties of yours and take care of your mom, and part of that is shielding her from all the emotions everyone in this town is throwing her way." Susan's tone has softened, her voice gentler than before. "Everyone loves your parents. In fact, I bet it's safe to say most people call them friends or consider them pseudo-grandparents, don't you think?"

Mia nods.

"Of course, everyone is worried. Of course, everyone wants updates. That's only natural, Mia. So, of course, most people will reach out to you, hoping for that update, and when you don't reply, they'll contact your mom because she's always been the one to contact.

It's true. Her mother has always been in the middle of things. She's generally the first person on the phone to organize meals, childcare, or whatever else needs done.

"I'll have you know my big girl panties are pulled up tight," Mia finally says. Susan's right. She does need to step up and shield her mother. "I just needed a moment, that's all."

Susan's shoulders melt as she gives Mia a smile. "That's my girl. I'll make it easy on you. Answer my texts or phone calls, give me the updates, and I'll pass the news along, okay? We've got a schedule to ensure you and your mom are being taken care of."

Mia's first instinct is to tell her that's unnecessary, but she knows it's the exact opposite. People need to feel needed, especially in times of emergencies. Her parents have always been there to help, support, and take care of others when it was needed. Now it's time for the town to take care of them.

"Thank you, that's what you want to say," Susan says with a smile.

"Thank you," Mia says, smiling back.

"There's a container with some snack foods, muffins, nuts, veggies, and such. Make sure both you and your mom eat, okay? When your father comes home, he's gonna need strong women to keep him from doing too much."

When...Susan said when, and out of everything that has been said to her today, that single, solitary word has tears pooling in Mia's eyes.

She steps toward the woman and wraps her arms around her. "Thank you," Mia whispers. "Thank you for everything."

"Oh honey," Susan eventually says, "you're never alone. I hope you know that. Your mother is the only person you need to be strong for right now. Everyone else will have your back, I promise."

Mia nods, too choked up to answer, and with one final hug, she retreats back into the storage room for a good cry.

A few hours pass as she catalogs, prices, and stores the items on the back shelves, and when she checks her phone, she feels twinges of guilt for having missed a few of her mother's messages.

Her father is awake.

CHAPTER TWENTY-ONE

ASHLEY

After dropping Jordan off at school to gather her things and say goodbye to friends, Ashley finds herself parked outside Brett's office building.

The woman looking back at her in the rearview mirror is someone she hasn't seen in a long time. "I've got this," she whispers to herself.

I'm in the parking lot.

It took her ten minutes to send him that text. Ten minutes of thinking about what Sylvia had said last night, how he didn't deserve the general niceties he thought he did.

Jordan doesn't want to see him. Not today. Not tomorrow. Not for a good long while, apparently. She made that clear the moment they were on the highway with a well-rehearsed speech. To be honest, she can't blame her daughter.

She really doesn't want to see him either.

I'm about to head into a meeting. I'll send someone down.

It's hard not to laugh at his reply. She knew he would do

this. Classic Brett. This would be so much easier if he'd just own up to the hurt he's caused, but no, he'll play the victim for as long as he can get away with it. If he's too much of a chicken to tell her face to face that he was leaving her, then there was no way he'd come down to retrieve his things this morning.

She kind of figured he'd do this, so she came prepared.

If you want it bad enough, you'll come yourself. Otherwise, it's all going in the trash.

Her fingers tap dance on the steering wheel as she waits for his reply.

Does she really want to see him?

No.

She needs to, though. She deserves to be told the truth, face to face, not via their daughter. She has the right to hear that he's been cheating on her, again, from his lips.

Five minutes later, his tall form exits the front door. He looks for her in the parking lot, hands jammed into his suit pant pockets, his stride nonchalant, as if coming to meet her is only one more line item on his agenda.

She steps from the vehicle, leaning against the door, arms crossed over her chest as he draws closer.

"Thanks for bringing me that file. I have a client coming in after lunch and wouldn't have been prepared."

He refuses to meet her gaze, surprise, surprise.

There's so much she wants to say. It all sits there on the tip of her tongue. She could be polite, not make waves, but is that the right thing to do?

She decides to let her heart speak. "You should have told me the truth instead of guilting me into believing you wanted something you had no desire for."

The smoothness on his forehead disappears as he frowns. "What are you talking about?"

"Our marriage." Ashley hates how her voice quivers ever so slightly.

"Don't place this on me." He steals a glance at her but quickly looks away. "You're the one who gave up on us."

Ashley draws in a long deep breath, mentally reminding herself not to be drawn into an argument. She is not going to allow him to guilt her or place the blame on her.

"I'm pretty sure you gave up on us when you decided to cheat. Again."

He flinches, and the satisfaction Ashley feels floods her soul. Did he not expect her to find out? Did he really think he could keep her in the dark?

"What? You didn't think Jordan would tell me?" She struggles to keep the anger simmering below the surface out of her voice. She will not lose her cool. She will not lose her cool. She will not—

"Where's my stuff?"

Ashley laughs. The level of sarcasm in that laugh isn't lost on Brett either.

"I don't need to take this," he huffs, his tone holding a level of threat she hasn't heard from him in a long time.

He didn't need to take...

Every single emotion she's struggled to contain since yesterday boils over.

"Excuse me? You don't need to take what, exactly?" She spits the words out like seed husks. "My reaction to your cheating? Or how I feel about you leaving me? How about the disturbing way you decided to parent our daughter by threatening her to keep your girlfriend a secret?" The rage bubbles over, with the heat level to scorch anything left between them to the ground. Somehow, by some miracle, she manages to tamper it down, and just in time, if the fisted hands at Brett's side are any indication.

He won't hit her, but he wants to. Oh, he wants to, she can see it all over his face.

"Tell you what," she says, swallowing back all the words she wants to say, knowing now is not the time. She's amazed at how calm she feels. Deadly calm. "How about I save all my thoughts and reactions for my lawyer?"

Brett's mouth opens and then closes, in sync with his fists.

"Your suitcase is in the back," she says, keeping an eye on his hands. "I also brought you those files. I'll let you know when I'm ready for you to come up to grab the rest of your things." She remains in place at the side of her vehicle while he heads to the trunk.

He's silent, and Ashley isn't sure if that's a good thing or not. It scares her almost as much as his fists do.

"There's nothing left of your stuff in our room," she continues, knowing he hears her as he unloads the luggage and bags from her vehicle. "I grabbed what I could from your office." She thought she'd been generous to pack his things. She even included photos of their daughter for him.

"Thank you," he said, more docile now. Maybe it's all sinking in, what he's done, the consequences of his actions. He gathers his things and stands there awkwardly as if trying to figure out what to say and how.

She doesn't help him.

She has so much she wants to say, so much she needs to get off her chest, to unwind the layers of knots inside, but both Nigel and Sylvia said something last night, something that made sense.

Place Jordan first. Don't let him goad you into making a bad situation worse. Before you unload even an ounce of anger and bitterness, get papers drawn up and make sure he signs them.

"This doesn't have to get ugly," Brett finally says. "I do love you, and I wish our marriage could have worked, but we've both know we've just been putting in the time for Jordan."

Her heart feels like it's being shredded and forced down a garbage chute.

Put in time? No, she was never just putting in time. She put a lot of heart and hard work into their marriage to make it work...for them.

"I wasn't," Ashley says.

"I'm sorry, either way." Brett stares off into the distance, not meeting her gaze.

She breathes in deep, needing to fill every empty spot within herself, but she might as well have been sucking from a deflated balloon.

"I'm not ready to accept that apology, Brett. Not yet. Neither is Jordan. You'll need to give us both time."

He sniffs, looking up into the sky and then back at his office building. She follows his gaze.

She wants to ask about the other woman. Who is she? Did she know her? Is she from work? A colleague or the receptionist? How long has it been going on?

What does this mystery woman offer him that she didn't?

She wants to know, yet...it doesn't matter, does it? The more she learns, the more she'd look back and wonder why she hadn't seen it, why she'd been so blind.

Maybe one day she'll find out the truth. If it mattered by then.

"Hurting you and Jordan is something I've never wanted to do...I hope you know that?"

She frowns. "What did you think would happen?" Ashley asks. "We'd throw a party? Be able to move on like our lives haven't been decimated? We're more than hurt. You betrayed us both. I hope you realize that." While she can see that this is probably the best thing for them, she will not make it easy on him. He cheated. He didn't just walk away. She would have fought for them no matter how tough things had been. He stopped fighting when he made a choice to betray their vows. "I hope you'll try to fix things with Jordan."

Something passed over Brett's face that gives her hope. Not for her and him, but for him and Jordan.

"What can I do?" He asks, to her surprise.

"Apologize."

"She's so angry, though. It's hard." He honestly sounds dejected.

"Of course she is," Ashley says. "What did you think would happen? She's hurt. She feels betrayed. Her white knight just fell off his pedestal." Does he really not understand the consequences? "You were never supposed to hurt her, and yet you did. It's going to take time."

It's a lot easier to discuss their daughter than themselves.

Ashley is surprised at the feeling that takes hold inside of her as they stand there in collective silence. It's small, like a seed, but it's there. It's a sense of freedom, like the birds flying above her head in the cloudless sky...a range of possibilities that are there, just out of reach, but there.

Without another word, Ashley climbs into her vehicle, giving Brett one last look, taking in everything that fills that moment between them, and accepts it.

They are done. He isn't coming home.

She's okay with that.

CHAPTER TWENTY-TWO

Ashley and Jordan walk the quiet hallway of the hospital.

Ashley carried a potted plant in a tea mug. Jordan is holding onto the gift bag full of different tea flavors. There might have been some individually wrapped pieces of caramel in there, too, something Ashley knows Weiss has a fondness for.

"Are you sure it's okay that I'm here?" Jordan whispers as their footsteps echo down the hallway.

"Yes, I'm sure."

Anna meets them in the hallway, having slipped out of Weiss' room at their approach. Ashley sent her a text when they first arrived, wanting to make sure they were still okay to drop in.

"What a stubborn fool that man is," Anna grumbles as she receives their hugs and gifts. "Scared the bejesus out of me, he did. The doctor gave him a talking to for not getting seen sooner," she continues as she leads them to a waiting area.

"Are you okay?" Ashley asks.

Anna looks worn out. Her bun is lopsided, with flyways all over the place. She's clutching her cardigan between her fingers, worrying the fabric.

"I'm tired, love. You wouldn't think sitting in a chair waiting for a grumpy man to wake up can be exhausting, but Weiss sure makes it to be." Anna leans back and rests her head against the wall. "I don't want to leave him alone, though. He may look tough, but he hates hospitals."

"Anna, we booked you a room at a hotel just down the street. Why don't we take you there so you can rest? I heard you and Mia stayed here all night." Ashley places her hand on Anna's arm and squeezes.

"Oh, that's lovely. Thank you. I'll wait until Mia returns, if that's okay. I don't want to leave him alone." She covers her mouth as she yawns.

"Why doesn't Mom drive you to your hotel, and I can stay with him," Jordan offers. "I can read to him if he'd like."

A warm smile grows on Anna's face. "He's sleeping, but I'm sure he'd love to wake up to your lovely face instead of my tired one." She glances toward Ashley, "if you wouldn't mind?"

Mind? Of course, she doesn't.

"While you sleep, maybe I'll indulge in some retail therapy and a good strong coffee from Starbucks." Ashley reaches over and gave her daughter's hand a squeeze.

Anna stands to her feet. "I'll just go grab my purse, and we can leave. Thank you," she says to Jordan before giving her a very long hug.

Ashley catches the sheen of tears in Anna's eyes.

They watch as Anna walks away, giving her time to gather herself and her belongings.

"That was really sweet of you, hun," Ashley says.

"I hope you didn't mind. She looks tired, and I have home-work. You don't need to rush back, do you?"

Jordan loves that her daughter can think of others, especially right now.

"I've nowhere to be but here with you," she gives Jordan a

side hug. "Well, and the shops on Main Street. I could do with a good walk through some of the shops. Especially the chocolate ones. There's nothing like fresh fudge."

Jordan's eyes light up. "Oh, could you get some turtle ones? Or even the mint chocolate one?"

"It might be a good thing you're not coming with me," she teases. "Let me see what I can do."

Jordan gives her a thumbs up just as Anna returns.

"You're sure you don't mind? He's still asleep, but I hate leaving him alone." Anna asks again.

"I've got homework to do, so I don't mind sitting here, honestly." Jordan gives her a brief hug before she heads down the hallway toward Weiss's room.

Anna checked her watch. "A power nap of an hour or so is all I need."

Ashley kisses her daughter goodbye and then stays by Anna's side as they head toward the elevator. She can't help but notice Anna's slow steps.

"You nap for as long as you need, okay? I'm in no rush to return to Innsbruck today, so please don't worry about us."

Anna hides another yawn behind her hand. "Are you sure? I don't want to put you out."

The elevator doors open.

"Honestly, I don't mind. I haven't had a good stroll down the main street of Banff in a long time. My first stop will be for a beaver tail. It's been a long time since I've indulged in one of those fried pastries, and after today, I could use one." Ashley bites her lip, knowing she's said more than intended, and unloading on Anna, especially right now, is the last thing she wants to do.

"Is everything okay, dear?"

"Just...one of those weeks, you know?" Ashley keeps it generic, choosing the safe route.

It wasn't until they were driving down the street that Anna chooses to confront that generic reply.

"I'm going to repeat something that an assistant of yours recently said to me. Don't be too proud to admit when you need help. Now, Susan and I go way back, so I didn't take offense. She knows me well enough to know I'd rather be helping others than receiving it myself. So, Ashley Tanner," Anna reaches out and gently lays her hand on Ashley's arm, "I'm going to say the same thing to you. Don't let that stubborn pride of yours get in the way of accepting help when it's offered, you hear me?"

Ashley's fingers tighten around the wheel, her eyes never straying from the road.

"Yes, ma'am," she says, soft and subdued. Sensitive to the fact that Anna probably needs to redirect her own worries and fears, Ashley swallows her pride.

If anything, the mothers of Innsbruck will surround them and be there for them both.

"Brett walked away from our marriage yesterday. He's... found someone else," she breathes in deep, "which is only an excuse for him deciding he wanted something other than us in his life."

"Oh, love," Anna's whispered words of warmth wrap around Ashley's heart, the heat a healing hug from heaven.

That's all it takes for Ashley's knotted shoulders to relax from the tension she's been holding in since picking up Jordan and pretending everything is fine.

"We're going to be all right," Ashley says, hearing her words come out more as a question than as an answer.

"Of course, you will. You'll handle this storm, not because you're strong and can get through anything, but because you will be surrounded by people who love you. Don't ever make the mistake of thinking you have to handle this yourself.

Promise me that. Don't be that woman who thinks she's so strong that she doesn't realize it's okay to be weak."

A lump of unspoken emotions and words all jumbled together form in Ashley's throat.

All her life, she's believed that to get through anything, she needed to be strong. Strong enough to weather storms. Strong enough to be the support for others. Strong enough to bend but not break.

That level of strength is exhausting, and when she fell in love with Brett, she thought he was the answer to keeping that strength, she could rely on him to hold her up when it became too much. And he had, for years. But, what about now? There's no one now to hold her, to remind her things would be okay...

Except, there are. There were women like Sylvia and Anna and Frankie who loved her. Her initial response is not to burden someone else with her issues but—

"I can see your brain spinning like a hamster on a wheel. Slow down, Ashley. Take a breath and stop trying to protect yourself in the future. Take each day as it comes." She stops as they pull up into the hotel driveway. "Oh, this is a nice one," she says as she stares at the rugged mountain façade of the hotel. "Weiss and I came here once for dinner. You spoil me." She pats Ashley on the arm.

Spoiling is exactly what Ashley was going for. The Banff Lodge is one of the oldest hotels in the town and had recently undergone a refurbishment. Other than being known for their farm-to-table menus, they're also known for their rustic charm and pampering amenities. If there's anything Anna needs during her stay, they will make sure she's taken care of.

"The room is already covered, along with incidentals. That includes food, Anna. Make sure you eat, please."

"You're such a wonderful caretaker, Ashley. Thank you. Listen, even if our worlds seem to be crashing around us, don't be afraid to lean on us for support. You are family, you and your daughter, and family is always there for one another."

"Thank you," Ashley says. Two simple words, but she means them with her whole heart.

"Now, instead of shopping, why don't you see if you can get into that spa over at the Banff Springs Hotel. You could probably do with a little pampering yourself, and those plunge pools are amazing. I'll text you when I'm ready to head back to Weiss."

Ashley whispers a small prayer of thanks as Anna heads into the hotel, clutching her purse between her hands. She's so thankful for the women in her life, their strength and love, and for always being there for her, without judgments. At times like this, she misses her mother with a fierceness.

Yes, she and Jordan will be okay. They'll weather this storm and come out stronger in the end. She knows it like she knows her daughter will enjoy doing a dinner and a movie before heading home.

CHAPTER TWENTY-THREE

MARLEE

Marlee listens to the kids share about their day at school with only partial interest. She can't stop worrying about Jared. She's been calling all day, leaving messages, then texting, but there's been no answer.

He always answers. Even if it's to say he will call her back.

She's worried.

The time with his parents hadn't gone exactly as planned.

Marlee had hoped that by being back in town, close to his parents, especially after the town hall, the idea of moving back would hold more appeal. It would solidify the idea of moving back home, but after the escalating conflict between Jared and Durwood over the weekend, Marlee doubts that will happen now.

"Mom, are you listening?" Julian taps her on the hand.

"Sorry, love. I was off in la-la land," Marlee forces herself to stop worrying over Jared and focus on their children. Dinner is a simple affair, spaghetti with a meat sauce.

"I said, I think Dad is home." He points toward the kitchen door that leads into the garage. Marlee cocks her head to listen, and sure enough, she hears the dull thud of his toolbox being dropped onto the worktable.

She rises from her chair and gets a plate ready for Jared. He's rarely ever home for dinner. Should she be worried?

When he opens the door, everyone is full of smiles, herself included, despite the anxiety that rises inside her like a boiling kettle.

"Well, isn't this a nice surprise," he says as their youngest launches herself from her seat into his arms. He avoids looking at Marlee, which just twists the anxiety that's razor sharp now.

She sets his plate on the table while he washes up in the sink, thankful that he's not rushing upstairs to wash or change right away.

She stays quiet, letting the kids steal his attention while they all eat. She doesn't say a word as she clears the table, or while she fills the dishwasher. Usually, one of the kids helps with clearing up after dinner, but tonight they're all gathered around Jared, talking his ear off as he takes it all in.

It's nice to have him home. However, that doesn't diminish the fear of why he is home early.

Please don't let him have lost his job.

Those words play over in her head as she keeps the smile on her face and the fear from her gaze. Those words play on a track repeated themselves over and over and over again as Jared led the kids outside to toss the ball, giving her some peace and quiet.

It's not quiet she needs, though. She needs her husband to explain to her why he's home, why he ghosted her all day and why he refused to look her in the face for any length of time.

Sipping a glass of wine in the living room, her cell rings, and the number on the screen surprises her.

"Hey, Dianne, what's up?" She'd just seen her friend earlier today at school. Dianne lives down the street but leads one of those busy lives Marlee is thankful not to have.

"Hey. Remember when I said my company was hiring?"

Marlee frowns. Yes, she remembers, but that was months ago. Dianne mentioned it in passing, wondering if Marlee wanted something full-time. She currently works part-time for a nursing home to help with some of the bills. She's lucky, to be able to schedule her hours so she can drop the kids off at school and pick them up. She's never questioned when she needs days off because one of the kids is sick or if she has to leave mid-shift to pick up someone from school.

"That was what, a month ago? I really can't handle full-time hours, Dianne."

"I know, I know. But what if I told you they'll work around your schedule, much like your current job, but with increased pay and more hours? You work like what, three days a week?" Dianne asks.

"More pay?"

"Yep. Five days a week. Marlee, they'll offer you five dollars an hour more than what you make now." The confidence in Dianne's voice when she drops that number shocks Marlee.

"You're kidding me."

"I'm not. Serious. I've bragged on you enough to my boss. She says the job is yours if you want it."

Does she want it? That's a great question.

Sipping her wine, she considers the options. It would help out financially in a huge way...it would mean Jared wouldn't have to work as many hours and could be home for dinner more often too. But...she likes being available for the kids, having the two days a week where she can volunteer in their classes. Is she willing to give that up?

"When do you need to know?" First thing first, she has to talk to Jared.

"As soon as you can. Honestly, it's a no-brainer to me, and they have the job posted, but my boss said you would get top pick if you wanted it." There's a sense of hurriedness in Dianne's voice that bothers Marlee. She doesn't want to feel rushed. She understands the situation, and realizes Dianne has probably put her neck on the line for her, but still...

"Let me chat with Jared tonight, and I'll get back to you, okay?"

"Sure, sure. Text me if that's easier. Honestly, I hope you take it! I know you've mentioned things are tight, and Jared is never home, this might be the answer to those problems."

Marlee is still seated on the couch, her wine glass now empty, when Jared finally joins her.

"I'll put the kids to bed tonight?" He says, casually leaning against the wall, hands in his pockets.

"Sure." Marlee peers at him. "Do I get a hello, sorry for ignoring you today, or anything?" She places a tiny tidbit of a smile on her face, hoping to dull the hurt in her voice.

In reply, he sinks beside her on the couch and leans forward, so his elbows rest on his knees.

"What's wrong?" Her concern notches up at least three more levels.

She places her hand on his back when he doesn't answer. Finally, with a deflation of his shoulders, he twists his head and gives her a rough grimace.

"Just a rough day," he mutters. "Sorry, I should have replied to your texts, but I just didn't have the energy to. I still don't," his head drops even further.

Now she's truly scared.

"What happened? Are you okay?"

The dark circles beneath his eyes stand out, and the weariness on his face enhances the exhaustion in his gaze. She's afraid to hear what he's about to say.

"Just a rough day. A lot of things went wrong, and I took the blame, even though I shouldn't have. They would have fired a guy at work otherwise, and he's just a kid with a new baby and a girlfriend who is struggling being a new mom. He needs this job...."

"And you knew they wouldn't fire you."

He nods.

There's something she wants to say, something that's on the tip of her tongue, but she knows he won't appreciate it, so she keeps the thought to herself.

He's more like his father than he wants to admit.

"I took the evening from the other job off, I know I shouldn't have, but I just wanted to be home, with the kids, you know? Remember why I'm doing this." His shoulders roll forward as if the weight of all their well-being rests on him.

It's not meant to be that way. They're a team, partners, and if it means she has to step up, then she will.

"Dianne called while you were outside," Marlee said. She explains the job offer, but even before she can tell him she's going to take the job, Jared's on his feet, shaking his head no.

"No. No. We agreed that your focus would be on the kids. The kids would be your top priority and not get extra work hours."

"That was before we understood the full sacrifice. You can't keep doing this, Jared. The kids need you to be present, and there's nothing wrong with me stepping up to help carry the load."

He shakes his head.

"You'd be at home. With the kids. With me. Think about that, please. If the pay is as good as Dianne says it is...."

He continues to shake his head as if blocking out her words, her plea. "It would keep us in the same position, except you'd come home exhausted daily rather than just three days a week. No. I'll look for something else."

"Something else? So, it's okay for you to be exhausted, never home, carrying the weight of this family on your shoulders alone, but I can't help?" She knows her words sting, but she needs to get through his stubbornness somehow.

He won't look at her. He won't reply, either.

"What about moving back to Innsbruck?" She offers this suggestion quietly. "We have a house there already that we can't sell, and I'm sure your dad would be more than happy to start his business back up again, knowing you'd be there helping him."

His brow bunches at the idea, but still, he remains silent.

"It could work...and you know the kids will jump all over the idea. They all want to move back."

They both hear a scuffle and glance up to find all their kids sitting on the stairs, listening in to their conversation.

"Please, Dad," Julian begs. "We want to move back home."

The others join in until Jared throws up his hands, not in a playful gesture but one full of exasperation.

"Get to your rooms, in bed...this isn't a conversation for you right now," he says, this close to yelling. The kids scamper to their feet and run, their bedroom doors slamming behind them.

"That wasn't necessary," Marlee says, getting to her feet. "I'll put them to bed while you cool off. Come up when you're ready to apologize to them." She doesn't need to say another word. They both know he went too far with his tone.

If he's upset, be upset with her, not the kids.

"I've no doubt Dad will restart his company. He'll be right in the thick of things if he can. But Marlee, you know Dad doesn't want my help anymore." Jared reaches his hand out, stopping her from walking past him.

Durwood not wanting or accepting his help bothers him –

it's in his voice, a deep hurt, whether he acknowledges it or not. He feels rejected, and that's something she should have realized. All she's focused on is the fact that the two men in her life have hurt their pride, but it goes deeper than pride. The rejection is felt by both.

"Your father needs your help, and he knows that. He's just too ashamed to ask for it. And we need to do something other than what we are doing because it's not fair...not to you with all the hours you work or to us as a family." She wishes Jared would look past his hurt and fear of rejection and see that moving back is the best thing for their family.

Why is he so blind to something she sees so clearly?

CHAPTER TWENTY-FOUR

With the kids all busy with homework, Marlee peers through the small window out into the garage to see Jared half bent over his worktable, shoulders slumped. One hand grips the table's edge, and the other holds his phone tight to his ear.

He's been spending a lot of time in the garage lately, and she hasn't mentioned it because she knows he's working off some stress. Stress he won't share with her. She gets he wants to protect her, but how can she help him if he won't open up to her?

She poured a fresh round of coffee into her mug, adding a splash of Bailey's, and snags a biscotti she'd picked up from Frankie's when they'd been in Innsbruck. She keeps her stash of secret treats tucked into the back of the freezer in a box for frozen meatballs. So far, no one has caught on about her hiding place, thank goodness.

Jared is still on the phone when she opens the garage door. He doesn't even notice, so she sits and waits, enjoying her coffee, savoring the cookie.

She rarely bothers him when he's working in the garage. For the past few months, he's been using the space to work on some side projects, forcing her to park in the driveway, but she doesn't mind. The area is an organized disaster zone, as she likes to tease him. He knows exactly where every single tool, screw, and piece of wood is located, despite the chaotic mess.

The garage is his sanctuary, as much as the lounge chaise in their bedroom was hers.

The moment she enters the garage, a chill settles across her shoulders, down her spine, and lodges in the curl of her toes.

There isn't much action happening in the garage. Jared's muscles along the back of his shoulders bunch as the grip on the table's edge tightens. She doesn't like what she sees.

He's not saying anything, just listening to whoever is on the other end of the conversation, but the way he's clenching his jaw isn't good.

She wants to cough, and make some sort of noise to alert him to her presence, but he twists to the side and throws his phone across the garage, where it hits the wall with a bang and lands on the ground.

He swears.

Marlee closes her eyes at the explicit, not because of what he said, but more for the hurt and anger she hears behind the word.

For some reason, she has a feeling she knows who was on the other line, and if she's right, they're about to have a conversation she's not going to like.

"Marlee, I..." Jared runs his fingers through his hair when he realizes she's there. "Damn it, I'm sorry. I didn't hear you come in."

Her grip on her mug tightens. "You seemed pretty engrossed in that phone call," she says, nodding toward the discarded phone on the floor. "Everything okay?"

His grimace says it all. "Good thing I bought a new case,

huh?" He says as he goes to pick it up, wiping any dirt off the case, not looking her in the eye.

"Good thing." His muscles bunch up even tighter beneath her touch when she places her hand on his arm.

"How much did you overhear?" He asks, the words coming out tight, taunt, and full of sadness.

"Nothing," she admits. "Was it your father?" That's the only person she knows who can work Jared up to the point of throwing his phone. Usually, he's levelheaded, able to keep his cool when dealing with suppliers, builders, and demanding clients.

But Durwood...that man has the power to throw Jared into a tailspin.

"I can't work with him, not again," he says, pushing his shoulders back and giving a slight groan at the pop from his spine. "He...crossed the line this time." His spaghetti-straight lips turn white from being so tense.

"Relax," Marlee rubs circles on his back. "Whatever happened, it'll be okay." She doesn't like seeing her husband like this, but she dislikes his words even more.

He shakes his head. "You don't understand, Marlee. He went too far this time." He seems like he wants to say more but stops himself.

He swallows hard, and a flux of emotions flits across his face, telling her more than she wants to know.

Whatever transpired between Jared and his father is bad. Really bad. Ten to one, something was said about her, their kids, or Jared's character. Those are the only lines she knows that aren't crossable for Jared.

"Just give him time," she starts to say, but Jared shakes his head, stopping her.

"Time isn't going to fix this," he says softly. "He'll never be able to take back the words. Not this time." The pain in his voice comes through with a swift thump of his fist pounding the table.

Marlee jumps.

He pulls her into his arms once he realizes he's scaring her, his hold tight, his face meshed against her shoulder. He mumbles something incoherent, something she can't make out, but she feels the tears as they slide down her bare skin.

Her heart stutters to a stop, then skips to a revving decimal that leaves her shaking.

"Jared?" She whispers his name, fear true and deep inside her.

He holds on for the longest time, and the fear gathering inside her is now combined with worry and concern. Her heart continues to race the longer he remains silent.

"You know I love you, right? There's nothing I wouldn't do for you. I hope you know that." He finally pulls away, enough so she can hear him, but not far enough for her to look directly at his face.

"Of course. You show me your love every day." A smile sputters on her face as she tries to mask her growing concern.

"You mean everything to me. You and the kids," he continues, as if he didn't hear her. "You come first. Before everyone and everything."

She nods. There's so much she wants to say, to comfort him, to affirm the love between them, but she holds her words, realizing he needs to say these words.

"I'm so proud of you. Have I told you that lately? You do so much for us, with the kids, putting up with me and my hours, plus working...I know you're tired. I know it's too much. I know that this isn't the life we wanted for our kids. You've always supported me, stood by me, been my partner in every decision..." he falters, unable to continue.

"Honey, what's going on?"

There's a twitch in his jawline as he pulls away. It takes some time for him to look her in the eyes, but once their gazes meet, the pain that radiates from his heart hits her with rocket force.

"Jared?" Now he's scaring her.

"We can't move back, not now. Now, after... he doesn't deserve you or the kids. I don't," he swallows hard, his voice falters, his words uneven. "You and the kids are my everything, and I'll protect you from anything ... you know that, right? Even if it's from my own family."

"What happened?" Protect her from his father? What did Durwood say?

His shoulders drop even more but only for a moment before straightening. He pushes his shoulders back, and his chin tilts upward.

"It doesn't matter what happened," Jared says, conviction now filling his voice, where before he'd only been full of pain. "What matters is our future. We can't go back to Innsbruck, not now. I know it's not what you wanted to hear. I know this life we have now isn't what we wanted, but we have to make it work."

Minutes ago, she'd come here hoping to talk about a possible future back home. Now that future is gone, all because of something Durwood said, something Jared seems determined not to reveal.

Through thick and thin. Through the good times and bad. That's what they'd promised to each other. To respect, to love, to be life partners. She doesn't understand the decision and can't agree, but she'll trust him for now. Trust that he's making the best one at the moment for their family.

Little by little, she sees her future dreams in Innsbruck, or maybe even of opening a campground and being part of the transformation disappear. And it hurts. Hurts to know it's out of her hands, that for whatever reason, this is a path they won't be traveling.

Despite the hurt, she pastes on a smile on her face and leans forward, resting her lips against Jared's.

"I love you. No matter what happens or what the future holds, as long as we're together, we'll be okay."

Inside she weeps, but on the outside, she does the only thing she can, the only thing her husband needs.

She smiles.

CHAPTER TWENTY-FIVE

ASHLEY

"Mayor, oh Mayor...."

Ashley hears her name being called after she walks into the Wandering Aisle during her lunch break. She's here for two reasons: one to talk to Mia about the Christmas Market happening in a few short weeks, and the second to find her daughter a small pick-me-up gift.

The past few weeks haven't been the easiest for Jordan, even with her switching schools. There have been too many nights to count where she's sneaked into Jordan's room to tuck her in, and she finds her daughter's pillow soaked with tears.

Her mama's heart hurts for Jordan, and she doesn't know what to do.

It breaks something inside her to see her daughter like this.

She accidentally picked up Jordan's phone from the table last night, thinking it was hers, and scrolled through her daughter's text messages. She still feels bad for doing so, knowing basically what she did was snoop, but when she saw all the messages

Jordan sent Brett and him not responding to a single one... it's like someone reached inside her chest, twisted the wrangled mess called her heart, and hasn't let go since.

Before bed, she's sent her own text to Brett, telling him in no uncertain terms how she feels about him being a coward and not replying to their daughter's messages.

His reply stopped her in her tracks: *I don't know what to say*.

Any response is better than silence; he should know that by now.

She owned up to what she'd done to Jordan this morning over bowls of cereal. She'd fully expected Jordan to lash out, tear a strip off her about respecting her privacy, so when Jordan came over and gave her a hug, she'd been caught off guard.

If she realized anything this past week, it's that regardless of what happens between her and Brett, even if their divorce becomes messy, angry, or hurtful, all she wants is for Jordan to be okay.

"Mayor, finding you here saves me a trip to your office."

Ashley turns and finds herself enveloped by Josie, with Durwood directly behind her.

Ashley hugs the woman back before shaking Durwood's outstretched hand. "You were coming to see me?" She had a free afternoon, her appointment book empty, and wasn't even planning on returning to the office today.

Josie's face glows with excitement. "Oh, yes. We have so much to talk about." She nudges her husband. "Do you have that folder?"

Durwood snorts. "No, woman." His face scrunches up, his nose flares, and the wrinkles on his face intensify. "Why would I bring it in a gift shop when all you're doing is buying a card? It's in the truck, where it belongs." He rolls his eyes, but Ashley catches the smile teasing his lips.

"Well, go get it," Josie tells him with a smack on his arm.

"Wait," Ashley interjects, reaching her hand out as if to stop Durwood from leaving, "why don't we go for coffee instead? I have it on very good authority that Frankie made scones today." Frankie had sent her a photo earlier, tempting her to come in.

As if she needs to be tempted like that. All Frankie has to do is tell her the scones are in the oven, and Ashley will be there to help get them out.

"How about you ladies chat while I head to the hardware store? I need to talk to Tomlin about bringing in some supplies, and we both know you'd rather be eating a scone than listening to us men talk about wood," Durwood says to his wife as he gently touches her cheek.

"You go do that, love." Josie's face beams a smile full of love, "the Mayor and I can chat, and I'll fill you in later." Josie rises to her tiptoes and kisses Durwood's wrinkled cheek. For a moment, there's a softness to his features as he stares into his wife's eyes.

A longing for that kind of love hits Ashley like a dart, her heart the unwilling target. It's been a long time since she's been looked at like that, and right now, she doubts she ever will again.

"What brings you into the store? Getting a card for Anna too?" Josie asks once her husband leaves.

"I actually need to chat with Mia about the Christmas Market."

"You're not bothering that girl while her father isn't well, are you?" The tsk she receives from Josie is loud and clear.

"No, ma'am. That's what I'm here to talk to her about," Ashley says.

"Good. That girl has way too much on her plate right now. Like someone else I know." Josie lightly touches her hand. "Don't worry, love, I know," Josie says softly. "You don't have to say anything. Durwood and I figured things weren't good between you and Brett. He's gone, hasn't he?"

Shocked, Ashley finds herself unable to find the words.

"Oh, come, child. I didn't raise six children and put up with Durwood all these years for nothing." Josie gives her a look that says more than words. "Grab what you need, and I'll be done in a few minutes here."

"Take your time. I just need to speak to Mia first." Ashley glances around and sees her friend organizing a shelf at the back.

"Of course, you know where to find me." Josie bends to pick up a basket at her feet and heads toward the cash desk where Tommi stands waiting.

Ashley takes a moment to refocus. The fact Josie figured out Brett was gone throws her for a moment or two. How did she know? What gave it away? Is she naïve in believing no one will know or that word won't get around?

Probably.

She pushes all that aside for the moment and focuses on her friend. Even from a distance, she notices the dark circles beneath her eyes and the sloop of her shoulders.

"Oh, sweetie," Ashley says as she goes to give her friend a hug. "You look like...well, you look like you need to curl up on a couch and binge Netflix for a full week."

"You and me both," Mia says. "I'm just not sleeping, that's all. How are you doing? You don't look any better, trust me." Mia nudges her in the side.

Ouch.

"I slept a bit better last night," Ashley admits. "Getting used to an empty bed isn't as easy as I thought it would be." Not that she's complaining. She much prefers having the bed to herself than sharing it with someone who was cheating on her.

"Do you need anything?" Mia asks while she goes back to readjusting a candle display.

"I could be asking you the same question."

Mia sighs. "Things have been nonstop since I got back from Europe." She inhales deep through her nose. "Life has thrown one curve ball after another lately to both of us. I can't believe the market is coming up. I've been dropping so many things... I'm sorry."

"That's actually why I'm here. Consider this off your plate for this year, okay? I've got it handled."

"Handled? How? There's still so much to be done."

"I know, but I've got it." Ashley infuses confidence into her tone, hoping it's enough to sway Mia into relaxing.

It doesn't seem to work. With hands on hips, Mia steps closer. "Did you get someone to take over for me?"

Mia's reaction is surprising. She thought she'd be relieved to have one less thing on her plate, but instead, she's obviously angry.

"No, nothing like that. I just—"

"What? You're going to take it all on yourself? Like you don't have a bazillion plates already in the air."

Ashley tries to argue, but the words are gone. She swallows hard and steps back, relinquishing control since this is obviously something Mia wants to do.

"Fine. If you don't want me to take this from you, then I need you to meet with Matt and finalize all the little details he needs. I'll forward his emails since there are a few, and you can figure things out with him, okay?"

"Fine." Something in Mia's tone is off, but Ashley can't quite figure it out.

"Okay then. Um," now this is awkward, "how is your dad doing?" Weiss is still hospital-bound, which is where Mia's attention has been the past little bit.

"Sorry," Mia rubs the back of her neck, "that was uncalled for. I know you mean well, but I could use a good distraction, and this Market is important to me."

"I know. It's okay. I was just wanting to help, that's all."

Mia nods. "I get that. You want to fix things, that's who you are, but there's nothing to fix here. It's a waiting game now. Dad will probably come home in a few days, I think, I hope. Mom is stressed, even though she won't admit it, you know? That alone is adding to my stress. Do you know how hard it is to care for a woman who refuses help? She thinks she can do it all, be with Dad while being involved in everything else, and she won't listen to reason."

"I know someone else like that," Ashley said, jabbing her friend lightly in the arm. Mia has the decency to blush.

"Um, do I really have to meet with Matt?" Mia won't meet her gaze, but Ashley sees the beginnings of a smile grow.

"Yes, you really do. Why don't you guys meet for dinner? Or maybe drinks? I can help set that up, you know?" She wiggles her brows just a little, totally enjoying her friend's sudden discomfort.

She'd love it if something were to finally happen between Mia and Matt. They're perfect for each other.

"Don't you dare. I'll email him, and we'll figure it out. Now shoo, Josie's waiting for you."

Ashley glances over to where Josie is standing. "Facetime over our show tonight?" They've been watching Bridgerton on Netflix together, one episode at a time, and if they can't watch it in the same room, they do it over video chat.

"You got it. I've got a fresh bottle of wine chilling in the fridge that will be perfect."

When she reaches Josie's side, the woman links their arms together. "Everything okay? Things looked a little tense for a minute."

"Guess she didn't appreciate me offering to take something from her plate," Ashley admits. She should have known better.

They first stop at Josie's truck parked outside the store, where Josie grabs a folder from the back seat and then places her bags on the back seat. "Oh wait, this is for Jordan." She hands her a small gift bag.

"What's this?" She looks inside, using her finger to push away the tissue to reveal a candle.

"Girls always love candles, don't they? My grandbabies tell me they love to light them while doing homework. You let her know my door is always open if she needs a grandma-type hug, okay?"

Ashley blinks back tears that gather before glancing up into the sky, inhaling as she does so. "How about a mama-type hug?"

"For you, always." Josie wraps her in a warm, welcoming hug, and Ashley has to swallow back a ball of tears. "Don't be afraid to cry when you need to or try to hide it from that girl of yours. Crying washes away all those ugly emotions we tend to bottle up inside."

"At this rate," Ashley says, "you'd think I'd be numb now, having cried out all those emotions."

"If only..." Josie tsks. "I'm sure you're missing your mama hard, aren't you? No matter how old we get, we always miss our mothers when they're not around. You know she's watching you, right? Rooting for you? Wishing words of wisdom into your heart in those quiet moments when you think you're all alone?"

She will not cry. She will not cry. Listening to Josie, hearing those words, they're exactly what she needs to hear right now. "Thank you," she whispers past a throat swelling with more feelings than she cares to describe.

"Now, now," Josie pats her back, "I'm here for you, child, you know that, I hope. Day or night. You come on by for some tea or coffee and just chat, you hear? My door is always open."

Ashley wipes the tears from her cheeks and attempts a smile. "Come on," she says with bravery in her voice. "Let's get into Frankie's so you can tell me about whatever's in that folder."

Ashley holds onto Josie's arm as they walk down the street.

"I've been able to chat with most everyone in town," Josie says. "The level of excitement over this idea, of transforming into a Christmas town, it's catching on. So far, we've got a family willing to turn their barn into Santa's toy factory, and a few families willing to turn their old family homes into quaint bed and breakfasts so that we don't need any chain hotels or people staying anywhere out of town." Josie taps the folder with her finger. "We've got a wood carver who is interested in making nativity scenes, a few different store ideas, a beer hall, petting zoo, and—"

"Whoa," Ashley interrupts, "are you serious?"

If Josie is, and there's no reason to believe otherwise, this is fantastic news.

In fact, it almost seems too good to be true.

The sparkle in Josie's eyes tells Ashley the woman is more than just serious; she's determined.

"Just you wait to hear what Frankie and I have cooked up. I had to get my oldest grand-baby to teach me how to use Google Maps and then spent hours researching those German towns focused on Christmas year-round. A research trip would be nice, but this costs a lot less."

Ashley makes an effort to pick up her dropped jaw as she holds the door to Frankie's café open.

She'd also spent a long time on Google Maps, making her own lists of ideas.

"Well, look who the cat dragged in," Frankie stands behind her counter, her smile as wide as Ashley's heart.

"You all just missed the big rush." Frankie rounds the counter and gives them both hugs.

"Does that mean we've missed out on your scones?" Ashley adds a little pout to her lips.

"Goodness, no. I made more than enough, trust me." Frankie pulls out a chair for Josie. "Your regular, love?" She asks Josie before looking toward Ashley. "In the mood for strong coffee, or do you need something a little sweet?"

Hard question...

"Before you answer, take a look at the menu board?"

Twisting in her chair, Ashley reads the daily menu and notices an addition under the *new* section. *Ashley's Brew – French press.* She preens a little seeing her name on the board.

"I don't know how you can drink that stuff," Josie says. "What's wrong with regular coffee from a coffee pot?"

"Have you tried it yet?" Ashley asks

Josie's eyes roll. "Yes. My one daughter brought one home for Christmas one year. By the time she poured me a cup, it was lukewarm. No, thank you." She pushes the folder on the table with her finger.

"Now," she says, "before we get into all the nitty gritty, I want you to know that Durwood is ready to start. All you need to do is say the word. He's been in touch with Nigel about budgets and pricing, and he has a roster of people ready to get to work. All locals, and all with experience."

Ashley rubs the creases forming on her brow. This is way more than she expected.

"I love your passion for this." She really does. She'd felt it in that first meeting with Durwood following the town hall, and she can feel it now. Josie and Durwood are like wild horses cornered by a farmer.

"I can't believe how much you've done and how fast you've done it." She sips at the water on the table. "I promise, as soon as

I get the go ahead, we will all sit down and discuss the steps to get started." She hates being responsible for the frown replacing Josie's smile.

She swallows hard, thinking of how best to tiptoe this minefield. "Mind if I take a look?"

Josie nods, watching her intently as she goes down the lists. Josie has so much on here, list after list, sectioned off into different categories: areas to be redeveloped, buildings to be remodeled, estimated costs, list of volunteers as well as those who should be paid, suggestions for future shops, street name changes and other ideas that Ashley hasn't even thought of yet.

She closes the file, feeling overwhelmed, her hands on top, clasped together, and takes a moment before addressing Josie.

"This is amazing and gives me so much hope."

Josie's smile returns.

"You know the town wants this, right?" Josie says. It came out as a question, but the statement is quite clear.

Ashley hopes she's right. "Not according to Marcus. He thinks this is a Hail Mary on my part."

"Oh, I know Marcus is trying hard," Josie worries her lips, "but he's not speaking for this town. Did you know he had a chat with Durwood? Told him he is too old to take on a project of this level." Josie's eyes blaze bright, her voice full of fight, "That man, he's got nothing on Durwood and me when it comes to passion for this town, and he's the last person to be telling my husband what he can and cannot do."

Ashley smothers her laugh. "Very true," she manages to say with a straight face. The Holms have always been a formidable family.

"This transformation is exactly what our town needs, and we all know it. You and the rest of the council have our backing. Not just ours, but most of those who live in this town, too."

"Agreed," Frankie arrives at the table, carrying a tray full of hot coffees and fresh scones. "All you need to do, Ashley, is let us start the preparations."

She doesn't like the sound of that, and her face must show it.

"Oh, it'll all be hush-hush," Frankie says, "nothing official until you get the final vote of approval, but we can at least get things going so we can start with a bang."

Ashley leans back, hands up. "I didn't hear that, okay?" Telling these two women no is like trying to stop a moving train.

Frankie shrugs. "Oh, come on, not like it's that big of a deal. Did Josie tell you about our idea?"

"She started to mention it on our walk here." Ashley is still trying to process that these two have gone ahead and done the very things she's been wanting to do but can't because her hands are tied.

The smile on Frankie's face is a mile wide and highway long. The excitement is plastered all over her face. "We're going to open up a few bakeries – aside from this one. I know, I know, competition and all that, but this town will be able to handle it, especially with how we want to structure it."

"I'm all ears." Ashley leans forward, elbows on the table, hands clasped beneath her chin. Frankie has her undivided attention.

"I know we have a few shops in town with kitchens, so we'll look at leasing them. We'll sell kitchen and baking products and see about ordering some original German items, too, like rolling pins, cookie cutters, that kind of stuff. Each bakery will have a different theme. One will be just for bread, we can have a chocolate shop, one for all things cake and pie related, all with their own distinct feel. We have a town full of bakers, so we'll utilize them to find some easy recipes to replicate day in and day out, and we'll then teach the staff how to make them."

Ashley nodded, liking the idea. Of course, as they grow, this town will need several bakeries, cafes, restaurants, and pubs... the list is endless.

"You aren't planning on opening them all at once, right?"

Frankie shakes her head. "No, no, we'll roll them out as things progress and when the demand is there. Don't worry, we've got a plan."

When it comes to this and to these two formidable ladies, being worried is the last thing Ashley feels.

The emotions she's experiencing is all about hope and excitement.

This is going to work. The potential is there. This town, their town, is going to be okay.

She carries this feeling with her as she heads back to the office. She initially wasn't planning on returning, but Nigel asked her to stop by.

His text was in all caps. Nigel only shouts at her when something is wrong.

CHAPTER TWENTY-SIX

There's an undercurrent of humming electricity as she walks into the office.

Is this a good thing, or has everything exploded in the past few hours since she's been gone?

Everyone is buzzing, busy with tasks, and the room's volume converges. Ashley pauses, taking it all in, trying to read the energy.

All she's getting is busyness.

Susan finally notices her and points toward Nigel's office.

"You need to see him," she mouths, her hand covering the phone glued to her ear.

She heads towards Nigel's closed door with heavy steps, suddenly worried.

She inhales deep, preparing herself for the worst. Something's wrong, she knows it.

Nigel rises from behind his desk when she opens his door. His face is a blank canvas.

Ashley instantly thinks of Sylvia, and her hands covers her already bruised heart. "Please tell me she's okay. And the baby, too, right?"

Nigel has this look on his face, like he can't compute what she's saying.

"Nigel, I need to know," she says, her voice soft, not wanting to spook him.

He shakes his head and looks at her with this weird expression before his eyes open wide with shock. "Oh no, no no, she's fine. The baby's fine. I scared you with my text, didn't I? Ash, I did it."

It takes her a moment to actually hear his words. Sylvia's fine. The baby is fine.

Wait...he did it? Did what?

"I did it," he repeats. "I found a compromise that benefits our town and still makes the retirement village a possibility. Plus, it will provide some of the funds needed for our reinvention. It's a win-win, and even Marcus is on board with it."

Ashley grabs the notebook he holds up and starts going over his notes.

She's not sure what she's more impressed by, the compromise he found, the fact the corporation building the retirement center agreed to pitch in for the town renovation, or that Marcus is on board.

Probably Marcus.

"I'm...more than impressed. I'm kind of speechless, to be honest." According to his rough notes, they project breaking ground within the year and have a multi-year building plan. Within the year is quick, and she can't see it being possible, but...then she also didn't think this idea would be possible, so what does she know?

Ashley gulps as she reads the price Nigel has circled in red. It's way more than she anticipated. "This is what they're offering? It's more than the initial bid."

"They have some special requests for shops within the community and other things. They upped their bid to help with the transition. We still have a lot of things to iron out, but, Ashley, this will work."

A spark of excitement nestled deep in her spirit bursts into flames, and Nigel's smile only adds more fuel.

"This is happening, isn't it?" She barely gets the words out before the tears swell. She blinks rapidly, not wanting to cry.

"You're not surprised, are you? I'm not. No one else is either. Do you know why? You promised to do everything possible to save this town, and look at what you've done! I couldn't be prouder of you or thrilled to work with someone like you on this." Nigel's words wrap around her like a warm hug.

Ashley laughs. "You have to say that. Your wife is my best friend."

"There is that." Nigel teases. "In all seriousness, I think it's time we sit down with Durwood Holms, create a plan and then present all of this at our town hall next week."

Everything is coming together, and it's all happening so fast.

Ashley pulls out the folder Josie gave her earlier. "On that note, I just had a lovely talk with Josie. Durwood is ready to start as soon as we give him the word. They've done a lot of the legwork for us." She hands it to Nigel. "I can't believe everything they've managed to do in such a short time. I wonder if we can get some preliminary drawings done to increase the excitement level for our next Town Hall?"

Nigel opens the folder and takes his time looking over everything. "It's all here, isn't it," he says. "From project targets to timelines and budgets...you'd think Durwood knew a thing or two about construction projects." He continues to go over the pages. "I'm really impressed with the level of detail," he says, his gaze never rising.

"He mentioned he'd already been talking with you about budgets?" She'd been a little surprised to find that out.

Nigel nods. "We had a beer one night and did a rough estimate. I like that he's been safe with his budget, knowing things inevitably pop up and will cost more than expected. He proposed a few stages of building, breaking things up into smaller projects throughout a three-year timeframe. He's got a good head on his shoulders."

"I agree. Okay, so the next step is to round everyone up for another council meeting, share the details of this fantastic collaboration with them and –

Her phone rings, and it's Jordan.

"Hey honey, everything okay?" Jordan should be in class right now, not on her phone, calling her.

"Mom, Dad just texted. He's coming by the house and wants to talk to me." There's a quiver of something in her daughter's voice that Ashley can't quite make out.

He what? Is he coming by the house? Without telling her? No, that's not okay. She made it very clear they needed time and space.

"Did he say when?"

"He'll be here for dinner. He's bringing pizza."

Ashley's first instinct is to say no, but she catches a hint of something that sounds very much like hope.

"Mom? Is it okay that he comes? Please?" The pleading in Jordan's voice is all it took for her to say yes.

By the time she hangs up, a headache forms right above her eyes. She rubs the spots where the pressure appears, but there's no relief.

"Everything okay?" Nigel asks.

"No." Ashley blows out a long burst of air. "Brett's coming for dinner. He wants to talk to Jordan, I guess. He can send her a text, but not me?" She worries her lips. "What's up with that?"

Nigel places his hands flat on the table. He seems to be weighing his words. "Have you guys talked since he left?"

"A little." She winces. "Nothing major since I saw him in the city. A few texts here and there."

Nigel hums and haws, obviously feeling uncomfortable.

"Just spit it out," Ashley says.

"I thought about texting him, but Sylvia said we're not playing sides. Brett left all of us behind, and we keep it that way, according to her."

"Really?" Why she's surprised, she's not sure, other than Sylvia hasn't said a word to her about it, and to be honest, she never thought to think about how her friends would feel.

"Thank you," she continues. "He's your friend, though, and I promise not to hold it against you if you stay in touch."

Nigel rubs the back of his neck. "Yeah, about that. We accepted him because you loved him. You come first."

"And yet, he's still your friend." She gets it. If anything happened between him and Sylvia...there's no way she could choose one friend over the other.

"Maybe I'll just mention I heard he was coming tonight, and if he needs any help packing up, I'm around," Nigel offers, the question clear in his voice.

"That's fair." She holds her phone and thinks about what to text Brett. Simple is probably best.

Heard you are coming over tonight for dinner??

The extra question mark should indicate she's a little surprised, right?

Sorry, I should have checked with you first. A storm is coming later this week, and I wanted to come out before it hits. Pizza okay?

Well, at least he acknowledges it.

That's fine. Let's schedule some visits with Jordan while you are here. It's only fair, after all.

He sends her a 'thumbs-up emoji, making her roll her eyes.

Ashley's stomach twists into million knots. She's not ready.

She still hasn't found it easy to breathe at home without him there. She finds herself searching for his warmth in the middle of the night, thinking random thoughts to share with him, and still programs too much coffee at night for them to share the following day. She doesn't miss him, though, not truly. Those nights when her legs stretch out, seeking his familiar touch, there's always this kick in the gut realizing someone else is probably doing the very same thing.

That kick brings anger, resentment, and betrayal.

Obviously, she was all over the place with her emotions. She misses what they had. What they could have been. She's angry at him for what he's done to her, to their family, to their dreams and plans.

Gah. She hates this twisty road of emotions.

She was going to go home, maybe make a cake or something to surprise Jordan, but not now. Now, she just needs to stay busy.

First up is a phone call to their local graphic designer. They'd had a meeting last week to discuss possible town looks, something to give people an idea of her vision. Now they need to add in the retirement village, but since she had spec drawings of that already in the previous bid, that shouldn't be too difficult.

"Hey, Liz? Do you have time to go over some designs with me? I'd like to prepare for our next town hall meeting. Just something to give people an idea of where we're going, as we'd discussed."

Spending the afternoon with Liz will keep her occupied and keep the focus on something she can change and direct, rather than what's happening in her personal life. Fingers crossed nothing happens tonight, and she can call their first family get-together since Brett left a success.

Fingers crossed.

CHAPTER TWENTY-SEVEN

Dinner had been everything but successful.

More like shallow and superficial, with stilted conversation and cold smiles.

Ashley finally left the table so Jordan and Brett could talk without her, claiming the weeds out in the front garden bed needed tending.

As an excuse, it's pitiful, but she couldn't handle another second of awkwardness at the table.

Elbows deep in dirt, the front door opens, and Brett emerges with a towel and two cups of coffee.

"Is now a good time to talk?" He sets the cups on the small table on the porch and sits in one of the wicker chairs.

Ashley pulls off her gloves, sticks them in her garden bucket, and dusts the dirt off her knees, not sure if now is a good time at all.

She doesn't say that. Instead, she joins him on the porch, reaching for her coffee cup. He'll be waiting a long time if he's expecting her to say something. He's the one who wants to talk, so he can break the silence.

"I didn't handle things well with Jordan before."

Ashley glances at Brett over the rim of her cup but doesn't respond. There's no need to.

"I apologized, and she said she forgave me. "

Ashley knows that conversation would not have been easy, so she's proud of them both for having it.

"I have an extra room in my apartment, so I asked if she would want to come and stay for weekends. I hope that's okay."

She somehow manages to squash the instant no that's on the tip of her tongue. Thankfully she'd anticipated this and already spoke to Jordan before Brett arrived. She has a feeling she knows how Jordan responded.

She keeps her peace and waits for him to continue. Her silence is all he needs.

"You already knew what she'd say, didn't you?" He winces. "That girl of ours, she doesn't hold any punches." He holds his coffee cup in his hand and sighs. "She's not ready to trust me yet, she says. She preferred to stick to every other Saturday for now that she has a life here she wants to live. Maybe she'll stay the weekend but only when she's ready."

From the look on his face, she knows he's hurting, and a large part of her is glad. She should feel guilty for feeling that way, but she doesn't.

"I miss her," he finally says. "And you, what we had. I... don't regret leaving, but I regret how I handled everything. Ash, you deserve better from me. I'm sorry."

Ashley almost chokes on the coffee she just swallowed.

"Wow, I...didn't expect that. I appreciate it. It... it could have been done differently, you're right." That was a given. "Give Jordan time, okay? This hasn't been easy on her for many reasons."

He plays with the cup in his hand, turning it one way, then the other. "I know. That's my fault too."

Part of her wants to say *enough with the sorries already*. But she doesn't. He needs to say as much as they both need to hear them.

A pickup truck pulls up.

"Nigel offered to help load the truck with my things in the garage," Brett says.

Ashley nod. "I know."

"Have you talked to a lawyer yet?" Brett shuffles to his feet.

"Yes." Thankfully she has enough contacts in the legal field, friends specifically who specialize in family law. "I'll send you a list of household items so we can figure out who wants what."

"I'm not going to make this difficult," he says.

"Good." That's all she'll give him. No promises or hints at what's to come. She won't be difficult either, but she will be fair.

"I do have a request," Ashley says as Brett starts to walk away. "When Jordan does spend time with you, make sure it's just the two of you, please?" She won't mention the girlfriend, not because she doesn't want to, but because she doesn't need to. He knows exactly what she's not saying.

Brett's mouth gaps open, and Ashley reads every thought crossing his face. The first is denial, followed by an argument, then acceptance.

"Fair enough."

With Brett in the garage with Nigel, Ashley goes back inside to check on Jordan, who's in the kitchen, music blaring on the Bluetooth speakers, arms elbow deep in dishwater.

"Dad gone?"

Ashley grabs a dish towel. "He's in the garage with Nigel." She wants to ask how the talk went, how Jordan feels, and what thoughts are going through her head, but she keeps her peace and dries the dishes, giving Jordan space to speak up when she's ready.

It doesn't take her long.

"I miss him, you know?"

Ashley gives her daughter a soft smile. "He said the same thing outside, that he misses you."

"Really?" Jordan doesn't look at her, but she doesn't need to. Girls need their fathers; if Brett is smart and remembers to keep his daughter first, they should be fine.

"Anytime you want to see him, say the word."

Jordan frowns. "I figured it would be one of those every-other-weekend type deal. That's what a friend of mine at school does."

"Is that what you want?"

Jordan drains the sink water and twists the dish rag of its excess water.

"No, "she says. "I don't want to feel forced either, you know? Can't we just be flexible? I mean, what if I end up babysitting on the weekends or in the summer?"

There's a knock at the door leading from the garage before it opens, and Brett steps in.

"I think I got everything I need. Thanks for boxing up so much of my stuff." He wipes dust off his hands and onto his jeans. "So, I am..." he stops, struggling to find the right words. "Jordan, I was thinking we could do some shopping followed by dinner and a movie sometime? Maybe next weekend?"

Ashley steps back, the action to show this is Jordan's decision.

Jordan doesn't answer right away. She glances over her shoulder at Ashley first.

"Can I let you know? I might have a sleepover with a friend."

Brett's face falls, and Ashley recognizes the signs that he's about to argue the point, so when he looks her way, she motions with her hand, a signal they always used with one another to indicate the need to slow down, remain calm, take a step back and breathe...

Brett's shoulder drops, but he takes her hint and doesn't fight their daughter on the issue.

Thankfully. Jordan is just trying to set boundaries, which Ashley appreciates. She also knows her daughter will go spend time with her dad, regardless of what she says right now.

Ashley nudges Jordan toward Brett for a goodbye hug.

"So," he hesitates, as if not wanting to leave, "I'll give you more notice next time, okay? "

Ashley nods. "I appreciate that, thank you. I'll keep the family calendar for Jordan updated, so you stay in the know with her schedule. "

There really isn't much else to say. As his vehicle drives down the road, Ashley takes a long, deep breath, holding it until her lungs ache from the pressure.

Her lawyer, an old high school friend, warned her there would be many moments like this. Moments of freedom, happiness, and of peace. The mantra is to live in the moment, to embrace these feelings because they'll quickly be followed by moments of fear, anger, and worry.

At the time, Ashley appreciated the honesty.

Realistically, she knows whatever happens with this divorce is out of her hands. There's only so much control she can maintain, but the tighter her grip, the harder it will be for her to adjust. There's no going back, no wishing for a different outcome.

Life will be better this way. It has to be. Both for her and for Jordan.

An idea pops into her head. "So...what do you think about getting a puppy?"

CHAPTER TWENTY-EIGHT

"A puppy? When did you get a puppy?" Sylvia's face beams as she's being slathered in puppy kisses.

Ashley still can't believe she adopted this wiggly mess. Talk about impulsive decisions, and yet, she can't imagine not having the little cuddle bug in their home. Jordan has been over the moon with this little thing since he came home.

Impulse or not, it was the right decision. This little Pomeranian Shit-Zu with cream-colored fur has stolen both their hearts, and rightly so.

"Jordan must be in love," Sylvia cuddles the pup against her chest. "He's so small, Ash."

"He'll probably only be between ten to fifteen pounds by the time he's fully grown."

"What's his name?"

"Snowball."

The smile on Sylvia's face blooms brighter than before. "Isn't that just about perfect? Omg, we have our own little town mascot now." She digs her nose into Snowball's soft fur and is greeted with even more kisses and nibbles.

"I think I'll need puppy therapy more often, just a heads up."

Sylvia called her a few hours ago, begging for company, crying of boredom. She hates being housebound, calling it her own personal hell, to please bring something sweet to eat.

Ashley brought cream puffs, brownies, and her new puppy.

"How about you pass me the pup while I pass you a brownie?" Ashley suggests.

"How about you pass the brownie, and I keep this little cuddler? He's about to fall asleep, and my lap is as good a place as any." She holds out her hand and wiggles her fingers in expectation.

"Craving sugar?" When she was pregnant with Jordan, all she'd wanted were olives. One night she'd eaten a whole bottle, drank the juice, and still craved more. The following morning, she'd been unable to walk due to swollen ankles.

"You have no idea. I'm not sure if it's a true craving or sheer boredom," Sylvia says, taking a nibble of her square. "There's honestly only so many romcoms I can watch, scarves I can knit, and coloring pages I can fill. I'm dying here..." she leans back in her chaise, one hand dramatically posed against her forehead.

"Hello, drama queen," Ashley says, filling her voice with brightness.

"Don't knock it till you try it," Sylvia counters. "I know, I know, stop complaining, right?"

"No way," Ashley shakes her head. "You complain all you need to. I can't imagine what life must be like, never having to lift a finger, having friends bring you treats, a husband who cooks and even carries you to bed every night."

Yes, she's mocking her friend, but it's all in fun, anything to keep that smile on Sylvia's face.

Sylvia being bedridden is for one reason and one reason only - the safety of her unborn baby.

"Whatever, mock all you want, but if you were in my shoes..." Sylvia lets the rest of the sentence hang, her left brow rising until Ashley nods.

She gets it. She's never been one to sit still either.

"How can I help keep the boredom at bay?" Ashley asks. She has a few ideas that have nothing to do with puppy sitting and everything to do with utilizing Sylvia's unique skills.

"Put me to work. Please? Don't make me beg because you know I don't do that well."

Ashley finishes the last of her mocha and eyes her friend, letting the silence build for a moment.

"You're going to make me, aren't you?" The eye roll Sylvia gives could have moved mountains, it's that large. "Fine, would you please, with chocolate syrup and whipped cream, give me something to do? Anything really. I'll transcribe your meeting minutes even...just don't make me knit another scarf." Sylvia's nose twitches with laughter, her eyes bright with joy.

"I was kind of hoping for a scarf, actually. Make one of those long ones with tassels? I'll even pick out the colors...oomph!" A pillow hit her square in the face. "Hey, what was that for?"

"How about I teach you to make your own bloody scarf?" The scowl on Sylvia's face soon gives way to a grin she can't hide.

"Actually," Ashley says, setting the pillow down on the floor, "I could use your help. It's in the area of more--"

"Yes."

"I didn't even finish."

"I don't care. If it keeps me busy, I'm in." Sylvia arches her back with a grimace. "I'd give anything right now to go for a nice long walk outside or do some yoga..."

"How about a massage? Can you get one of those?" Ashley suggests.

"I get one every night along with a good rub down..." the

twinkle in Sylvia's eyes confirms to Ashley everything she already knows. Sylvia is being well taken care of.

"How does creating a community calendar sound?"

Sylvia perks up. "Paper or online? For the whole town or for a particular project?" She gingerly reaches for a notebook on the side table, careful not to wake the pup snuggled on her lap.

"This is where your marketing expertise will come in handy...so you tell me." Ashley leans forward. "Ideally, we want one for the whole town once everything is ready to go, a consistent schedule that doesn't change," she started.

"Something that we can place on brochures and online, something people will remember year after year. Like Christmas parades, ice sculpting contests, weekend hayrides..." Sylvia writes like a banshee, filling lines with ideas as they talk.

"How's the Christmas Market looking? Any last-minute hiccups?"

Ashley leans back in her chair, pulling her up legs beneath her. "Well, I convinced Mia to work with Matt and then took a step back." She can feel the grin grow on her face.

Sylvia rolls her eyes. "You're not still playing matchmaker, are you?"

Silly question. "They're perfect for each other, but they're also both very stubborn. All I'm doing is providing opportunities for them to realize what we all see."

There's a look on Sylvia's face that says way too much, and it has Ashley squirming in her seat.

"Out with it. I know you have an opinion."

"More like an observation," Sylvia says. "Your personal life is falling apart, your professional life is full of stress, and let's face it, not something you can control, so you focus on things that you can...things that you really shouldn't be."

Sylvia's words hit like a dart. Ouch.

"I don't know how to respond to that, mainly because you're right."

Sylvia nods. "I know."

"Do you want Jordan to help with your booth? You should probably stay home, right?" Ashley tries to change the focus of their conversation.

"I'll be there, but yes, I'd love her help. Nigel will be there with me, but this will give him space to walk around and chitchat with everyone. I'm sure everyone will have many questions and ideas after tonight. Speaking of that, are you ready for tonight?"

Ashley sighs. This week leading up to the Town Hall meeting has been chaotic, and throwing a new puppy into the mix has only added to the craziness, and yet... it's worked.

"I'm as ready as I can be. We've got a win-win solution on the table, and all the drawings are mounted for viewing. At this point, I'm not sure there's much left to do other than officially vote." Ashley knows it'll go well, but her stomach is still a jumbled mess of nerves.

"It'll go well," Sylvia says. "What could go wrong?"

What could go wrong? Why did Sylvia have to say that?

"Calm down," Susan says, nudging her in the side. "Everything looks perfect."

"You think so? You don't think we have too many drawings? Does it look too busy? Like I'm trying too hard?" Ashley peruses the room once more, suddenly worried she's gone overboard with the visuals and people will think she's desperate.

"Are you kidding me? They're going to take one look at the drawings and go bananas with excitement." Susan says, her voice full of all the confidence Ashley isn't feeling.

Liz worked a miracle. Following their original talk, Liz created rough drawings of what Ashley envisioned for the main downtown area. She hit the nail on the mark with perfect precision.

Liz drew scenes with Bavarian-inspired facades to cover every building, trim around the windows, and wood cut-outs to help give each storefront that Christmas-cottage vibe. The streets are lined with trees covered in lights, wreaths hanging from street posts, and old-world shop signs hanging over each storefront.

There were designated park areas where they would have Christmas wood carvings and picnic tables, helping to create an overall feel of a fairytale Christmas, and Ashley couldn't be happier.

"It's perfect," Susan says. "I'm excited, actually. This may seem overwhelming but in a good way. After speaking with both Nigel and Marcus, I also updated some talking points for you."

Nigel has worked a miracle. Not only with the retirement village agreeing to have their buildings themed to the town along with gardens and trails, but they also agreed to help budget wise.

Leasing the land will help the Council start earlier than she'd initially projected. According to Durwood's projected project timelines, they should have enough funds for at least three years' worth of work.

All that will be discussed tonight, along with store suggestions, voting in project heads, and ultimately the final vote.

Ashley remains at the back as people mill in, watching reactions from those heading from one display board to the other. So far, the room is full of *oohs* and *ahh's*, along with a lot of excited chatter, which makes the smile on Ashley's face permanent.

Frankie appears from out of nowhere. "This all looks fabulous. I can't believe what you've pulled together in such a short amount of time."

"I had help." There's no way she could have done any of this alone. This is all just the start...the start to something that is both exciting and overwhelming at the same time. The scope of what she wants to accomplish is mind blowing on the best of days, but when she actually stills herself and really lets it all sink in... there are moments of panic.

What was she thinking? How could she possibly pull this off? Thankfully, she's not doing this alone.

By the time the meeting begins, the room vibrates with a sizzling amount of energy, and Ashley is buzzing.

Marcus starts off the meeting by announcing the retirement village and what it means for Innsbruck. Ashley wanted Nigel to be the one to share his accomplishments, considering he's the one who found the compromise, but Nigel insisted Marcus get some time in the spotlight.

From how the man beams as he talks, Nigel was right, again.

Liz follows shortly after to share how the design concept will work and what it will mean to re-create the town into a Bavarian village. Ashley is careful to watch the room, gauging reactions by the smiles, and is secretly thrilled. She doesn't expect everyone to love the new look, but it's still only a concept that can change.

It's not until when Nigel approaches the podium that Ashley feels a little tense. His role tonight is to discuss the financial aspect and give a broad overview of the projected timeline. Everyone loves ideas until they consider the cost involved. If anyone is going to raise objections, Ashley knows this will be when it happens.

Surprisingly, no one says a word. Everyone remains in their seat, not interrupting, listening attentively.

Is this really happening?

She feels a deep sense of kinship with these families she's known all her life when she steps up to the podium.

She's glad she didn't listen to Brett and walk away from all of this. She would've tossed away her life, career, home...for what?

For nothing.

She takes a moment to frame the words perched on the tip of her tongue, but before she can utter a single word, people stand to their feet, clapping, a few even uttering sharp whistles.

Her face burns from embarrassment. They're celebrating her, congratulating her, when she wasn't alone in this. She might have come up with the idea, but without the others around her, this idea would have no feet.

She turns toward the council members behind her and claps, adding her praise to the sound resounding throughout the room.

These are the ones who deserve the praise. Them and others.

"I made you a promise," Ashley raises her voice to be heard over the continual clapping until the applause slows down, "that I would work hard to bring about a revitalization plan for Innsbruck. This isn't a promise I can make on my own, though. What's about to happen in our town doesn't rest on just one person's shoulders. As much as I want to think I'm like Wonder Woman, or maybe Lois Lane, I'm not. I'm a daughter of Innsbruck who loves her home and the community here, and if this is going to happen, it's because we are all a family."

She pauses, reading the room, and a swell of emotions

pushes tears to the surface. "If there's anything I've learned over the years, it's that Innsbruck is indeed a family, and family is always there to help, support, carry...." It's hard to continue. "All I did was plant a seed of possibility. It's because of people like Anna and Weiss, like Josie and Durwood, like Frankie and Susan and Marcus and Nigel and...." she sighs, taking the time to grab a tissue and dab at her eyes. "We have a town full of miracle workers, and I couldn't be prouder!"

Another minute of cheering starts up, and thankfully, Ashley isn't the only one with tears.

She shares a look with Sylvia, sitting in her wheelchair, her hands full of bunched tissues, then she smiles toward Susan, who waits off to the side with some volunteers.

"You've all heard about our plans, hopes, and dreams...but now it's time for us to hear from you. To make this official, we need to vote."

A man stands up at the back. "Raise your hand if you want this to happen," he calls out.

Stunned, Ashley can't believe it when she sees every single person's hand raised in the air.

"Does that work for a vote?" A voice calls out.

Ashley laughs, her relief real as her gaze weaves through the crowd, the smile on her face growing.

"To make it official," she says because she can see the panic covering Susan's face, "how about everyone hand in their ballot as you leave?"

Susan is a stickler for the fine details, and not having actual pieces of paper to indicate a formal vote will drive her crazy.

Not to mention, the bylaws require an actual count of votes.

This is happening. It's really happening.

Innsbruck is saved. It will be a long road, and she understands it won't always be smooth, but this is happening. Gah. She'd do a little dancing jig if people didn't give her funny looks.

Their quiet little town, the town that's been dying a slow death, isn't going to be so quiet anymore. It's going to thrive, grow, expand...a light fills her on the inside that expands until she has no doubt she's glowing.

Glowing with happiness, belief, and excitement. Glowing just like every other person in the room with her.

CHAPTER TWENTY-NINE

8 MONTHS LATER

ASHLEY

Days, weeks, and months roll together until there have been times when Ashley can't tell one from the other.

In the past few months, it's like this little mountain town has been preparing to give birth, and they're all just waiting for the big day to happen.

It's been amazing. Everyone wants to play a part, and it's everything Ashley has dreamed about.

Tomorrow is the groundbreaking ceremony for the new retirement village, Christmas Spirit Retirement Village. Ashley loves the name so much that the road leading up to the village will be called Christmas Spirit Lane.

Work on the store facades began sooner than expected, thanks to the personal donation of Weiss and Anna Becker.

Ashley wanted to wait until everything was finalized with the retirement village, but Weiss insisted.

Considering the man had a heart attack on the heels of recovering from pneumonia, saying no or suggesting they slow down wasn't an option. He's been Durwood's shadow, not lifting a hammer but offering suggestions, helping with the teams. Thanks to both these men, the downtown core of Innsbruck is starting to look more Bavarian than ever.

The promise of Christmas is very real in Innsbruck, and Ashley can't be happier about it.

There's only one itsy-bitsy problem that she is not quite sure how to fix.

That itsy-bitsy problem is why she's sitting in Frankie's café waiting for Josie Holms to join her.

Josie's husband is the problem, and it's Ashley's job to find a solution.

All day she's dreaded this meeting.

She's gone from one meeting to the next, overseeing one project to another, checking on the progress, and going over lists and schedules with Susan about other things, but in the back of her head, all she can think about is this meeting and how important it is.

If she screws it up, she could be screwing everything up.

It's after hours in the bakery, but despite Frankie sneaking pours of Ashley's favorite type of Bailey's – Lux Chocolate that is only available in Europe — into her hot chocolate, Ashley can't stop fidgeting.

Yes, she's nervous. Yes, she's worried. And for the love of all things Christmas, yes, she's definitely stressed.

"Don't you sigh at me like that," Frankie snaps before forcing another snickerdoodle into Ashley's hand. "I'm here to help, not hinder."

Frankie looks as frazzled as Ashley feels, which isn't good.

Grey ringlets of hair have escaped a hasty bun, her apron is streaked with chocolate, and no matter how often Ashley points to a spot on her friend's face, the flour smears won't disappear.

It takes a few sips of her cocoa before being able to give Frankie an apologetic smile. "I know, you're right. It's just that...."

She can't finish her sentence. Not that she doesn't want to, but speaking it means breathing it into existence, and the last thing she needs is one more problem becoming her reality.

The bell over Frankie's cafe door jingles, and both women turn to greet Josie with a slight wave.

"I already know what you're going to say," Josie says as she pushes the door closed with the heel of her foot. "Durwood is being a cranky old jackass, and you need me to sort him out, right?"

Ashley's cheeks bloom bright red, like she's been caught red-handed in the biscotti jar.

"When isn't Durwood a grumpy old man?" Frankie pushes herself away from the table and heads toward her counter. "I made Ashley a special cocoa. Want one too?"

"You know I won't say no." Josie pulls out a chair opposite Ashley. "Do yourself a favor, girl, clean your face, and change your apron. You're a mess."

Ashley averts her gaze at the sight of Frankie's scowl. Someone had to say it, and thankfully it wasn't her.

"Listen," Josie holds up her hand, demanding Ashley's focused attention. "Durwood isn't an easy man. We all know that. Retirement and age have only made him worse, not better. You can't think this will go smoothly because we all know it won't. But he'll do a damn good job, won't let you down, and his heart is in the right place."

With Josie folding her hands on the table, Ashley takes that as a sign it's her turn to speak.

How much does she start with? All of it? Some of it? Tiptoe into the truth or hedge around it?

"I'm worried it's too much for him," she says, deciding the truth is better than tact and probably appreciated too when it comes to Josie.

Josie shrugs her shoulder. "Possibly."

Possibly? Is she agreeing or not? Ashley can't tell.

"I don't want the stress to affect him." Ashley can't help but think about Weiss.

"Don't compare him to Weiss. Everyone is, and it's getting on his nerves. His heart is good, he's got a lot of strength in his muscles, and the doctor said doing nothing will kill him faster than any project he might take on."

No matter what Ashley might say, Josie will have a comeback.

"He needs to play nice." Frankie approaches the table with an overflowing mug of cocoa topped with whipped cream.

Josie laughs. "When has Durwood ever played nice? He's a contractor, not a salesman."

Here lies the issue. "I need him to play nice, though," Ashley says, lifting her mug for another sip. "That's what's causing the problems."

Since day one, this has been building into a growing snowball of conflict. Specifically, issues with Durwood respecting the town's direction and design. He changes everything that the council and engineers have settled on.

Every. Single. Thing.

"You know what would fix all this?" Frankie leans back in her chair, arms crossed over her ample chest.

"What?" The wistfulness in Ashley's voice is bright. She has a funny feeling she knows the answer. It's probably the same suggestion she wants to make herself.

"Having someone else run the operation, be the front

person, while Durwood focuses on project management." Frankie looks directly at Josie.

Josie throws her hands up in the air. "You, of all people, know I'd love to have Jared and my grandbabies back home." Josie shakes her head and heaves a *don't-you-think-I-thought-of-this* kind of sigh.

Jared and Marlee moved years ago due to a lack of work. Jared helped his father run Holms Carpentry but moved his family to the city, where they could find work to pay bills.

They'd been just one of many families to leave Innsbruck over the years.

Hopefully, they'll be one of many returning families to come back, too.

"So how do we get all these families to come back? Not just Jared and Marlee, but all the others too."

Frankie's question has Ashley wanting to duck and cover from their pointed glances.

This is something she's been working on for the past six months or so, but so far, she's barking up a dead tree. "I'm trying, guys. I really am." Ashley rolls her shoulders back and groans at the crack-crack-crack.

Frankie pats Ashley's hand. "I know, dear, that was unfair of me."

No, it wasn't unfair. Frankie's just being honest and plain, and Ashley will never fault her for that.

"So, what are you doing then?" Josie's chin juts forward. "Our transformation is a good idea, and I know of a few families who are planning to return, but what are you doing about the rest of them?"

Ashley plays with her mug, turning it in circles and smearing drops of chocolate on the table. "We sent out a mailing to all those who'd left and let them know about the Christmas Spirit Village employment opportunities." This village has been a blessing in disguise, and she's so thankful for Nigel making everything happen like he did. Their team in charge of building the village and integrating it into Innsbruck have been phenomenal to work with.

"We provided a link to their hiring page," she continues, "and I've signed quite a few letters of recommendations too. At least a quarter of the new hires are from those who are moving back to the area," Ashley can't help but let the smile on her face grow with that news.

Josie's brows ride up like a hot air balloon.

"Honestly," Ashley continues, hoping that Josie believes her. "I was half expecting Jared to apply for the site supervisor position or one of the carpentry jobs."

The high brows disappear with that remark. Josie snorts. "Do you know what they offered for payment? Less than what he's making in the city."

"For just one job, or all of his jobs combined?" Frankie's voice is lower than usual.

Ashley winces. Tricky question, but these two women aren't known for skating over topics.

Josie waves her hand in the air with a dismissive attitude. "He's working too much," she says, her tone more agreeable than Ashley expected.

"He does realize that the cost of living here, compared to the city, probably means he wouldn't have to?" Frankie mentions.

Ashley is thinking the exact same thing.

Josie rolls her eyes. "Men and their pride. Trust me, I'm working on it. I'd love for him to move back and help his father, but Durwood needs to be the one to ask for help."

Ashley reaches for the last cookie on the plate and sticks it in her mouth before she says anything. What she wants to say and what she should say are two very different things.

She wants to beg Jared to return home and take over from his father.

She wants to remind Josie of the impact she has on her family. If she says it, her son will listen.

She wants to ask for another cocoa, but this time with more Bailey's.

Instead, she keeps all these thoughts to herself.

"Tell you what? Why don't you two ladies create a plan where Ashley can offer him a job without Durwood realizing what's happening, while I refill our mugs. And then, once you've accomplished that, you can help me strategize how I plan on taking over the baking world within our small town."

CHAPTER THIRTY

MIA

What is going on at her parent's house?

There's a white pickup full of building materials in the back of the cab, her father's garage door is up, all his tools on full display for the taking, and the ground is covered in sawdust.

As she steps over pieces of discarded wood and stacks of lumber, she tries to wrap her head around what she's seeing while struggling to reel in the instant anger and panic sneaking in.

Her dad had better not be doing any of this work. She gets so angry at him for overdoing things, especially when he knows he's not supposed to. His heart isn't as strong as it used to be, and she is not ready to go through the anticipatory grief of thinking she's about to lose him, not again. It was bad enough the first time he was sent to the hospital for pneumonia, but when he collapsed a month later while in the garage due to a heart attack, she wasn't sure she could handle it.

Sure, she's overreacting.

Sure, she's jumping to conclusions.

Sure, she's being overprotective, but someone has to be.

As soon as she steps up to the porch, she sees what's going on – Dad is tearing it apart and replacing it like he's wanted for the past few years. This is one of the many projects on her mother's *honey-do-list* that anyone, but her honey, should be doing.

She hates the idea, but her mother is still gung-ho about pushing ahead with the whole bed and breakfast idea, and she has no choice but to accept that it's happening, grudgingly.

These last few months, it's like life is spiraling out of control, and Mia is really struggling. Everything is changing – her friends, this town, her parents, even her business – everyone is being swept along with the tide and somehow staying afloat while she's flailing in the shallows. How is that even possible?

Mia drops her bag on the upstairs steps and heads into the kitchen, where she hears a murmur of voices.

The minute she recognizes the bowed head of Matt Pablo, her heart does this little ridiculous triple-beat which she quickly squashes.

Matt made it very clear he wasn't interested. The day before the opening, she'd asked him out for drinks to celebrate finishing on time, and he'd turned her down flat.

"Good morning, honey," Mom says with a bright smile. "You're just in time for fresh coffee. I made some new creamer this morning. I found this recipe for an almond mocha cream." Anna gets up from the table and pours Mia a cup.

"Mia." Matt pushes his chair back as he stands. He's scruffy, with sawdust in his hair, and her fingers make this little twitch motion as if itching to feel his hair against her skin. What the heck is wrong with her?

Stuffing her hands in her pockets, Mia gives him a nod and steps out of his way as he brushes past her.

"Thanks for the coffee, Anna. It was just what I needed." He gives Mia a brief smile before walking away. She finds it a little difficult to look away, something her mom obviously notices by the smile on her face.

"He's a nice man, dear." Anna's eyes twinkle.

"Sure, when he's on a job site and speaking with clients." She doesn't bother to hide her eye roll.

"Try the creamer, dear," Anna says, nudging the glass container toward her.

Mia pours some of the homemade creamer into her coffee, watching the mixture swirl before taking a sip.

Her mom has been experimenting with homemade butters and creamers. Mia has so far enjoyed her role of taste tester... until today.

One simple sip is too many. "Whoa, this is way too sweet." Mia heads over to the sink and dumps the coffee.

"Really? Matt seemed to think it was just right."

There's no hiding the twinkle in her mother's eyes. They're shining brighter than the sun coming through the windows.

"Well then, that explains everything," Mia mutters.

"What's that, dear?"

"The man doesn't know a good thing when it's in front of him." Mia pours herself a new cup, adding about half the sweetener this time to her coffee.

"So, where's Dad?"

"I would assume outside, helping Matt with the front porch. Didn't you see him?" Her mom reaches for a stack of papers and starts going through them.

"No one was out there," Mia says.

"Hmmm. Well, he's out there." Anna picks up a pen and twirls it in her fingers. "Your father decided he wants to add on an addition to the garage so it can be used as a guest house. What do you think?"

"I think that's a big undertaking." She needs to be more supportive, but building an addition when they already have three extra bedrooms in the house that they are renovating? Seems like a bit much to her.

"That's why we hire help, dear. Plus, it'll keep your father busy. You should see the drawings he's come up with for changing the front section of the house to accommodate a proper check-in area." Anna flips through a few sheets and hands one to Mia.

She reels back a little. What Mom is showing her isn't a small change. It's a massive alteration to the house she's always called home. No. She doesn't like any of this. Not one bit.

"Oh, stop frowning, dear. It's not very becoming. I know you're not a huge supporter of change, but this is what we are doing. You can either be happy for us, or you can continue to become a grumpy old maid. The choice is yours."

"Excuse me?" Did she just call her an old maid?

"Well, it's true. You've become rather grumpy lately. Even your father has mentioned it."

"I am not grumpy." She takes offense to that.

She might be overwhelmed, struggling with all the change happening, maybe even a little disgruntled that her parents are turning her home into a bed and breakfast, but grumpy?

Absolutely not.

"Then why can't you be a little more supportive? This B&B is a good thing, Mia, you know that. And it's not like it's affecting you. There will still be personal space in this house for you, separate from our guests when they arrive." Anna reaches out. "This will always be your home, love."

She hates how her mom can look deep into her soul and see the underlying issue.

"But it's not going to be home anymore. It'll be a business

where you have living space. I mean, is Matt going to be here every time I come over, working on one project or another?"

"It will be home, because it will be our home that we open to guests, when we feel like it. And whether we have someone helping or not, is really none of your business, Mia. You moved out and have your own place that you call home, or did you forget?"

Ouch.

Anna jumps up as the oven timer goes off. "Oh, good timing. I made a new breakfast casserole dish I think you're going to like. Frankie wants me to supply a few different recipes for our cooking classes, but I'm not sure about this one."

"Cooking classes, as in plural?"

Anna cocks her head. "Yes. Oh, come on, we talked about this, Mia. You know the cookies and cocktail class we're testing tonight? Like that."

It took Mia a good five seconds to remember the conversation while remembering she'd agreed to take these classes with her mom as a sort of mother-daughter bonding time.

"You forgot, didn't you?" Anna's hands settle on her hips as she gives Mia a typical motherly frown.

"I didn't forget," yes, she totally did, "I just didn't realize that was tonight."

"Uh-huh." It's obvious Anna doubts her words, and to be honest, Mia doesn't blame her.

"Okay, you're right. It totally slipped my mind, but I'm all for it. I mean, cookies and cocktails - who wouldn't jump to join that class?" Hopefully the smile on her face negates the tinge of sarcasm in her voice.

"Mia."

Nope, Anna still heard it.

"How many classes are you taking on?" Mia asks, totally ignoring the warning in her mother's tone.

"Why do you ask? Are you thinking of hosting one?"

Mia's about to answer until she sees how her mom's eyes light up, with a sparkle and an idea. Mia doesn't want to hear whatever she's about to say.

"Oh honey, you should. It would be great marketing for the bookshop. You could do some themed ideas – from some of the classics or centered around genres or..." as Anna talks, she reaches for her notebook and starts writing things down. "Actually, this is a great idea, and I'm going to suggest it to Frankie. She's going to love it."

A bubble of panic takes root within Mia.

"Wait a minute, Mom, let's slow down, please... I'm not volunteering for anything—"

"I've noticed."

"I was just...wait, what? You've noticed? What does that mean?"

With a sigh, Anna sets down the notebook and retakes her seat. "Mia, it means I've noticed that while you say you're excited about the new direction our town is taking, so far, it's all talk. You do the absolute minimum when it comes to planning, you never seem to make any of the meetings I invite you to, and when I convince you to join me for something, it's like I'm forcing you out of your comfort zone."

"You are." The words pop out before Mia has a chance to swallow them.

Anna's eyes narrow. "Since when?"

Mia's about to give an answer, then realizes she doesn't have one.

Anna reaches across and wraps her hands around Mia's.

"For someone on the town planning committee, who organizes the Christmas fairs and set up a very successful annual outdoor Christmas Market, you've been absent from what's happening recently to our town. Why's that?"

There's no judgment in her mother's voice, no condemnation, just pure speculation, and care.

Mia releases her hand from her mother's hold and rubs the back of her neck, feeling very vulnerable, very seen, and very uncomfortable.

"A lot of my excitement was overshadowed by Dad's health issues."

The look on Anna's face tells Mia that's not a good enough excuse.

"The Market didn't fall apart only because of Ashley. That had nothing to do with me."

"You took care of everything up to that day, or am I wrong?"

No, she isn't wrong. Dad had a heart attack the morning of the market opening, so technically, everything was already done and set up. Ashley just had to ensure everyone was at the right booths and they were taken care of.

"Things have been a little busy since then, Mom. You, of all people, know that. I mean, Dad's health comes first, right?"

Anna nods. "First for your father, yes. That's on him. Not you. We appreciated your help in the beginning, hun. We really do. But, you can let go now."

Mia struggles to process what her mom is saying.

"Yeah, but—"

Anna shakes her head. "No buts. Your father is an adult and fully aware of his limitations. He doesn't need you, his daughter, constantly reminding him of them."

"That's not what I'm doing..." her voice trails as she thinks about it more.

No, that's exactly what she's doing.

"Oh honey, it doesn't matter how old you get, you'll always be his little girl, and dads like to think they'll always be their daughter's white knight, up on a pedestal where she knows he's always there to protect her."

Mia swallows hard, a swell of tears forcing her to blink rapidly.

"But he…"

Anna holds up her hand, stopping her. "No. There's no buts. Just support your father as best you can and let me take care of him, okay?"

She hears her father's voice coming in through an open window. He's laughing with Matt, joking about something to do with the size of wood, and Mia can't help but smile.

"Taking care of this house, taking care of me, it's what keeps your father going lately, hun. Then, we'll have the odd customers, not overfill our calendar, but have enough to keep your father busy and fill this house with a little bit of noise. It'll be good."

This kind of caught Mia off guard. She always thought her parents enjoyed being empty nesters, that being on their own, able to travel whenever they wanted to, was exactly what they wanted to do with the rest of their lives.

Maybe once upon a time, that had been their dream.

Maybe their dream has changed. That's not always a bad thing, right?

CHAPTER THIRTY-ONE

ASHLEY

Ashley can count on two hands the number of times she's had a cordial conversation with Marcus.

She's lost count, however, of all the times simple starts to their conversations end up in sarcastic clashes, leaving them both beyond frustrated.

He tends to buck her ideas, left and right, regardless of how much they will help their town. Not because they're bad ideas, but because they weren't his ideas.

Today, however, there's no frustration, no arguing, nothing but smiles, congratulatory claps, and champagne.

A wide, warm, and welcoming smile spreads across Marcus' face as Ashley holds a bottle in her hand.

This is his moment, and she has no problem letting him know it.

"Marcus," Ashley raises her voice to be heard in the room, "you've worked hard on getting our new zoning passed. Thanks to you and your initiative, every new building within our town limits will be constructed in the Bavarian style. I have to admit, I wasn't sure you would embrace our new town vision, but you've not only done that, you've also taken the reigns and made our look even more distinctive."

His smile grows from his lips to his eyes, encasing his whole face.

"If I'm not careful, you'll be running against me again in the next election," Ashley continues, adding a teasing tone to her voice. The nod he gives her isn't a shock, she's fully prepared to run against him again, but her heart still jumps as if jolted with a battery pack.

"Not this time. Consider me the perfect partner in this endeavor," Marcus takes the bottle from her before it slips from her grasp. "Don't worry about me, you're the one spearheading this change. We're all here to support you."

Ashley's jaw drops. Susan has to nudge her before she closes it. Nigel snickers to the side.

"I've never been your enemy, Mayor," Marcus says, "even though sometimes I know I haven't appeared that way. You need someone to make you look at every angle, and I felt that was my role. I've never hidden that."

She dips her head in a nod, copying his earlier gesture. "How about you open that baby so we can enjoy a glass?"

At the sound of the bottle's opening pop, everyone laughs as Marcus leans over the tray of glasses and pours the bubbly elixir.

Despite the town's vote to change the focus of their town, once people started to see and understand the scope of change, a few balked. Even with the retirement corporation helping to cover the cost of the updating, a few sticklers refused to play nice.

It was Marcus' idea to create the new zoning bylaw.

"Can we unveil now?" Susan whispers after sipping her champagne.

"Oh, yes," Ashley totally forgot about this surprise.

She made her way to the large, covered surprise mounted on the office wall. It's huge and something everyone will notice when they walk into the office.

"If I could have everyone's attention," Ashley calls out. "We've all dreamed about what this town will look like when it's completed, we all know that it will expand and grow as we grow, but I thought it would be better to see our vision in person."

The hush in the room softens as voices lower.

"We used to be a logging town. We come from good stock, hard workers who know the value of family and dedication. I'm not sure they ever saw this future for us, but I, for one, am as excited about our journey as a town and our destination." Ashley pulls at the large red bow holding the two sheets of craft paper together, revealing an illustrated map of their town.

Even though she's seen the map a zillion times during its creation, her breath still catches.

A low murmur of oohs and ahhhs fill the room, the sounds draping across Ashley's back like a fine velvet sweater, making her feel warm and cozy.

In all its Christmas Bavarian glory, the town of Innsbruck beckons like a platter of sweet treats. From Santa's Village on the outskirts to the parks, trails, cafes, and beer halls, it's all there. Christmas shops, craft markets, and especially their new town center.

She's so excited about their new town center. All their future Christmas Markets will be held there, weekly fire pit gatherings, but most importantly, their new town cuckoo-clock, complete with wooden characters, will be the focal point.

This clock is truly a piece of art, and it's all thanks to Anna and Weiss, who graciously donated funds toward it.

"Isn't it all amazing?" Ashley gestures toward the large map, "I know this is huge, and not everything will be completed within a few years, but eventually, we will get there. We have a lead, or I should say Nigel has a lead, on a sponsor for our cuckoo-clock, which will be handcrafted in Germany and shipped here." She looks to Nigel, who steps forward.

"The traditional name is Glockenspiel," Nigel explains, "and my lead is still in the infant stages of planning, but I've been in contact with a builder, and we're discussing prices. There are a few variations of clocks we can go with – a tall one that stands above the buildings and is seen from miles away, or a two-level building created with the clock as the focal point and used as a museum tourist piece that visitors can walk in and see it working from a different viewpoint."

"The cost?" Marcus asks.

"Not in our budget, I will say that," Nigel says. "I'll share more at our next meeting, if that's okay?"

Ashley nods. Sylvia has been busy trying to find different sponsors for the clock, and until there are more details, she would prefer Nigel not to say much. She doesn't want to jinx things too early.

Susan keeps eyeing her watch, a subtle reminder to Ashley that she has an appointment.

Ashley sips at her bubbly before placing the glass on the table. "If I'm not back in forty-five minutes, call me." She says quietly.

"Done." Susan hands her an envelope and gives her a thumbs up.

She's going to need it.

She's off for her daily intervention, or inspection, with Durwood Holms, a meeting she dreads more and more each day.

CHAPTER THIRTY-TWO

MARLEE

Her phone lights up like a Christmas tree at night from the plethora of messages from Josie. She loves her mother-in-law, but right now, she can't handle another update about Innsbruck.

She's homesick. It's been six years since they left, but there hasn't been a day she hasn't daydreamed about returning.

Now is the perfect time, too. She knows it. Josie knows it. Her kids even know it. The only one ignoring all the waving flags of opportunity is her husband and his father. Both are strong-willed mules.

"Hey, Mom, I think Nana really wants to talk to you," Lilianna, her oldest daughter, says as she walks by.

Marlee takes a look at her phone again before turning it upside down. Out of sight, out of mind, right?

"Well, that's rude. Wait till I tell Nana on you."

Marlee sticks her tongue out at her teenager, who only rolls her eyes as a sixteen-year-old can. "You know she doesn't like tattletalers, Lily," she says.

Lily wrinkles her nose. "Yeah, but she loves me more than she hates tattletaling."

Her phone vibrates, then rings, the sound of Minions' laughter, the ringtone the kids gave their Grandmother, growing louder and louder.

"Hi, Josie," Marlee says, finally answering. "How are you?"

"Didn't you see my text messages? I figured it was easier to just call. Besides, I have a list of things to do today and don't have time to wait for you to respond." Josie jabbers like a magpie, her words going a mile a minute.

"I was just talking to Lily, so I haven't had a chance to look them over," she says with a wide grin to her daughter, "what's up?"

A loud harrumph comes across the line. "I know you don't want to get involved, but this has gone on long enough. These boys need an intervention. Durwood needs Jared, and I'm tired of waiting for him to admit it."

Marlee feels a glimmer of a headache forming right between her eyes. "We can't, Josie. We both agreed not to step in."

"Fuddle bugs. I think we've given them long enough, don't you? Haven't we all paid enough for their stubbornness?" Josie asks.

Paid enough? They've more than paid their fair share.

"Tell Durwood to call him." Even saying that Marlee knows it will never happen.

Josie laughs, the sound reminding her of a bark.

"Have you gone to the doctor about your cold?" Marlee didn't like the sound of it. It reminds her of when the kids would get croup.

"Yes, it's just a wee cold, don't worry about me. Durwood won't call Jared, Jared won't call his father, so it's up to us." Josie pauses, and a slight tap-tap-tap sound can be heard. Marlee can picture Josie sitting at her kitchen table, tapping her pen against the table, deep in thought.

"Why don't we have a sleepover with Grandma and Grandpa?" Lily speaks up, her voice loud enough for Josie to hear.

"Oh, I like sleepovers with my grand-babies. That's a great idea," Josie's voice brightens up right away. "Oh, and it's perfect timing because we have some kid baking classes that I'm leading, and I would love the kids' input. Oh…and now that I'm thinking of it, we have a class on making outdoor gnomes that I need someone to host. Jared would be perfect for that since he's the one who made the pattern for me."

Lily snickers as Josie charges ahead with making plans for everyone.

"I'll talk to Jared and see if he'll do the class. Either way, we'll come up." Marlee isn't about to argue, but she will give Jared the chance to say no, if he dares to.

"Oh, don't you worry. I'll tell that son of mine I need him and expect you all for Friday night, does that sound good? He'll need to cut all the wood, so coming Saturday won't work." She pauses for a second. "Yes, I think that will work perfectly. It's a full class, so I might just need to get Durwood to help too."

Marlee isn't about to promise anything when it comes to Jared. He's managed to find one excuse or another not to join them whenever they head up to Innsbruck to visit on weekends, so this is all on Josie.

"All right, I'll send my son a message, and you start getting ready to come up. It'll be good to see you. Love you, Lily," Josie yells loud enough that Marlee has to pull the phone away from her ear.

"Love you too, Nana," Lily yells in return.

Hanging up the phone, Marlee scrolls through the numerous text messages Josie sent, many photos of the latest facades built over the buildings in downtown Innsbruck. She loves the new look. It's so quaint and mountainous and invoked an instant feeling of being someplace else.

Lily hangs over her shoulder, looking too. "We should move back," she says, her voice full of nostalgic dreams.

"I know, baby, I know." She wants to. They all do. Even Jared, even if he won't admit it. Things haven't been going in the direction they'd hoped. Even with her working more now, it's not worth everything they gave up. Moving to the city was the answer, but it's looking more and more like it's a mistake.

It's not until after eleven at night that Jared finally gets home. He drops everything on the floor before sinking down on the couch, his legs outstretched, arms flung to the sides. He looks exhausted.

She closes her book and curls up beside him as best she can. He wraps his arm around her, head resting on her, and they remain that way for a few minutes, in silence, something they've started doing the past few months, just to reconnect.

"I missed you," Jared mumbles. "I've been looking forward to coming home to this for hours."

"Long day?" Marlee threads her fingers against his, her thumb lightly rubbing his skin.

"Something needs to change. I can't keep doing this."

Marlee hears everything in his voice. Tiredness. Hopelessness. Grief. Heartbreak.

The past six months have been really tough.

"I'll see if I can pick up more shifts at work," she offers, yet again, even though she knows how he'll react.

"No. The kids need at least one of us home. It's bad enough you had to pick up a job, to begin with. That was never the plan. I'm going to spend some time putting out resumes tonight. Maybe it's time to call it quits and admit I can't hack having my own business. Guess Dad was right."

Marlee sits up, the palm of her hand on his chest.

"Since when did you start doubting yourself? It's the economy at fault, not you. And you're not a hack. Think of all the individual contracts you've done yourself. The first couple of years here were okay...."

He shrugs. "Okay, but not all right."

"Better than if we'd stayed in Innsbruck." She hates saying the words even though they are the truth.

"There was nothing there for us." Jared reminds her.

"Not then, but maybe now?" She's been wanting to broach the subject for weeks, but the timing has never been right.

Jared places his lips against her forehead and leaves a kiss. "You've been talking to Mom, haven't you?"

Marlee doesn't need to answer. He's always been able to read her.

"It seems like Mom has been talking to everyone but me," Jared said, his voice a little worn, a little tired, and very disappointed. "I wish she'd talk to me instead, you know?"

"Maybe she doesn't think you'll listen?" Marlee yawns. "Why don't we go upstairs? You can have your shower. I'll watch you from the comfort of our bed, and then we can talk about this tomorrow."

Jared pushes himself to a sitting position. "When tomorrow? After my double shift again? We never see each other. We never talk. I hardly know my own kids anymore." He rests his elbows on his knees and buries his fingers in his hair. "This isn't working, Marlee, and it's time I suck up my pride and admit it."

Even if Marlee wanted to say something, the words are twisted around her tongue, and her lips remain sealed.

"I'm not going home, not unless Dad..." Her husband shakes his head, not finishing his sentence. "I can't keep doing two jobs, pulling double shifts with only a few hours of sleep a day. I'll look for something else, do whatever it takes."

Marlee swallows the gum ball of hope lodged in her throat. "Okay. If you look for something, I'll look on my end. In the meantime, did you hear from your mom about this weekend? She needs your help and asked the kids to come for a sleepover.

"She left me a message about gnomes, and since it's my template, I'm responsible. What else did she say?" Jared's brows group together like a fuzzy caterpillar.

She sighs. Of course, Josie wouldn't fully explain things. "Remember how your mom was talking about setting up a bunch of different workshops and classes? Well, she's got a few on the go this weekend, one the kids can help with, and the other...she needs you to cover. Guess she's out a host, and since it's a wood class and it's to make those lawn gnomes of yours...."

"She wants me to do the class. Right. In other words, she's trying to find ways to convince us to move back."

Marlee shrugs, neither agreeing nor disagreeing. There's no point. Josie isn't being too subtle about it.

"I think it'll be fun," Marlee says. "I was looking over the website of all the classes they offer, and there's a few I'd love to get involved in. I mean...I would if we lived there, at least."

The look Jared gives her says all the things a husband wants to say to his wife but knows he shouldn't.

"Come on, you know it would be fun, right? Going up will give us time to check out the town, see all that's happening, for ourselves."

Jared drops his head and rubs the back of his neck. "Why do I have the feeling this is only the beginning?"

"The beginning of what?" She adds a little hint of teasing to her voice.

"I don't want you to get your hopes up, Marlee. I don't know if there's a place for me back there, you know? Not with Dad, at least."

She wants to say a lot, but she holds her peace. Instead,

Marlee stands to her feet and holds out her hand. "Come on, you big lug, let's get upstairs before you fall asleep on me."

"You can't tell me you'd want to be surrounded by Christmas all year long," Jared says, his voice hidden behind a yawn.

"Are you crazy? That's like living in a wonderland. Of course, I want that." Christmas is her favorite holiday, and she already has ideas of how to get involved once they move back.

Once they do. Not if they do. That thought alone places a huge smile on her face.

CHAPTER THIRTY-THREE

ASHLEY

Ashley's desk is covered in random stacks of papers, sticky notes, printed photos, and more than three almost empty mugs of coffee.

Almost empty because she hasn't had time to finish a cup before it goes cold. While she may enjoy a nice glass of cold brew coffee, she's not a fan of cold coffee that once was hot.

There is a difference, ask any coffee addict out there.

"Maybe we should head to the boardroom to go over all the permits that have been approved this past month," Susan suggests as they both look at her desk with a mixture of dismay and laughter.

"If I leave, someone will notice and corner me before I can even set foot inside the boardroom, and you know it." She grabs the coffee mugs, knowing their removal means nothing in terms of how clean her desk is about to get.

"Give me those," Susan says, offering her hands. "I'll put them in the kitchen while you move the stacks. Place them on the floor if you need to...but please keep them in piles. I worked hard on organizing those."

Someday she'll get organized. Someday, however, is not today.

Ashley makes her piles, puts away the pens, gathers all the sticky notes, and waits for Susan to return.

"I'm about to get stomach rot if I drink more," Ashley complains as Susan brings in two new cups of coffee, setting them down on her somewhat clean desk.

"Which is why I also brought these." Susan pulls out two granola bars from her pocket.

For the next half hour, the two go over the various lists Susan brought in. Ashley can't get over how many permits have not only been applied for but handed out as well.

Her smile is about to create a permanent crease on her face.

"This is really happening, isn't it?" She whispers under her breath. It's a phrase she has found herself repeating over and over for the past nine months. At times, it hits her the extent of what all has been accomplished and what's still to happen.

"It really is," Susan agreed. "I don't know how, but this has some good legs."

The two look up at the same time, see matching smiles on each other's faces, and burst out laughing.

"What's with all the noise?" A gruff, grumpy, and graveled voice interrupts their joy.

Durwood sounds worse each time Ashley sees him. If she didn't know better, she would have sworn he was a smoker, the way his voice rumbles like a freight train.

Susan steps to the side while Ashley leans back in her chair, fortifying herself for this unexpected visit.

"Durwood, this is a surprise." Ashley hopes her voice is light and friendly rather than snippy and curt. Why is he here?

"You weren't answering your phone," Durwood ambles his

way into the room, grabbing onto the back of the chair in front of her desk. He doesn't sit, for which Ashley is thankful.

Ashley glances around her desk, then the floor, then to Susan, hoping she'll know where her phone is. She doesn't remember her phone ringing. In fact, she's not even sure where her phone is at the moment.

"Check your top drawer," Susan says.

Sure enough, there's her phone. She gasps at the notifications lighting up her screen.

"Ten messages?"

Durwood just shrugs his massive shoulders.

"This is important."

"One would have been fine. I'd have called you back," Ashley reminds him, the words sounding vaguely familiar since this isn't the first time this has happened.

"Eventually." The disapproval in Durwood's voice reminds Ashley of her father. He'd hold that same tone when he was disappointed in her.

"If you don't need me," Susan speaks up, an apologetic tone to her voice, "I'll head to my desk and get back to work."

It's not lost on her that Susan didn't bother to wait for a reply before bolting from the room.

"You're being overcharged." Durwood crosses his arms over his chest. "Being suckered like a sunfish about to snatch a worm off the hook."

Ashley tries to hide her sigh, but from the scowl on Durwood's face, she isn't doing a very good job.

"If you don't care about where your money goes, fine." He turns to go, his obvious disgust with her response evident in his side glance.

Rebuffed, Ashley feels tainted, like she's been caught wearing a sweat-stained sweater too many days in a row.

"What company?" Ashley stops Durwood from leaving her office.

"The one doing all the cutouts. I told you it was a mistake to go with an outsider."

Ashley thought back through the multiple discussions with Durwood about vendors. Yes, it's an outside company, but they could mass produce the cutouts for all the building facades, thus saving them money.

"How am I being overcharged?" She crosses the room to the drawers full of files and searches for the company name. She remembers pricing out the cost of buying the wood and the time it would take for someone to cut them versus going mass. She also recalls it being comparable - that is, as long as there were no hiccups along the way or mistakes likely to happen if someone on Durwood's crew did them.

Durwood pulls a scrap of paper from his back pocket and unfolds it for her.

She takes the paper, casually glancing, then riffles through the file to find the original pricing comparison.

"I can save you about three dollars per unit being cut. Now, that might not seem much," he says, "but considering how many we need, that will add up and can be used elsewhere."

Very true. It would add up and could be used elsewhere but is it worth it?

"Can you guarantee that? What happens if a cut goes wrong and you have to redo it? That's lost material. And what if it takes longer than you've estimated here? That money you think you're saving me could quickly be eaten up, Durwood."

The deep scowl on his face says everything he doesn't verbally speak. *Don't question me-I know what I'm doing-who are you to doubt my skills?*

Ashley rubs her forehead. Lately, he's been the cause of her headaches - not her pending divorce or even her attempt to slow down on the wine she drinks each night. Durwood. He's the reason.

"Durwood," she says, hoping none of her frustration comes out. "Have you thought more about my suggestion to get help? Someone to run the crews while you oversee everything to keep it on schedule? Every time I see you, you're elbow deep in either cutting wood, attaching it to the buildings, or painting something. You're doing everything when you should just be focusing on one thing."

"And what exactly is that?" His eyes narrow until his wrinkles almost hide them.

"Making sure we stay on track," she said. "Making sure we're not being overcharged," she raised his scrap piece of paper, "like this." She smiles then, hoping to pass along the message that she is on his side.

She's not sure it worked.

He *harrumphs* with so much force, his shoulders jerk forward, before turning on the ball of his foot and leaving her office.

"Durwood?" She calls after him, but he's already walked far enough away that she knows he wouldn't turn around even if he heard her.

And she knows he did.

Damn that man.

CHAPTER THIRTY-FOUR

MARLEE

This could be the beginning of the end. All the signs are there.

The end of living in the city.

The end of feeling sectioned off from family and friends.

The end of all the stress that's managed to creep into their house, their family, and even their marriage.

Marlee doesn't want to jinx things, but she feels really good about this visit. Maybe, just maybe, it will be the beginning of the end of this rift between father and son.

Ever since approaching the outskirts of Innsbruck, the slow transformation of the town is clearly visible, with teasers of what's to come, hints of that year-round Christmas feel everyone loves.

As far as Marlee is concerned, she's sold. She's all for the Christmas in July idea, personally.

It's not until they come to the new welcome sign that things feel even more real.

It's a large wooden sign with a wooden wreathe hanging off the corner, invoking a smile and a sense of nostalgia.

She loves it.

Mere seconds after the sign, the road is lined on both sides with Christmas trees.

Marlee turns in her seat. "Wouldn't it be fun to decorate all those trees in lights?"

Lily leans forward. "Can we? For reals?"

"Wouldn't it be fun if we could? Maybe we could ask Grandpa and see if they have a group lined up to do that."

"Don't get their hopes up," Jared whispers to her softly.

She ignores him. It's obvious to everyone that all their hopes are up. Well, everyone but Jared, apparently.

Josie waits for them, standing on the lawn, and waves for them to hurry from the vehicle. The kids all launch at her, and her sound of laughter is like a dart to the heart. Jared feels it too. She can tell.

"Did you have a good drive up?" Josie asks once they reach her side.

"Traffic wasn't too bad," Jared says, giving her a hug.

"Take those bags in the house and then come back out here. I've got things to show you before I can focus on these grandbabies of mine." She gently pushes him toward the direction of the house while giving Marlee an exaggerated wink.

"Alright, here's the plan," she says once Jared is in the house. "I want you two to go for a walk. Take a look at all the changes and see if you can stumble upon Durwood. When you get back here, I'll put him to work cutting all the wood for tomorrow's workshop. Be sure to stop in and see Frankie. She's packaged some treats for me and will have them ready for you."

"Are you wanting us to see Durwood?" Marlee's trying to wrap her head around this plan of Josie's and why it's important.

"Of course, I do. I want that son of mine to see just how

much his father needs him."

Jared walks out of the house, wiping crumbs from his lips.

"Jared Holms, did you eat some cookies I left to cool on the stove?" Josies' hands rest on her hips as she gives her son a fierce glare.

"Maybe?"

"Serves you right for not asking then. Those were dog treats, you silly goof."

Jared's eyes round into saucers, and it takes him a minute to react.

Marlee would be gagging. Jared just shrugs. "I think you've got a winning recipe then, Mom." His eyes twinkle as he wipes his hands on his pants. "I feel you're about to put me to work, aren't you? Exactly how many cut-outs do you need for this workshop I'm doing tomorrow?"

"Well, here's the thing...." Josie looks off into the distance as if she doesn't want to share this next bit of news, "it's a full workshop, with about a dozen attendees. I thought I'd have a few people to help with the class, but... it's just you."

"And how many gnomes are we making, Mom?"

"Oh, you know...well, one gnome was included in the price, but so many people loved your idea, and they asked if they could do extras, so...."

Jared's eyes narrow as she hedges around the answer.

"How many gnomes, Mom?"

"Everyone bought an extra gnome. I didn't think it'd be that big of a deal, right?"

By his eye roll, Marlee isn't sure if it's an issue or not, but before anything more can be said, she decides now is a good time to change the subject.

"Before you get started on that, let's go for a walk and see what all has been done. We won't be long, but your Mom needs us to pick up something from Frankie's, okay?"

She links her arm through Jared's before he has a chance to disagree and drags him down the street, her excitement building with each passing minute.

It feels good to stretch their legs, walk through their old neighborhood, and see the small ways their town is finding its way. Besides, it's a gorgeous day to spend outside. There's nothing like summer in the mountains. It's not scorching hot like the city can be. There's always a nice breeze, and everything just feels so alive.

Jared may remain quiet during their walk, but Marlee doesn't let that stop her from pointing out every single Christmas decoration she discovers – from every tree, ornament, and painted cut-out that's been added to houses of people they used to call neighbors.

She loves it. Loves how the town embraces this change and wishes they were part of it. She thought it might feel weird to be in a town that is so focused on Christmas, but it isn't. It feels almost natural.

She's having a severe FOMO moment – fear of missing out – and she doesn't like it.

Jared's cataloging everything. She can see his brain working a mile a minute, noting his father's handiwork or ideas to improve what's been done - which is exactly what she wants to happen.

She needs him to become invested, see a future, and discover a desire to be part of the change happening in their hometown. She needs it more than she wants to admit.

"A penny for your thoughts?" She finally asks as they stand at a crosswalk.

He lets out a deep sigh. "Not sure they're worth a penny at the moment."

This has her worried. She's been hoping for a level of happiness, contentment, a sense of something...but his brows crease together, and the worry in his voice...she doesn't like what it could mean.

She looks around them, at the buildings, the street, the people out walking enjoying the sites, like they are. She's home. They are home. Can't he sense that? Doesn't he feel it, too?

"It's too much," he says, his grip on her hand tightening as they cross the street.

"What's too much? The decorations? I think they're perfect." She loves how the buildings are starting to look like real mountain chalets. There's this general feeling of a gingerbread house, and she's all for it.

"Everything looks great. I think they've done a good job in such a short time." Jared doesn't sound happy, though.

"But?"

He shakes his head. "It's too much for Dad. Sooner or later, he will drop too many balls, which will be a catastrophe."

Yes – this is precisely what she's been hoping would happen - that he would see how much he's needed with his own eyes.

"Then help him." Marlee stops and faces him, looking deep into his eyes. "We can do it. You can do it."

He shakes his head and looks around them. Everything she sees as progress, he's viewing through skewed eyes.

"Could we do it? Sure. Do we want to? Yes, of course, we do. Moving back is something we'd do in a heartbeat, but it's not going to happen, Marlee, not like this."

"Why? I don't get it."

With a sigh, he takes her hand, and they continue down the sidewalk. "Why? It's simple. Dad. I'm not sure he wants my help or even realizes he needs it," he says.

What can she say to that? She knows Durwood. Understands how stubborn he can be. Whatever has happened between father and son is only going to get worse before it can get better. She just hopes the fall-out isn't too damaging.

CHAPTER THIRTY-FIVE

MIA

It's been a long day, and all she wants is to go home, sit out on her back deck and watch the sun set over the mountains, but instead, she's headed to her parent's house, and for some reason, this puts her in a mood.

She thought the walk here would do her some good, getting out of the stuffiness of the shop, getting some exercise, but nope, her mood is like that first taste of a sour candy.

Puckerish.

Maybe it's the headache she's struggled with all day. Maybe it's the need for quiet after listening to the pounding hammer from the store next door. Maybe she's just peopled out.

There can be a number of 'maybe' reasons for her headache and attitude, but she knows one thing: seeing Matt work on her parents' front railings isn't helping.

What is it about him that sets her on edge? Even with his shirt off, his tanned skin glistening in the dwindling sun...if he says one wrong word, she's ready to rip a strip off him, which doesn't make any sense to her.

It's not like she'd been turned down before. Sure, she thought they had a thing or could have a thing, but they don't, so it shouldn't matter, right?

And yet, it does.

Maybe she should just go home. She hesitates, in the middle of the act of turning around, when Matt notices her and waves.

He waves. Like, what the actually? Why would he do that?

Now she has no choice but to wave back and continue, make some awkward small talk before heading into the house to chat with her parents about what she's not sure about.

Mom sent a text asking her to come by after work. That was it. No reason. No time.

She should have said no.

"Hey Matt," Mia says as she heads up the walkway. "Wow, you've got a lot done. Looks great." She's impressed with the amount of work Matt has completed in such a short time.

The whole front porch, steps, and railing have been replaced, but he didn't stop there. He's in the middle of building a wraparound porch, and as much as Mia wasn't sure she liked the look, she's not to proud to admit when she's wrong.

"Thanks. Your dad has been a great help." He removes a cloth from his back pocket and wipes the sweat on his forehead.

"Not too much of a help, I hope. I mean, he's not paying you to watch him do the work, right?" She knows that didn't come out as she intended, but it came regardless. "Sorry, that wasn't necessary."

"No, it wasn't." He turns and starts picking up some loose pieces of wood. "Your parents aren't here, by the way. They had to rush out and said to tell you to stick around, if you didn't mind."

"Those were their actual words?"

He shrugs. "Not really, but the message is the same."

"What did they really say?" She cocks her head, imagining what they would have said. Anything from...no, they wouldn't, would they?

"For you to keep me company, maybe have a beer, and catch up until they get back."

And there it is. Her parents are playing matchmaker.

Sitting and chatting, shooting the breeze, as her dad would say, isn't really something she's in the mood for, especially considering how awkward things seem between her and Matt.

She lets out a long sigh, purely unintentional.

"Sounds like you're the one who could use the beer. Don't worry about me. I'm about done for the day, anyway. Give me a few minutes to clean up, and I'll be out of your way."

He moves to the side, giving her room to pass. She doesn't argue, instead appreciating someone not requiring something from her.

Her mother taught her better, though, so after dropping her purse on the floor, she heads into the kitchen and pulls out two beers.

She wasn't raised to be rude, and ignoring him would eat at her.

She pushes the front screen door open with her forearm, and he glances up in surprise.

"Beer is always required at the end of a day, don't you think?" She hands him a beer and then sits down on the step, making sure there's room for him to join her.

See, she can be nice.

"Cheers to that," he says, clicking his bottle with hers. They sip in blissful silence, and it's not lost on Mia just how nice it is to sit with someone who doesn't feel the need to fill space with pointless words.

"Your parents aren't crazy, you know," Matt breaks that silence. "What they're doing... it's smart if you think about it."

She nods. That doesn't mean she likes it.

She could argue that they're too old to take on this new venture, that they're throwing money away for no reason, that they're jumping in with blinders to a dream that might not even happen...and yet none of that would be true.

No one is ever too old to pursue something new. It's their money to do with as they choose, and this dream of Ashley's, this reinvention of their town... it's a smart one.

So, what's the issue then?

"I know it is. And of anyone I know to own a B&B and thrive as hosts, it's them."

"So, is it just me you object to, then?"

The fact he comes right out and says this surprises her. She turns to look at him, but he stares straight ahead.

It's on the tip of her tongue to deny and argue, but why bother?

"No, it's not you. Honestly. It's just...so much change at once, I guess."

He nods. "I get that. You were under a lot of pressure about the Christmas Market, and then your dad got sick, then all the changes with this town...life probably feels a little messy."

Messy. That's a good word for it. Out of her control would be another way to phrase it.

"I'm a bit of a—"

"Control freak?" He says for her.

She nods.

He shakes his head. "You look at that as a bad thing, don't you? Why? Look where it's gotten you. You run a successful business and started a new tradition for the town when you created that Christmas market. From what I've seen and heard, people tend to come to you for help with their problems, knowing you have a take-charge attitude."

She remains silent, unsure what to do with this praise. It feels...uncomfortable.

"If you don't mind me saying, stop beating yourself up for what you can't control. If my mom were still alive, I'd probably react just like you...wanting to smother her with care and caution."

Smother? She snorts at the word, knowing he's right.

"Between us, your father likes the attention he gets from you. He barely picks up a tool until he knows you're close by. Ninety percent of the time, he's out here giving me pointers, telling me stories...he just puts on a show when you're around."

Mia can't believe what she's hearing. "He does not."

Matt takes another chug of his beer. "He likes being coddled. It shows him that you care."

"Of course, I care. The idea of losing my father... I'm not ready for that. My world will be crushed." Her throat chokes up with emotion at the memory of just how scared she was.

"No one ever is," Matt says softly.

There's so much in his voice, words he doesn't need to say out loud.

"I'm sorry about your mother," she says, realizing how inadequate the words are yet not knowing what else to say. She doesn't really know much about Matt. He came to town a few years ago, lives above one of the shops downtown, and keeps pretty much to himself.

He clears his throat. "Thanks. She's been gone a while now, but the ache is always there. You learn to live with it, but it never goes away."

"I'm not sure I can learn to live without him," Mia's whisper soft words leave an ache in her heart.

"The cycle of life wields a cruel hand," Matt says. "You'll

figure out how to live with the loss, or you won't, but I think... well, I think you're stronger than you give yourself credit for."

How is she supposed to respond to that?

"So, did my parents happen to mention where they were headed?" She changes the subject to something more comfortable and far less personal.

Setting the bottle down on the porch, he stands and wipes his hands on his pants. "Honestly, I'm not sure, but they headed toward the church if that helps. Looked like your mom had some baking in her hands...." He starts to pick up things from the front yard, tossing pieces of wood into his truck bed and the odd nail into a bucket.

The church? She tries to remember if there's anything happening tonight and remembers Mom mentioning she's volunteered to bake some muffins and cakes for some youth fundraiser.

She heads over to the sidewalk to see if she can see them returning. The church is only a few blocks away, but more than likely, they'll end up talking and volunteering to do something else.

Her parents like to keep busy, that's for sure.

"Mind if I ask you a personal question?" Mia stands close to Matt, hands in her back pockets.

"Ask all you want," he says.

"How come you're not on one of the crews for the downtown restoration or the village center?"

He barely gives her a glance as he slams the trunk gate closed.

"Most everyone is, which means there's no one around to handle all the little jobs. Like helping your parents and others needing a handyman," he says. "I keep busy enough on my own, and it's a control thing, you know? I like working for myself, choosing my own jobs, and my own hours. The onus is on me to find the work or not."

She can understand that. She has an idea, something she wants to do in the shop, but she will need help, and maybe Matt is the answer.

"Listen, I'll see you, okay?" Matt hops in his truck with a brief wave, leaving her standing on the grass feeling like she'd said the wrong thing.

Maybe she had? Or maybe this was just Matt?

CHAPTER THIRTY-SIX

ASHLEY

Coffee in hand, Ashley can't dim the brightness of her smile even if she tried to - which she won't.

It's a gorgeous evening with a warm breeze brushing against the leaves on the trees.

When Jordan yelled down the stairs that Frankie had some croissants at the shop with their names on them, Ashley rushed to the door, eager for the chance for both the fresh baking and spending some time with her moody teenage daughter.

Snowball is even excited, twirling in circles as they walk, giving little yips as he sniffs at everything and anything on the path.

"When things are up and running, we should do a Christmas in July event, Mom. I mean,... that's a thing, right?"

"I'd say so." All summer long, all that's been advertised on tv and social media is the idea of Christmas in July. She has it on her list to approach Hallmark about possible movie locations, considering they'll have that whole Christmas vibe...

"I can't wait to see how everything will look when it snows." Jordan's voice is high with wonderment and happiness. "It's going to be so pretty, don't you think?"

"I know it will." Ashley links arms with Jordan as they head downtown.

So much has changed and still needs to change, but it's all starting to look amazing.

The local hardware store built a small Bavarian chalet in their window, almost an exact replica of the drawings Ashley made up for their town.

"Wow." Jordan leans forward, her nose almost touching the window. "It's so detailed! It reminds me of one of those old Christmas villages you see in stores, you know?"

"Like the ones my grandmother used to have?"

"Yeah, like the old ones." Jordan's eyes twinkle, so Ashley holds back her comment and heads into the store, waiting for Jordan to join her.

"Oh, fabulous," Basil Jack, the owner, calls out. "Just the person I want to talk to." Basil wipes his hands on the grey apron around his waist. "Well, hello there, Snowball. I've got just the thing for you," Basil says as he pulls a treat from a pocket. He leans over, holds his hand out, and waits for Snowball to sit like the good boy he is.

Everyone in town has embraced the pup, and he's loved everywhere he goes.

Basil doesn't look a day over forty-five despite being close to sixty years old. His smile, along with his laugh lines, wipes years off his weathered skin.

"What do you think of the first building?" He motions for them to join him at the window display. "I tried to make it as detailed as possible without going overboard, you know?"

"It's amazing," Jordan speaks up. "You made all this yourself?"

Basil puffs his chest out a little, fingers wrapping around the suspenders holding up his jeans. "Sure did. That's when I came up with an idea..." he turns to Ashley, "I could do some classes on woodworking and carving. Start with something simple, do some cottages, etc. I'd pre-cut most of the wood, so it's just a matter of putting it together and then painting it. People can create their own little villages if they want."

Ashley's smile grows wide as she listens to the pride in his voice. It's the same sense of pride she's been hearing in most everyone's voice lately, too...pride in their town, work, and involvement.

"I love it. The idea, the steps, the village...I love it all," she tells him. "Why don't you put your idea down on paper, give me more details, and I'll have Susan add it to the schedule, okay?"

"Really?" Basil's voice almost breaks as if he can't believe she's going along with his idea. Why wouldn't she? The more people invested in this transformation, the better.

"You said wood carving, too?" Jordan tears her attention from the display.

"Yep. You interested? I was thinking of carving nativity scenes or doing a Santa's village thing. I've been looking at different carving kits you can order, or I might work with someone to create my own. We'd start with the basics, and if there's enough interest, we'd keep going." He takes a toothpick from one of his many pockets and sticks it in his mouth.

Jordan turned toward Ashley, a beseeching look in her eyes. "Can I take one of these classes? This is so cool!"

"Of course," Ashley says. "Actually, consider both of us your first two students...I love the idea of learning how to carve. My dad used to do that. I still have a little sheep figurine he made for me."

Basil nods. "Yep, I remember that. He'd come in here Sunday afternoons, and we'd do some carving together. Do you remember that you begged him one year to move to a farm?"

Ashley laughs. She'd forgotten all about that.

"A farm? For reals?" Jordan's eyes are wide with disbelief.

Ashley nods. For a whole year, she'd begged her parents to move to the foothills where they could have some land and all the pets she wanted.

Dad would never leave Innsbruck, so instead, he did the next best thing. She couldn't have a dozen pets in the house, so he carved them for her, giving them to her for Christmas one year.

She only had the sheep left. She lost the others somehow.

"I have the horse, cow, and chicken." Jordan offers up that little tidbit of news with a pixie-ish smile.

That explains a lot.

Shortly after her parents had died, she started noticing things going missing around the house, specifically items that used to belong to her parents. She found them all in Jordan's room – in her closet, on her shelves...she said she felt better surrounded by the things her grandparents had touched.

Ashley let her keep most things. Some she took back. Like a few picture frames and her little sheep.

With a promise from Basil to send her more details on his idea, Ashley and Jordan continue on their walk. Jordan kept up a steady stream of monologue with Ashley adding in her 'uh huh, yeah, sounds good' comments.

There's so much going through Ashley's head as they pass the different stores. She's trying to stay present, and in the moment, but she can't stop noticing things she will have to address soon.

She is so proud of how people have embraced all the changes, but there is still so much to do...and the one thing that really stands out is that they are so behind on so many projects.

From going over the schedule as often as she has, she knows the number of projects they are behind on. Their timeline wasn't tight as it was, but more and more, she's seeing numerous items that are only partially completed or projects that haven't even been started.

Her muscles tighten, her shoulders tense, and her chest expands with pressure the more she sees what hasn't been done. They have a timeline for a reason, and even minor projects not being worked on can have a considerable impact.

It looks like she's going to have another talk with Durwood.

Maybe she should start pushing these meetings off to Marcus, or even Nigel. She has no idea why there's an obvious disconnect between her and Durwood, but it's there.

She knows the solution to her problem, or rather, she knows who the solution to her problem is...and her heart skips a beat as she realizes that answer is walking toward her right now.

CHAPTER THIRTY-SEVEN

MARLEE

After being engulfed in a hug that seems to last forever, Marlee looks at her friend, noticing a vast difference from the last time they were home.

As Ashley turns to Jared, there are telltale signs of stress and a slight hint of panic that gets overshadowed by a small measure of hope.

"I can't believe you are here," Ashley says after giving Jared a hug. "I've been struggling to figure out how to get back on track, how to handle your father...and you are here!"

Jared looks around. "No one really handles my father," he says.

Marlee hears the caution in his voice, but she knows Ashley is oblivious to it.

She knows something she's been keeping from her husband: Ashley is desperate to convince Jared to move home and work alongside his father. She has been begging Marlee to help her.

Everyone wants her help in convincing Jared to move back home. She wishes it were that easy.

"We're just here for the weekend," Marlee injected before Jared can say anything else. "The kids are here for a sleepover with Josie and joining in on some classes," she explains. "Josie kicked us out of the house, so we thought we'd take a walk and see the progress." She takes Jared's hand in hers and squeezes it tightly.

"It looks great," Jared says, his voice garbled like he's trying to speak past the boulder lodged in his throat.

"Your dad has done a great job," Ashley says.

The 'but' that is coming next almost doesn't need to be said.

"It's exactly what this town needs." Marlee stopping Ashley from saying what they all know anyway. "I can't believe how far along you are." The lie in her words lay there at their feet.

Will any of them pick it up and confront it? Speak the truth? What could possibly be said?

It's impossible to hide just how far behind Durwood is. So many projects are half completed, things that Jared pointed out as almost done or other comments like he would have done it this way or that way.

"Dad's a handful, isn't he?" Jared finally utters the question Marlee knows he doesn't want an answer to.

Marlee is actually surprised he even asked it...knowing it's not a question he wants answered. Hearing the answer means he'll take responsibility for an outcome she's not sure he wants.

Seeing the struggle Durwood may be having is different than actually being told he's struggling. The former...Jared can ignore. The latter – he won't. She knows her husband too well.

The way Ashley's lips quirk says it all.

"I wish I could help you, honestly, but..." Jared lifts his shoulders in a shrug, and Marlee has a funny feeling he's hoping this is the end of the conversation.

He should know better.

"You could help by taking over," Ashley says the thing that needs to be said. "Please? Your father is great with ideas and saving money, but..." she lifts her hands and points toward the many unfinished projects in view.

"It's not that he's too old for the scope of what we need, but..." Ashley doesn't finish her sentence, letting the words trail off and hang there, like a string that, if pulled from a sweater, could cause irreparable damage.

"Until he realizes he's out of control, there's nothing you can do. Unless you take the project from him entirely and hand it over to someone else. Another firm maybe," Jared suggests.

Marlee stares at her husband, trying to decipher his thoughts but unable to. His face is a mask of indifference, making her extremely uncomfortable.

What is he thinking?

"I won't take it from him, not like that. I just...well, could you talk to him, maybe?" Ashley asks.

Marlee chuckles, she can't help it. Jared is obviously surprised by her outburst, but it doesn't take long before his lips tug upward. Ashley's as well.

"Okay, okay...I realize he probably doesn't want your offer of help or suggestions. Your father tends to be a bit...difficult when it's pointed out he's in the wrong," she says with a little shrug.

"Listen," Jared leans his head one way then the other, looking up and down the street as if trying to determine which direction to go with what he's about to say.

Marlee hopes he goes in the direction that will ultimately lead them back home, here, to Innsbruck.

"The best way to deal with my father is to be practical. He won't listen to emotion. Make a list of the issues and possible solutions, or...ask him for solutions and ways to fix his mistakes. That's the smarter option, in my opinion. Make a list," Jared continues, "of the things he's behind on, the things that remain incomplete, and then remind him he probably agreed to a schedule -"

"He provided one," Ashley interrupts.

"Then ask him what he plans to do to get back on schedule."

It takes everything for Marlee not to laugh at the way Ashley's lips thin. She can read everything her friend wants to say but isn't.

The way Jared lists out the solution seems simple enough, but the three of them know it won't be that easy.

"Why can't you just help him? He's your father. You're his son. Why can't you work together as a family?" This simple question comes from Jordan, who has, up until now, remained silent at her mother's side.

Out of the mouth of babes...Marlee has to turn slightly away to hide her smile.

"Have you ever worked on something only to have your mom or dad attempt to tell you to do it differently?" Jared asks her.

Jordan thinks about it for a moment before she nods. "Yeah, I get it, but still...you are family. You should try to work together."

Ashley places her arm around Jordan's shoulders and leans her head gently against her daughter's. "If only it were that easy," Ashley says.

"It should be." Jordan counters.

The look Ashley gives Marlee is priceless. Like mother like daughter.

"Families are always difficult, but I think Jordan's on to something," Marlee says. "The simplest solution is often the best one." She gives her husband a quick little jab on his arm, but he ignores her.

"Sorry guys," Ashley gives them both a sheepish look, "this

is my problem, and I need to deal with it head-on rather than trying to get others to do it for me." She twists her wrist to look at her watch. "Jordan, if we hope to get some of those croissants from Frankie, we'd better get our butts in gear."

"Tell her to save some for us." Marlee's stomach rumbles. "We'll need a big box of her baking to take home. I've missed it," she admits. The idea of indulging in Frankie's muffins, desserts, and cookies has her mouthwatering.

"I'll mention you'll be along," Ashley says, giving Marlee another quick hug. "You have no idea how much I've missed you," she whispers.

Marlee pulls away. "I've missed you too. Phone calls just aren't enough, are they?"

Marlee feels the deep, shoulder-dropping sigh, Ashley releases. "Please, think about coming home? Not," she looks directly at Jared, "just to work with your dad. There are other things you could do, you know? In fact, I've got a whole note-book full of ideas for businesses if you are interested."

She leaves that tidbit of info there for them to consider as she walks away.

It takes everything for Marlee to remain silent, not call Ashley back, and not badger Jared about the possibility and probability of returning home. Her grip on his hand tightens, though, as excitement builds up inside her, thinking about what they could do, things they've discussed,...gah, the words just want to pour out of her mouth, but she can't.

Not yet.

Not as their footsteps inevitably lead them toward the main square where Durwood is working.

He's surrounded by tools, wood, and copious coffee cups. A tarp lay on the grass, a saw bench in the middle, and a makeshift table on the edge. Durwood has his back to them, bent over the table with a pencil stuck behind his ear.

He's also very much alone, which has Jared mumbling too low for Marlee to make out what he's saying.

"Hey, Dad," Jared calls out as they approach from the side.

Durwood's head lifts, and for a brief second, Marlee swears she sees a smile before he quickly masks it into a frown.

"Come to check up on me, have you?" His gruff voice is enough of a push to get rid of most people, most people but family. Marlee recognizes his gruffness as a mask.

"Mom kicked us out of the house," Jared answers honestly. "Plus, I've been wanting to see how far you've come along, see it with my own eyes, rather than just through the photos mom sends."

Durwood stands there, arms crossed, saying nothing.

Jared takes his time, really paying attention to his father's work. "You've done a great job, Dad." His voice breaks with only a hint of emotion, but Marlee catches it. So does Durwood.

Durwood clears his throat, shuffling his feet before his lips turn back into a grimace. "Glad it meets your approval." He then turns from them and refocuses on the drawing on his table.

Marlee is more than happy to remain in the background while father and son attempt to find some solid ground.

Jared joins him over at the table, and Marlee follows, wanting to see what Durwood is so focused on. It's a drawing of something unrecognizable to her, but from the nod on her husband's face, he clearly gets what he's looking at.

"You gonna offer a solution or just stand there like a fool," Durwood grumbles.

Marlee zones the men out and relaxes on one of the folding chairs as they discuss measurements and whatever else. Everything looks so different from the last time they'd been home.

The change is substantial, enough so that she catches the passion behind the vision, feels the drive everyone in town seems to have. From the trees covered in lights, wreaths hanging on doors and signs, the displays in store windows that scream Christmas... it's all there. She sees it, feels it, and breaths it all in.

There's a desperation inside of her to be part of this change, so much so, that she chokes up for a moment and dabs at the tears pooling at the corners of her eyes. This is home. Jared must see it, feel it, too, doesn't he? She's at a loss of what else she can do, what else she can say to convince her stubborn husband that this is where they belong.

She didn't realize how much time had passed until Jared pats her on the shoulder. "Mom called – she needs you to stop at Frankie's before you head home."

She lets him pull her up from the chair. "You coming too?"

He shakes his head. "I'll stay and help Dad a bit. He may seem grumpy, but I think he appreciates the help. I'm not sure why he's alone today."

"Maybe because it's the weekend?"

He frowns. "If they're behind, then they need to put in the hours to catch up. He could have a skeleton crew on at least, rather than insisting on doing it all himself." He threads his fingers through his hair. "He's as stubborn as..."

"As you." Marlee finishes for him. "Like father like son. If it were your crew, you'd have told them to enjoy the weekend with their families too."

He looks like he's going to argue, stopping himself just in time before he says something ridiculous. They both know she's right, only because he's done that very thing time and time again.

"Don't be late, okay?" She's glad he's staying behind, helping Durwood. Healing has to start somewhere.

"We won't. Mom gave strict instructions we are to be home for dinner."

If there's one thing Marlee knows about the Holms men, when Josie gives an order, they jump and ask questions later.

Marlee takes a mental photo of the two men working side by side. Regardless of how much Jared complains about his dad, this is where he's most happy...working side by side with the man who taught him everything. He isn't happy living in the city, struggling to make ends meet. She's not either.

Somehow, she needs to make the idea of moving back home their reality. She just isn't sure how.

CHAPTER THIRTY-EIGHT

Taking the dish Josie hands her to dry, Marlee remains quiet, knowing now is not the time for small talk.

It's not just the way Josie pinched her lips together as she angrily scrubs the dishes in the soapy sink but also in her sharp, tight, and quick movements.

Josie hasn't said a single word since they started cleaning the kitchen, but she hasn't needed to either.

Even while she and Jared started dating, Marlee learned two things about Josie: when she's angry, she's hard to handle, but when she's quiet angry, Josie is downright dangerous.

"We'll wait for Grandpa and Dad before we have cake, right?" Julian stands in the doorway, his hands dangling at his sides.

Josie's head lifts, and a bitter smile grows over a clamped jaw. "Of course, sweetheart. We'll wait for the two knuckle-heads. I'm sure they'll be here soon. You've all been a great help. Now run outside for a bit, all right?"

The kids leave one by one until it's just Josie and Marlee in the kitchen.

Marlee waits to see if Josie will say something first, but the woman is still too focused on scrubbing dishes to say a word.

"All right, Josie. What gives?"

"I was very clear with that son of mine. I wanted them both here for dinner." Josie dips another dish in a hot sink full of water and bleach and hands it to Marlee. "What's so important they have to miss a meal with their family? It's not every day you guys are here to visit, and I'd like a proper meal. Is that too much to ask? They'd better come up with an excuse better than their phones died. I swear..."

She stops as angry voices drift in through the kitchen screen door. Marlee notices Jared and Durwood approaching them, their voices rising the closer they get until they stop and face one another, their hands flinging about in all directions as they attempt to get some sort of point across.

Marlee glances at Josie, who's watching the interaction with an intense frown.

"Want me to interrupt?" Marlee asks.

"You'll probably be politer than me," Josie says.

Marlee tosses the dish towel over her shoulder and heads to the door. She hesitates, listening for a break in their argument before shoving the door open and popping her head out.

"You're late. I'd suggest you leave whatever you are arguing about right here at the door and deal with it later after you've both cooled off." Marlee holds the door open with her hand, indicating to the two frowning men that they need to enter and enter quick.

Jared has the decency to look ashamed.

Durwood just grumbles as he walks past her. He casts an unreadable look toward Josie before muttering something about cleaning up and heading up the back stairs to their bedroom.

Marlee returns to her post beside Josie at the sink, taking the next dish Josie hands her, wiping it clean with circular motions, as Jared stands there looking sheepish.

"I don't ask for much from you, Jared Holms. So, when I ask that you be here for a family dinner," Josie emphasizes the word *family,* "am I making an unreasonable demand? No, I don't think I am."

Jared is smart enough to just nod his head. "You're right. I'm sorry, Mom."

"You need to apologize to your wife and children too. You both let us down, and that's not acceptable."

"Don't you think you're—"

Josie splashes him with water from the sink. "Don't you dare finish that sentence," she warns him, her voice vibrating with pent-up emotion.

Jared glances toward Marlee, but she looks away. Nope, she wasn't getting involved in this.

"Go get cleaned up. Your children made a cake."

They made it through the dessert with little fanfare. The kids seemed to understand something was going on, so as soon as they could escape the room, they did. Every so often, Marlee would catch silent exchanges of frustration between Jared and his father, followed by Josie slapping Durwood on the arm.

It's not until later that Marlee corners Jared. "Is everything okay?"

"Mom hasn't been that mad at me in a long time," Jared says.

"Jared, she was vibrating with anger. What's going on? We called, texted...why didn't you answer?"

"Dad and I..." he shakes his head, fists clenched tight but doesn't finish his sentence.

"Dad and I...what? Were you too caught up in work? Actually, getting along? Lost track of time? Had someone stop by, and you were chatting?" She tries to imagine what could have detained them for more than an hour.

"We were fighting." Jared runs his fingers through his hair. He drops down onto one of the kitchen chairs and leans back, tipping the chair, so it's only on two legs.

"It won't work, Marlee."

"What won't work?" This is not what she wants to hear.

"Us. Here. With Dad. It won't work. He...I know you...I just can't..."

Marlee holds up a hand, stopping his stuttered attempt of an explanation.

"What did you and your father argue about?" She asks. She isn't going to spend time guessing since it could be any number of subjects that set them off. Or rather, set Durwood off.

"What didn't we argue about? He asked for suggestions but then would tell me why those suggestions were wrong," Jared sighs. "But the main argument was over why he's so behind. He's got a million and one reasons, but any time I offered up a solution, he'd wave his hand, dismissing me each time."

"Sounds to me like you butted heads over male pride," Marlee offers a suggestion that is probably closer to the truth than either male wants to admit.

The downward tilt of Jared's lips confirms her suspicions.

"He created a schedule with the expectation he'd have men who knew what they were doing, men who knew their way around tools and diagrams and drawings. Men who could take a measurement, who understood even the simplest of functions, but...."

"But what?"

Both Marlee and Jared turn at the sound of Durwood's voice.

"Go on...but what? Since you're Mr. Big Time City now. You've got all the answers, haven't you?"

Jared lets out a long groan, raking his hands through his disheveled hair before he pounds the table with his fist.

"There'll be none of that," Josie says, following behind her husband. "Why do you have to be so cantankerous," she says to Durwood, "and why do you have to be so stubborn?" She asks this of Jared.

"You need a crew who knows what they're doing," Jared says.

Durwood grumbles something under his breath.

"Well, no one can hear that, can they?" Josie throws her hands up before taking four coffee cups from a cabinet and placing them on the table. She reaches for the coffee canister and fills each of their cups. "If we're going to settle this, then we need to start acting like adults."

"Nothing needing to be settled. Mr. Big Shot here will head back to the city, and I'll continue what I'm doing...my bit to save this town." Durwood's lips clothes lined shut as he takes a cup and holds it between his hands. "Would prefer beer," he mutters.

"Coffee is all you need. Be good, and I might let you have some Bailey's," Josie pats his shoulder, the touch a tad harder than her normal pats.

Josie sets the chocolate Luxe Bailey's down on the table with table cream and spoons, then pulls out a chair opposite Marlee. The look on her face says no one is leaving the table until things have been discussed.

The Queen of the Holms family has taken control.

"I just want to help," Jared starts the conversation, his voice softer than before.

"Help? By telling me what I'm doing wrong? How is that being helpful? That's just judgment, and I thought I raised you better than that." Durwood's frown covers his face, from the deep furrowed brows to the downward slant of his eyes.

"Then help me to understand."

Durwood grunts.

"Oh, for Pete's sake," Josie's voice carries the frustration they all feel up a notch. "Jared, your father is doing the best he can with the people he has. Surely you, of all people, can understand that. We don't want Mayor Ashley to be hiring an outside firm, we want the money used for Innsbruck to stay within Innsbruck, and a lot of the people here could use that help." She takes the bottle of Bailey's and pours a generous amount into her cup.

"Does the Mayor know you have a crew full of newbies?" Jared asks this question to Durwood.

The look on Durwood's face hasn't changed. "She knows I'm hiring townsfolk."

"But does she understand what that means?" Jared leans forward, arms resting on the table as his full attention is focused on his father.

Marlee understands what Jared is trying to get at. At least, she thinks she does.

"Hiring local is awesome," she says, trying to create some retainable sense of peace. "But that must be daunting, Durwood, to constantly train the men. It's probably why you're so behind, isn't it?"

Again, Durwood just grunts.

Josie huffs a sigh.

"Who on your crew is helping you, Dad? You can't be doing it all..." he then leans backward, the frustration etched on his face from earlier gone, and in its place is exasperation.

There's a fine line between frustration and exasperation, but the line is there.

"I don't need that tone from you," Durwood says, his voice rising. "I'm doing what I can with what I have." His lips pinch together until they resemble a stitched wound.

"But does Ashley know and understand?"

"Do you think I like being behind? Stop micromanaging me. I've got this covered." Durwood pushes his chair back, the bottom scraping on the floor with a loud screech sound.

Everyone remains silent as Durwood leaves, the screen door slamming behind him as he heads toward his garage.

"Go to him," Josie says to Jared.

"Why? He doesn't want to hear anything I have to say."

Josie takes her son's hand in hers. "Then listen. Just...listen. You don't always have to have the answers." The look she gives him has him pushing back his own chair, grabbing both his and his father's coffee mugs, and taking them outside.

Marlee wants to say something...to tell her husband that his mom is right, that he doesn't have to try to fix everything, but she remains silent, sipping her coffee instead.

"It's obvious those who bull-headed men of ours need help fixing this situation," Josie said, giving Marlee a deep nod of her head. "I think I know the answer too."

Intrigued, Marlee rests her elbows on the table and holds her cup, waiting for whatever idea Josie has.

"If Durwood won't ask for Jared's help, fine. Let him fix the situation himself. But I want my grandbabies back home, which means we need to figure out how to make that happen. I've been thinking...remember those cabins we'd discussed?"

Marlee's eyes widen with excitement, having an idea of where Josie is going with this.

"I think I figured out a way to make that idea happen."

CHAPTER THIRTY-NINE

MIA

Curled up on her couch with a glass of red wine in hand, Mia pulls up a text from Ashley.

We should discuss the upcoming Christmas market soon.

Yes, they should. The next market is only a few months away, and they've already rented out at least seventy-five percent of their stalls.

Whenever you're ready. Mia texts back.

She pulls out her laptop and opens her market spreadsheet. Most everyone has placed their deposits for the stalls. She just needs to send out a final reminder for payment before she opens those stalls back up to the waiting list.

After last year's success, they had almost double the number of requests from vendors, and then as word continues to spread, more and more requests come in.

The last thing Mia wants for this market is to feel like it's an outdoor dollar store with cheap trinkets bought in bulk from overseas. She carefully vets each vendor, wanting to ensure the wares being sold are distinct, hand-made, and not something found during a shopping spree in the city.

Within minutes, Ashley calls, and they quickly switch to video since they both seem to be on their computers. Mia moves from the couch to her kitchen table, pours herself a new glass of wine, and pulls out a notebook.

"I was thinking," Ashley begins, which has Mia groaning.

"Please stop. Every time you say that, you add something more to my list of to-do's, and honestly, we're out of time adding new things."

Ashley leans in close to the screen, her face filling the screen. "That's fair, but I promise this is a good idea."

Mia leans back and crosses her arms. "Let's hear it then, but I may use my veto card and tell you no."

"How long is your waiting list?"

Mia doesn't have to look at the number, considering she just looked at the list.

"I've about twenty-five applications waiting. Why?" The suspicion in her voice is genuine. Ashley isn't about to suggest what she thinks she is, right? There's no time.

"Why don't we ask Matt to build more stalls for us? There's room in the park, and—"

Mia leans in close so all Ashley can see on the screen is her face.

"Are you kidding me?"

No. No, no, no, no. She will not ask Matt to build more stalls, let alone over twenty of them. Is Ashley crazy? There's not enough time.

"I'm serious. Thanks to Durwood, we've got the wood all ready, so it shouldn't take too much, right?"

Breathe in through the nose, breathe out through the mouth. Count to five before you even think of answering...remain calm...

Mia repeats this to herself rather than vomiting all her reasons why this was a bad idea to Ashley.

"Whatever you want to say, let it go. Seriously, Mia, it's a good idea. If Matt can't do it, we can ask Durwood's crew, or even Jared...he might take on the project."

This catches Mia's attention. Does this mean Jared and Marlee are moving back?

"It's not just the wood, Ashley. It's the facades, the lights, the greenery, redesigning the layout to accommodate the new stalls..." even as she says it, she knows how weak her argument is.

"I seem to remember Matt giving me a detailed inventory, and I've even a note that we had excess design elements," Ashley counters.

"Okay, but..."

"But what? Come on, Mia, this is a no-brainer, don't you think?"

Mia hems and haws, trying to figure out what exactly she is objecting to.

"It's not Matt, is it? Cause if there's something going on between the two of you, like I said, we can ask Durwood's crew or Jared...."

"Something going on? No, absolutely not. Why would you say that?" Flustered, Mia grabs her ponytail and plays with the strands falling over her shoulder.

The look Ashley gives her is priceless.

"Fess us, Mia. What's going on?"

Mia stops playing with her ponytail and grabs her wine glass, taking a long sip.

"I've got all night, girl. Jordan is upstairs, and I just opened up a bottle of prosecco."

Mia gives off another groan, reaches for her own wine bottle, and shows it to her friend.

"Take another drink then and spill the beans. What's going on between you two?"

Mia does precisely that, but instead of a simple sip, she drains the rest of her glass and then refills it...again.

"Nothing. Absolutely nothing is happening between us." She gives a very long sigh, one that starts in her bones and is felt throughout every single vein. "He's working on some projects for my parents right now, and he's there every time I drop by. Like, every single time, Ash."

"That's great – gives you two time to get to know each other, right? Small talk and all that."

Mia snorts. Yeah, like that's happening.

"I'm more of a prickly pear. Everything I say comes out wrong, to the point that if he had any hint of interest, I've probably wiped it out. I mean...he was very clear last year when we were getting things ready for the market that he wasn't interested, so why would I think he is now?" The embarrassment from that interchange is still very real, still very present, and still very cringe-worthy.

That look of surprise on his face, how he turned beat red and turned away from her, then started packing up his tools and throwing out his distinct *no* over his shoulder before hopping in his truck and leaving her in the dust.

"Have you asked him?"

Mia closes her eyes, not appreciating the simple and direct response.

"No, of course, I haven't asked. Getting turned down once was enough, thank-you-very-much. Can we change the subject now, please?"

"Well...since you see him often, can you ask him about putting together more stalls?"

"Come on, Ash," she seriously did not just ask her to do that.

"Fine, I will, but I want you to contact those on the waiting list and see if at least fifteen to twenty would be interested."

Fifteen to twenty? Does she understand what she's asking?

"Ashley, for some on the list, there's not enough time for them to procure enough stock. That's not being fair to them."

"It doesn't hurt to ask, though, right? You don't know if they have enough stock or not...."

Mia wants to roll her eyes but doesn't.

"Just see, okay?" Ashley asks. "Susan says she's been seeing threads in different groups she's in online that people are looking for last-minute openings to markets, so the interest is there. Susan can even put a call out, if you want, just in case?"

"Fine. I'll send out the email and see what happens. But you'll talk to Matt, right?"

The smile on Ashley's face grows. "Thank you. This year is going to be amazing; I know it. So many businesses are gearing up for the season, it'll be our first one looking like a partially put together Bavarian town – I'm excited. You've got all your stock, right?"

Mia nods. "My backroom is overflowing with shipments. You should see the stuff I have for my stall and my shop."

Ashley rubs her hands together, like a kid finding out she gets two treats instead of one. "I can't wait to see it all. Oh...that reminds me. Susan was asking about your shop, she says you haven't submitted your ideas on how to rebrand, but she's got you on the list...so... what's going on?"

Augh. She's so not wanting to discuss this right now. Mia rolls her neck, hearing the cracking as she stretches the muscles. "That's because I can't decide on what I'm going to do."

"What do you mean you can't decide? I thought we'd talked about this? You had a page full of ideas...."

Mia shrugs. "Nothing is really speaking to me, you know?"

"No, I don't. Why haven't you mentioned this before?" Ashley's voice is full of concern and worry.

She doesn't like knowing her friend is worried about her. Considering all that Ashley has on her plate – from her divorce to the town...she doesn't need to add one more thing.

"I can't seem to commit to one definite idea. I mean...I could do Santa's living room where Mrs. Claus reads kids' books, or I just have a dedicated Christmas book section, or I turn the whole store into a Christmas bookshop or...I don't know, Ash. I know I need to get more involved; I know I do, but I just...the idea feels overwhelming."

Mia looks away from the screen, thinking about that page where she'd written down all those ideas. Where had she placed it? She glances behind her toward an old antique cabinet she refinished a few years ago.

"Hang on, will you?" Not waiting for Ashley's reply, she gets up and heads to that cabinet, opening drawers and rooting through all the papers.

"What are you looking for?" Ashley asks.

"Ideas. I know I have that piece of paper somewhere...."

"You don't need that paper, Mia. Come back to the computer," Ashley says.

Mia stops rooting around in the drawers and looks over her shoulder toward the screen. Ashley is sipping at her wine, waiting.

"Go back to the beginning. Your first idea to me was to become a Christmas bookshop. I remember how alive you became every time you discussed the different ways you could transform areas in your store. You were going to create an elf room for the kids, a fireplace area, a kitchen area with cookbooks and some hardware...remember?"

Mia can't stop nodding. Of course, she remembers. She also remembers how overwhelming all that feels.

"You can't do it all at once. That would be ridiculous, but one area at a time, right?"

Mia rubs her face, a sure sigh she's getting tired. "Tell Susan I'll get back to her, okay?"

She signs off, considers shutting down the computer and climbing into bed with a good book to read, but she can't stop thinking about how to transform her store.

Ashley is right. Way back when, when they were spitballing about what they'd love to do... she'd mentioned if she owned a shop in one of the German towns they loved to visit, she'd make it all about Christmas – Christmas stories, cookbooks, gifts... Christmas all the time.

So, what's stopping her? Lack of vision? Lack of energy? Lack of...what?

The transition wouldn't be all at once, and she has a lot of products as it is...she could ask Matt if he'd be interested in another odd job too...

She must start to embrace all the change. She needs to. This version of her isn't one she likes... she's always been gung-ho, the first to volunteer to help, and this version of her that's stuck in the mud, grumpy, and not embracing change... it's a version that needs to disappear.

She searches up Christmas bookshop ideas, but all she gets is actual book titles.

Well, that's not going to work... she's a visual person and needs to see some actual display ideas for her imagination to take over.

Her fingers start their tap dance along the keyboard, and as she pulls up image after image, an idea begins to form, one she finds herself getting excited about.

CHAPTER FORTY

ASHLEY

Ashley manages to step out of the office without anyone stopping her, a feat unheard of for the past few weeks, especially on a Monday.

Susan saw and just waved her off with a smile.

There are benefits to having a competent office manager on staff.

She skips down the steps of Town Hall, sidestepping a couple looking at something on their phone, and makes her way down to Gingerbread Tea Room, a new tea shop close to opening.

The theme is a Lebkuchenhaus, a gingerbread house focusing on all things gingerbread. Even thinking about it brings a smile to Ashley's face. When Gabriella first came to her with the idea, Ashley hadn't been sold. Frankie convinced her that having multiple bakeries, coffee shops, and restaurants would benefit the town.

Every small town needs a tearoom, is what Frankie said.

Ashley agrees, especially now that she's here and she sees what it entails.

The shop resembles everything you'd expect from a gingerbread house, all the way down to the white icing decorations around the windows and doors. The framework around the doors looks like candy canes, with cutouts of gingerbread men for corner pieces and what she assumes to be gumdrops lining the bottom of the walls.

Inside, well, it's candy heaven. Calling this a tearoom doesn't cut it. There's so much more to this little shop, so much that she loves. Shelves lining the walls with jars full of candy, china cabinets and tables holding an assortment of handmade and wood gingerbread houses – with kits for sale. There are even heart-shaped gingerbreads hung from the walls, much like you'd see in a traditional German Christmas Market.

"Well?" Gabby asks, a wide smile on her face.

Ashley can't get over how amazing it all looks. "How soon till you're open? This is amazing." She knows this shop will be a hit, probably one of the more profitable businesses to open.

"Next weekend, actually. Just waiting on a shipment of tables and chairs, plus some quaint dinnerware I was able to order from a supplier straight from Europe." Gabby rubs her hands together in excitement. "Remember that one room I'd said I wanted to create? Come look..." She leads Ashley around the corner and stops at the edge of a smallish room.

The room is outfitted with a large table that takes up the middle of the room. She immediately knows this to be a classroom considering all the icing equipment on the table.

Each wall holds three extended white shelves. The far wall has been fitted with a sink and cabinets. Hooks with adorable aprons hang on a separate wall along with a cubby space, which Ashley assumes is meant for students to store their bags and such.

"You're really going to hold gingerbread-making classes?" Ashley's mouth salivates with anticipation. She remembers making gingerbread men with her grandmother as a child and can still taste the molasses cookie on her tongue, and smell that sweet aroma as her grandmother mixed all the ingredients from a recipe passed down from mother to daughter.

She needs to make those cookies with Jordan this year.

"Sure am. And thank you for Sylvia's information, too. I've been in touch, and we've been working on some creative ways to advertise."

Ashley breathes in a shuttered breath, unable to contain all the excitement coursing through her. It's one thing to have already existing businesses embrace the new vision, but it's another to have new businesses begin because of that new vision.

It's exciting and scary all at the same time. What if this all fails? What if something goes wrong and stops everything in its tracks?

"Will you let me know if there is anything I can do to help?" Ashley asks, breathing in the scent of gingerbread spice.

"Actually..." Gabby links her arm with Ashley and leads her back to the main room, "I was hoping you'd be in one of my first classes? We could make a gingerbread house together? I've lined up someone from both the local and city paper to be in attendance as well. It would make for great PR."

The idea sounds like something Sylvia would suggest. If that's the case, Ashley has a feeling she'd be taking part in all of the classes soon to open within the community.

"Of course I will! I have fond memories of making gingerbread with my grandmother," Ashley says as she eyed one of the large hearts that hang from hooks on the walls. "You know, I remember seeing photos of similar hearts from different

Christmas Markets in Germany when I was doing some research. Did you make those yourself?"

"The Lebkuchen? Of course, I did." Gabby sounds almost affronted at the question. "They're a staple when it comes to Christmas Markets. The most popular recipe is really inedible, in my opinion, but these ones aren't that bad. Want one?" She reaches for a large heart with the edges outlined in icing ruffles and the word Danke written in icing in the middle. "Some have words in German, others in English."

Ashley takes the heart and heads to one of the cabinets, where various loose teas are located. "Will you be selling tea to go, or is the focus on table seating?"

Gabby joins her at the cabinet and lifts a lid off one of the jars. "I plan to have a small take-out section by the door, just waiting on all the equipment to arrive. I had thought about having a small window open to the outside so people can order on the go, but then they wouldn't see everything we offered," she gives a slight shrug. "I'm going to have different gingerbread houses on display along with the tea service."

"Coffee too?"

Gabby shakes her head. "Tea and gingerbread only. I know, I know... I'm limiting myself, but..." she glances around the room, and Ashley can see that her heart is here.

"No, you're making yourself exclusive. There's a difference. I think it's a good idea," Ashley says, fully confident in Gabby's idea. "I'll be here often for tea; you can be sure of that."

Gabby's arms wrap around Ashley. "I can't thank you enough," she says, her voice filling with emotion that tears Ashley's eyes. "This is something I've always wanted to do, and you made it possible." Gabby gives her an extra squeeze before releasing her. "There's no way I could have afforded to open this store in the city."

Ashley wipes her eyes, not afraid to show her emotions.

"Anything I can do to help, I'm here. I want you to be success-ful, I truly mean that."

Gabby nods, swallowing hard. "Actually...I do need help with another thing. I just hate to bring it up." She bites her lip, and Ashley can tell whatever she's about to say won't be easy... not just for her to say but for Ashley to hear.

Her stomach churns as she waits for the inevitable shoe to drop. It has to, doesn't it? Nothing can ever just work in her favor. There has to be one thing or another pop up to catch her off guard.

"It's the outside façade. I have a vision for what I think it should look like, which I laid out clearly in my proposal to you when we first met. Do you remember? I wanted it to look like a real gingerbread house?" Gabby leads her to the front door and outside, so they stand on the sidewalk.

"I remember. I thought it was a charming idea, different than what we had for other stores, and would help to make your shop stand out," Ashley says.

"Mr. Holms doesn't agree," Gabby says, saying the words Ashley really doesn't want to hear.

Her heart sinks as she forces the frustration that floods her to flee from her face. She pastes what she hopes is a *tell-me-more* kind of smile to her lips.

"I want it to look like dripping frosted icicles are hanging from the top, but he refuses, saying that it's too complicated of a look and that it would put him behind even more than he already is." She won't look Ashley in the eyes as she says this, as if complaining about Durwood is the last thing she wants to do.

What Ashley wants to say and what she can say are two completely different things.

"I was hoping," Gabby says, stopping her from saying anything at all, "if it would be okay if my family took over finishing up instead? My brother does woodworking on the side, and my Dad is a painter, and they've both offered to come and help me on the weekend. My brother doesn't think it would be too much to do." Gabby's voice holds that *please let me do this* plea.

"Of course," Ashley said, pleased she's able to keep her voice upbeat and positive, whereas inside, she's fuming with fury she can't wait to unleash on Durwood Holms.

Gabby sags with relief. "Oh, thank you." Her cell starts to ring then. "Will you excuse me? That's my father now. I'll let him know we have the go-ahead."

Ashley waves goodbye as Gabby rushes back into her shop. Without thinking, Ashley makes her way down the street until she's standing in front of Frankie's shop. She pushes open the door and sits at one of the empty tables, not really paying attention to anyone or anything around her.

By the time she notices anything, Frankie has already placed a cup of coffee in front of her. Josie is seated across from her, both women waiting patiently for Ashley to be ready to speak.

"I haven't seen you this angry in a long time," Frankie says, her voice full of worry. She reaches out and gently touches Ashley's hand.

Ashley blinks away the cascading tears gathering in her eyes. She isn't angry, she's furious and frustrated and full of so many things she can't put words to.

First things first,...why is Josie here?

"Have you guys been to the new gingerbread tea house?" There's a mixture of excitement and exasperation in her voice, but she tries hard to ensure the enthusiasm comes through.

Frankie nods. "I love it," she says, her warm smile softening the worry on her face. "Gabriella has done such a great job. We've chatted over shared recipes and ideas for classes and whatnot."

"So, you're not concerned about competition?" Josie's hands wrap around her mug of coffee, her tone suggesting something Ashley can't quite put her finger on.

Does she know what's going on? Does she understand why Ashley is so frustrated?

Frankie laughs a full-throttle kind of laughter that is almost infectious.

"I asked her the same thing too," Ashley offers.

"Take it to the bank and make a full withdrawal," Frankie adds. "I think her idea of having a gingerbread tea house to be fantastic. It's perfect for our new vision, don't you think? She showed me the drawings for how she wants it to look on the outside, too, it's an honest-to-goodness gingerbread house most kids would die to make."

And there it is. The issue at hand. "Would be nice if it looks like that too. Will it? That's a different question."

Frankie's eyes narrow as she leans forward. "What's that supposed to mean?"

Josie's eyes widen. "Oh, he didn't...." She whispers loud enough to have Ashley nod.

"That's why you're so upset. My husband isn't playing nice."

Ashley doesn't really feel the need to answer.

Josie's lips mesh together as she plants her palms straight on the table. She pushes down hard, her fingertips going white from the pressure.

"Whoa, there," Frankie mutters.

"That man just doesn't know when to accept he needs help," Josie grumbles, her cheekbones pulsing with what Ashley could only attribute to frustration.

It was nice to know she isn't alone when it comes to that feeling and Durwood.

"Please tell me Jared is moving back home." Ashley presses

her index finger tight to her forehead. She's starting to get a headache, and that's the last thing she needs right now.

"I'm trying," Josie says.

Frankie clears her throat. "I think you need to work harder, love. That man of yours is ruffling quite a lot of feathers lately."

Josie gathers up her purse, which has Ashley reaching out.

"Please don't leave, Josie." She doesn't want the woman to think she's mad at or blames her for Durwood.

In all honesty, this is all on her. She knew Durwood would be a handful. She just didn't realize how bad it could get.

"Oh honey, don't you worry. I need to head to the doctor's office." She brushes her hand in the air. "He wants to place me on new blood pressure pills, but between the three of us, it's not the medication I need to alleviate stress."

Frankie stands and places her arms around Josie in a hug.

"He has a heart of gold, you know that, right?" Josie asks of Ashley.

Of course, she knows that. He's placed this town first and foremost, and she's so grateful for everything that man has done for this town.

She just wonders if he understands his own limitations - because to her, they're as clear as the sky on a warm summer day.

"Oh, he's aware. He's also too stubborn to admit them in public." Josie says.

A flush of heat rises on Ashley's face. She didn't mean to say that out loud.

"It doesn't help that he's also working with a crew that...are limited on their own, right?" Josie continues. "He will only hire local, you know that. Unfortunately, not everyone he has hired has the experience needed. It's why he's so behind."

"And probably the reason for some of the changes he's made

lately," Ashley muses, understanding more and more. It all makes sense, every single thing.

"He never said a word to me, Josie. I wish he had."

"Of course, he hasn't," Josie scoffs. "He's a ball of frustration, I get it, but he's doing the best he can. I know he needs help. He knows he needs help, but he's also the last person who will ask for it." Her grip tightens around her purse. "I'm trying to get my son here, trying to mend a fence long broken...just give me a little time, please?"

CHAPTER FORTY-ONE

ASHLEY

It's not until end of day that Ashley manages to clear her desk so she can tackle a new project: Project Help Durwood Holms.

Enough is enough. She's tired of feeling frustrated, annoyed, and dealing with complaint after complaint after complaint. Obviously, their original timeline is garbage. They're so far behind that all they can do is look ahead, and she realizes the only way to keep a semblance of a timeline going is if she helps Durwood with it.

The question is how.

She's so glad Josie finally admitted why Durwood is so behind. It all makes sense. Her respect for him goes deeper knowing he's remained stoic in only hiring local help, even at the cost of completely missing deadlines.

She appreciates that he continues to stand by his words and goes beyond the pale to ensure things get done. She can understand that type of commitment.

What bothers her, throughout all of this, is the toll this

project seems to be taking...not just on him, but on his family, on her, on their town.

Maybe she made a mistake in not hiring outside help.

Earlier, she'd asked Susan to get copies of all the old and new drawings that Durwood is working with, and that's what Ashley's looking at now.

Her goal is to better understand the scope of work, as well as figuring out the changes Durwood seems to make without notifying her.

One of the things she's noticing is how simplified things are becoming. Ornate designs are simplistic in nature now. Sure, they can add and change things design-wise as time goes on, as their town grows and as more skilled workers move back home, but then they wouldn't be offering the magnificence of the vision for their town. She's okay with things being done in stages...but those stages must be completed to the best of their ability.

That's not happening – and she only has herself to blame. She should have been more on top of what's going on, known why Durwood is behind, caught on to the simplistic design changes, and stepped in a long time ago.

She's been more worried about a man's ego than anything else, which changes today. Today she takes over, pulls up her big-girl panties, and adjusts her mayor cap.

Today, she puts her foot down and makes sure she gets what she wants when it comes to this town.

What she wants is Jared Holms.

What she needs, what this town needs, is for the Holms men to work together.

She picks up her phone and makes a call.

It rang three times before a voice answers: "Mayor Ashley?"

She pauses, taking a moment to determine the reaction expressed in the voice. Is it surprise? Offense? Irritation? Or is it a mixture of hope and suspicion combined in one? She can't tell, to be honest. But then, when it comes to Jared, she's always had to rely on Marlee to read him.

"Jared. I hope I'm not calling at a bad time."

There's a moment of silence, followed by a slam of what sounds like a truck door.

"Just on break. I have a few minutes. What can I help you with?"

She lets out a gentle breath. "I think you know why I'm calling."

There's no reply.

Fine. "I want to officially offer you a job. Project supervisor."

Still more silence.

"I'm not firing your father, if that's the concern. More like... moving him into a new project management position, something that's more suited to his skill set."

The silence is getting awkward.

"I'd have you be hands-on, doing the work, watching over the men, helping as needed, hiring and such." She continues, the words tumbling from her lips as she struggles to fill the silence.

She just wants him to say yes.

"The pay is good. Your father isn't taking a pay, which he won't budge from, but you would. We'll take care of all moving expenses as well."

She realized the risk she's running, going behind Durwood's back and essentially offering his son his job, but she'll talk to him later. She has no doubt he'd be fine with it, even if he doesn't say so.

"What did my father say?"

Finally, he speaks.

"I haven't actually talked to him yet. I'm just going over the recent changes he's made, without approval, and realizing he doesn't have the help he needs. I'm working on that...first, by getting you here. Then, by trying to find more skilled laborers. The goal is to get families to return, families who have the skills needed to do the work."

"But my father doesn't know? He has no idea you've offered me his job?" His tone is less surprise and more disappointment.

That bothers her.

"I will tell him." She doesn't need Durwood's approval.

"It might backfire, you know. You, offering me this job, without talking to him?"

She nods, then realizes he can't see her. "Yes, but it won't." She hopes he hears the confidence she suddenly doesn't feel.

Why does she feel like she's doing something wrong? She's not. Durwood isn't in charge of this project. She is. If she needs to make changes, she will.

He doesn't say anything for several minutes, leaving her feeling extremely uncomfortable. She doodles in her notebook, her scribbles starting to look like *please and say yes*.

"I'll take the job, but on one condition," Jared says, his tone heavy with assumption.

Ashley almost drops the phone. She honestly never expected him to say yes so soon. She thought she'd have to give him time to think, consider, and weigh the options before he accepted.

Thank you and amen.

"What's the condition?" She's almost afraid to ask.

"You let me talk to my dad. We'll pretend this conversation didn't happen, for now."

His workaround, the one condition, is perfect. She feels terrible at first for not taking responsibility, which she has no problem doing, but hey...if he wants to do the heavy work at first, fine.

"If he asks me, I won't lie to him," she says. "I also don't need you to cover for me."

"I won't lie. I also won't cover. But I know my father better than you do, and if you want him to continue this project, you'll let me take the lead on this."

"Okay, then," Ashley finds herself smiling. "Welcome aboard," she couldn't hide the relief in her voice even if she tried. "How soon can you start?"

Jared chuckled. "Yesterday, if it were up to my wife and mother. Let me have a conversation with my father first, and I'll get back to you. Okay?"

In other words, keep this between them. She has no problem with that request and says so. By the time she hangs up, she's ready to dance a jig from excitement. She can't believe that worked but is so glad it did.

Knock-knock. Susan nudges the door open, a somber look on her face. "You busy?" She asks.

Ashley waves her assistant in. She gets up from her seat and joins Susan at the table where she spreads out all the drawings and plans for the town.

Susan will be just as ecstatic at this news as she is.

Susan points to the farm just outside of town. "We've got a problem," she starts.

Nope. No problems. She will not entertain any bad news, not right now.

"That's for another day. Listen, I have the best news...." She then told her the news of Jared moving back to help.

For the next few minutes, both women stand there, looking at one another with goofball expressions, believing all their problems have just been solved.

CHAPTER FORTY-TWO

MIA

Spending the morning going through the books, Mia tap-tap-taps her pen against the table as she reflects on the next stages of her store. Things are going well, better than anticipated if she were being honest. This is a nice feeling, one she hopes continues through the next few quarters.

She glances at the video feed and sees Ashley with Jordan entering the shop.

"Good thing I've got an update on the new vendors for the market," she mutters as she gathers all her papers. She had a feeling she'd be seeing Ashley at some point today.

"Just the person I was hoping to see," Ashley greets her as Mia closes her office door.

"I've got good news," Mia says, going through her papers to find the ones with all the new vendors listed. "You were right. People jumped at the chance to join the market. I've got a solid eighteen who have placed their deposits."

The smile on Ashley's face is bright and bolstered with confidence that's very Ashley-like.

"I knew it," Ashley says. "I chatted with Matt briefly, and he says he can start working on them this weekend and will have them done in time. Why don't we get together one night, and we can rework the vendor map together?"

Mia chuckles. She's way ahead of her. She pulls out another sheet, handing it over.

"Oh, you've already taken care of that...this looks great, and I love that you added another branch off the main market square. You know," Ashley pauses, "we could probably take over the whole park and really make it look like you're walking in a winter wonderland, don't you think? A few extra fire pits, maybe some photo op locations...." Ashley's eyes sparkle, and Mia can only guess the ideas flooding her brain.

It's like Ashley never stops, rarely relaxes, and she's always coming up with ideas on something. To Mia, it would be exhausting. For Ashley, it's invigorating.

"I have some photos of different markets we visited in Germany a few years ago. Why don't we go through them for some ideas?"

"Sounds like the perfect excuse for wine." Ashley's phone rings, and Mia steps back to give her some space to answer it. Ashley notices and shakes her head, pocketing her phone at the same time. "That call can go to voicemail. I put out some feelers to some realtors to see if anyone would be interested in helping set up some empty homes in town as vacation rentals...but most everyone is from out of town. I would really like someone local, you know?"

This is news to Mia. "That's a great idea, actually."

Ashley shrugs. "Blame your parents. Them opening their home as a B&B is what gave me the idea. I've been in touch with a few families who have moved away, and there's enough interest in renting their homes out, so why not?"

"I still can't believe my parents are doing that. At their age, they should be traveling or something, you know? Not entering the hospitality industry."

"Oh, honey," Ashley gives her this look that tells her she's sounding childish. "From what Anna's told me, they don't plan on operating a full house. Besides, she's going to have help, right?"

"Help?" This is news to Mia. "She's not hiring anyone, not that I know of."

Ashley frowns. "Hmm, I could have sworn she told me she was considering hiring some teenagers to help when they have guests. You know, like help with the cleaning, serving and such."

Yeah, she gets it, and it's something she should have thought of, but now she's feeling like she's being left out of the loop, and this is not a feeling she likes experiencing, at all.

"Stop. I can see where your mind is going. There's no secrecy happening. I checked in on them today, just to see how they were doing, and we got talking about one thing and another, that's all."

Mia nods. "It's fine. It's no secret that I haven't been the biggest cheerleader when it comes to this idea, so why would I expect her to ask for my opinions or even for my help, right?" She glances around the store, "did you come in for a reason, or just to chat?" She knows she sounds short, and it's not intended. "Sorry, Ash, I just...."

"I get it, I do. Change is hard."

Mia frowns. "Why does everyone assume I find change hard? You should know me better than that." It's starting to get frustrating; the more people bring it up.

Ashley remains quiet.

"What?" Mia says, knowing her friend wants to say something but isn't.

"Do you want an honest answer or need me to be an enabling friend?"

Mia throws her hands up in frustration. "How about we just drop the subject completely? I know I will eventually need to deal with whatever issue I have regarding my parents and this new venture...but today is not that day."

"When you're ready, you know I'm here if you need me." Ashley glances around, "I need a new notebook, and I'm hoping you have a few hidden away for me?"

"A few? Girl, I keep your favorite brand in stock all the time. But, seriously, I got some good ones in. You should check them out." Mia leads her over to the stationary section stocked full of notebooks. There are so many to choose from: solid black covers, leather, soft covers with embossed sayings, ones with tabs built in, unlined...Ashley isn't the only one who has an addiction to notebooks, thankfully.

"Seriously, Mom? How many notebooks do you need?" Jordan appears, carrying a stack of books.

Ashley gives her daughter a side-eyed look which has Mia chuckling.

"So, where are you two headed after this?" Mia asks as she packs up their purchases.

"Just heading to Frankie's. Why don't you join us for a quick coffee?"

Mia looks around the shop, see's Tommi stocking shelves, and decides an impromptu coffee break is exactly what she needs.

Besides, she needs to visit Frankie – there's a book club happening in her coffee shop later today, and the ladies all placed book orders she'd promised to hand deliver.

Frankie must have known they were on their way, because

she's at the door, piddling with her chalkboard sign as they approach.

"Oh good," she says, handing Jordan the chalk. "Can you do this up for me? I don't care what you put on it as long as it brings people in for coffee." Frankie wipes her hand across her forehead, spreading a trail of either chalk or flour on her skin. "What a day. If something goes wrong, it's going to happen today." She frowns before urging everyone to follow her in.

"I hate doing this, but I need help, and I need it fast." She beckons them into the kitchen area, which resembles a disaster zone

"What happened in here?" Ashley asks, setting her purse down on the counter.

"Failed recipes, that's what happened. I thought I'd try something new...." Frankie glances around the kitchen with dismay. "Note to self, do not stray from what works on days you have bookings in the restaurant."

Without even being asked, both Mia and Ashley roll up their sleeves and get to work. Mia starts with the pots and pans scattered all over the place and fills up one of the sinks with hot water and soap. Ashley focuses on the disastrous baking tables.

"My helper called in sick, so I know better than to try new recipes, and yet, I did it anyways. That's what I get for staying up late searching Pinterest for recipes." She hands Ashley an apron and then helps Mia secure hers.

Jordan eventually joins them and pitches in right away. Within no time, Frankie's kitchen is back to working condition.

"What were you trying to make, anyway?" Mia asks.

"A savory scone, but I didn't have all the ingredients, so I was substituting...never mind now. Listen, I'm glad you're here because I have an idea." She glances at the clock and grimaces. "Jordan, would you mind putting on a fresh pot of coffee for the front? The book group will be showing up soon."

Once Jordan is out in the front area, Frankie opens her notebook full of scribbles and drawings. Ashley leans forward, her attention piqued. Mia pulls out a stool and waits.

"What would it take to lease the old Sunset restaurant? I'd like to turn it into a working kitchen where cooking and baking classes can be held. Not just for me to teach, but for anyone in town. I thought about calling it "Gretel's Kitchen, as in Hansel and Gretel?" Frankie shows her the page where she wrote down all her notes, including a little sketch she'd made, and then points to the name.

"I love the idea," Mia says, butting in. Ashley nods.

"I love it too, I love everything about it, but I'll be honest, the last time we looked at it, it was quite outdated. It will need a lot of work to bring it up to passing standards."

Frankie waves that concern away. "I've talked to several people who are interested. They're all willing to pitch in to help cover the renovation costs, too. Between the six of us, we can fill a monthly schedule with two to three weekly classes. We'd have everything from starters to desserts and make it available to rent out to others if they wanted to use it for a party or gathering."

As the two women talk, Mia feels like retreating. Compared to these two, she's doing absolutely nothing. Organizing the Christmas market doesn't count, considering it's only a yearly event. What Frankie is proposing is a full-time thing, apart from owning her shop, and from everything she's hearing, Frankie has other ideas, too, ideas that are only benefiting the town.

What is wrong with her? Why isn't she jumping feet first into this renovation? Why can't she see beyond her own store?

"Frankie," Ashley says, her head bowed over the notebook, "you know my answer. Go for it. Put in the official paperwork, and let's get this thing passed. I can even see if the council would be willing to help support it too."

Jordan pushes through the doors and peers over Frankie's

shoulder. "What about asking the media class at school to help? My teacher has been wanting to take on a new school project, and this sounds fun."

Ashley nods. "And you could coordinate with Sylvia, who is helping with marketing for the town."

The more they all talk, the more minuscule Mia feels. She's tired of whatever this is that's going on with her. Change happens when you jump, at least for her, so that means it's time to jump.

"What can I do?"

The moment she utters that phrase, it's like chains she had no idea bound her up, loosened. She gets off her stool and goes to look over Frankie's notebook.

Ashley beams a smile at her, and Mia, for the first time in a long time, feels right.

CHAPTER FORTY-THREE

ASHLEY

Despite the bright smile on Sylvia's face, Ashley reads the exhaustion in her eyes.

"How's my goddaughter?" Ashley reaches out for the squirming bundle in Sylvia's arms, itching to smother those chubby cheeks with kisses and inhale that fresh baby scent.

"Well, her mother is ready for her to nap, but this little stinker," Sylvia leans forward and little tickles her daughter, "has other ideas. Maybe Aunty has the magical touch?" Sylvia yawns as she leads the way into her kitchen.

Ashley trails along, not paying attention to where she's going, focusing entirely on the little bundle of waving appendages.

"Has her sleep pattern changed?" Ashley asks. She lets little Jem, short for Jemilynn, play with her fingers.

"No, just mine. I was up way later than I should have been finishing a book. I know, I know," Sylvia holds up a hand, "my own fault. But I can't get enough of Anita Hughes and her Christmas books. Seriously, you need to read them."

"I have her newest one on preorder. I was the one who told you about them, remember?" Ashley helps herself to a glass and fills it with water. "No, you probably don't, considering you have baby brain."

Sylvia grimaces. "Pregnancy brain, then baby brain...am I ever going to go back to normal? I'm starting to miss me, you know?"

Ashley can totally relate. "It took a while for me to feel like I was even close to normal, but you'll get there. Enjoy this time, Syl. You'll miss it, I promise." She can't stop staring into Jem's eyes, marveling at just how precious and beautiful this little girl is.

"I treasure every moment, I swear, but I need more moments than just staring into her eyes, you know? I know that sounds horrible..." real genuine anguish fills Sylvia's voice, and Ashley hears the desperation.

Desperation not to sound like a horrible mother. Ashley takes her focus off the baby and goes to give her friend a solid hug.

"Oh honey, don't ever feel guilty for needing to be more than just a mother. It's okay, and it's healthy to need more. You are so much more than just this...more than a wife, more than a daughter or friend or new mother, but you need to remember you're not Wonder Woman either, even though you might want to do it all, you can't and shouldn't. I know you, Sylvia...."

Tears gather in Sylvia's eyes and start to fall, one by one, onto her cheeks. Sylvia turns to wipe them away, and Ashley retreats to give her friend some space.

As she does so, she rocks Jem in her arms, and slowly the little girl's eyes begin to flutter until they eventually close.

"Let me go put her down," Ashley whispers. She walks

through the house until she finds the bassinet in the living room. She gently lowers the baby and immediately regrets it. It felt good to hold a baby again.

She always wanted more babies, a full house of laughter and screams, and the busyness that comes from having a large family.

She'll settle for a busy life and a fantastic daughter, and enjoy these moments with Jem, instead.

"Why don't you go lie down," Ashley says once she's back in the kitchen. "I can come back later."

Sylvia looks like she's about to agree but pauses. "You mean you didn't just come to see Jem and me?"

"I came to see if you had some time for a new project," Ashley says with a smirk. Sylvia has been badgering her for the past month for more work, but Nigel kyboshes her at every corner.

"Do I have time for a new project? That's like asking if I need coffee every single morning?" Sylvia's voice drips with sarcasm. "Lay it on me."

Months ago, Sylvia created an online community calendar, and it's been working like a charm, with the little bit they have on there. Now it's time to expand it to be utilized in a broader spectrum.

She explains what she wants, the idea of adding cooking classes to the calendar, and Sylvia's eyes light up with excitement.

"This is brilliant," Sylvia says as she writes notes. "Frankie mentioned wanting to do this, but I didn't realize we were going forward with it. There's that new tea house that will be offering cookie decorating classes, I've been working on creating a schedule for that, but this...having a rotation of cooking classes will sell out, I know it. We need to have authentic German cooking classes, not just cookies but savory dishes too. And baking classes. Gingerbread houses and..." she stops talking as she writes things down.

Ashley leans forward to see all the ideas, but Sylvia turns the page too quickly, her pen scratching furiously on the paper.

"You know who needs to be part of this conversation?" Sylvia finally pauses.

"Who?"

"Frankie. You should text her to come by. Call it a planning session, especially since this is her idea."

Ashley feels guilty for not thinking of that.

It only takes a minute for Frankie.

"So?"

"She's on her way," Ashley says. "I also mentioned there's a sleeping baby, so to come on in."

By the time Frankie arrives, the two have come up with a rough outline for a few community classes that can start right away.

"I can't believe you all started without me," Frankie says as she tiptoes into the kitchen. "Where that sweet baby anyway? Shouldn't her nap be over by now?"

"Don't you dare wake her," Sylvia says, her voice a mixture of panic and threat.

Frankie wrinkles her nose. "Fine, I'll let her sleep, but I'm going through withdrawal, I'll have you know."

"You just saw her two days ago," Sylvia says.

"And she's probably changed so much in that time. All right, what have you got already?" Frankie reaches for the paper Sylvia had outlined the calendar on, hands on her hips, and frowns.

"Nope. You're not allowed to frown like that. This is just a rough idea of how things will look." Sylvia says. "What's the matter?" She's biting her nails while waiting for Frankie's reply.

Frankie taps her finger against the paper. "This is too all

over the place. We need to simplify things, like...create a theme."

"A theme?" Ashley is trying to understand where Frankie is going, but she's feeling a little out of sync.

"Each month should have a different focus. We can't always be offering cookie classes. That will get boring. We want to produce a need and build excitement, right? We can have a month focused on chocolate, German cookies, appetizers, wine pairings from the Mosel regions..." she taps her finger again against the paper.

"I like where you're going with this," Ashley says. February could be all about chocolate. October needs to be focused around Oktoberfest and such.

"This isn't just for our community, right? I mean, you want to advertise these classes, have tourists sign up, right? Are we a day trip destination, like Banff and Lake Louise, or do we have any hotels in the plans?" Sylvia brings up a good point, one Ashley has been stressing to the council. There's an opportunity here they don't want to miss out on, but they have to do it carefully.

"Marcus is taking care of this. We've had a few requests from some major chains, but..." she pauses, not wanting to say too much. "I would prefer to have more B&B's, or vacation rentals in town than a hotel. Especially in the beginning." She has a few applications for more B&B's, which is exciting.

"Those would be great for couples. Or if we did some girl-friend weekends, don't you think?" Sylvia asks. "We could plan some weekends around that idea, actually. We could do a wine and chocolate pairing weekend with some baking classes?" She looks to Frankie, who's nodding.

"How long will you need to set it up?" Ashley asks.

"A month." Sylvia gives a slight shrug.

"That soon? Do you think you could get people to come?"

To say she's surprised is an understatement. She expected Sylvia to say three to four months.

"Actually, I think I have the perfect idea for our first themed weekend. The ladies who hold their book chat at the cafe mentioned they were tired of going into the city for author events. One of the ladies mentioned they knew some authors doing a joint book tour...maybe I could see about them adding Innsbruck to their itinerary? We could build around it."

"Where would they stay?" Sylvia asks. Ashley is actually thinking the same thing.

Frankie just smiles.

"What do you know that I don't?" Ashley gives the woman a look. She really doesn't like being kept in the dark.

"Janice Dixon is thinking of coming back and opening up her home as a B&B again," Frankie says with a hint of satisfaction.

Ashley's brows rise way past her hairline at the news. Janice used to run a successful B&B years ago until, like most things in town, people stopped visiting. She moved into the city to live with her daughter and help take care of her grandchildren.

Janice has been on Ashley's list of people to contact, to see if they would think about returning. Having Janice back, that would be...well, it would be amazing and a miracle.

"I should have told you, I'm sorry," Frankie continues. "I wanted to wait until Janice knew for sure. I'm supposed to talk to her tomorrow."

"I'll forgive you, if you can make it happen. Tell her we'll speed up any permits she needs as well as licensing." Ashley doesn't bother to hide her joy at the news.

"It wouldn't take her much to get up and running either," Sylvia says.

"Would it help if I call her?" Ashley doesn't want to step on toes, but...

Her phone rings just then. She's about to ignore the call, then notices it's Susan.

Excusing herself, she wanders onto Sylvia's back porch before answering the call. "Everything okay?"

"Josie is here," Susan says in a whisper. "She needs to talk to you right away."

Right away? This can't be good.

"Code red," Susan says.

Shoot. Code red isn't good.

"I'll be right there," Ashley promises.

CHAPTER FORTY-FOUR

ASHLEY

By the time she walks into her office, Josie has a cup of tea in her hand and appears calm.

"Everything okay?" She pulls a chair closer to Josie's so their knees almost touch. The whole ride over, she couldn't stop stressing over what could be wrong.

"I'm a silly old fool, breaking down like that with Susan." Josie's hands shake as she holds the teacup close to her lips. She blows a breath over the steam still billowing over the cup. "I should have just stayed home and minded my own business. I miss my son and his family. Is it so wrong that I'm trying to do everything I can to get them to return home? They're struggling, even if they won't admit it. This is home. This is where they need to be." She stares down into her cup, sudden tears trailing down the lines in her face.

It breaks Ashley's heart to see Josie broken. Gone is the strong, opinionated, mother bear she's known to be.

Ashley wants to say something, to tell her Jared is coming back, but even though the words are there, they won't come out.

"Durwood... he's off the rails," Josie finally raises her face. A million emotions were swirling in the older woman's gaze. Embarrassment, heartache, and sadness, to name a few.

There's so much Ashley wants to say, so many questions she wants to ask, but instead of giving in and letting the words blurt out, she bites the inside of her cheek and forces herself to remain silent.

"He needs help. That's no secret. I know you thought Jared coming home was the answer, but my..." Josie stares up toward the ceiling, her lips tight together, nostrils flaring as she breathes in deep. "My stubborn, obstinate, foolish husband just kiboshed that idea, and there's no coming back from the hole he jumped into."

Jared's not coming back? What?

"I don't understand. Tell me what happened, please."

Josie swallows. Gone are the tears. In its place is rage.

Ashley's a little taken back, unsure how to accept this change.

"Instead of accepting help and listening to his son, who is also stubborn and too proud for his own good, he blustered and said things he not only doesn't believe but knew he shouldn't have said." The cup shakes in Josie's hand.

Ashley takes the cup and sets it down on the table.

"He won't apologize either, will he?" Ashley isn't sure why she said this, except deep down, she already knows the answer.

Anyone who knows Durwood can answer this.

"Apologize? He's basically told me I'm not allowed to talk to my son and daughter-in-law!" Josie's face is bright red.

Not liking what she's seeing, Ashley takes Josie's hand in hers. "Breathe, please," she says, practically begging the woman to relax. The last thing she wants is Josie to have a panic attack, or God forbid a heart attack.

"Whatever happened, it can be fixed," Ashley says, hoping to help the woman calm down, but she apparently says the wrong thing.

"Fixed? No, not this time. Do you know what he did? He attacked Marlee. Can you believe it? The mother of our grandchildren, the woman who works so hard, always supports our son. He attacks her and tells Jared that it's her fault they're struggling." Josie's face continues to grow a deeper shade of red, her chest heaving as she breathes in and out.

"Breathe, Josie, please." That's all Ashley cares about right now. Not Josie's words, but the color of her face, the heaving of her chest, the panic in her eyes. Ashley rubs Josie's hand, never taking her focus off the woman's face.

"He doesn't realize what he's done. He knows better," Josie's grip on Ashley's hand tightens. "If his father had done that to us, Durwood would never talk to him again. How could he do that? To us? To them? He was frustrated and afraid to accept Jared's help. Stupid, pig-headed, stubborn man."

By now, the tears don't just trickle-down Josie's face, they cascade down her skin like one of the many waterfalls in the mountains. Ashley places a tissue in Josie's hand.

Little by little, the redness in Josie's face subsides to warm pink, her chest doesn't heave as heavy as before, and Ashley's concern for Josie's wellbeing loosens.

"I love my husband," Josie says.

"I know."

"But I hate him right now." Josie averts her gaze at this admission.

Ashley understands that sentiment all too well. She's close to the same feeling toward Durwood. Things can't continue the way they have been, being behind schedule, him going behind her back, and changing looks that had been approved by the town council.

Durwood has a good heart. She knows this, but lately...Innsbruck needs more than just a contractor with a good heart.

"I don't know why I came here. I'm sorry." Josie pushes herself to her feet, but Ashley stops her.

"I think we both know why you came," Ashley's voice is whisper soft.

Josie came because she needed Ashley to step in, to take the stand that she can't.

Josie nods.

"Here's what I know, Josie. I know your husband has a good heart and that he's the first to offer help when it's needed. He's single-handedly brought back families to our town, so I will never be able to thank him enough." She pauses, watching a timid smile grow and settle on Josie's face.

She hates to take that smile away.

"We're at the point where we need more, and I think we both know your husband has taken us as far as he can."

Josie breathes in deep, her chest filling as she holds her breath.

"I don't know what he did or said to Jared, but I want you to know this. I will take care of this town and make sure we get back on track." She doesn't know how, but she'll figure it out. "I appreciate you telling me that Jared won't be coming back. Honestly, I don't blame him." Yes, yes, she does, but she'll never admit that. "I've got this. I promise."

She helps Josie to her feet and gives the woman a long, tight hug.

She isn't sure what she's going to do, isn't sure how she's going to handle the situation, but somehow, someway, she will.

She has to.

CHAPTER FORTY-FIVE

MARLEE

With a rare afternoon off from work, Marlee does the one thing she's wanted to do all week but hasn't had time to: call Josie.

Life has been crazy with school meetings, picking up extra hours at work, and reworking their home budget in the evenings. Not just busy, but stressful. For the past week, it feels like she's been walking on eggshells around Jared, and she's not sure why.

"It's about time you called! I've been wanting to talk to you all week, but the stubborn man I call husband, well, he's forbidden me from calling." Josie barely takes a breath once she answers the phone.

Forbade her from calling? And Josie actually listened?

"What is going on, Josie?" Marlee hates being in the dark. Jared still refuses to talk about his last conversation with his father.

Without communication, without clearing the air, contact with his side of the family will disappear, and Marlee won't accept that. Her kids deserve better. They all deserve better.

Without family, without the benefits of grandparents, who are they?

They're alone. That's who they are. Alone when they don't need to be. She knows what it's like to not have parents or grandparents to lean on, and she doesn't want that for her own family.

"You mean you don't know? Jared hasn't said anything?" There's a slight hesitation in Josie's voice, as if she isn't sure of her next words.

Since honesty is always the best policy, Marlee goes with the truth.

"I know words were said. I know that my husband has told me he can't work with Durwood again. I know we won't be moving back to Innsbruck to help rebuild the town."

"But you don't know what was said?" Again, Josie hesitates, drawing out her words.

A sick, twisted sensation settles in Marlee's stomach. "I don't."

Her words are met with silence.

"What is going on, Josie?"

The silence on the other end of the phone grows.

"Has Durwood forbade you to tell me? Is that why you're not saying anything?"

"Oh honey, no... that's not it," Josie finally says, releasing a long breath as she does so. "I just... I'm thinking this is a conversation you need to have with Jared. He needs to be the one to tell you."

Marlee nods to herself. With those words, her fears are validated. Whatever has been said, whatever's happened, it's bad.

"Things happen in the heat of the moment, you know that, right? Things are said that aren't meant."

"Out of the heart, the tongue speaks," Marlee says softly. Regardless of what's been said between Durwood and Jared,

Durwood meant every word. He might regret it now but at the time...

"Oh, honey..." Josie's voice is full of tears. "If he could take it back, I know he would. He's been absolutely miserable since that phone call."

"I don't know what you want me to say, Josie. Am I supposed to offer forgiveness? I can only assume the conversation was about me since everyone seems to be trying to shield me, but..." she's at a loss. "What do we do?"

"Have Jared call his father," Josie said, offering a suggestion they both know won't happen.

Jared takes after his father. If Durwood is too stubborn to call and apologize, what makes anyone think Jared will?

Marlee doodles on a scrap piece of paper. It's aimless doodling, the goal to keep her hands busy while her brain struggles to work through the problem, except...without all the information, it's like trying to cook a three-course dinner with her hands tied behind her back.

She ends the call with Josie, feeling even more frustrated than before.

Without thought, she texts Trina.

Twelve seconds later, her phone rings.

"Hey," Trina says. "Have I told you lately I miss your face? You need to hurry and move back. Listen, I've got about ten minutes to chat, and then I'm helping in Lauren's class today. Fun times...the cupcakes I made taste like sawdust. Do you think they'll mind if I pick up some store-bought ones? I know the treats are supposed to be homemade, peanut free, but..." Trina chuckles as if she really can't care.

"Just take them out of the store packaging, place them in a container, and no one's the wiser," Marlee says from experience.

"Except the teacher. She'll know. She always knows. She looks down her long nose at you, silently judging your skills, and

I'm sure I get a two out of ten regardless of how hard I try. Why do I feel like I'm being graded every time I volunteer there?" Trina babbles on with nervous chatter.

"I'm sure you're not being judged. I'm also pretty sure she's just happy to have some help, you know? Besides, even if you were being graded, you'd come out with flying colors."

"Oh please, I never got good grades in school, you know that. So, what's up?" Trina asks.

Marlee sighs, saying more in that one long breath than she can with words.

"What happened? Whose butt do I need to kick? Please tell me not Jared. He's got buns of steel if I remember correctly."

If Marlee had taken a sip of water right then, she for sure would have spat it out.

"Holy...I totally forgot about that!" She giggles from the memory of when Trina had actually kicked her husband in the butt. He'd been hanging shelves in the mudroom just after moving in and placed his hammer in his back pocket when Trina walked into the room and butt kicked him. She left their home with a bruised foot that night.

"No one's," Marlee says. "It's just been...a day, that's all."

"What's going on?" Trina's voice is barely loud enough to cover the ding of her car door opening.

"I wish I knew. Something's happened between Jared and his father, but no one will tell me what. It's bad enough that Jared says we won't be returning to Innsbruck--"

"What?" Trina interjects. "That's crazy. Of course, you're coming back. You have to come back. Jared has to take over for his father... that's crazy talk. Take it back."

"I wish I could."

"I'm serious, Marlee. Take that back. I've been telling everyone the rumors aren't true, that Jared is the one coming in to save the day...so help me, I'm going to lose it if you tell me that's not true."

"Rumors? What are you talking about?"

"Oh, you know how small towns are. Any hint of discord and the crazy talk all comes out. Apparently, someone from that retirement home they are building above the town works on a crew and overheard his boss say they were bidding on the town reconstruction."

Bidding on the reconstruction? Why would Ashley have bids out? Unless...no, she wouldn't do that. This can't be happening.

"What? That's not true!"

"I know that. You know that. You know how the gossip mill works." Trina's voice holds a hint of disdain.

Nope, this is not okay.

"The thing is," Trina continues, "that crew, most of them are bussed in from the city. There aren't many locals, you know? So, if it's true, many jobs will be lost."

Every rumor starts with a seed of truth, right? So, what's true? What's not?

"I'm telling you it's not true. No one has mentioned that to us. Not once."

"Phew. So, whatever is happening between Jared and Durwood, they'll work it out, right? And you'll move back home, hopefully before Christmas? Please tell me I'm right. If you don't, I'm hanging up," Trina threatens.

By Christmas? No, that's not going to happen. Not anymore.

"Trina, come on..."

Click. Just as she'd threatened, Trina hangs up.

The rest of the day, while preparing for dinner, helping the kids with homework, and then cleaning up, all she can think about is what Trina said. The rumors can't be true, can they?

Maybe it's a new development from this week. Maybe Jared has already talked to Ashley and explained the situation, and maybe Ashley has no choice but to bring in outside help.

So many maybes. They all make her sick to her stomach, knowing that somehow, for some reason, all of this is centered around her and something Durwood said.

What could he have said that would push Jared away like he did? Nothing makes sense to her.

By the time Jared comes home, she's a ball of nerves.

"Sorry I'm so late," he calls out quietly as he walks in. "Kids in bed?"

While he showers, she pulls out two beers from the fridge and waits for him at the kitchen table.

"Long day?" She asks as he takes a long drink of the beer.

He nods.

"I'm about to make it longer, I'm afraid." She plays with the bottle in her hand, twisting it first one way, then the other, thinking about how to bring this up.

"I figured. What's going on?" There isn't a sense of censorship in his voice. Instead, he appears rather calm, and patient, as if he'd been anticipating this moment for a while now.

"I need you to be honest with me. I promise you, I can take it. It's better than the alternative."

The look on Jared's face tells her she doesn't need to elaborate. He knows exactly what she's talking about, and she can tell he's finally ready, or resigned, to discuss it.

"If you attempt to apologize for your father for whatever he did or said, I'll dump the rest of my beer on your head," she warns, able to read him with clarity.

"Now that would be a waste of a good beer." He cracks a smile, but she knows it's only a surface reaction, not one felt inside.

"Dad said he wasn't one to hand out charity."

Charity?

"Since when have we ever asked for their help?" That doesn't make sense to Marlee.

"Also said he didn't raise me to hand it out either. You work for what you got," Jared continues, ignoring her question. "Whatever situation we're in, it's of our own doing. We are the ones who decided to leave our family and move to the city. We are the ones who took on the debt of living above our means...so why should he be the one to rescue us?"

The way Jared speaks, low, unclear, as if each word physically hurts him.

He's not telling her everything.

"Did he blame you, me, or both?" Marlee has no idea where that came from, but there it is.

"Does it matter?"

Does it matter? Of course it does, and he knows that.

"For whatever reason, he has it in his head that you are the one who pushed us to move to the city and forced me to leave him and the business."

Marlee plants her elbows on the table. "Me? Why would he think that?" She tries to recall every conversation she's had with his parents around the time of their move.

She always supported Jared, never once stabbing him in the back. So if that means it was her idea, because she never said otherwise...

"Doesn't matter," Jared says. "He doesn't have the right to blame you for anything."

"He must have done more than just blame me." Marlee can feel the permanent scowl on her forehead as she desperately struggles to comprehend where all of this is coming from.

She'd never wanted to move to the city. In fact, she'd been against it from the very beginning. But she only ever said that to Jared, never to anyone else. As far as anyone else is concerned, it was a joint decision, sometimes even over-emphasizing how they were making the best decision for their family.

Maybe that's why Durwood blames her?

He's only ever heard her talk positively about the move.

But that still doesn't explain things, not properly.

"I can see your brain overworking, trying to figure out how we went from A to B, aren't you?" Jared leans back in his chair, taking another drink of his beer.

"Don't overanalyze, okay? You know how Dad is. When he's upset, he stops thinking and just talks. He said things I know he regrets, but it's not an excuse. Don't ask for specifics because I won't tell you. Ultimately, it doesn't matter." With his arms across his chest, he's giving her a look that reminds her all too much of his father.

She lets that sit, knowing she may never know what's been said about her, not truly. She allows it to sit and accepts it, accepts that she really doesn't need to know, that it's okay to let her husband fight this battle on her behalf.

"I love you," she says, pouring all of her feelings into those three words. She means it, loves how he always places her first, her and their kids, even when it means hurting himself.

Because she knows that ostracizing them from his family hurts him deeply. She can see it in his eyes, read it in his face, and feel it in his embrace.

She wants to pound her fist against the table and say *screw it, screw Durwood, screw her dreams of moving back to Innsbruck*, but she can't.

She can't and won't because it isn't just about them anymore. It's about his family, their friends back at home, and the people who work with and rely on his father for income.

Once she explains that to Jared, she knows he'll feel the same way too.

CHAPTER FORTY-SIX

ASHLEY

The house is eerily quiet, and it's times like these that being alone makes her skin crawl. She doesn't do well with silence and the feeling of loneliness.

Never has, never will.

Even though Brent was rarely home when they'd been together, just knowing he could walk through the door at any time made all the difference between feeling lonely and being alone.

Technically, she's not alone tonight. Jordan's home, but other than the few dishes she left on the counter by the sink, she might as well be in a different country.

Ashley's...restless. She's been looking forward to a day off, a day to herself, but now it's here...being alone is the last thing she wants to be. She can call any number of people and suggest meeting for coffee or guilt someone to go on a walk with her, but that will negate the idea of enjoying a day to herself.

Her fingers tap along the wood rail of the staircase...does she go up and beg her daughter to join her on a walk, or should she bake something enticing to draw her out of her room?

One means possible rejection, the other potential company to kill the boredom.

She spends the next fifteen minutes preparing cinnamon sugar muffins and is just about to place them in the oven when her phone rings, and Brent's number pops up on her screen.

"Hey, everything okay?"

"Sorry to call. I know you're probably busy," Brent said. It's rare for him to phone her, choosing instead to send texts or lengthy emails.

Her first instinct is to tell him she's not, but she holds her tongue. Boundaries are a good thing, especially for them.

"I wanted to chat with you about Jordan. Is she okay?" His voice is filled with concern.

"She's fine. Why? What's up?"

"She keeps canceling our weekends together. Which makes me think she's avoiding me or something."

Ashley swallows back her chuckle. Avoidance and Jordan go hand in hand lately.

"She's a teenager. I can almost guarantee it's the something," Ashley says. Truth be told, it's probably a combination of both: avoiding her father and something else is going on.

"It's not just that. We've talked about how things can be taken wrong through texting and email."

"So, call her then."

"That's the issue, Ashley. She's not taking my calls." Frustration laces his voice like spoiled cream in coffee.

There are two options available for Ashley. She can get in the middle, something she works very hard not to do, and attempt to get Jordan to see her father, or she can listen and do what she's done in the past...suggest Brett keep trying.

She really doesn't want to get in the middle.

"Just keep trying. That's all I can suggest. Listen, if it makes you feel better, we're not best friends right now either. Most nights I'm having to drag her to the table so I'm not eating alone."

The buzzer on the oven went off, and when she opens the door, she's covered in a waft of steam.

"Dang it," she mutters as the heat hits her full in the face.

"Everything okay?" Brett asks.

With the phone tucked tight against her shoulder, she sticks her hands in the bright pink and yellow oven mitts Jordan bought her as a Christmas gift one year.

"Yep, all is good. Just pulling out some muffins."

"You're baking?" Brett's voice holds both a hint of laughter and concern mixed in.

Ashley quirks her lips at his question.

"Yes, I'm baking, okay. You're not the only one missing time with Jordan." She glances over her shoulder, hoping that her daughter smells the delicious aroma of cinnamon muffins, and comes down.

Sadly, that doesn't appear to be the case.

"Will you talk to her for me?"

"No." Ashley doesn't give herself any time to think about his request. Their separation hasn't been easy, but she doesn't hate him. "As much as I'd love to help you build that relationship with Jordan, there's only one person who can do that, and it's you."

"You don't think I've been trying? God, Ashley, there's only so much I can do, you know." His words shoot a barbed wire straight through to her heart.

"Actually, Brett, you could be doing a hell of a lot more, and you know it." Once that barb made its mark, all bets were off. She's tried, she really has tried, to push the pain from their failed marriage down deep, but all it takes, apparently, is him playing the victim, and whatever lid holding down that hurt and anger she's been holding, disappears.

"Whoa --"

"Nope." Ashley interrupts. "The rift between you and Jordan has nothing to do with me and everything to do with you. I don't appreciate you trying to pull me in, expecting me to fix everything for you. I don't come whining to you every time she yells at me, slams the door, or plays possum, do I? If you want a relationship with your daughter, it's going to take a lot of work on your part." She slams the cooling tray for the muffins down on the counter.

"I know that, Ash, trust me."

"Really? You may say that, but you don't believe it in your heart. If maintaining a relationship with our daughter is a priority, then you'll do everything you can to see it happen. Don't forget, I know you, Brett. I know how hard you work at something once you've put your mind to it."

Ashley throws open the fridge door and searches for the bottle of Reisling she knows is in there. She can do with a glass of wine right about now.

"Fine."

Ashley snaps her mouth shut to keep from saying more. Did he just say fine? Like fine, fine...you're right, fine...or fine, I'm done talking, fine?

"I just sent our daughter a text. I'll be there in less than two hours. I expect her to be waiting for me." With that, Brett hangs up.

Ashley closes the fridge door and looks around, stupefied by Brett's reaction. He hung up on her. He'd actually hung up on her, not because he's mad, but because she's right, and he knows it.

She let herself process that while melting butter and mixing together cinnamon and sugar in a small bowl. She brushes the tops of each muffin with the butter before dipping them into the sugar mixture, making sure they are nice and coated.

There's nothing better than a freshly baked muffin, especially these ones, while they were still warm. Ashley places a few on a plate and makes her way up to Jordan's room, taking her own advice to heart. She has to stop waiting for Jordan to come to her.

"Hey, sleeping beauty, are you awake yet?" Ashley knocks on her daughter's door and opens it slightly.

Jordan's sitting there, legs curled under her, phone in hand. Music plays in the background, but surprisingly, not at full volume.

"I made some cinnamon sugar muffins. Thought you might want one while they're still warm." Ashley sets the plate down on the bed before perching on the edge.

"Dad is coming." Jordan drops her head.

"So, I hear. Any plans, or just hanging out?"

"Well, I had plans, but now I have to cancel them, I guess," Jordan grumbles as she plucks a muffin from the plate. "Why does he have to come? He didn't even ask."

After hearing the uncertainty in Jordan's voice, Ashley waits.

"Well, okay, I guess he did, technically," Jordan admits. "But if I don't answer, he should take that as my answer. I don't want to see him."

"Does he know that? Or have you just been playing the ignore game?" Ashley breaks off a piece of her own muffin and savors the taste.

These are her favorite muffins, more so than chocolate chip, lemon, or pumpkin swirl. They remind her of time spent with her grandmother in the kitchen. She'd been tasked with dipping the warm muffins into the sugar mixture.

They are comfort muffins. Not just for her but for Jordan too.

"I don't like him. Everything else comes first for him until it's convenient that he remembers he has a daughter, you know? Then to assuage his guilt or something, he expects me to drop everything the minute he says so. Um...no. That's not my responsibility."

Ashley's impressed with Jordan's insight.

"You're right. It's not fair of him to place that on you. But...he's making an effort today to right a wrong. Maybe he realizes..."

"That he's a shitty father?" Jordan finishes her thoughts with an accuracy Ashley will never admit out loud.

"Come on, Jordan. You have better words you can use to describe him. Swearing is a cop-out."

The eye roll she receives is epic.

"Fine. He's a negligent, self-absorbed father who will never win a father-of-the-year award from me, is that better?"

Ashley tries to hide the smile on her face, but she's unsuccessful.

"You know it's true," Jordan's lips broke into a similar smile.

"Word of advice?" Ashley offers. "Maybe don't tell him that unless he specifically requests feedback."

In reply, Jordan pops the rest of her muffin into her mouth.

"Is there more?" She asked in between bites.

Ashley stands, takes the plate, and gives her daughter a wink. "They're downstairs," she says. "Your dad will be here before you know it, so come join me for a snack, then you can get ready." She doesn't wait for a reply.

The fact her daughter wants more muffins and jumps off the bed to follow her downstairs is all she needs.

CHAPTER FORTY-SEVEN

MARLEE

The house is quiet, blissfully quiet. Unable to sleep, Marlee creeps out of bed, careful to not wake up Jared, and heads to the kitchen, where she pours herself a glass of maple whiskey.

Durwood's disapproval hangs over her like a winter fog. If she doesn't do something about it soon, she'll be buried beneath its heavy weight. She loves that Jared stood up for her, but she knows the cost is just as burdensome on his heart as it is on hers.

She's been playing with an idea, something that won't leave her thoughts, and the more she works on a solution, the more she realizes it might just work - if she can convince Jared to go along with it.

Deep in thought, she jumps out of her chair when a hand lands on her shoulder.

"What's all this?" Jared plants a kiss on her forehead before pulling out the chair next to her.

"Did I wake you?"

For a second, the idea of gathering all the papers and

ignoring his question sits in her mind, but she brushes it away. Secrets always do more damage than initially intended.

Rather than answer him directly, she pushes a sheet of paper his way. She enjoys a sip of whiskey, needing a bolster as Jared studies the drawing she's been working on, a rough outline of what the Winter Wonderland Cabins and Park could look like.

"So...cabins, huh?"

She can't read anything in his voice, which is a little unnerving. Is he upset? Excited? Does he understand where she's going with this idea, or is it a complete surprise?

She sits back when he pulls the sheet with all her number scribblings and waits for him to walk through things. She'd looked online for a simplistic cabin kit, figuring out how much it could roughly cost, and then compared it to buying everything separately. The cabin isn't elaborate. It's a simple space for couples and families with small children. As they grow, they could expand and build larger sites and such. The alpine look, complete with a fire pit, will work for now.

Jared points to the available cash flow line. "Where did you get this number? We don't have that in our savings."

She wasn't sure if he'd catch that or if he'd focus more on the cost of lumber versus the kits.

"True, our savings is nowhere near that, But it's available to us, nonetheless. And it's enough for us to build three cabins, even leaving us a bit of a cushion." She plays with the glass in her hand, turning it round and round, anything to not look her husband in the face.

"Where is the money coming from?" He leans back in his seat, angling his head toward her. She's uncomfortable under his scrutiny and stares downward.

"A silent investor." It takes her a bit, but when she finally peeks up at him, expecting to see him frowning, she's surprised to catch the twinkle in his gaze.

"Let me guess, this silent investor goes by the name Josie?" He returns his attention to the sheet, his finger going along the numbers and calculations she'd made. "I can probably get the supplies cheaper than what the kits are going for, so that would shave off a bit of the cost, but if you add in labor..." he grabs the calculator and punches in some numbers.

There's a bead of hope inside Marlee that this will work, that Jared sees the potential and doesn't toss the idea to the side. She has to squash her growing excitement, not letting her thoughts dwell on the fact that they just might be able to move back home.

Home. She'd give anything to do that. They have a mortgage-free house that's sitting empty despite being on the market for all this time. They rented it out for a few years to a family that had since moved back to the city for the same reasons she and Jared had packed up their family. At that time, there was nothing in Innsbruck to provide adequate income for their family.

"Who came up with the idea?" Jared leans back in the chair and has this expression that says he already knows the answer but wants to hear it from her anyway.

"Well..."

He stops her. "No, wait, let me see if I can guess. You've been trying to think of a way for us to move back, something that has nothing to do with my father. Mom was able to weasel the idea out of you and then offered the money she's been placing away for a family trip. How am I doing so far?"

If it wasn't for the twinkle, she'd think he was either upset or annoyed...she isn't sure which is worse.

"Pretty close, actually. How did you know she'd been saving the money for a family trip?"

He takes her glass of whiskey and drains it. "Because she's always talked about doing a family trip to Disney with the grandkids, and the last time we were home, she told me she wanted to give us the money instead."

Josie did what?

"I told her we didn't need it, that we were fine."

He stands, pulling her along with him. "Have I told you lately how much I love you, Marlee Holms?"

She rises to her tiptoes and plants a soft kiss on his cheek. "So, does this mean you aren't upset with me?"

"Well...that depends. When were you planning on telling me about this hair-brained idea you cooked up with my mother?"

"Once I knew it wasn't hair-brained."

"Then I guess my answer is no." His lips taste like delicious whiskey when he kisses her. "What about Durwood?"

Marlee scrunches her nose. "Josie says he doesn't get to be part of this, that the money is hers to do with as she pleases, and he lost the right to interfere."

The twinkle disappears from Jared's eyes. "No. No way. If we do it, it's on the up and up. I'm not going behind my father's back; my mother should know that. We're not taking their handout."

She knew he'd react this way. She reaches for one of the sheets he hadn't seen and hands it over.

"No handouts. I told your mother that too. I worked out a repayment plan, giving ample breathing room in case things are slow at first."

Jared looks it over, nodding his head a few times before dropping it on the table, the sheet fluttering until it lands.

"So, we're on the same page, good. I'm still not sure how I feel about leaving Dad in the dark." He looks toward the ceiling, sighing as he does. "Let me work through some pricing on my end, and then I'll set up a meeting with Ashley, okay? Maybe the town will be willing to partner with us, tossing in some cash to get some of the reservation revenue."

Marlee snuggles into her husband's chest as he works out a solution to their problem, the worry, the gnawing doubt dissipating as his hold on her tightens.

CHAPTER FORTY-EIGHT

MIA

Turning up the volume to finish listening to one of her favorite true crime podcasts, Mia isn't paying attention as she leaves the grocery store and walks into the solid brick wall of a man's chest.

More specifically, Matt's chest.

His hands reach out to steady her, and it takes a split second for her to adjust to listening to how a man stalked his next prey to hearing what Matt is saying.

"Oops, sorry," Mia says as she pulls out her earbuds. "I need to pay better attention to where I'm going."

His hands drop from her arms, and she immediately feels the absence of his touch, which is ridiculous. She needs to stop this, whatever *this* is that happens inside her whenever she's around Matt. It's obvious he's not into her and that nothing will ever happen between them. Maybe if she stops making things so awkward between them, they could end up as friends...not quite what she'd wanted originally, but at this stage, anything is better than nothing.

"What are you listening to?"

The question catches her somewhat off guard until he points to the earbuds in her hand.

"Oh, only the best true crime podcast ever. My Favorite Murder, have you heard of it?"

The way his brow arches tells her he has no idea what she's talking about.

"I know, listening to people talk about serial killers is odd, but hey, it's about the only excitement in my life right now, so I'll take what I can."

"The only excitement? That's not the Mia I'm familiar with. Seems to me you're always busy, rarely ever taking time off for yourself." He steps off to the side, and she finds herself following him.

She scoffs at his words. "There's being busy for a reason and being busy because you're lonely." Her face warms as she's more honest than she'd ever intended. "In my case, it's more a habit than anything. You know my parents...do you ever see them relaxing?"

The smile on his face welcomes her own.

"No, your parents never stop. If they're not doing something around the house, they're out and about helping someone else. Who knows," he shrugs, "this B&B might be the best thing for them, you know, force them to slow down a bit."

"Wouldn't that be a miracle? Although even Dad will admit he wasn't his best self when forced to slow down, heart attack and all." Maybe some people just aren't made to relax.

"Some men are happiest when they keep busy. No reason. It's just who they are."

"So, you're trying to tell me that sometimes, there's nothing wrong with being busy." She hikes her bag over her shoulder, feeling the weight of her groceries.

He shrugs again. "We attribute guilt to things too often, I think. Busy or not, does it matter if you're happy?"

He stares at her with this look that's trying to say something, except she can't read him.

At all.

"Are you happy, Mia?" His voice drops a little as he asks. In her mind's eye, she sees him reaching out, lightly touching her arm as he asks this.

It's all in her imagination, though, because that doesn't happen. His arms remain at his sides, but the concern in his eyes is real and genuine.

The immediate response is to say, of course, she is. How could she not be, but she stops herself because she wouldn't be speaking the truth, would she?

Regardless of what is going on, or instead, not going on between them, the truth deserves to be spoken.

"Honestly, I don't know. I should be, I want to be...maybe I'm trying too hard to feel something beyond reach, you know? I mean...can you truly be happy?"

He takes a step back as if what she said repulsed him.

Did it? Maybe she shouldn't be so honest. She holds tighter to her bag and glances at her watch.

"I should go," she says, barely looking at him. She doesn't want to see whatever expression is on his face.

"Are you in a rush? Somewhere you need to be?" His voice is a little...coarse, like he's saying words he didn't expect to say.

"No...." Where is he going with this?

"Do you have time to grab coffee or something?" He swallows hard, and for a second, Mia thinks he's asking her on a date.

She's got all those fluttery butterfly feelings in her stomach as she struggles to hide her smile. Was he actually—

"The Mayor called and wants me to build more stalls. I just

figured you're running it and all, that maybe we should chat about what's going on and stuff."

Just like that, the butterflies spiral down and drop en mass.

She needs to stop getting her hopes up. Time after time, he's made it clear there's nothing there, that all of this is coming from her and her alone.

She should say no. She should reschedule, have him come by the shop, keep it impersonal and low key.

What she should say and what she actually says are two different things.

"Sure, I've got time for coffee." It's on the tip of her tongue to suggest heading to Frankie's, which is just down the street a bit.

"Have you ever tried that new Dutch place that just opened? They have this amazing pannenkoek that I can't get enough of."

She'd heard of the Pfanntastick Pannenkoek Chalet and has been meaning to stop in. According to her dad, pannekoek is something between a pancake and crêpe but is more addictive than imaginable.

"That's the same place where Dad says he can't get enough of the shredded potato, onion, bacon, and cheese one, right?" They start walking, their steps slow and measured, neither one in too much of a rush.

Matt nods. "It's become your dad's secret pleasure, or so he says. He tries to get me to go for lunch a few times a week. The place will be a huge hit once word gets around about how good these things are."

It surprises Mia just how easily they can keep the conversation flowing as they walk together.

Stepping into the restaurant is like stepping into a kitschy Dutch shop in the Netherlands. The Delft pottery that covers the walls and shelves is iconic, along with the various clogs and windmill decorations. The staff wear aprons and the smell has Mia's mouth-watering.

"Oh dear," she murmurs.

"What's the matter?" Matt turns to her in alarm.

"I really hope they have horrible coffee, otherwise, Frankie won't be seeing me as often," she says as they head to a booth.

Matt chuckles. "Don't worry. They don't hold a candle to her coffee. It's drinkable, but not Frankie worthy."

Her first sip of coffee confirms Matt's words. It has a burnt taste and is an average blend, the type that will produce gut rot after a few refills. No, Frankie for sure has nothing to worry about.

It doesn't take long for their casual chit-chat to become a little more serious.

"Were you aware of the additional stalls for this year?" Matt asks as he stirs another package of sugar into his coffee.

"Do you mean before or after Ashley came up with the idea?"

He shrugs.

"We'd discussed growth, but I didn't anticipate it until at least next year. Ashley, on the other hand...." Mia can't help but smile.

"The Mayor anticipates growth to happen right away, and she wasn't wrong, was she?" Matt sips his coffee before he pushes it to the side. "Should have ordered a Pepsi," he says.

"Once she heard we had a waiting list, she was all over it. It's not too much, is it? The market isn't that far off, and I feel bad we've asked you to put more stalls together."

He waves his hand, fending off her concerns. "I had it planned in my schedule anyway. I thought I'd get the request sooner, but it's fine. I would like to start setting up earlier this year if that's okay? I had some ideas for different settings we could put into place – more fencing, a few extra fire pit areas, and some kid-friendly areas, too. I thought it would be fun if we had an area where kids could make snowmen and such."

Mia is all for his ideas, especially if he's willing to take on the responsibility of seeing them through.

"I'm excited about the market this year, of actually being part of it, you know?" Her voice catches a little as the memory of why she wasn't part of the festivities hits her. *Dad is fine. Dad is fine*, she repeats to herself. This year will be different.

Matt's hand reaches across the table and then retracts, almost as if he was going for her hand.

"We were all scared," Matt admits. "It's been nice getting to know your father. He was always this name to me, a name that meant something, but…your father is a special man, Mia. You're lucky to have been raised by someone like him." There's more that's being said, more that's hiding behind his words, more than what she can understand.

"He's not perfect. Let's not kid ourselves," Mia says, trying to lighten the space between them, "but I couldn't have asked for a better dad, that's for sure."

Their food arrives, and those first few bites are heaven, delicious, savory, smothered in sour cream heaven.

"Told ya," Matt mutters in between bites.

"Oh my goodness, you weren't kidding about how good this is," Mia finally says after feeling slightly full from basically inhaling her meal. "Listen, while I have you here, there's something I've been meaning to talk to you about."

Matt's head rises with a rush, his eyes flaring, and he swallows hard. "Listen, if it's about me –"

"I'd like to…." Mia says at the same time.

They both stop.

"Sorry, you first," he says.

"No, it's okay. What were you saying?" She leans in,

curious as to what he was going to say before she spoke over him.

He shakes his head. "No, please," he waves his hand at her, "please go ahead. You wanted to do something?"

It takes her a moment to switch the direction of where her thoughts were heading.

"Um, well…" she plays with the food left on her plate, sorting through her words. She can play it safe and discuss the store, or she could be bold and say something about last year, about her thinking there was something there…

"I was actually wondering if you could help create a new display area in the store," she says instead, going with the safer topic.

Matt leans back, and for a moment, he looks about as disappointed as Mia feels.

"Yeah, sure. What were you thinking?"

She details her vision of Santa's library, complete with a faux fireplace, rocking chair, and large rug on the floor for kids to sit and listen to Mrs. Claus read stories.

"What about creating a false front to the bookshelves? I could do some design work and give it more of a Christmas feel. Like rotor a Christmas tree in the corners or something?" He pulls out a napkin from the dispenser and draws a rough design.

She leans forward for a better view and instantly likes what she sees.

"That's perfect. It's not too much, is it? I don't want to pull you away from other projects," she asks. Their heads are so close, their foreheads are almost touching.

"No, it's fine. As long as you're not in a rush, I should be able to get some of this done in time for the market. I'm assuming that's when you'd like to have it ready for. Of course, it won't all be done, but we can do it in stages. The fireplace will be first, and it won't be too hard. Know any students who like to paint? That might speed things up since that's not really in my wheelhouse."

"That's perfect, really, and yes, I have someone in mind," Mia says. "Now, what were you going to say before I cut you off so rudely?"

He plays with the napkin before folding it and placing it in his back pocket.

"Nothing rude about it. I think we both had something to say, that's all." He pauses as a server comes to their table and clears up their dishes. She also brings their bill, and before Mia can reach for hers, Matt whisks them both off the table.

"My treat," he says. "It's not technically a date, but I did ask you here, after all." He doesn't look at her as he says this, which is probably good since Mia knows her face has turned blaring red in color.

Not technically a date? Did that mean it was close to one? Or that maybe there will be one?

Could he be interested? If he's not, then he could have remained quiet, let her pay her portion, and they could go their separate ways.

Stop. She can't let her thoughts go there, even though she's all twisted in knots now and feeling like she's on the edge of a waterfall, unsure if she can actually jump.

"On that note," Matt says, clearing his throat, "I've been too much of a coward to bring this up before now, and for that, I apologize."

It's on the tip of her tongue to say something, but she keeps her comments to herself, as hard as it is.

"Last year was...well, it wasn't a great time for me. I was about to leave Innsbruck, had a place lined up in Vancouver, actually, and was only sticking around until after the Christmas market in case anything came up that needed fixing."

He was going to leave? She didn't know this, right? She couldn't have.

"That's why, when you asked me for drinks, I had to say no...I didn't want to start something with you that I knew couldn't work."

If she thought her face was red before, it's probably turning a nice shade of scarlet about now.

"It's okay, I ahh..."

He reaches out and gently touches her hand. "No, it wasn't okay. I can't tell you how many times I kicked myself for doing that. I wanted to call, to say something but then...well, things with your dad and then this town reinvention and ...."

"It just got easier to say nothing," Mia finishes for him.

Matt nods.

She asks one of the many questions swirling in her mind. "How come you didn't leave?"

He starts playing with the cup in front of him, turning it in circles on the table.

"I was leaving because there was no work. Then, suddenly, there's so much work. Innsbruck became home, and truthfully, I really didn't want to leave."

A smile blooms on Mia's face. "Well, even though nothing happened between us, I'm glad you didn't."

He looks her direct in the eyes then. "Something could, though, right? I mean...if it's not too late to give it another try?"

He's still interested? Despite how awkward things have been between them? How she's treated him every time she comes by her parents' house?

"I mean, it's okay if it is. I get it. I just thought..." his voice trails as he doesn't finish his sentence, and Mia realizes just how vulnerable he's being with her.

How he's always been with her. Even when she was rude, even when she was reacting out of fear, he's always been honest with her. He didn't have to be. He could have been cold, distant...but he never was. He gave her space, sure, but he was always honest, never mincing words.

This time, it's her reaching out to lightly touch his hand.

"I'd love that, Matt. I really would."

CHAPTER FORTY-NINE

ASHLEY

Her next appointment is one she's been looking forward to all week, from when Jared called to say he had an idea he'd like her input on. All week, she's been racking her brains trying to figure out his idea, knowing taking over for Durwood wouldn't be it... she's accepted that reality.

"Do you need anything before I head home?" Susan pokes her head into Ashley's office.

Ashley waves her away. "Go, enjoy your weekend." Her desk is a measured mess, with folders scattered everywhere. Chaotic but controlled. "I've got everything covered here."

"Great. Jared's here."

Ashley stands and lightly stretches the kinks out of her back. "It's about time. This day has felt like it would never end."

"Sorry for coming so late," Jared says. "Even with leaving early, traffic out of the city is crazy."

"There's some art festival happening in one of the parks," Susan says. "All the hotels in Banff and Canmore sold out weeks ago." She gives them both a wave before closing the door behind her.

Ashley heads to her office window and looks out over the main street. Innsbruck has also seen some traffic today from those coming to the festival, which is nice. The street below is busy with parked vehicles, those driving by to see the different facades on the shops...their early marketing efforts paying off just as intended.

A few weeks ago, they'd started a marketing campaign through social media, inviting people to take the drive to discover their transformation, to watch history in the making. The few baking classes they advertised, just as a test, have been filling up nicely, too.

"Town is looking great," Jared says, settling in the chair. "I can see the difference, even from when I was here a few weeks ago."

"Your dad has been able to hire a few more skilled workers, which has made a huge difference. We're still behind schedule, but not by much anymore."

Jared clearly wants to say something to that but keeps his thoughts to himself. He leaned back, hands on his thighs, fingers drumming a little da-da-da-da on his jeans.

Ashley sits close, arms resting on her desk, a waiting smile on her face. She can easily fill the silence between them, but he's the one who requested the meeting, so she'll wait till he's ready to speak.

"The land up on the hill, have you thought about how you'd like to utilize it yet?"

Ashley pulls herself closer to her desk, her shoulders hunched up close to her ears. Yes, she's had many thoughts on that land usage. She wonders if maybe their ideas are similar and if so, he's the perfect person to take on the job.

"Have you seen the map we placed in the sitting area?" She asks him.

Jared rubs his hands along the back of his neck. "Yep, took a look today. That's been up for a while? You've got some grand plans there. Figured that's where my mother got the idea."

Oh, this sounds promising. That area on the map has been designated for a camping area. Ashley pushes her chair back and folds her hands on her lap. Her expectations are rising, but she doesn't need to show him that.

"Do you have anyone in mind for building that campground?" Jared's stare is direct, just like his question.

"We are looking at leasing it out to a charity organization. Why?" She lets that little bit of information sit between them. "Do you have a different idea?"

Jared dips his head in a slight nod. "I'd like to suggest a partnership. A holiday-themed campground with rustic cabins. Marlee and Josie came up with the idea, and I think it'd fit. Rather than leasing to a charity who'll use the campground a few months of the year, we'll make this open year-round."

Ashley writes down notes in her notebook, the idea very appealing.

"How would this be a partnership?"

"You help with some of the initial setup costs, let us build on the land, and in return, receive a portion of each reservation we take in. Things will be slow at first, but in time, I think it'll be a popular option for travelers." He pulls a folded piece of paper from his jacket pocket and holds it out. "We could have an area for campers and RVs to park. Considering how quickly campgrounds in the National Park fill up, this could be a huge hit."

He hands her a basic drawing of what he has in mind. It's rough, but she can see the gist and likes it.

"We have enough financing for three cabins. Nothing fancy, one bedroom, bathroom, kitchenette. We'll need help with furnishings and such. We'll start out basic, and as we grow, we'll enhance the cottages so they are larger, more elaborate, and offer more amenities."

An idea blooms in Ashley's mind the more he talks. More lodging with different options is really appealing, especially if the town gets a cut on it too.

"I'll have to look into zoning, but Jared, I'll be honest, I love this idea, and I feel the council members will too. So, just one question to start…"

A distinct change occurred in Jared at her words. His shoulders drop, his lips lift, and the tension creases around his eyes disappear.

"How soon can you start?"

Before he answers, there's a knock on her office door. It opens before she has a chance to open her mouth. Durwood blocks the entrance, his arms crossed over his red plaid-covered chest, a fierce frown on his face.

"That's a great question I'd love to know the answer, too." He says, his voice a growl matching the look he gives them both.

Jared almost jumps in his seat.

"Durwood, I wasn't expecting you to come in," Ashley says. He's actually the last person she thought would walk through her door at this hour.

Any appearance of happiness is stripped from Jared's face. He lifts his hand in a greeting, but he doesn't turn to look at his father.

"Saw my son's truck outside," Durwood says, not leaving his post at the door. "Figured I'd come and say hi in case he left without dropping by the house."

"Of course, I'll drop by. Marlee and the kids are there, and we're staying for dinner."

"Harrumph. Didn't know nothing about dinner plans."

Jared shakes his head, as if he isn't surprised at the news.

Ashley brings her hands up close to her face in a relaxed fist, dropping her forehead to rest on them for a moment. She's struggling to think of how to handle the obvious tension between the two men.

"Seems I'm interrupting some business between the two of you," Durwood says. "Should I leave?"

She knows Jared is staring at her, she can feel the heat of his glare, as if he's imploring her to step in between them, but she knows from experience how ugly misunderstandings between these two men can get and doesn't feel like getting caught in the middle, again – especially when this time isn't her fault.

"It's fine, Dad." Jared eventually speaks up. Ashley finally looks up to find Jared on his feet. "Come, sit. I'm not hiding anything from you."

"Really, because that's how it feels." Durwood doesn't move from his spot to the seat Jared offers.

"What exactly do you think is happening here?" Jared asks.

Ashley pretends to write notes as if the confrontation doesn't concern her. From Durwood's pointed glances, she knows he blames her just as much as his son. For what, she isn't sure, but she's being lumped into the equation all the same.

"I think you're about to move back home. That's what I think is happening. I know our wives have concocted a plan that will benefit your family and this town. I also know I want in, but only if you give me an honest answer." Durwood steps into her office then, fixated one hundred percent on his son.

"Why would I lie to you?" Jared's shoulders stiffen at the accusation.

Durwood's face pinch together at his son's reaction. It seems to Ashley that he hasn't thought through the words he used.

"I didn't mean that."

Jared crosses his arms. "Sure you did. If you spoke it, you meant it. Isn't that what you've always taught me?"

Durwood gives off a sound as if he's being strangled.

Ashley expects Jared to step in, to smooth the path for his father, but he doesn't. She isn't sure what's going on between the two men, but the power struggle is real and affects both men in different ways, from what she's noticed.

"Son, I've..." Durwood stops and hangs his head. His arms drop to his sides in a defeated stance.

Ashley's never seen Durwood look so lost and broken before. Something inside her wants to speak up, to break the tension...the words are all there, on the tip of her tongue, ready to make the jump, but they won't come out in the end.

Whatever happens, has nothing to do with her and everything to do with a strangled relationship between a father and son.

"Don't bother, Durwood. I think you've said enough." Jared turns his full attention toward her, unmistakable pain in his eyes. "Mayor, why don't you get back to me after you hear from zoning?" He leans forward as if to shake her hand, but Durwood bolts into the room, his large body blocking the handshake.

"My wife has informed me that it's time I let go of imaginary hurts and man up. Which is why I'm here. I'm not questioning your honesty, son. I just need to know, did you ever plan on telling me you were going into business with your mother but not with me?"

CHAPTER FIFTY

MARLEE

Marlee is nursing her second round of coffee while Josie stands at the window, anxiously peering out.

"Are you waiting for the kids to return with treats from Frankie's, or are you worried about Jared? The meeting is going to go fine, you know that, right? It's a solid plan, and we both know Ashley will jump on board."

When Jared first dropped her and the kids off at his mother's place, Josie was full of smiles and chatter, and Marlee appreciated the ability to sit back and enjoy her coffee while Josie fussed on the kids.

But ever since the kids left to grab cookies from Frankie's, Josie's gone silent and hasn't sat down once. First, she made a batch of muffins, which are baking in the oven right now. If she isn't cleaning something, she's at the window, her fingers curling around the fabric as she waits for someone to return home.

"You know we love you, right?" Josie asks, slowly turning from her post at the window.

Marlee cocks her head to the side. To say her mother-in-law

is off today is too obvious. "Come sit," Marlee taps her hand on the empty seat beside her.

Josie ignores her, focusing on the muffins instead, opening the oven door. "Oh good, they're done," she mumbles, avoiding Marlee's gaze.

Marlee waits until Josie is finished fussing before she decides to respond to her mother-in-law's question.

"Josie, you know I love you, right? That both Jared and I love you and Durwood with all our hearts." She pushes her half-drank mug of coffee to the side and gives Josie a smile full of that love.

Josie's eyes well with tears. "Oh love, I know that. You kids...I just miss you all. I really hope this idea works, that you'll be able to come back home. This is where you belong."

Finally, without a look outside the window, Josie joins her at the table.

"And yes, I know you love us," Marlee finally answers Josie's question.

"But, do you know, here, deep in your heart," Josie places her palm on Marlee's chest, "that we love you, Marlee Holms, as if you are our own daughter?"

Marlee covers Josie's hand with her own. "Of course, I do. You're the only mother I have left, and I will never give you up."

"And Durwood..." Josie's voice is full of uncertainty, insecurity, and hope.

Marlee takes a breath, holding it for a brief moment, before letting her eyes speak for her. The tears gathering in Josie's eyes journey down her worn face, curling in the lines of her laugh wrinkles, gathering in pools at the edge of her jawline before dropping, one at a time, onto her sweater.

Marlee hands her a napkin, all the while curling her own

tongue over the words that need to be said but intuitively knowing now is not the right time.

"He knows." Josie stares at the table, her head bowed, her lips trembling.

"What does he know?" Marlee asks, trying to follow along with Josie's thought pattern.

Does he know that Marlee knows about his conversation with Jared? That Jared has been offered his job? He knows why they are here today?

"He knows about our idea. He left the house just before Jared dropped you off."

Marlee automatically reaches for her discarded coffee cup. It's like she needs something in her hands for her to think clearly.

"Okaaayy," she draws the word out slowly. "We figured he knew or that he'd know after today. Why do you make it sound like it's a bad thing?"

"Oh, honey. Once he found out the truth, he stormed out of here like the hellhound nipped at his heels, and I'm afraid he's headed to interrupt Jared and Ashley's meeting." The quick corner glance she casts toward Marlee is enough to put Marlee on edge.

"Josie...what happened exactly?"

Josie swallows hard before she goes to jump up from her chair.

Marlee's hand shoots out, grabbing the woman's arm and forcing her into place.

"Oh no, you don't," Marlee says through gritted teeth. "Sit that tush of yours back down and tell me exactly what happened."

While Josie hedges and tries to mask her emotions, Marlee starts to understand things are bad. Like, really bad. Josie isn't one for running from confrontation - she's more the charge-ahead type of woman.

"Things were all fine this morning. We drank our coffee, talked about dinner, and then Durwood had to ask me what we had in the savings account. The man knows I sock money away for rainy days or whenever I feel like using it, that I've been saving for a family trip, but that's my money, and he rarely asks about it. So why today?" Josie stares up at the ceiling, head shaking, as if the ceiling holds all the answers.

"He apparently has an idea for that money, something he just talked to me about," Josie continues.

Marlee holds her tongue. The same can be said for Josie and her idea, but it won't help progress this story.

"What kind of idea? Or should I not ask?"

Josie shrugs. "We didn't quite get there. When I didn't answer him about the money, he got all in my face, and you know how I feel about that." Josie's hand wrap around the back of her neck. "I'm so tight now because of him. I need a massage."

"Josie..." Marlee keeps her voice low, expectant, pushing Josie back toward the topic on hand.

"Fine. First, I told him that what I do with that money is none of his business, which, looking back, is the wrong thing to say, but I wasn't ready to tell him the truth, not just then." Her lips ground together, reminding Marlee of a spoiled child not liking the answer no.

"When I told him that I was giving the money to you guys to start up a camp and that Jared is meeting with Ashley to discuss, he gave me this look," her body shakes with tiny tremors, "then left without another word to me."

"Oh, Josie..." Marlee wants to wrap her mother-in-law in a big warm hug. She'd been worried that the money might become an issue between Josie and Durwood, and they'd almost said no for this very reason.

"I'm sure it'll be fine." Marlee tries to muster up the belief that everything will be fine, even though she has a feeling it won't be.

"Jared warned me keeping this a secret could cost me." Josie blinks several times. "I should have told Durwood. It's not like he wasn't going to find out eventually..."

Marlee grabs her cell phone to see if Jared sent an update on how the meeting went. Surely, it has to be over by now.

Nothing. Not a single word or emoji. Just complete silence.

While Josie sits there now, looking a little shell-shocked, Marlee is the one fidgeting like crazy, her leg bouncing, her fingers twitching, her heart rate racing...scenarios and more scenarios racing through Marlee's imagination, none of the outcomes being salvageable.

"I should make cookies." Josie jumps up from her seat.

"The kids will be back with cookies, remember?" Marlee reminds her.

"Then I should get started on dinner."

"You promised the girls they could help you make dinner," Marlee says.

Josie stands there, hovering, her hands settled firmly on her hips. "Well, I need to do something. I can't just sit here and wait for word. I stress bake, you know that."

"What about a pie? What's Durwood's favorite? Jared hinted he really hoped you'd made a Dutch Apple Pie for dessert."

Josie's eyes light up as large saucers. "That also happens to be Durwood's favorite. Maybe I'll make a few for tonight and one for you to take home." She glances around the kitchen, at the large basket of apples on the counter, fingers stroking her chin. "I should actually make three. Leave one here for

Durwood to nibble on after everyone's left, but I'm not sure I have enough apples for that."

Josie heads into the large walk-in pantry Durwood finally finished last year. "Well, don't you know it, I have more than enough to work with. I forgot about these." Josie walks out of the pantry carrying a large burlap bag of apples.

"Sometimes words aren't enough," Josie mutters to herself.

"What do you mean?"

Dropping the sac on the counter, Josie pulls out a large bowl, a cutting board, and peelers. "Here, why don't you help me peel some of these."

It isn't until Marlee is into her fifth apple that Josie finally answers her question.

"Words aren't enough. It takes action, something that requires work and commitment from us to really say we're sorry." Josie wraps the pie crust she'd been working on with saran wrap and then places it in the fridge to cool. "When Durwood screws up, he can say I'm sorry all day long, but it's not until he's gone out of his way and done something that makes him uncomfortable, like spending time reading through a bajillion cards to find the perfect one, and pick out a bouquet of flowers he knows I'll love, that I know the apology is real."

Marlee completely understands, recognizing Jared is the same.

The silence between the two is reminiscent of the early days when Marlee was a young bride. It was Josie who taught her to bake, to clean a kitchen, to say *I love you* and *I'm sorry* through food.

The front door slams just as Josie sets the pies in the oven. Both women freeze, the heavy steps announcing their husbands, are back.

CHAPTER FIFTY-ONE

"Honey, we're home." Jared enters the kitchen, his face as solid as a slate of wood, and Durwood follows close behind. His expression reveals even less. "Where are the kids?"

Marlee tries to get a read on her husband, but he's giving her nothing. Not a sweet thing.

"Marlee? The kids?" Jared repeats his questions.

Marlee grabs her phone and pulls up Frankie's message from a few minutes ago. "Mom sent them to Frankie's to grab some cookies, and now she's giving them a baking lesson. They'll be back in an hour or so, Frankie says."

Jared nods, taking the offered mug of fresh coffee his mother pours for him. Josie repeats the process for Durwood.

"What is that I'm smelling?" Durwood's head tilts up as he sniffs the air.

"You know exactly what it is," Josie says, wiping her hands on her apron before taking the seat next to him.

"Huh. So, it's like that, is it?" Durwood says, one brow lifting.

Josie gives him a timid smile before staring out the side

window as if truly fascinated by what she sees beyond the blowing curtains.

The men are quiet. Both sip their coffee, eyes down, shoulders tense.

It's Jared who breaks the silence.

"So, Dad joined my meeting with the Mayor today." There was a lot he doesn't say in that sentence, too, a lot that Marlee hears.

Expectation. Disappointment. Hurt. Hope.

It's the hope she grabs hold of. *Please let things be okay*.

"And how did that go?" Marlee directs her question first to her husband, then to Durwood, when Jared doesn't answer. She's kind of glad he didn't answer, that he's giving his father space to say something.

If Marlee's honest with herself, she's struggling with her feelings toward her father-in-law. She's been hiding these feelings from Jared, not wanting to add more fuel to the fire, but the feelings are there nonetheless.

She loves Durwood. Of course, she does. That will never change.

She respects him, because she'd been raised to respect an elder, and he deserves that respect.

It's the trust she's had in him that's the issue. Until now, she always believed he'd be there for them, always look out for them and protect them as a father would. Now? Now she's not sure.

He hurt her. She doesn't need to know what's been said to feel that hurt.

"You all have come up with a good idea," Durwood finally utters, his voice gruff, ground with hidden meanings.

"Well, of course, it's a good idea." Josie acts affronted. Marlee recognizes this as her way of protecting them, her children.

The issue is they don't need to be protected. Not anymore.

Especially not from Durwood. That's something both she and Jared have come to realize.

"Durwood, I'm sorry if you felt out of the loop." Marlee starts off apologizing, knowing he deserves that apology. Being left in the dark over anything isn't a fun feeling, one she knows from experience.

Durwood turns toward her. She can't read his face. There's no hints to what he must be thinking or feeling.

"I was out of the loop." Durwood finally breaks. His head bobs as his chin quivers. "I deserve it, don't I?" He sneaks a look at Jared before staring at the table. "I lost my temper. I admit it. I said things I should never have said, all because I was afraid. I am afraid." He clarifies. He's staring deep into his coffee cup as if ashamed to admit his fears to them.

"Afraid? Why Durwood, why would you be afraid?" Josie lays her hand on her husband's arm, concern shining through her touch, her gaze, her words.

Marlee notices Jared's face is as blank as it was earlier. He does, however, reach for her leg beneath the table and squeeze her thigh, leaving his hand to rest there.

He's been quiet. Too quiet. She wishes he would say something. Anything instead of remaining silent.

"I'm getting old. Too old to be trying to rebuild a town. Instead of admitting that and accepting help, I thought others were deciding it for me." His shoulders lift in a shrug. "You all know how much I love that." He attempts a chuckle, but it falls flat as everyone remains silent. "I ahh...I lashed out, not because it's what I really believed but because I knew it would hurt you as much as you were hurting me." His voice breaks as he turns his attention to Jared. "Except, I was wrong."

"Yes, you were." Jared finally says something. He doesn't give away much in the tone of his voice, but Marlee knows how hard it is for him to confront his father like this.

Marlee squeezes his hand, offering support.

"Dad, you said things that a lesser man would find unforgivable. You raised me to believe family is everything, yet you almost destroyed yours with your words. If you demand that I choose between you or my wife, I'll always choose my wife. Always." He leans forward. "Because that's how you raised me." He stresses those last words.

Durwood nods deep at his son's words while Marlee's throat swells with choked emotion.

"I was wrong. I'm sorry. So very, very, sorry." Durwood bites his lips as tears trickle down his face.

That's all it takes for her husband to break. He throws himself out of his chair and wraps his arms around his father. The men sit like that for the longest time.

Marlee can't contain her own tears. They flow down her face, dripping from her chin until Josie hands her a napkin.

"I want you to come home, to where you belong. I just haven't known how to make that happen," Durwood says once the tears and sniffles stop. "I didn't want you to work for me or with me, because you don't need to run things with your old man. You need something of your own...and I was going to chat with the Mayor to see what we could do."

"I was a step ahead of you, love," Josie says, her face beaming bright.

"As you usually are." Durwood reaches over for his wife's hand. "You shouldn't have had to go behind my back, though. Not sure I'll ever forgive myself for that."

Marlee turns toward Jared, wanting to give the older couple a little privacy, and leans in close, keeping her voice down. "How did the meeting go?"

"It went well," Jared admits. A sense of peace and excitement accompanies her husband as he says the words, a sense she hasn't felt from him in a long time.

"Ashley likes the idea, actually. We can probably start with more than three cabins, thanks to the funding she thinks she can provide. She's a step ahead of us, that's for sure. You haven't been talking to her?" A smile plays on his lips, like he's expecting her to say yes, but she shakes her head instead. "Really? Huh. Well, she had sketches already drawn up."

"Well, that's not surprising. Did you see that map she has in her office? That woman has huge expectations for this town." Durwood interjects. "She asked for ideas from the townsfolk and has been trying to implement as many as she can. It's a hassle, actually, from my standpoint."

"Too many cooks in the kitchen and all that," Josie says.

Durwood nods. "I try to tell her, but..."

"What do you think of the name Candy Cane Cottages?" Jared says to Marlee, obviously ignoring his father's grumbling. Marlee tries to stifle a grin but struggles. Jared rolls his eyes at her. "You should ask her to send you a photo of the map she's got. There's cabins, lanes, a tent area by the stream, and even a concession stand. I'm quite impressed, truth be told."

Candy Cane Cottages. It's cute. Cute and perfect for the reinvention of Innsbruck.

"I'd like to talk to your brothers and see if they'll come on board. Make this a real family thing," Durwood says. "That is...if you want."

"Now, Durwood...the money is just a loan." Josie's voice is full of warning. "The kids have a plan to pay us back so we can take that Disney trip with the grandkids."

Durwood waves her concerns away. "There's no need to pay us back. If you feel you must, save the money, pay for the vacation, and bring us along. This family has always stood beside one another, shoulder to shoulder. Why should this be any different?"

"Because it's not our decision," Josie said, hopefully

stressing the words with enough force for Durwood to get the message.

Marlee isn't sure he is. His forehead creases together, creating ruts on his face to match his frown. "Why are you making a big deal about this?"

Marlee is shocked at how surprised Durwood actually sounds.

"Dad, let's take one step at a time, okay? No hasty decisions right now. Plus, you have your own project and crew to run. I've got this. If you and Mom want to be silent partners, that's one thing, and I'm sure Marlee and I will have no problems with it."

"Harrumph," Durwood grumbles beneath his breath.

"Oh hush, you old fool. For someone who wanted to retire years ago, you sure like to keep yourself busy. Leave the kids alone." Josie pats his hand before standing.

There's a glimmer of a smile on Jared's face. That glimmer grows until it fills her heart and soul with hope and joy. It's overwhelming, and she doesn't bother to hide the tears that pool.

"We're coming home, aren't we?" The words slide off her tongue with a welcome sense of ease.

Jared pushes his chair closer until they are side by side, wrapping his arm around her shoulder, pulling her close.

"We're coming home, baby," he whispers into her ear. "We're finally coming home."

CHAPTER FIFTY-TWO

ASHLEY

She's on a mission. Heading down the street, her focus is solely on one store and one store alone.

She'd asked Mia to join her for the Cookies and Cocktails class tonight, the first one she hopes is a standing event, but she has this funny feeling Mia will stand her up, claiming to be too busy or too tired or too something else. She's not about to let that happen. It's been too long since the two spent time doing something fun, and tonight's class is sure to be more than just fun.

What's more fun than a room full of friends, sipping cocktails, and baking cookies? If this goes well, and there's no reason it shouldn't, the class will be a success. There's already a small waitlist for future classes.

Pushing in the door of the Wandering Aisle, Ashley walks into a bookshop full of people.

Mia waves at her from beside the cash desk, where she's chatting with customers.

Ashley takes her time walking over, looking over the new display tables set up in the front area. They're a mixture of holiday fiction titles as well as different Christmas cookbooks.

She immediately picks up a cookie one and starts to flip through, seeing so many recipes she'd love to try.

"Oh, that's a good one." Mia appears at her side. "I had to put in an order for more. It's been selling so well. These are all I have left. Mom bought the first copy when it came in, and actually made those last night. She doubled the amount of almond extract, though."

"Jordan mentioned she wants to do more baking this year." She closes the cookbook, holding it close to her chest as she looks over the other selections.

"Honestly, you can't go wrong with that one," Mia says. "It's Mom approved, so you know it's good."

"Mom approved is all I need to know." She glances around the shop. "Do you have a sale or event going on that I don't know about?" She counts about half a dozen or so crowded around the counter.

"Book club order came in," Mia says with a smile. "It's been like this all day. I was just about to sneak out when you came in."

"Sneak out?" From the slight grin on Mia's face, she's about to do more than just sneak out. "I thought you were coming with me tonight? Or wait...please tell me you have a hot date instead, right?"

Mia's eyes widen just slightly, but enough for Ashley to grab her arm and give her a slight squeeze.

"You do, don't you? Have a hot date? Please tell me it's with Matt." She's just about given up on these two becoming an item, even though they're perfect for each other.

"Of course, I'm coming to the class. Cookies and cocktails...

hello? Like I'd miss that. I seem to remember being forced to promise to be your date to these adult-focused classes."

Ashley hears the words, but she's more focused on the slight blush creeping along Mia's face.

"What aren't you telling me?" Ashley leans close, keeping her voice conspiratorially low, knowing Mia has a secret she needs to share.

Laughter erupts from the back of the shop, catching both women off guard. "I love it when my shop is busy," Mia says before linking their arms together, "but if I don't leave now, I may never escape." Mia pulls Ashley out of the store.

"Mia, wait." Ashley forces Mia to a stop. "I left without paying for the book." She holds up the cookbook with a giggle. "Does this make me a shoplifter?"

Mia laughs, waving away her words. "Bring me coffee in the morning and pay for it then. It's not like I don't know where you live and work." She takes the book from Ashley's hands and stuffs it into Ashley's bag. "There. Out of sight, out of mind."

"All right, woman, spill the beans," Ashley waits until they've passed a few stores before she pulls Mia in close.

It's cute how Mia's steps falter. It's even cuter as she struggles to find the words to admit to something Ashley hopes has to do with Matt.

"Matt and I—"

"I knew it!" Ashley lets out a whoop, interrupting Mia. "Took you guys long enough, like seriously."

Mia giggles like a schoolgirl receiving her first Valentine's Day card. "Can I finish my sentence at least?" She glances around to make sure no one is in earshot.

"Spill the beans, woman. I've been waiting almost a year for this news."

The epic eye-roll from Mia does little to damper Ashley's

excitement. "We went on an unofficial date and decided to take things slow and see where it goes."

Mia tries hard to contain her smile, but Ashley notices the deepening dimple. Rather than saying anything out loud, she squeezes her friend's arm.

"You guys are perfect for each other."

"So, you've said, repeatedly," Mia says, leaning her head on Ashley's shoulder for a brief moment. "Thank you for trying to play matchmaker, even though it didn't work out like you thought it would."

"Wait, what do you mean? I thought it worked out perfectly."

They're really close to the new community kitchen, but Ashley wants to hear all the juice bits before they turn their focus to whatever delicious treats they're about to make tonight.

"Perfectly? You expected it to take us a year?"

"Well, no," Ashley admits, lifting her shoulder in a shrug. "But you're dating, right? There was no timeline...well, not for me at least. Everyone else might have bet on how long it'd take, but..."

"You...you bet on us?" Mia's eyes grow the size of toy teacups.

"I didn't, no," Ashley says, trying to placate her friend, even knowing it's no use. "Everyone else, though? Maybe...listen, none of that matters, right? Bottom line...I knew the two of you would make a great couple, and it's about time you two realized just how awesome my match-making skills are."

Mia tosses her hands up in the air, visibly frustrated as they cross the street. "Ashley...girl...I have no words."

"That's fine. Save them for when we're in class." Ashley gives her a wink, thoroughly enjoying just how flustered Mia is.

"Why?"

Ashley waits until they're inside the building and take their seats before she leans over and whispers into Mia's ear.

"I made a promise to everyone you'd be a couple in time for Christmas, and you know how important it is that I keep my word."

EPILOGUE

DECEMBER 1st

It's a perfect evening with a smattering of snow in the air.

Bundled in a thick winter jacket, complete with hand-knit wool mitts, a hat, and a brightly colored scarf, Ashley is prepared for a magical night.

It's their first Christmas as a themed town, and while everything isn't yet complete, they're more than on their way to that full-on Bavarian feel.

Every town has their traditions when it comes to Christmas, and Innsbruck is no different.

Tonight is all about the tree-lighting ceremony, but this year it's extra special.

It feels like the whole town has turned out for the celebration, and Ashley couldn't be happier. Ashley gazes out into the crowd with her daughter at her side, her heart swelling as she sees the expectant faces of so many families who recently returned to their small town.

A year ago, she promised to save their small town. Seeing all these people turn out tonight is proof of a promise kept.

Little by little, as word spreads, more families move back, and that's exactly what Ashley was hoping for. This town is meant for families, for families to call it home, and finding a way to make that possible...she wipes the tears that pool on the edges of her eyelids as happiness spreads through her.

"You're not crying, are you?" Jordan asks with a bit of mortification in her tone.

"Maybe," Ashley admits.

"Moooooommmm, stop it," Jordan hisses, sticking her hands into her jacket pockets. "That's so embarrassing." She half turns her body, putting a little distance between them, but Ashley doesn't mind. She caught the slight tilt on her daughter's lips.

This past year hasn't been easy – between her marriage falling apart, her daughter struggling with her own hurts, and all the growing pains associated with turning the focus of this town...but it's all been worth it. Her friendships are stronger, her relationship with her daughter is tighter, and she's no longer struggling with her purpose. She's found it... she's living it...this is it – building a home for a community of families.

Susan gives her a brief wave, their prearranged signal to alert her to the five-minute warning mark.

Tonight is all about their town. Lighting this tree signifies their rebirth of Innsbruck and starts their annual Christmas Market. As soon as the tree is lit, they'll all walk over to the park where the market stalls have been set up, but from what Susan told her earlier, there's already a crowd there, sipping hot cocoa, surrounding the fire pits as they wait for the official opening.

She could squeal with glee, knowing this will be the best Christmas yet, and every year will get better and bigger.

"Well, hello everyone," Ashley says into the microphone. "Can you believe the size of our tree this year? When I asked

Susan to find me the tallest and biggest tree she could find, she sure didn't disappoint, did she? Isn't this tree amazing? Wait until you see it all lit up! I hope you'll join us over at the expanded Christmas market tonight. I have it on good authority Frankie has a booth with her best hot chocolate yet. Okay," she looks out into the crowd with a smile, "who's ready to see this gorgeous tree all lit up? On the count of three. One....two...."

The oohs and ahhs as a brilliant display of white lights cascade their way down the tree, covering every branch, is music to Ashley's ears.

There's a reason she loves Christmas so much, and it has nothing to do with gifts.

Christmas is about family, about community, about a sense of wonderment and excitement. Christmas is a promise of things to come, of giving yourself permission to dream and for resting in the peace and hope of what's been promised.

Pulling Jordan close in a hug, Ashley knows they are where they belong, where they've always belonged, and that for years to come, this place will be home to generations, just like it was meant to be.

...THE END

Author note: wouldn't it be fun to do a reader weekend in a Bavarian town located closer to home? Would you join me if I did? If the answer is YES or MAYBE...do me a favor and join my travel email list and let me know?

https://www.steenaholmes.com/lets-travel-together/

FRANKIE'S HOT COCOA

FRANKIE'S FAMOUS HOT COCOA

Who doesn't love homemade hot cocoa? Especially when it's topped with delicious homemade whipped cream!

This recipe uses cocoa and chocolate chips and it's delicious!

For extra fun when you have kids around or company... create a tray with fun sauces to add, different toppings...use your imagination and have fun!

INGREDIENTS:

4 cups creamer (can use milk)
¼ cup unsweetened cocoa powder
¼ cup granulated sugar
½ cup chocolate chips or chopped chocolate bar
¼ teaspoon pure vanilla extract

STEPS:

1. Place milk, cocoa powder and sugar in a small saucepan.

2. Heat over medium/medium-low heat, whisking frequently, until warm (but not boiling).

3. Add chocolate chips and whisk constantly until the chocolate chips melt and distribute evenly into the milk.

4. Whisk in vanilla extract, serve immediately.

TIPS:

* I love to use cream (makes it creamier/thicker) but you can use milk or add 1/2 and 1/2 creamer. You could use almond milk too. The choices are endless.

* Use semi-sweet for a sweet taste.

* Want less sweet? Use dark chocolate.

* Use your imagination for flavoured hot cocoa! Peppermint extract, almond extract, Kahlua, Baileys...enjoy!

* I love to top with whipped cream, but you can use marshmallows, crushed candy canes - the list is endless on how to create the perfect hot cocoa.

CINNAMON SUGAR MUFFINS

ASHLEY'S RECIPE FOR CINNAMON SUGAR MUFFINS

I love these muffins. They are soft, sweet and have the consistency of a donut...and who doesn't love donuts! These are my favorite because they're dipped in melted sugar and then dipped again in a cinnamon sugar mixture.

Whenever I make them, they never last! And...if I'm being completely honest with you...sometimes I make them and don't tell my family! (which means, yes, I eat them all! but not in one sitting...)

I hope you'll try them...and I know you'll enjoy them when you do!

FOR THE MUFFINS:
   1 1/2 Cups All Purpose Flour
   1/2 Cup Granulated Sugar
   1 1/2 Teaspoons Baking Powder
   1/8 Teaspoon Salt
   1/2 Teaspoon Ground Cinnamon

1/4 Teaspoon Nutmeg
1 Teaspoon Vanilla Extract
1 Large Egg
1/2 Cup Milk
1/3 Cup Butter, Melted and Cooled

FOR THE TOPPING:

1/3 Cup Granulated Sugar
2 Teaspoons Ground Cinnamon
5 Tablespoons Butter, Melted

BAKING INSTRUCTIONS:

Preheat oven to 350 degrees. Grease muffin cups or line with paper liners. Set aside.

In a large bowl whisk together the flour, sugar, baking powder, salt, cinnamon, and nutmeg. Set aside.

In a small bowl beat the egg. Add the milk, vanilla extract, and melted butter and mix well to combine.

Add the wet ingredients to the dry ingredients and stir just until moistened, being careful not to over mix.

Spoon batter into muffin cups about 1/2 - 3/4 of the way full. Bake in preheated oven for 20-25 minutes. Allow muffins to cool for 5 minutes before removing from pan.

TOPPING INSTRUCTIONS:

In a small bowl mix together the cinnamon and sugar. In another small bowl melt the 5 Tablespoons of butter.

Dip the muffins into the butter, then roll in the cinnamon sugar mixture.

PANNEKOEK RECIPE

STEENA'S FAVORITE PANNEKOEK RECIPE

I love these...you can go savory or sweet. Of course, I like both (who doesn't like the idea of melted chocolate, strawberries and whipped on something a little thicker than a crepe?

First – what is a pannenkoek? It's dutch for pancake, basically. It's a delicious crepe with a variety of ingredients cooked right into the batter. In the Netherlands, this is lunch or dinner...or dinner and dessert.

My absolute favorite – the one that has me headed to a local Dutch restaurant in town is this savory one. I promise, you will love it. Think of it like a pierogi with some shredded potato added in.

INGREDIENTS:
   2 eggs
   2 cups milk
   2 cups flour
   2 pinches sale
   ¼ c crumbled bacon (cooked)

¼ c shredded cheese (and then more because you'll need it later)

¼ c shredded potato (you could add onions too)

STEPS:

Beat the eggs in a large pouring bowl.

Add the milk and mix together with a whisk.

Combine the flour and salt to the batter, mixing until incorporated but still slightly lumpy.

Prepare toppings.

Place a 12″ non-stick frying pan on a medium burner with 1 tablespoon butter.

Pour about 1 cup of batter over the melted butter to cover the bottom of the pan.

Add filling ingredients such as ham, asparagus, bacon, onion, pineapple, etc.

Shake the pan gently from side to side to loosen the pancake as it cooks.

Look for tiny bubbles appearing and the edge of the pancake to start browning and drying (about 3-5 minutes).

Flip the pancake and cook on the other side for about 3 minutes.

If adding cheese, flip the pancake again and spread shredded cheese on top and turn down the heat to low while the cheese melts (about 3 minutes).

Plate and add any additional toppings (me, I like to add sour cream)

ABOUT THE AUTHOR

The Personal Bio:

Who am I? I'm just a girl addicted to chocolate, travel, reading and my fur babies (I share too many photos on Instagram of them, I know...but...).

I love to write stories that deal with family secrets and how those secrets affect lives. I also love to add chocolate, coffee and other personal passions into my stories.

Did you know I love to travel too? I love going on trips and started 'reader trips' where you can come with me as we explore Europe and more!

You're probably wondering here have we gone / where are we going? ... well, we've done a Christmas Market River Cruise in Europe, a Sweet Tour of Paris, a Chocolate & Tulips River Cruise, we'll be headed to a Chocolate Resort and so many more places!

If you want more info...join my newsletter or find me in my Steena Travels FB group. I'd love to have travel with you!

Now onto the official bio...

Official Bio:

New York Times & USA Today Bestselling Author!

With 2 million copies of her titles sold world wide, Steena Holmes was named in the Top 20 Women Author to read in 2015 by Good Housekeeping. She continues to write books that deal with issues that touch parents heart, whether it is through her contemporary fiction or psychological suspense novels.

To find out more about her books and her love for traveling, you can visit her website at http://www.steenaholmes.com

2012 NATIONAL INDIE EXCELLENCE BOOK Award for her bestselling novel Finding Emma

2015 USA BOOK NEWS Award for The Word Game,

2015 USA BOOK NEWS finalist for The Memory Child.

Instagram: www.instagram.com/steenaholmes

Facebook: SteenaHolmes.author

Twitter: @steenaholmes

Email: steena@steenaholmes.com

For softer, sweeter stories with a hint of chocolate, a lot of coffee and communities you want to live in, look for her stories under the name STEENA MARIE.

DON'T MISS THE FOLLOWING NOVELS:

Second Chances at the Chocolate Blessings Cafe

Finding Emma

Emma's Secret

The Memory Child

Stillwater Rising

The Word Game

Saving Abby

Abby's Journey

The Forgotten Ones

The Patient

The Perfect Secret

Lies We Tell Ourselves

The Halfway Series - start with Halfway to Nowhere

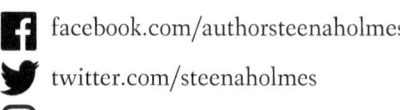

facebook.com/authorsteenaholmes

twitter.com/steenaholmes

instagram.com/authorsteenaholmes